How to Outthink a Wall:

An Anthology

Marvin Cohen

VP Festschrift Series:

Volume 1: Christine Brooke-Rose
Volume 2: Gilbert Adair
Volume 3: The Syllabus
Volume 4: Rikki Ducornet
Volume 5: Raymond Federman
(Edited by G.N. Forester and M.J. Nicholls)

Reprint Titles:

The Languages of Love
The Sycamore Tree
The Dear Deceit
The Middlemen
Go When You See the Green Man Walking
Next
Xorandor/Verbivore
by Christine Brooke-Rose

Three Novels — Rosalyn Drexler
Knut — Tom Mallin
Erowina — Tom Mallin
The Greater Infortune/The Connecting Door — Rayner Heppenstall
The Penelope Shuttle Omnibus — Penelope Shuttle
Conversations with Critics — Nicolas Tredell
The Utopian — Michael Westlake
Image for Investigation: About my Father — Christoph Meckel
Meritocrats — Stuart Evans
Bartleby — Chris Scott

New fiction:

Mirrors on which dust has fallen — Jeff Bursey

other Verbivoracious titles @
www.verbivoraciouspress.org

How to Outthink a Wall:

An Anthology

Marvin Cohen

Verbivoracious Press

Glentrees, 13 Mt Sinai Lane, Singapore

This edition published in Great Britain & Singapore

by Verbivoracious Press

www.verbivoraciouspress.org

Text Copyright © 2016 Marvin Cohen

Cover Art © 2016 Miguel Figueiredo

Author photo (from 1976) on p.464 © 2016 Tom Gervasi

Proofreading: Siobhan Strode & Bianka Nedjalkova

ISBN: 978-981-11-0118-2

Printed and bound in Great Britain & Singapore

First published: *The Monday Rhetoric of the Love Club*, 1973, Rapp + Whiting (UK) & New Directions (US), *Fables at Life's Expense*, 1975, Latitudes Press (US), *The Inconvenience of Living*, 1977, Urizen Press (US), *How the Snake Emerged from the Bamboo Pole, But Man Emerged from Both*, 1978, Oasis Books/Earthgrip Press (UK), *Aesthetics in Life & Art*, 1982, Gull Books (US). All the stories from *Dialogues* (1967, Turret Books) were republished in *Monday Rhetoric*.

CONTENTS

A *Disrespectfully Short but Exceedingly Well-Intentioned Introduction*

Who is Marvin Cohen? A tousle-haired New Yorker who from a period spanning 1967 and 1982 published surreal and whimsical fictions, many in the form of 'dialogues' between two unnamed interlocutors, and published many of them in prestigious magazines along the lines of *Ambit* and *The Transatlantic Review*. Several collections appeared in hardback from famous outfits such as New Directions and André Deutsch (US & UK publication), and one novel (*Others, Including Morstive Sternbump*) was released from Bobbs-Merrill. This anthology of short fiction represents the two modes of Cohen's writing: short 'dialogues' with fantastic titles such as 'On the Clock's Business and the Cloud's Nature' and 'The World is Cluttered With Objects' which operate in the manner of an Ionesco or Beckett script, turning language on itself with an eschatological hopelessness, revelling in life's absurdity, rather than despairing. The longer stories such as 'Saving Art for Tourism in One Tragic Lesson' and 'Love by Proxy of Solitude' showcases Cohen's knack for bending language into new shapes and his unique style: his repetitions, random exclamations, and taking abstract nouns and bestowing them with abstract qualities ("Open to whisper of love's quiet reason, cooling rampage of love's sour fever?" / "Bugles blared out the creeping closer of danger's crawling demon.") His focus on creating abstractions pulls the focus to the dancing prose, pirouetting on each page, always humorous, often beautiful. Cohen has an ear for the music of the absurd on a par with Donald Barthelme, particularly in stories like 'Listening to Herman', mixing the flip whimsy, astute and wry observation, and verbal heft of that long-gone short fiction master. His fondness for paradoxes and intellectual riddles, and incessant probing into the weird crevices of existence makes reading Cohen a perpetual pleasure. This omnibus collects the four volumes of short fiction and two pamphlets Cohen published, alongside new material written in the last few years. Leap into the volume at random, read strictly linearly, or start backwards. Delights abound.

—M.J. Nicholls

THE MONDAY RHETORIC

OF THE LOVE CLUB

AND OTHER PARABLES

For my mother and father; also for Audrey Nicholson who kindly helped edit this book.

On the Clock's Business and the Cloud's Nature

What is a cloud?

A cloud is a clock on vacation.

Oh. It wanders irresponsible?

Yes, it relaxes.

When does it return?

When the clock has to start working again.

For whose benefit?

For the office clerks whose foreman is strict about time.

Oh. What happens to the cloud that the clock *was*?

Its vacation was dissolved, and so it was restored into a hard clock.

With any sign of regret?

Not visibly. It must be wound up and click like clockwork, so it had no time to mourn the passing of its cloud self.

It sounds pretty busy.

It *is*, and meets itself at the end of a circle.

Where is *that*?

Depends on what time it is; it's got to be accurate.

Why? Why the precision?

The commercial world would collapse without it. A *cloud* can go gather its wool, but a *clock* has got to be on time. And there's no second thought about it, or a moment's hesitation. It's up to a clock to prove itself, and be on the wall. (I mean 'ball,' but 'wall' too.) If the office workers are caught watching it, the foreman will punish them.

For that matter, if those office workers look out the window at the *cloud*, and gaze in reverie, doesn't the demon foreman give them punishment for *that*? Clock and cloud have a point in *common*, there!

Yes, but don't confuse the two. A clock is a clock.

Oh, so what's a cloud?

A clock on vacation.

Then a clock is a cloud whose vacation is over. Back to the old office routine. Is that right?

Yes. Business goes by clocks. Leave the *poets* to the *clouds*.

Are poets, by nature, idle?

Sure. Hence their addiction to clouds.

Oh. Then poets are rovers.

Purposelessly. But: who goes by a clock, has got to be on time. He's *appointed*.

Oh. What appointment does he have to keep?

It's urgent, whatever it is. The clock would guarantee that.

Oh. Whereas a cloud — is a lack of stress.

Slack, I'd call it. And lazy.

Oh. The cloud has license?

It lingers the day long. It loiters. It plays hooky, and gets away with it. Really, it's aimless.

What's business's aim?

To justify the clock.

For how long?

Indefinitely. Businesses are self-perpetuating. They operate on their own profit.

What does a *cloud* earn?

Nothing. It *is* earned.

How?

It's a vacation. You must *earn* a vacation.

How?

By working hard for it!

How?
By going round the clock.
Oh. Is a clock round?
Yes. And continuous.
When does it break off?
For a vacation.
Oh. It softens up?
Yes. It floats away. Cloudlike.

The Truth Preserved in Verbal Cubicles of Ice, To Freeze Out the Melting Charges of the Crime of Gossip

I

On a ship traveling in the North Sea, two of the passengers were women gossips, who talked along the whole route. Beginning from the bottom of Africa, and continuing high up the North Sea. Their babbling went on and on. They outbabbled the waves.

It got colder and colder, the more and more northern they sailed, but on they blabbered, taking no notice.

Meanwhile, they kept on drawing north. Nor did their talk decrease. It increased.

The route sailed colder and colder. But bare due north, the boat continued to travel.

The other passengers huddled in their cabins, to keep warm. The *crew* were wise enough to keep indoors, as well.

But not those two women gossips. Impervious to the chill, they were warmed up by the heat of their conversation, which flared *incessantly*, without letdown. No silent syllable was heard.

The North Pole grew near. Still, the boat climbed. With the women gossips exposed on the windswept deck, like weather-beaten fixtures, the whole route long.

They reached a frozen climate. Still, they yapped on. The waves tossed ice at them.

The atmosphere changed. A dangerous level had been reached. Exposure had been carried too far north.

Something happened to the two women's words. The words were all freezing, in mid-air, just as delivered. Long words, short words, words of every description and vowel, without exception — they all froze.

And then, subsequently, their *echoes* froze. The women, animated, prattled gaily on. They were suffused with the ardor and sweat of their discourse and interchange.

But words of ice can't be heard. So they began not to hear each other.

This imposed a silent pall on the conversation that otherwise had been so lively.

II

The boat docked on the North Pole, through ice floes. Penguins and seals, millions of years old, were fresh preserved by the extreme cold. Like food kept alive in a refrigerator.

The ship's business was done. Then all passengers reboarded, after their chilly touring excursion, for the trip due south.

The return voyage was merry. The frozen words and their echoes that the two gossips had uttered on deck now began to thaw. And when they melted audibility was sounded in an incessant rain of prattle to drench and deluge all ears. So the flood waxed, as the tide turned mirthfully.

III

The words melted so well, that not only were they fluent, but fluid. They were from hot Latin Mediterranean tongues.

All the passengers crowded the decks to overhear last week's words of ice now turned to melted sound. But what was said hardly could be said to melt the passengers — or the crew, for that matter! The gossip was exposed. It was like a playback from a concealed tape recorder, and those two gossips had shrilly, even maliciously, concocted scandal to spice the fiction of each passenger and crewman. How unpopular the gossips now were, their lies exposed to blatant indignation! They were harangued, crowded to the rails, spat at. The passengers, to a man, vowed revenge. Even the captain, whose character had been maligned and morality impugned, was not loathe to stick out a plank for the gossips to walk blindfolded on, to tumble drowningly at the end. It was an unruly mob of passengers, thirsty for revenge. An improvised court tried the gossips, and a guilty verdict had plentiful evidence, for some of the harder-frozen bits of gossip and iced echo cakes were only now turning to melt, revealing such busybody tongues of wicked reincarnation as to stun the righteousness of each Godloving victim. Half of the passengers understood the gossips' language and were only too glad to translate for the other half. The translation made the tone more devastating, and the content filthier.

The gossips were accused of being gossips. They were both a middle-aged lady. The husband of one had been killed in a war, the husband of the other was in jail. Their children already had just married, so they were free, these ladies, to injure the reputations of whoever they found about. And what better source material than an oceanliner?!

IV

The accused now pleaded their defense. Their only defense was: "It was nothing but truth that we said. So why punish us? Why waste ice to preserve a lie? Ice is *valuable*, it keeps food fresh. It was the *truth* we froze, and not anything we made up."

One by one, the passengers, shamefaced, had to drop the case, and withdraw their prosecution. Also were the crew members abashed, and ceased from pushing their legal action (roughly unofficial as it was, so crudely improvised), as a tacit confession, amounting tantamount to an admission, that alas the gossips were correct, but let nothing more be said about the matter, and may vapor wisp the words away. The crestfallen passengers were proved guilty.

How did it all come about? The gossips had big ears. They heard. With their big eyes, they saw. With their brains, they cynically compounded. And how did the elements cooperate, in working out, in stages of state, what these ladies took pains to discover, and convert to the merciless veracity of tongue?

From air to ice to water, was the process and revelation of their grave words damning and defeating those passengers condemned to what they did by the observant factfinding gossips. Anything committed had found its way into the gossips' net. Unearthed. Air first the gossips spoke. And ice it turned to. And fire made water out of it, like tears of guilty confession, when temperate suns melted those tales told of temptations so undergone that the damage was done, and the chronicle made available by the voluble pair of historians. Having melted, may those words evaporate. Once released, that record can't be repeated. And the southbound ship, with the gossips vindicated, grew into hot climate. But not so hot as what had been divulged, on the passage north.

The Saving of Surrealism

Who was feeding Surrealism while all the poets were taking the afternoon off to watch the conclusive championship ball game on millions of identical television sets? I was one of them, I was watching too, when in alarm, and a deadening pang, I realized that Surrealism was being left unattended, and was missing the many warm meals it required just to stay alive on one Sunday afternoon! I panicked. Should Surrealism die of this mass criminal neglect, all the poets would have to fall back to imitating Alfred Lord Tennyson, which would be a blow against the future and an unexpected square meal fed to all the ghosts of reaction. (And that would be all those ghosts would need to come alive and haunt us in their bodies again!) So there was no time to lose, an emergency was at hand that gave even me a sense of responsibility. I left the television set still giving out the latest images of the game in progress (which was so exciting that it tempted me to remain, so I had to tear myself loose like Odysseus resisting the Sirens), and ran down the apartment building till I alighted on the street. Then without stopping I ran to the Surrealism Center, which is a big building with a cell in the middle, where the Surrealism unicorn is kept in strict and well-fed custody by its devoted guardians. Much to my horror, all the guardians had gone off to watch the game as well; and it gave me a cosmic stomach ache to see the Surrealism beast lying on its side, belly swollen, with an emaciated look in its eyes, and the boils of starvation growing regularly between the hairs of its skin. I had to rescue it, or the entire Avant-Garde would go down the drain! There was no time to lose, as the death rattles were growing closer. No food was handy, so I would have to feed it myself — first I put an arm in its mouth, and slowly it sucked it off. That was an appetizer, or an hors-d'oeuvre. Then went in my whole leg on the same side of me as that eaten arm. The monster of Surrealism made quick work of that dainty leg, taking a nice hunk of nourishment by gently amputating it right up to the corresponding ball on that lateral side of the body. It was making a quick recovery; and modern poets would have my martyrdom to thank when critics would attribute their styles to the surrealist influence. I was saving the world for Surrealism — or was it vice versa? But History was angry at me, for History would have liked to close the case on Surrealism to have it done with to make a serene verdict on that period or art movement from an interpretive and analytical position in the rectitude of retrospect. Momentarily, I had deprived History of this advantage, but didn't fear retribution from *that* quarter, as I had Surrealism already at work devouring me in the present, which was mentally distracting to say the least. My other leg was now eaten up, for Surrealism's greedy and vigorous appetite was enjoying a speedy recovery. At this rate, I would soon be no more. I then began to spend more concern on Survival, for my own sake. It was selfish. I wanted to live, so as to be able to find out the result and details of the all-important ball game that was being decisively enacted on the television sets of poet and non-poet alike. I wanted the Yankees to win. I was already fed up with Surrealism. If only Surrealism could have been fed up with me! But no, it kept chewing away. All the pieces of me were absorbed in its digestive system. My problem was to put myself together. To my great and very good fortune, I found in the central pit of its belly a working television set. I turned it on, eagerly, and enjoyed, down to the last play, the entire second half of the ball game whose progress I had been forced to abandon when realizing that my current devourer (whose lodger I was) would be dead of starvation unless I acted. Well, I *had* acted. My promptness had saved all of poetry from an unmitigated disaster, as well as art of course. But it had cost me the wholeness of my body. (Nothing good or heroic is without its awful price.) Yet it hadn't deprived me of watching the crucial climax of the ball game, thanks to the interior preparedness and sporting domesticity of my homekeeping monster of Surrealism. I had my cake, and was eaten too. The story ends happily, I'm glad to say. The Yankees won the championship, and that drove me mad with delight. It was a disembodied glee, a pure spirit of floating Yankee ecstasy as their posthumous rooter and well-rewarded fan, that dirged me melodiously — or all that remained of me — to a fulfilled grave on the Yankee side of Surrealism's ample plot. That's from where my voice is issuing, there being nothing else left of me but a saintly fame as the Saviour of Surrealism, and renown as a Yankee fan to the very death. Peace to all those above. I rest content.

Listening to Herman

After dinner, we all sat around. We were gasping for our thoughts. A silence circulated, with comfort, and not anxiety, as the sponsor. Our bellies bulged in storage of recent acquisitions neatly stacked. Wine had induced optical swirling: the square ceiling revolved in slow circles. Drowsy waves of alert vitality subdued the circuit of tension. The blurred clarity of sweet images drooped on us. We chewed on candy, or sipped drops of burning brandy from glasses of transparent tulip. Our feet were not under us, but far forward.

Who spoiled our fine feast of contentment? Herman, the loquacious bore. "That reminded me," he said, apropos of nothing outside his head. "I was traveling, and had arrived at the station, when —" The rest were just banal words. Severing themselves from meaning, they floated in vocal clusters, sounds hazy in vapors of dull abstraction. Curse them: they all but murdered my serenity!

Indolence is so nice! The tranquility of lethargic musing. Bloated with eating, we dozed, or chased the soft butterfly from a dream suspended above. The fabric of woven imagery, so lovingly stitched together, was punctured by the uttered mutterings of vulgar tedium that Herman distributed with infinite largess. "The shoes this year are much more in fashion, don't you think, than those brogans or clods we tripped in last year? Slim shoes think, then . . . impart grace to the dancer — a partner congratulated me, and she said how soft I tread. But I *do* love spectator sports, don't you? Freud thinks that games are a substitute for war. I'm not as fit as I once was, but in my day I was considered a splendid athlete.

I held a collegiate record that was only recently broken. Ah, say what you will, the current generation will be served! The papers report of a scientist with a new theory of death — a version so pessimistic, that it ought to drive people to religion. Heaven knows I'm not a churchgoer, but materialism is far too superficial to satisfy my mental needs. A philosopher said the other day that the soul was only a shallow pool. Well, I hope he slips in and drowns himself. This evening, I thought the fish course was excellent! And that white wine was so delicate! My diet has to observe a few restrictions, but otherwise the doctor is lenient. I caught a cold last week, but drowned it in citrus juice. I stayed home from work, and wiled away some delicious hours with a novel that ought to be banned for being erotic — though I'm plenty liberal, I can assure you. My wife and I consider ourselves humanists — right, dear? — and we're always warning whoever we can against confusing mere machines with the sacred souls of men. But in my opinion, the technological age contributes a prodigious amount to progress — and I defy any cynic to belittle the importance of scientific advancement. I bought my little tot a junior science set, and it intrigues him by the hour. He's quite talented when it comes to art, as well. The little heathen painted a nude female — I was shocked. But thank God it was almost abstract.

"Ah, it's so comfortable just lounging here. Excuse me. I opened the window a wee bit. Our health will circulate better now.

"You know, I must confess that I have a passion for music. I heard a symphony on the radio, and I hummed bars of it today. They flowed forth, as if my head were some uncanny phonograph needle. I'm also an excellent amateur photographer. I drove my family to the park last Sunday, and I shot nature in the raw — the trees were so natural, that they didn't seem posed. Nothing beats realism. Painting is at a dead end. And the prices in the art galleries! Fabulous! There must be a conspiracy. There's a culture boom. Reminds me of those war profiteers. Human nature is growing more corrupt by the minute. It makes you think twice, before accepting evolution. Last month I took my kid to the zoo. At one of the cages, he and a monkey whipped up a rapport. It was fun, and I felt very paternal for the both of them."

Herman's droning continuum was a verbal study in perpetual motion. He skipped from one subject to another like a frog in a fickle multitude of ponds. The host should have shut him up — but he was too polite to be obvious, and Herman ran on like a transcontinental train whose engine plows its own tracks. We were awake, and perfect passive captives to this monologue den of torture. All the air in the room was just a vocal passageway for Herman's tiresome pluckings of words out of context. The cliché machine bounced in abandon, to cover all subjects known to man. We were surfeited sick. We would turn desperado, and gag that compulsory maniac of talk. The rambling was non-stop in its voluminous greed.

Guest by guest, we all got up to leave. Herman took the cue in kind. To his taciturn wife, he gestured the 'let's go' signal. (Why hadn't he *said* it to her? I never could figure it out.) Our fatigued host thanked Herman for leading conversation into delightful broad byways. Herman was profuse in accepting this.

My wife and I got home, and released the babysitter. I couldn't sleep. Herman was speaking, in that unmistakable tone. Like a car siren that kept screaming, through mechanical default. Visually auditory words kept pouring from Herman's mouth. The monotone of rigid variation. My balance fell apart. I was going mad.

For distraction, I woke up my wife. She was sleepy, but a good sport. We had a tumble, but it barely entered into pleasure's zone. Like the cackle of static on a ruined radio program, Herman's voice zoomed up a steady staccato of interference. His voice was a rumbling world, roaring in at either ear. I couldn't shut off this deafening obsession.

Ear plugs were pathetically futile. The core of my skull was submitting these sounds.

Wave on wave: like an endless torment of hornets, swept down from clouds to sting and plague. The lips of articulation: Herman audible.

Not a snatch of sleep. Morning was a fuzzy day. It was grounded on Herman's undertone. Not a let-up. Within this repetition, insanity's independent rhythm grafted on a hookup, while I swayed. Bound by Herman's vocal cord, I endured an apprenticeship to lunacy, with monolithic perseverance. Heartlessly, I was barred from all variety alien to the intimacy of Herman's voice. In the wild din of silence, I heard it.

My wife worried to a hysterical pitch. To rid myself of those reiterative echoes was the puzzle pounding on me with a panic's gong of vibration. My system was pumping glandular heaves to the tone of that organic poison. My wife arranged a psychiatric appointment. But the psychiatrist was interested in recitations of my *childhood!* "That's *before* the fact, and bears no consequence," I rebelled. He insisted that his professional method was the correct one. Herman drowned him out. I abruptly left, without paying.

Anxiety for me made my wife neglectful of our boy. The problem was blown up into a domestic crisis. This acceleration was nightmare material.

After my second sleepless night, my wife's hysteria was converted by necessity into inspiration. The husband desperately needed rescuing. My work had been falling off, for the office was one loud buzz of Herman the day long. The boss had been alerted, becoming distrustful of my fidgeting, with the commercial minimum of sympathy. I was about to lose my job. Acute desperation, alarming her instinct for family survival, enlightened my wife with emergency's bolt of inspiration. "Go and visit him!" she declared. "Listen to him talk, all night. The reality will saturate, clutter, kill your memory. The obsession that's haunted you can only be purged by the real thing. Only Herman's presence can create a catharsis." Authority had made her summons imperious. I must heed it, to terminate delirium's crucifix that doubled between ordeal and agony.

I phoned up Herman. "Let's get together," I suggested. He invited my wife and me to dinner for the following night. I couldn't wait, so I asked him to visit us now. "That's impossible," he declared, "I have a one-day attack of tonsilitis." My third sleepless night equipped me with special energy. Dinner with Herman would be curative, or else, I hoped, kill me off in haste. My ears were leaking pus. Cancer globules were forming there, breeding psychic pathology in all those little work cells. They were adroitly spelling out my doom.

I was wound up, as never before. Like an ancient Chinese scroll of bureaucratic length being unrolled for academy inspection, the Herman machine unfurled the relentless intricacies of its tune. A pitiless unfolding, in murderous intensity. A compulsive mercilessness, scurrying in the sharp breeze of frenzy. It was too glaring for the dull solace of dizziness. Billions of infernal word variations were spawned on the eggnest theme of the chronic headache outbreak. The ruthless Hermanization of my head was proceeding on a national front, with strains of international grandeur intermingled. It was no simple jingle or pure melody. It was hell, boiled into sound, dripping slender serpents of malice, stirring the vipers' drops of a deadly vengeance.

We were at Herman's doorstep well before the appointment time. In ringing anticipation, his voice was making a production of my ears. My head was the gong, where he clanged all day. Like a metallic battering ram, the bruise rubbed precision on my nerve. Like a street drill or the dentist's instrument, it went like a wicked streak through my body.

"Come in," he welcomed, "right in here, where my wife is preparing drinks. My bout of tonsilitis has subsided. Heaven knows why I had it in the first place. The weather has been running eccentric these days, hasn't it? I can remember the weather of every day of my life — it's an uncanny trick of memory. But I wouldn't want to bore you with the recitation. Years of weather reports and outcomes are on active file — my head is a veritable weather bureau, but confines its forecasts to the predictable accuracy of the past. That reminds me that tomorrow is expected to be cloudy. No wonder my lumbago wart is stirring. I can stare at the clouds all day. It's fascinating, the number of patterns in all that shifting panorama. But at heart, I'm a sun-worshipper. I can lap it up. I go to the shore for it. I never vacation in the mountains. I love to go for a swim, and then let the sunbeams swim on me. Do you admire my tan? I'm glad, because I do. I always like my friends to share in my opinions. This confers a greater air of intimacy. And as we all know, harmony is the antidote against war. Do you know that the President was taken ill the other day? But the papers hushed it up. An acquaintance in the diplomatic corps discreetly informed me. The state of the economy is breathing too fast: I go in for a *gradual* fluctuation. When it comes to politics, I'm moderate right down the center. With this safe approach, I'm immensely farsighted. Foreign aggression is so potentially dangerous, I think the matter should be discussed in Congress. The United Nations has only feeble option to resist the inevitable dilemma that the world is facing. I just heard a television commentary warning against complacency. The speaker had a fascinating style of delivery. His hair I think was too much combed on one side. But my wife decided that he really had a handsome face. When it comes to men, I think women are better able to judge our appearance than our own mirrors. Do you like this suit? It was a bargain. Mostly, I'm ignorant of clothes; but I sure like what I wear. The other day I was walking down the street, and got stared at — by an impressive-looking woman! I was so flattered, my masculine pride went up. As a rule, it doesn't take much to keep my vanity alive. But I hate people who are sometimes slack in paying attention. Courtesy and consideration are only my due. I'm only human in asking for this right. I was told I talk too much, but only by an envious admirer whose mouth was too small to withstand the fatigue of enduring his own voice. My little son feeds a bird out the back window, but lately the bird hasn't reported for its meal. Perhaps it's a migratory tramp or something. My son's appetite has suffered. But at least mine is plainly all right. My wife eats whatever I do. That makes it so convenient.

"There, take that chair please. Begin eating, at once. I insist on no ceremony! We must be forward about these things.

"My dear, you're improving as a cook! Hearty congratulations are in order. I think food is basic to life, don't you? What can a starving man do? He's practically helpless!

"The more I think about it, the more my life is a fascinating achievement! When I was born, I was so inconsiderable! My mother, were she alive today, could talk for hours about my unrobust state of childhood. I spent my infancy with the tears rolling down my cute red cheeks. That was hardly fun, for the sensitive condition I was in. But *now* look at me! Who gets more out of life? I ought to be copied as a standard model. Fools would become wise, if they chose aspects of my life to studiously emulate. Not that I'm any sort of genius! No, I'm just *too* normal! A terrific combination of ingredients makes me dynamically balanced — I could go on and on. It's a subject I never tire of, so inexhaustibly manifest with possibilities that compel contemplation. But what about my dear guests? Are they having fun? What an insult to my elaborate hospitality, if this isn't the case."

My host was continuing. My head pounded its sockets loose. My wife looked at me with alarming concern. I stood up, and outshouted Herman, gaining the floor. It was the time the coffee was served. I went on, and kept going.

Herman was furious, but I didn't stop talking. What I spoke about was immaterial. I drew out its interminable length. The fury increased my pace.

My rate skyrocketed a verbiose marathon. My words packed space densely, like a huge monopoly machine. Herman's gorge choked to the brim with moral indignation.

While I kept sputtering out, Herman was on the phone to the police. He took an hour and a half explaining what he was complaining of, stopping occasionally to digress and branch out with chance expansion. Meanwhile, I was rivalling him in our joint counterpoint that shared a hideous assassination-rape of the mangled body of silence. Who knows whether the police sergeant had already hung up? Herman was pouring it on. His wife submissively smiled throughout. *My* wife tried a trivial interference. She was out competed, in a rugged contest of men locked in the no-rules mortality of a tongue-war.

Dawn was closing in. Neither Herman nor I could stop.

Wouldn't his throat choke of apoplexy? Wouldn't his throttle explode suddenly? Not his. He was brutally endowed.

Our sprawling wives slumbered in their chairs. Herman's kid was asleep in another room. At *my* home, the babysitter hadn't been relieved!

My fourth night of no sleep had passed. I flamed into an embattled mass of fire.

I traded Shut up's, with my adversary. His practice and experience were beginning to tell. He slipped in several words for my one. My defense was slacking. The note of triumph entered Herman's voice.

I called on all my verbal reserves, and fought back with the weight of a rapidly decimating dictionary. Herman chose his words from a richer fund of resources. They lighted on me, like a pack of indiscriminate birds. His tongue was like a weather vane, tossing in a month of wild wind.

The spittle and the spleen also rose. The exchange closed quarters.

Then Silence crashed, like a lead ball, smashing the splintry floor. Our mouths kept moving, but all in a dumb-show. Phantom words were not given their heard bodily weight, but were mimed in the inarticulate panic of lips. Herman was like an epileptic. His oral pantomime screwed itself gulping. He strained to uncork the sound barrier.

Silence was vanquished. The words streamed at me, non-stop. (My own had ceased, like trickles from a dried-up river.)

Excruciating vowels were ejaculated, and jibbering consonants. I was being slaughtered, sent rocketing into annihilation!

Not a pause to break rhythm or rest its swell. Herman's being heard. Herman, I'm hearing you! Your wavelength is the sole one operating. You come through, sound is only you. The drum is rolling. My body is a splinter network of slightly-hinged bones. Each bone is your sound's familiar. Especially my top bone, with its revolving sockets. Oh Herman, I can see your sounds! Each one is a special burial bone!

The Balance of Power
(Violence Without Meditation)

I met an important man. He looked down on me (a difficult accomplishment, considering my height) and when he spoke these words, they were underscored by command: "Go away." As we were in the free public street, owned jointly by policemen and politicians, I conveyed a note of courage in the answer, "No."

He hit me. With dignity and money, he hit me. While the hurt raised embarrassment from my blush, he snapped back his arm, preparing to repeat. My anger crushed him down, and when the blows stopped falling, he turned his surprise on me, and began retreating. I chased him, just for fun, since triumph delayed my step.

How proud I felt. How easy to survive. While returning home, I met an unimportant man. With insolence, I told him to go away. "Not right now," he answered.

A policeman took me to the hospital. It wasn't funny, but they had me in stitches. When released, I felt totally neutral.

The next man I saw, I said to him, "Don't be funny." "But I'm a comedian," he answered: "my livelihood." "So you're a professional," I retorted, and let his blood bounce softly off the pavement.

Next, I encountered a boxer. "Boy, you're strong," I said. "I must be," he replied, while a quick reflex made me dodge. Too late, and at once I found my skull. "You're hard," I cracked. "I must be," it answered; "and you're thick yourself."

With my skin loosely patched, I pounced along the street, alert to the trouble soon to assault me.

I made a fist, and kept it clenched. This squeezed the blood away, and soon the white knuckles grew blisters. Thus handicapped, I fell easy prey to my next would-be victim. My arms and legs lay sprawled beside me. After an imperfect matching job, I staggered upright, with a proud scorn twinkling in my virile eye. "How survived I am!" I managed to utter, just as my collapse caught up with me.

The hospital was white, like snow. I shook off the hovering angel, and sprouted new muscles. I walked out a new man.

"You're new," said the important man. "How changed," said the unimportant man. "Incredible," said the comedian. "What a comeback," exclaimed the boxer. "How annoying," crowed my would-be victim.

They made a path for me, while I chopped down a tree and poured the chips over my shoulder. "Knock it off!" I yelled. They fought among themselves, to be the first one.

Realizing that my legs were new, I tested them by running. They refused to stop, until safety was clutching at me with her ferocious arms.

Now, when I make love to safety, she calls me her favorite coward. I tell her what a wonderful nurse she is and she blushes.

A Movement, in Several Short Pauses (Concluded by One Interminable One)

Let's go somewhere.
I don't blame you.
Are you ready?
Not if you are.
Then we're all set.
That's for you to insist.
   (Pause)
What shall we do on the way?
Shop for an article.
A newspaper article?
No, a purchasing commodity.
You're too deep for me.
Yes, but I *feel* shallow enough.
   (Pause)
We've been walking.
I can tell.
Why? The distances we've covered?
Fatigue: Don't forget to mention *that*.
No. It's cost me my energy.
   (Pause)
I'm going to buy a left-handed handkerchief.
But what if your *right* nostril is on fire?

Tough. It fends for itself then.

Are you *always* this unfair?

That's not a fair question, I warn you.

Then I'll disregard the answer you're not going to give.

(*Pause*)

Have we arrived?

I don't know. What's our destination?

It depends on where we're going.

Depends! Can't you be sure about *anything*?

Not when *uncertainty* casts its ugly doubt.

(*Pause*)

Let's stop. We've walked enough.

Why? What tells you that?

The perspiration is using my clothes as a sieve.

What *more* evidence do you have?

The bottom of my feet are where my soles used to be.

Then put on your shoes, next time.

(*Pause*)

Are we there now?

'There' can be anywhere. So 'here' is no better than the next place.

But not worst neither, no, sure?

Don't get plain with *me*.

I'm only helping out.

Yes. That's why you're a hindrance.

(*Pause*)

It's my limit. Not a step more.

Are you *stubborn*, or merely *obstinate*?

Whichever way resists any further advance.

Then you force *me* to stop, as well.

Why? Are you a *shadow* of some sort?

Granted. But more substantial than its object, if you're the object I cast.

Don't confuse me. I don't know light from dark.

No need to, if you can tell time.

But my clock always stops.

That means you don't *feed* it enough.

Why should I? It's only a *small* one.

   (Pause)

Are we at the end?

Yes. The road stops where I stop.

Is your approach to geography *always* so personal?

When I'm tired, geography quits whirling and settles down.

But people *depend* on geography for their whereabouts. When you stop, you stall billions of lives.

Blame the *earth*, if it puts *me* foremost.

You're not foremost: I'm *equal* with you. *(They're parallel to each other; they stand without moving)*

Not one more step forward.

How long will our stillness last?

Forever, provided I say one word.

What magic word is that?

This: *Curtain!*

(Curtain)

Rain's Influence on Man's Attitude to Art

A man and wife hated culture. But it suddenly rained hard, while they were passing a museum. So they only had a dry reason for entering.

Is that how the conflict was solved?

Yes. They shook some of the rain off on culture, while culture gave *them* a brief soaking.

Who gains, in the long run?

The rain. It lasts longer.

Than the couple?

And than the priceless treasures in the museum.

Oh. Where *was* the museum, by the way?

In the middle of an empty desert. *True* art is hard to come by.

But doesn't the attendance suffer, when public art is isolated in an ivory tower?

That protects art's scarcity. Once its rarity is ruined, devaluation would set in.

Would that depreciate the assets?

Yes. Products become cheap, when too much democracy is inserted.

Oh. Where did the culture-hating couple go, once the rain dried up?

They were offered jobs as mummies. Their future was guaranteed.

So it was fatal for them to enter the museum.

Yes, but it beats standing in the rain.

What harm could rain have done? Is water impure?

They would have become fishes. That would have stunted evolution, reversed its laborious growth, and necessitated its beginning all over again, from the sea on.

That's tough. Another museum down the drain.

Yeah. What time gives, time can take away.

Who loses, in the end?

People, and their predecessors.

Is it so sad it's hopeless?

More than that. It's miserable.

God. I'm raining down tears.

You need distraction. I'll take you to a museum.

What's there to see?

Nothing, unless you mop out the ocean that swims in little waves from those prehistoric craters in your eyes.

I wish something wonderful could devour me.

Only because you've failed to *be* the devourer of something wonderful.

Oh. Why were they married, by the way?

The couple who were buried in the museum to avoid the rain?

Yeah.

To form a cultural unit, an institution so self-sufficient that outside culture wouldn't be necessary.

Yeah, but the culture they hated wasn't outside. It was *inside* the museum.

Sure. Art is too delicate not to need a roof.

Like man an umbrella.

Right. It's destructive to be too vulnerably exposed.

Then you condemn the elements?

Sure. Rain foremost.

Confusions for Embroidering Detective Intrigues

There's an exclusive detective who only takes on cases that have *already* been solved. I admire his ingenuity.

Yes, but his soft job is a lazy sinecure. Does it require any skill?

No, only audacity.

And it's devoid of *thrills*, isn't it?

Yes. There's not much suspense in it.

(Pause)

I know a detective who's so exclusive, he only handles cases that don't even have a *problem* to be solved.

Then why are they called 'cases'?

Short for 'briefcases'. You see, he carries a portfolio without being an ambassador.

Oh. That explains it.

(Pause)

I know a detective who's investigating himself.

On what grounds?

His own. He does it in his own back yard.

Why? Can't he afford an office?

Yes, but he insists on operating a *charitable*, rather than profitable, business.

But—
And 'charity,' he declares, 'begins at home.'
Oh. Has he found any evidence?
Yes. The investigation has been successful. He's been placed under house arrest.
What evidence incriminated him?
The hunch that he had done something wrong.
But what did he do that was wrong?
Nothing. But he needed practice.
  (*Pause*)
Won't his career suffer?
No; it was a brilliant piece of detective work.
Was it written up in the newspapers?
No, they had already gone to press when the publicity was released.
Oh. Then with no fame, who will hire him?
He *invents* clients.
Invents! Does he have a license?
That's invented, as well.
Doesn't he take too much on himself?
That's his style. And a man's style is his signature. You can't argue with it.
You mean he has a *signature*, as well?
Yes, but only when his name is working.
  (*Pause*)

The World is All Cluttered with Objects

The world is all cluttered with objects.

Where? Isn't this stage bare?

Well, *we*'re here, aren't we?

We? Who are we?

We're the ones who, if it weren't for us, the stage would be empty.

That's not a flattering function, as a reason for my whole existence. Just to take up space isn't why I'm proud to have been once created.

But you're solid. The air stops flowing, when it bounces off your surface. It can't pass through you. You're so opaque, the audience can make you out. (*Looks at audience with look of sympathy*) You're as physical an object as a stage prop. And even more personally real, when you consider your animation. Your properties are those that belong to the living. But enough of you. I had meant to mention things more general than yourself alone.

I'll do you the same disservice, some day.

My subject had started out to be the world at large, with the various things in it.

Sweeping generalizations will get you nowhere.

But still, the world is a striking fact, if you get around to it.

The *world*? Oh, it's *there*. (*Shrugs complacently*) But why bother to acknowledge it?

So as not to be ungrateful. We wouldn't have a leg to stand on, if the world didn't help to support it.

Well, your theories sure aren't groundless, anyway.

The world is the undeniable basis of all reality.

Yes, it sure does interfere with my dreams.

Dreams? Why waste time dreaming, when the world offers more truth than we can ever learn in a total lifetime of years?

Truth is dull, when it gets plentiful. It's really a diluting agent, like water in a whiskey glass. Dreams keep us drunk. You, you can drink water. But being sober isn't so much fun. The world appears better, when converted to imagination: it's more translated in terms of *us*. Me, I'm the measure of the world, by passing it through my dreams. Otherwise, truth is merely a dull irritant.

But are you insulting reality?

Reality is too well established to stop operating on the strength of a passing insult. Leave me to my unreal mind. If the world amuses you, you can keep *my* portion, too. Just stop referring to it. Thank God, our stage is empty. It's more than I can merely bear, to suffer us alone.

There's more than just us. What of the clothing we're wearing? They're our closest approximate environments. They're our outward trappings, our physical surroundings. Look, watch me move: (*Waving arms, walks a few paces*) Where I go, they go, too.

That limits your constitutional freedom. But dreams exist in a rare purity, devoid of a cluttered environment. It affords peace, for concentration.

In a vacuum?

No. The material is plentiful, I assure you.

Well, it's the world for me.

Take it. I'll go the other way. (*They part, each going off to opposite end of stage. Bareness remains, then curtain*)

A Shadow Speech Play

If a shadow is developed in a darkroom, it can cast an *object*.

Does it cast the same object that *it* was cast by when out in the sun?

Oh, stop being technical. It *forgot* what it came from. It only wishes to create.

An artist? But an artist paints a *picture*, not an object.

No. This is a *shadow*, that creates a specific object.

Isn't that overdoing the *modern* bit?

So what? Progress has *got* to be made.

   (Pause)

Why are you so interested in shadows? Your fascination is almost morbid.

Because they're cooler and darker than the freckle-faced world. They're underdogs, as well. Everybody's treading them underfoot.

Why can't shadows fend for themselves, instead of being helpless?

Because they practice humiliation.

Why don't they rise and revolt? They suffer the sun's yoke.

To overthrow what they're dependent on would be to slice off their own necks. A parasite's survival depends on keeping the thing it leeches off so healthy, that there's surplus to afford.

But don't shadows play primarily a secondary role?

Only compared to the sun-lit objects that are predominant. Subordination doesn't *keep* the shadow down: it develops the shadow's profile, and fills it out with sweet fat.

Then shadows, like beggars, must thrive?

Sure. But their masters must do so first.

(Pause)

My vision is elevated. It's the *sun* I'm thinking of.

As long as you remain modestly *thinking* of it; don't fall into the error of assuming that you *are* it.

No. I know my place. No good to get elevated ideas.

Quite right. You don't want to burn yourself out when you're so young.

Yes, that would be a mistake.

Be cool, and play it safe.

I'll accept my lot's being humble. Let those who wish to stumble seek more exalted footing.

Yes. But don't become complacent for being so *low*.

No. That's only adding *perversion* to arrogance.

You're getting sensible.

That's what comes with agreeing with you.

Then are you ready for my quiz?

As ready as summer is, to locate the sun so democratically central that most nations on almost all the continents can be kissed by radiance of so well-distributed a bestowal.

You gild your rhetorical lily. Come down, and sniff a little moonblaze. You have a gold-stroke, that only silver can remedy. The sun is cracked with some of your craze.

Then quench my glaze with a little question's glitter; unless it fazes me, I'll catch it with a quiver.

You see those long inclining shadows? *(Points)* Filling the alley's dusty emptiness? Isn't that somehow a *Sunday* scene? But fact dictates this day as Wednesday. Why are *Sunday* shadows different from Wednesday ones? — assuming equality in season and hour of afternoon.

Because they've had four days to complete their decaying.

You reply too cynically. Here, try this: De*fine* a shadow. I mean its inmost, non-surface, self.

A shadow? Why, that's a soiled replica of the original object. It was cast, but not as solidly.

But why is an object more solid than its shadow?

Because it's flattered with more direct personal attention by people. This inflates its pride, and makes it a substantial citizen.

Somehow, you're not being scientific.

No need to be. Objects and shadows speak for themselves, separately. I eye them with spectator disdain. But were I *them*, I'd feel haunted with paranoia.

That's too human an attribute for them to assume. But if you were the *sun*, what would you say?

I'd say not once, but continually, "Why can't I ever find an object to be an intermediary between myself and my shadow?" Frantically, I'd question the air. But not one human sprite would venture even a *puny* reply.

But what language would you, as a sun, be speaking?

(Imperiously) Total language.

Very impressive. But is your 'total language' visual?

It lies bleeding in the sky, scourged by innumerable semantic battles.

Then will you retreat, and undergo a sunset?

Certainly. It's my grand coup. For, once I've set, all four horizons, that eye can see at one fill, are plunged purely into the total darkness of shadow. My deputy, the moon, has but a wan rage. Mighty night is my blackest creation. Against it, man defies with thousands of neon bulbs. What candle is that trivial defiance of my intense power! *(Walks haughtily off)* Good night.

    (Darkness)

Becoming a Building After Considering an Approach to a Previous Building

I

Have you been to that big wonderful building yet?
(Looks at it)
No. I'm waiting for *it* to come to *me*.
You might have to wait a long time.
(Looks at watch) Well, I've got fifteen minutes, anyway.
But the building is a couple a centuries old.
So?
Well, that tends to cripple its moving. It can't get around now so much, you know.
What a senile old stick-in-the-mud!
Still, even *modern* buildings don't move around much.
Laziness! The present generation is the idlest—.
But some *prefabricated* houses are mobile.
Well, good for them. They're enterprising.
Do you see *everything* in business terms?
No. I consider leisure completely separate.

II

Come, aren't we going to that splendid building?
What! Are you *still* reminding me?

But you don't know what's *inside* it.

I only know things from the *outside* first. I approach things gradually.

That's mighty cautious of you.

Yes. Even people. First I see them from the outside. I know their superficial appearance before I know them inside.

Good. Then you're no intruder.

No. I wouldn't presume.

Is there *anything*, or *anyone*, you first knew from the inside before knowing from the outside?

Yeah. My mother.

Which did you prefer?

In, frankly.

But wasn't there a relative lack of objectivity?

That was hardly my concern, at that time.

When did you *begin* burdening your shoulders with responsibility?

As soon as there was *room* on the shoulders.

Why? What had to be removed?

Chips, you see.

Oh. Now shall we approach that building? *(Looks at it)*

No. Let's wait for it to come this way.

But we might have to wait *forever!*

No. I'm a busy man. I can't be bothered.

Then we'll visit the building?

Yes. On our own steam.

Well? Why don't you begin walking?

(Legs are gone. Concrete rectangular tube up to the torso, instead) I can't. I've just become a building myself — more recent than that one.

Then you must be given a postal *address*.

Sure. My name would make the beginnings of one.

Where? I don't see any sign.

(Other man has become a building, about eight feet tall, with a flat front and large windows. It doesn't move. The lights are on; then they blank out)

Image Streamlining

I was once a public relations man. My first client was a cockroach. I was so surprised to see him.

Him?

Well, *it*, I suppose: it's hard to tell.

Go on with your story.

As I said, I was in public relations. I had just opened shop. A cockroach — dressed quite well if you please — walked in nonchalantly.

Why nonchalantly?

It was his cool approach.

Oh. *(Pause)* Continue, please.

The cockroach spoke quite distinctly. I was grateful: usually I have difficulty with foreigners.

But a public relations man is supposed to *adjust*.

Well, so I entered business under a slight handicap.

Enough of *you*: tell about the cockroach.

"Can you improve our image?" he asked. "Whom do you represent?" I replied, with professional detachment.

So what did the cockroach say to *that*?

He said, "I represent the United Cockroaches of America. We're a thoroughly unionized organization. We're even a chartered corporation, to please the capitalists."

Clever, those cockroaches. So what did *you* answer?

I said, "To the point: What do you want?"

Go ahead.

So the little insect replies, "Sir, we seem to disgust people. They don't see how harmless we are. They're squeamish, they look down on us. Those stuffy morons! We want to be more seemly. We want to erect our dignity on a noble carriage."

Did the cockroach go to *school?* — that's quite a mouthful.

He was educated, all right. But I didn't feel inferior: after all, I towered *over* him.

(Looking at other) You're a brave man, all right. *(Pause)* Were you of any help to him?

I quoted my fee. I said it would involve extensive research. But that I would give him most considered and careful advice. He persisted, that he *did* require my services. So he signed a contract to that effect.

I'm glad to see that you don't discriminate against clients.

Of course not. Prejudice is fatal, businesswise.

But didn't the *nature* of your client sort of give you the creeps?

I repressed it; I acted like a routine course was pursued.

Your professional ethics are excellent. Did you carry on the market research campaign? Was it exhaustive? What were your findings?

I did all that. I spared no method, down to the finest detail.

Then did you call the little squirt in?

I did: he was breathless with panic. I had to lend him a damp sponge: he was soaking with liquid excretion.

Ugh! A little accident of nature.

I did him the courtesy of pretending ever so faintly not to notice.

Weren't you too conspicuous about it?

Don't be ridiculous. "Your result!" he clamored. Cautiously, I began: "Publicity is not an exact science. In *your* case, it's the *lack* of publicity that is here heartily recommended." "But doctor — my species can hardly make themselves scarce — there's too many of us. Doctor — it's our *image* we want to improve." "Pay me the fee," I said, "and receive the findings." It was an exorbitant amount. With meticulously enunciated agony, choked with a note of despair, the little creep again asked, "Doctor! Advise us!"

This suspense is awful! What *was* your advice?

"In the interests of your public image," I said — and here's the crux of the matter — "Off with your legs?"

(*Aghast*) And how did he take it?

Bit me . . . Here. (*Showing cheek*)

Well — those are your occupational hazards.

(*Proudly*) It's worth it! I'm entirely devoted to my job!

Saving Art for Tourism in One Tragic Lesson

Deep in one of this world's wealthiest, most ancient and traditional continents (famous for its variety of national tongues, especially those of the western Romance languages) stands a town not quite large enough to be called a city. This town, set by an idle, mud-pent river between a sloping range of valleys, would have been obscure and undistinguished; and it is, except for a unique item in it, prized beyond the rest of its drearily unextraordinary self.

Somewhere approximately to the middle of the town's center stands — or pretends to stand — a venerable religious relic mentioned reverently in all tourist guide books as a universal attraction for visitors. All other buildings contemporary with this shrine have long since been dissolved in time's dust. But *this* antique has weathered all the ages. Successive coats of paint have faded into one another, the wood has peeled, the metal has splintered, the stone is pore-riddled like sponge, the ornamental surfaces are rubbed away; but there it is, having tolerably survived, to its increasing fame and glory, a requisite 'must' for foreign culture-addicts.

Otherwise, the town itself is dull. The other buildings are all shabbily recent, of an uninspiring motley of architectural drabness. The movie theatres play antiquated Westerns born at the inception of cinematic mediocrity. Go along the streets: the ice cream parlors cheat you, for cheap bread-crumbs are intermingled in so-called ice cream. The coffee is so stale that the locals call it tea. The beer tastes like semi-urinated lemon water. The wine must have been blood crushed from ants by the coarse, unshod feet of drooping-jawed rustics. As for the 'meat', steers would die laughing, and steer clear of the dubious incest of 'eating' this unrefrigerated breed of extinct leather.

Internally, the town was not a money-maker; its own citizens were not good domestic providers. The only dependable revenue was its tourist trade, all due to that particular monument for which every conscientious traveler routes his global itinerary. But since conscientious travelers are too few, or are not wealthy enough to make the out-of-the-way scenes and so must confine their holiday excursions to the great old large cities where so much is concentrated in one whirling visit, the scale of tourism for this town was modest, its natives subsisting on the margin of poverty's eking standard.

The Chamber of Commerce makes a small, neat profit. The restaurant, café, hotel, postcard, and souvenir trade keep the coffer tills just full enough with shekels from international sightseers. The religious building is their golden calf. It's invaluably old: its decay works for them. (In the town, old people are given the right of way in the streets, hats tipped off to them.)

But things that decay are likely to fall, soon or late. This is one of nature's laws that are artificially defended against, in the prevention-over-cure creed of conservation. Municipal watchdogs keep a weather eye on the precarious monument. A crack electrician is hired on a round-the-clock basis to divert any bolt of lightning from that delicate edifice. The town has commissioned an anti-war lobby in the national legislature, since a bombing raid would doom the precious attraction, level it from sight and destroy its utility as an unbeatable fund-raiser. Geology experts scratch the soil with anti-earthquake rods that thwart excitable rock. Barricades to keep out natural hazards have been precisely instrumented. No bacteriological colony of virus, capable of contaminating obsolete matter by malignant agency, may be bred to infest these carefully sterilized premises. Tourists must take a health test (sneezing and coughing illegal on forfeit of fine) before being permitted so far as the highly sanctified inner gate, where a binocular view hints at the riches in store. Germ carriers are weeded out in a ruthless warfare of chemical censorship. Suppression of alien infiltration spares only the bona fide tourist, on a generous quota system of widely popular exclusiveness. Nothing remotely harmful may venture close to that sole source of fitful income for the total inhabitants of a town. The very weather is daily checked by umbrella-clad philosophers whose theories conservatively practise a dry goal. Rainfall is forbidden to molest the natural self-weathering of this time-hallowed shrine, this mecca of the tourist sport.

One day, an alarmed guard reports to the Mayor's vigilant committee of minute-aldermen that the foundations are gradually giving way. The building seems in a slump. Its base-support slopes; the land seems to slide free. Stones are slipping loose: pebbles shoot out from underneath. Moss slime and the pus of moody vegetation betray a decomposing factor: putrefaction confounds esthetically scented nostrils. "It's a rotten matter," tersely concludes the report. The heavens frown ominously. Test winds are unleashed. The building totters with every sharp breeze, swaying like an aspen, quivering like a tubercular epileptic.

Venerable decay, or the evidence thereof, is excellent for tourism; but the very existence itself of the relic must surely be preserved from perishing! Or else the town's economics would dip below zero freezing!

Clang went the emergency gong; to their collective feet rose a community. On the unseen enemy, it was all-out war!

This celebrated temple of an outmoded religious function from a holy era, seems not long for this world! Quickly, a panic conference is called by the local chieftains. If tourism's source is cut off, the town itself is due for the poorhouse, a charity case beyond redemption.

This building, however infirm, must hold the fort, whatever the windy odds! Economic survival is at stake. The town's inconsequential name would be wiped off the revised editions of every self-respecting map atlas! (Rarity ceases to be dear, when the rare object loses its existence; the word's ungrateful memory demotes it to a myth.) To cope with this desperation, the town's most powerful heads linked brains in a crusade, a campaign of great renown: 'To conserve' was the verb these burghers agreed on. Now only technical execution became the abiding problem.

Outside the town, a different type of excitement was working. A flurry of fermented agitation was converging broadly on that archaic magnet that worried the town fathers so! An ingress of money was on the way!

Rumor spread with rampant acceleration. Its hot news penetrated all travel agencies within the commercial spread of civilization. Contagion spawned foamy waves of culturemania; a splash of hysteria drowned mankind in common. All feelings were washed into one tide.

Everybody knew it: this crumbling memento to a devoutly dedicated past was doomed. It must be visited in immediate terms of now-or-never. Soon was it due to collapse, like man's own mortal heart and his bag of emptying lung-wind.

The international proliferation of such ecstatic despair brought tourists rushing in like Indian tribes on tracks joining to a mutual warpath. This out-of-season frenzy jumped up the town's treasury booming. The world over, booking agencies were stampeded for tickets; a farewell crusade poured in by boat, plane, car, and train, by bus and by foot, for the sentimental nostalgia of bidding a monument of dead spiritual magic goodby. A single destination was central to a myriad passages. Only the migration of birds can parallel this vast breadth of unanimity.

Itineraries were rapidly rerouted, business timetables suspended, deadlines postponed; vacation schedules were altered, holidays adjusted, for this necessary of all trips. Plans and directions were recharted in one concerted hurry. A mass pilgrimage flowed its relentless flux on this vanishing mecca. Their object would imminently be no more for material eyes.

Babies prematurely leapt to adolescence, just to reach an age that would glimpse the tiniest appreciation of their era's final link with a genuine historic relic. Monks and nuns came with vials for tears, and mimeographed prayer sheets to chant from. Vulgarians and philistines were infected by the culture-rage, and left their bourgeois pursuits of gain to jump on the bohemian bandwagon and come to swoon before this fashionably doomed altar. The publicity image of this homage would advertise and sell in bulk all their crass products and services. Martyr-like sacrifice was bound to boost business through exemplary prestige. From all lands, the well-dressed and those in rags arrived to bloat the tourist rate of a grieving town whose rehearsed mourning concealed tears smiling from fortune's glittering bliss.

Every nation was represented, some by official committees, some by regal visits of state, some by ranking ambassadors, some by busloads and planeloads of clubs, groups, organizations, and schools. Ladies of fashion and the jet set arrived with their entourage. Squads of reporters and photographers came on behalf of communication media. The number of academics and clerics staggered the imagination. Even curious foreign animals managed to swim or climb across, proving that Evolution was enjoying an upswing in cultural participation, even those species designated as low creatures, such as colonies of migratory ants that diligently made the journey with numbers that increased along the way. Fish crawled up the river for a view.

Creeping things and swinging were chartered cheaply on a cut-rate voyage or came with richly endowed luxury. The town was milling with them, exceeding spatial capacity, accommodations, or sanitation. Nobody minded. It was festival time, like a comet's visionary appearance on the sky's lower show window once or twice in a decade of centuries.

There were so many languages there that one would have thought that the declining tower was none other than that of Babel.

The town's mayor and monument's curator were given celebrity status, as befitted their improved standing in the world's gazing eyes. They were subjected to highly flattering television interviews, fawned upon, and lionized out of all restraint. Their autobiographies were serialized by an eminent ghost writer, then translated into all dead or recent languages. They were proclaimed international heroes, and presented with brand new wives, as status symbols or live medals. Their every word (whether an informal utterance or prescribed doctrine) was recorded for posterity's heeding ears, and analyzed with various metaphysical interpretations, according to the most semantically brilliant meanings possible to ascribe.

During all this, sight was not lost of the prime Cause of this hullabaloo, the religious edifice being chewed up by tragic decay of time's splendid indifference.

Like a Presidential Convention or Coronation or Inauguration, this Celebration was a phenomenon that would spoil a town in the miraculous benignity of pampering.

This modest town was beset by tidal popularity. It became the focal radius for all local cosmic reference. Without abstention, the universe's majestic varieties jumped in, and landed where everybody else was going. Like those minor animals below on wing, fin, gill, fur, or bone, immense stars and distant moons whizzed closer with flapping wind for a favoured spectacular theatrical view of the extravaganza of an old ruin soon to topple and dissolve in particles of smoke.

The journey of the Magi, laden with gifts and awesome offerings, to a humble Nativity stable, was repeated in this hectic tableau, where Modernity consummated its highest spiritual orgasm in the post-Christian era.

It was rumored that the downfall of Religion itself was symbolized in the impending collapse of this antiquated shrine. Then all theology will become a historical figure of obsolescence.

Empirical archaeologists confirmed this view. Scholars and scientists disputed this technical issue, or debated whether indeed the Death of the Spirit of Immortal Man was implicated in the crumbling plaster. Viewpoints were aired from polarities of eccentric extremism that clashed in an ideological imbroglio. Stale ideas were led to this field heaped with fresh slaughter.

Reigning royalties and their courtly pomp honored this supreme occasion. Even the Congress of Vienna was not nearly so gilded with ostentatious splendor.

But the true lover of beauty and worshipper of the past was, as well, abundantly in attendance. Genuinity vied with the sham, in deriving a pleasurable thrill from the circumstance of an ancient monument being gradually eased out of the present. Nothing could be more solemn or grander than that. Temporal drama was being woven, as a passing construction, before spectators who marvelled with well-informed respect for the magnificent significance of the moving stationary vertical procession of a rusty old building about to call it a day by kicking the bucket and giving up the ghost. Souls were stirred, and God Himself was moved.

The latter Supreme Gentleman suspended the arduous tasks of His current labor, putting it aside for a more pressing engagement. His delegates preceded Him, arranging for a Celestial Visit of State, a signal honor conferred on the town whose only boast was this authentic shrine of times gone by. God made ready to descend. In an age nostalgically devout, this memorial now passing away had been consecrated to His Everlasting Glory — a dedication that *these* days were deficient in emulating. Few buildings of modern times paid Him that glowing tribute, on which His reputation was established in our world of men. With worthy resolution, God has to struggle to uphold His own Honor, due to the slackness in the demand for His Sovereign Presence or existential Existence that characterizes this debased decadent age's impious, dissolute indifference to the reputed idea of Deity. In a day when He was out of fashion, God condescended to visit this swollen town for the privilege of watching His monument die.

As for the local Chamber of Commerce, heaven was right now, on the instant. From high, low, far, and near, their beloved town was besieged by visitors fanatic enough to come with bulging wallets. Right and left, good wholesome money was being spent. An orgy of consumption multiplied a town's rallying revenue. Commercial hearts lifted in gratified prayer. Hotels and guest houses, though charging double, were thanked with smiles of deference, so essential was any roof for a sleeping visitor's head. Restaurant and cafeteria prices soared above exorbitant. The food was so lousy that customers varied the trash, after leaving a briefly sampled plate, by ordering a second and equally obnoxious meal. Plaster souvenir models of the town's benign reason for fame were being purchased swifter than a factory production rate goaded by the bonus of overtime incentive. The printing press cranked away non-pause on explanatory catalogues, brochures, and picture postcards representing tinted photographic images of the ageing wonder. Swamped with every-swarming tourists, this place loomed larger than real life. The overflow sprawled with gaping humanity. Tarts didn't have to *solicit* patronage, but were *begged*: the customers chased *them*. Traditional outlets like prostitution and gambling enjoyed a greatly enhanced custom. The closer to the monument, the more thickly packed the congestion. This dense cultural jungle was a revolutionary event, something almost too legendary to be true.

This modest town's earning power skyrocketed simply astronomically. The concession industry and the pickpocket trade benefited hugely. Miraculous feats of commerce were a daily commonplace. Business surpassed the most prosperous optimism. Records were broken, currency floated like the breath of air. The town fathers exulted. Happiness was acquiring its most impressive definition. It was too much to bear, and sensitive businessmen openly wept in their fever of unbroken joy.

God's glorious bounty of abundance! An impassioned religious fervor was restored in every breast.

For this extremely welcome stampede, indebtedness was owing to what beatific source? All praise was due, in general thanksgiving, to that electrifying rumor of announcement that an important building's fatal days were numbered to some few tragically remaining heart-beats. The Board of Trade computed a boom popping with unprecedented proportions like muscles that conceal an athlete. Greed compelled an attempt to guarantee perpetuity. This was predictably human avarice.

The gold and silver was coming in from all foreign directions east south north and west of a well-rounded compass, converging to a magnetic center. *Preserve* that magnetic center, then: that's logical.

Material lust contaminated that town. From within, of course. From outside was where the market moved in. What a pull, what a draw!

The elders of enterprise were seated at the conference table; in attendance were their apprentice juniors.

Should their buckling breadwinner, erected before anybody's ancestral tree sprang up, deteriorate without their allied resistance? Should the communal origin of income go dry and flake off in annihilation? As yet even, it wasn't too late to prevent this major disaster. The magnet of a solvent finance budget had still not come apart. While good fortune had not fallen, every effort must go up to keep it standing. Diseased ancient chemistry will be combatted by modern achievements of scientific ingenuity. The past can only be saved by means of the present.

What's needed right now was obviously the most radical policy of prompt, instantaneous conservation. To this solution must be added a liberal dose of progressively status-quo maintenance of a thing as it already is (or was a month ago, before the foundations were imperilled). Hordes of people are now crowding about the monument. Revenue is exuding from their pockets; spending is protruding from handbags. There's quite an admission charge, in addition to the town's general facilities for purchases on the necessity, luxury, and impulse levels. God Himself donated these people to the town's thriving welfare. All very well, but they must be pushed back. The rescuing crew must get in there, where the flocking is most central, to begin work on salvation of equal magnitude to the Savior's salvation of the fallen apple of man's degenerate soul.

The committee acted, and acted quick. (This wasn't time for shirking amid the cloud-packets of theoretical verbiage.)

Requisitioning funds from salted-away mines supplying storehouse vats of deeply deposited reserves where the town's buried resources of safely invested capital wealth are sealed in secretion against just such an allocation of emergency usage for survival's rare dearness, the executive committee of elders on the Board of Trade went out and did a good job of hiring. They didn't stint as to cost, either. They contracted a crack team of engineering geniuses specializing in preservative restoration of accredited antiquities. These timely and highly-skilled experts were imported one by one from all over the inside of the world — some being summoned from even remoter places, of astral habitation, so angelically merciful was to be their crucial mission in saving tourism from losing a perfect gem. They were hailed as saviors by a grateful public body. Mass prayers were served, to get God on their side, as Foreman-in-Chief. For these special engineers, the possible was the *least* that was expected of them; the *impossible* was the *real* challenge, a test of almost exhilarating difficulty. Nature's decay must be halted by way of a miracle — a *planned* miracle, with blueprint deliberation. Natural law must be opposed to the full, by a constructively enlightened artifice. Art must save art from losing its battle against natural time. It was a task built on classically heroic lines. Only utmost genius was qualified to succeed. Their labor of invaluable salvaging was directed to a very frail edifice indeed. Bending in some dishearteningly gnarled directions, its spiral seams twisted with columnar disintegration in cracks treacherously leaking rot, the structure had a center which somehow wouldn't last out or hold. Ravaged by time, the sagging building swayed like a tender string suspended in a high storm range between parting clouds. Those chemical engineers faced the pressure of having to work quite fast. This project wasn't intended for lazy bones. Look overhead: A circle of vultures swirls in descending spirals, patient for their fell appetite of a plunge. These ugly winged beasts of foul prey scent a soon-to-be corpse of culture to feast on with gruesome glee, grimly chewing up chunks of historical flesh and spewing out as rejects the bones that myth must make its sparse picnic on. Oh, chase the sky clear of these gloomy birds heralding darkness; and may our sun shine on this old temple cleanly new and sound!

The engineering associates had to order their materials from a list of top-notch manufacturers, mindful that the monumental patient of their surgical know-how was plagued with overlayed encrustations of age's ancient burden. They acquired internal beams of durable quality, though at a discount for the product's firm being publicized in this newsworthy venture. They bought steel-tipped nails of sterling precision. Hinges, so oiled that they were slippery, were a further necessary article. Cement advertised to harden any concrete mold, was also ordered, by the can. Since lace curtains were on sale, some fine patterns were acquired for morale-lifting decoration by a somewhat effeminate member of this brilliant engineering combine. Paint was bought, for some good stiff coats to be applied. (The color scheme was worked out by votes, with the result that the harmony was the least offensive to the average esthetic taste of those practical technicians.) Concealed props and wall girders next were lent to the well-buttressed effect of stability that would prevent this creaking temple from caving in. Herculean glue helped to join together some shy individual parts. Insect exterminators were found so useful that a deal for bulk quantity was most economically arranged. Undeciphering ointment was wedged into carved scrawls of dates and initials. Hairpins, candy wrappers, cigarette stubs, and other defacing marks or unsightly blemishes were plucked loose, swept clear, cleansed free. Indentations were filled up. Care for the surface was an investment in depth dividends. Disposed-of details totalled back a recaptured whole. Magnified piecemeal progress was cumulative. Busy haste enforced wise patience in a fussy pile of proven results. So far, so good. These engineers were just what the doctor ordered for a sick building. Moreover, they were the doctor himself. Color floods the monument's cheeks; health stirs. It has relinquished that ghostly pallor. Despair is converted to hope, as a town warms its concern in the flames of a cunningly wrought deed. Matter is submitting to man's masterful brain!

These gifted engineers were hardly idle. They ordered lots of elastic supporters to keep their restored structure from lapsing into an unsightly middle-aged sag. Adhesive devices of tensile strength proved valuable matchmakers between lonely sections of the hallowed edifice; individual panels, so forlorn before, now participated in group relations in an over-all system of therapeutic interplay: to behold it was an inspirational stroke of organizational revelation. The rehabilitation of key areas of this architectural wonderpiece proceeded at perfection's stepped-up pace and steadily monotonous rate. The busy squad of experts took heart with increased zeal of industry, encouraged by each patch of success to the ardor of craftsmanship, work well done as a reward and stimulant for continuation of same. Pride and achievement reinforced each other; how well was the temple being put together! It was conforming to the original shape its inspired builder had had in mind and executed so many centuries distant back along the invisible reverse of time's abstract path! The ancient was newly visible! Art's mighty endurance was holding out!

An architect long long dead was being artistically revitalized! Oh how binding art is! It literally unites man!

Superlative rendering by a past, forgotten architect — your work entrances today's eyes with modern naive sophistication of admiration!

Your conception bred a form, and the form holds good, containing your conception to the full — it hasn't leaked out!

You imparted life to something, then died yourself. What has survived manifests your spirit yet! It was a *soul* you were fortunate to articulate. It's a soul that hasn't become fashionably dated. You who perished, made what endures! You commanded art, and retain your noble rank. What commotion you cause! Crowds are cheering outside. The engineers are performing a eulogy for the unknown architect who never envisaged what a vulgar age would grow around his masterpiece. The town is banal. Immortal folly is old, new, the same. Another today punctures an indefatigable world.

The engineers are reviving the inanimate old thing, so that it holds firmly. Endless adulation is accorded to them. Their honors multiply, their fame mounts in proportion to the amount of enthusiasm circulating in the combined cavities of all breasts of human diameter!

They *replace* the ancient architect. They either represent him, or really *are* him. Praise is lavished, as their efforts are cheered to completion.

They have resurrected beauty! They have dared, in terms of sustained scientific objectivity of realism, to invoke Magic's aid in a feat that incredibly extends restoration's honorable old boundaries. Or so it seems, judging by an overwhelming response by people interested in tourism, commerce, beauty, and other forms of human endeavor, however mundane in versions vulgarized by corruption. (Appreciation these days is conspicuous. But rejoicing occurs to hearts in their *private* capacity, as well.)

Ply on, great engineers! Gallant men, your humane deed shall nobly reward you. Magnitudes of gratitude wait to adorn the success of the bold labor in progress. Don't let go. Surely you're far ahead, you're winning!

But no complacency, just yet! Keep it up, you immortal friends and benefactors of time-invincible beauty!

It won't slip away. You're erecting the thing solid again!

They work with unabated vigor. They employ anything handy, utilize all tools of ordinary household maintenance. They twist screws in where needed. They solder, weld, and meld, with plastic fixatives, standard joints, curative sprays, lime-base mortar, patches of miscellaneous material, from repair kits for the homey mechanic or the thrifty housewife with a spool of thread and her camel's-eye needle. Physics, chemistry, and allied disciplines are referred to; the results are outstanding. Not even a beaver-eyed critic can fault their detailed accuracy. They were paid for the job they're doing so well; they're fulfilling *their* end of the contract. Having taken a complex structure and overhauled it, they allow to take place the reflecting, back to recognition, in a modern mirror, of an antique that connoisseurs had given up on. Surely this accomplishment is not of a small order? More than a semblance of the original has been resuscitated. Were the past still to have eyes, those eyes would behold, against the strange background of a changed world, an image once familiar in early rays to those eyes, and now strikingly refamiliar, a re-creation free from the impediment of transmission. As before, it stands, the monument. The surrounding town and world are different utterly, but here's this object, still taking up the same space. A corner was torn off time, and made consistent to a knot.

Had these engineers resorted to crime for a base career, what immaculate counterfeiters they could have been, or undetected pickpockets, or confidence tricksters of agile facility in the guile of a cunning craft. Instead, they devote their skills in virtue's efficient service, to boost the common good. They're no impotent arm in God's power to help man in his bungling struggles to achieve recognition in the status of a civilized animal.

Toil on, they do. They fuse, repair, spray, connect, smooth out, re-activate, set operative, lacquer, polish, finish, straighten, solidify, turn into joining, impose pattern, correct, convert, alter, rectify, mend, align, reconstruct, round out, clear up, file down, bind fast, tighten, tone down, heighten, lighten, weigh down, secure, liberate, install into place, sweep, comb, pack firm, uncongest, set off, tidy up, deodorize, repel (insects), purify, cleanse, purge, offset, alleviate, compensate, bring forth, materialize, introduce, set up, put back, shift, renovate, re-arrange, replace, spruce up, forge, even out, place into order, beautify, sterilize, unify in effect, free from erosion, render whole, emancipate, make immune to decay, refurbish, knit together, mold into harmony, make radiant, reconcile, conciliate, select, reduce, add, combine, release, harden, lengthen, truncate or curtail, systematize, wrap going, confine, unblemish, awaken, brighten up, unplug, highlight, emphasize, relegate, sacrifice, stress, choose, restore, unleash, restrain, manage, deepen, find, uncover, unfurl, reveal, translate, illustrate, freshen, spring into organization, renew, revise, discover, innovate, improvise, interpret, explain, block out, restrict, suppress, show clearly through, filter, bring into being, make into steadfast durability, actualize, concretize, complete, succeed!

It's done! A transparent lineage to the past!

They came down from the scaffold, and had to enter a file of elongated queue, to be embraced or shaken by the hand. The ordeal of a heroes' reception. Mayor, Curator, elders, proprietors, a Chamber of Commerce in full force, the beaming townsfolk, the entire population itself, committees from all over the world, inspectors, journalists, television hawks, turnouts of opinionated blocs, a mob of tourists, the stalkers of publicity, the exploiters of fanfare: all proffered congratulations in a gruff concord of vulgarity. The religious monument seemed to recede, as the engineers took a primary foremost in the precedence of scope. Second to the sun, their notable blaze fanned the universe.

The town's holy shrine realized a permanent second youth.

Archaeological antiquarians were consulted. They calculated that the restored monument will not merely endure, but prevail as well as survive. The term was fixed somewhere between forever, eternally, and endlessly. Thus, longevity would be no problem, but a blessing of long standing.

It was estimated that a dynastic succession of reliably tireless janitors should be on hand to ensure thorough upkeep. The precious building should never be neglected. History wouldn't have the heart to condone a town's responsibility for the anticlimactic ludicrousness of an ill-timed second collapse. (Even though the first collapse was averted by those dashing young engineers under veteran supervision; they'd scattered now, and all gone home, dragging honors, trophies, medals, wealth, and most-merited conceit in their applauded wake.) Sensation would be too jaded to witness attentively the drawnout crisis of a second threat to the building's impeccable integrity (now established beyond immediate doubt, relaxing tension and soothing scarred nerves).

Precautions should still be taken, as formerly, against natural hazards and unnatural predicaments perilous to the shrine's safety. Demolition bombing would be a destructive eventuality, if advocates of war ever took control. Peace must be maintained at all times; even local outflares should be stamped out and blotted with ashes. Earthquakes must be promptly extinguished, as well as volcanic eruptions belching a coarse digestion from intestinal roots mangled by malcirculation. Hurricanes; forest fires; tornadoes; epidemics; crop failure; spells of black magic; mass misfortune; biblical catastrophes both prophetic and diabolical such as the forecast end of the world and a general uprising of dead spirits to plunder and rape in anarchy's mismanagement; a deluge of baptismal drowning: such phenomena are to be held off, repulsed, and circumvented. Unlikelihoods are to be treated with distrust. Careless habits are to be abolished. A stern prudence will preside over the gift of this building to extensive mankind's growing generations. The renovated structure is expressly intended as art's dowry to a philistine future.

Its safety was snatched from the peril of emergency's teeth. Reinforced now, with pads of protective fat and strips of surface armor (transparent, to allow the beauty to shine through), this cellophane-secured, plastic-covered, cobweb-wrapped feature of any tourist's itinerary bulges vertically erect with erotic pride; stroking the sky, it caresses some virginal clouds accessible to its arching reach of supreme, masculine art.

Listed in guide books as an 'immemorial memorial', it's the focus of paternal attitudes by the relieved town fathers who undertook the expense of its fabulous salvation. These materialistic entrepreneurs proclaim hypocritically that their noble town attraction was restored at high cost to benefit 'posterity': by 'posterity', however, they mean, bluntly, 'prosperity', which *sounds* close enough. Money supersedes art, in their psychological motivation register. They own an interest in a famous shrine for private gain, cashing in on the selling power and surprising commercial pull of something old enough to be ruled as 'cultural' by esthetic historians. This is an acceptable fact. After all, they *live* there.

Their luck doesn't hold out; momentary comfort is dispelled. Some air hisses loose from the secure inflation in their bankbooks. An unforeseen decline takes place, touristically, in that dependent town. This trend scares them, and reverses all previous optimism.

In droves, the tourists stay away! The demand vanishes. Who wants to go and see, from miles abroad, what's permanently accessible now that it's safely restored? It was all the rage for sightseeing fashion when its existence dangled precariously on death's cliff. But that's all over, for the romantic danger has given way to a snug fixture. Why rush to see this relic, when one can afford to take a whole lifetime about it, since the structure was repaired with immortality as its built-in ingredient?

It was bound to outlive any potential tourist; immediacy having lost its lure, and urgency its piquant goad, why not wait, and see other things first? Life goes slowly by, and is long.

Tourists will get around to see it when they're dying — but that's far off.

Other preoccupations were much more compelling. No need to bother breaking a gut to hurry off for the sake of some dull tourist trap that's finished gnawing the dry dog's-bone of its day.

A shroud of voguelessness (like those vultures, now departed, at the time when decay seemed to be winning its internal destruction) encircles our barren relic. It's not even guarded any more, so deeply it's plunged into unpopularity's staunch solitude. No echo can recall those vanished mobs. No sign remains, to indicate the former fame. Only *it* is left behind, unseen by lengthily traveled eyes. Here's time's ignored trophy.

Memory, like art, is but a short song. Undefended by hearty throngs of tourists, this monument is invaded effortlessly by Time's near-by battalions. Abandoned by both its commercial and its art-crazed friends, deserted to the weedy field of fate, this solitary building develops a stooping droop. Rats chase each other in its merry basement.

No new crowds nourish architectural vanity; probe the marks on those vast interior surfaces; explore details subtle to architecture's art; study the uncanny spiritual effect of harmony, decked out in the radiant mysteries of an absolute essence.

The poor town begs for relief. Its country puts it on charity. Red Cross ambulances bring apples and donuts to stave off starvation.

The Mayor and Curator are sent packing to disgrace. Their exile is *imposed*, whereas the other townspeople are *voluntarily* banished. A folk-drained town is soon self-emptied of the humanity born to it.

The bigwigs have gone bankrupt. Unemployment causes a wholesale evacuation. Steadily, the aura of a ghost town replaces what was once a highly-prized stop-off in the wanderings of world-cluttered tourists, for the sake of one gem of monumental architecture.

Occasionally, some visitors still do arrive. But they're only old. (No vendors molest them, since the town is commercially defunct). The feeble and the infirm are the last faithful tourists. Tottering as the shrine itself once did, these ancients hasten to pay, not their last respects to a doomed antique, but a personal visit before the world sees *them* out. They come to see the dismal old ruin not for fear that it will perish, but in the dark conviction that they themselves are the ones doomed, and without engineers to restore them (in a job of salvation-renovation acclaimed for its perfect haste of timely brilliance by a universe that then proceeded to pay no further heed to a safe, newly-painted old bore).

To what's old, only the old come, to wrinkle irony tragically. Perhaps the skeleton crew of the former Chamber of Commerce should build a burial ground behind that bothersome monument, and an old-age home for senior citizens as well, who stray in from abroad with senile veneration for art and set about the laboriously delaying decay of death's mechanical animation. Having come from so far, they wouldn't be able to make it back home again. So here, under the shadow of what was once rotting, and is now bereft of care or preventative treatment, these sleepy travelers would protract their disintegration in a setting suitable to their ceremonious motion into a cemetery's haven of rest.

Otherwise, how could business be revived? No magic halo is sported by that superannuated religious relic. It would not do as a miraculous healing shrine such as Lourdes in France, which has profited exceedingly from the custom of the superstitious of all nations, those hysterically afflicted and sufficiently devout to procure the private benefits of a cure.

Tourism is a highly difficult art. But art is no perfect assurance of a high touristic turnover. Ascertainable predictability lags behind.

The tourist market brutally fluctuates, in its fickle application of fashion to art.

Can a town recoup its losses? Hardly. Its greedy capitalists miscalculated. But they did do one thing: unwittingly, they saved a monument for posterity to conserve. (An international team of restorers is moving in, with the latest in anti-decay devices, to consign the shrine to immortality — again! It's a different engineering unit this time, employed by a World Body for Cultural Preservation. The slumbers of the dying worshippers — those elderly immigrants who camp along the site — will be momentarily arrested; then they'll be left to fall back to the peace of corpsey stillness.)

Posterity, in the long run, won. But *prosperity* for those town leaders in the venerable, brittle art of commerce? — no. They're martyrs, while Art marches on.

The Art of Concealed Abortion

Crippled by life's agony, the man sat on his brain for an hour. This more or less smothered several oversized thoughts. When this reverse hatching occurred, only broken eggs remained, like worries with their skulls cracked.

He met a girl, and kissed her through a swift abortion, while they held hands. Working with all their might, they produced a dead life. From then on, their smile tilted to the ugly side.

Then, to forget, he turned artist. He fought against colors, and stabbed the canvas, where muddy blood formed as a protest against meaning. He copied nature, and in retaliation, spring was delayed by a month that year. Then poverty crushed his art, and the crumbled bones formed a neat skeleton where he fell. He looked like a motheaten self-created work of sculpture, and was put on exhibit underground. His girlfriend, spry after her abortion, and already bearing the seed for another one, scattered her feminine tears along his anonymous plot. His paintings went for firewood, in the municipal dumping ground. A journal was found. In it, there was evidence of mental deterioration. Its words were clumsy, but had origin in the dictionary, whereas his thoughts and paintings were obscure in their reference, depending on bare ideas of nature and his past.

His girlfriend claimed the journal, underlined her own name where mentioned, and, because of her higher education, completed sentences, inserted commas, and rounded out the tragedy. Delayed by her second abortion, the work was completed some time afterward. Through a lucky series of contacts, from lower to higher agent, in which the sale of her love was included, the script became a famous movie, a popular box office hit, and soon there was a stupendous demand for the paintings of its poor subject. Phantom auctions were created, and genuine originals became a fabulous obsession of every art dealer. Hundreds of ghost painters were employed, each representing a different phase of the artist's development. Museums were clamoring for a sample. Art hysteria hit our country, ruining the careers of current artists, looking beyond life for the works of a dead man. The girlfriend was now known as his wife, in a posthumous but hasty marriage. A sequel to the first motion picture, by popular demand, projected a great genius into the history of our culture; and stuffy old Europe, with its outmoded art, looked toward these shores for its legendary universal image. The fan clubs were by now international.

The actor who played the hero had to be retired from the screen, to preserve the triumph of his role, and keep the movie ever identified with its subject. There was a movement to kill the actor, and thus have his death conform to the real-life death of its original, linking the actual world with its immense satellite, Hollywood. But the actor, protected by several aliases, slipped into oblivion, and was unrecognized except for his black glasses. He commissioned an art instructor, and is now painting in precisely the mode of the myth-like man he had portrayed.

Meanwhile, a technicality developed. The abortionist threatened to sell his story to the press, unless the great man's wife divorce her dead husband and marry him. The ensuing legal problems, clarifying the fidelity of a widow, freed the woman to marry her abortionist. She then paid to have her new husband sent through medical college, where he graduated as an M.D., much to her pleasure. Then they carefully produced a baby, and it was actually born. They named it in honor of the great man who had brought them together. True, they lived in his shadow, but the shadow was paved with that comfortable substance, wealth. Art had profited, too. Everybody was now imitating a certain artist, and amateur brushes and palettes were in evidence everywhere. Luckily for the human race, the artist had for some reason never mentioned abortion in his journal. Either that, or his girlfriend had discreetly attended its removal.

Love by Proxy of Solitude

Along the journey of reminiscence, Billy-Boy summed up his life so far. There he was, almost at life's halfway point. Three times, love's arrow had scarred him "permanently"; four times, it had nicked him seriously; seven times, it had nipped him to an outcry of pain. Once, it had been mortal. He'd recover in the depths of death's tomb.

That should be six years ago. Since then, Isabel had been made into a mother twice. Billy-Boy had been superseded by a double fatherhusband who took marriage institutionally. Isabel was cemented fast beyond reclaim.

Billy-Boy had accomplished an unyielding bachelorhood. For this feat, he was awarded solitude's silver trophy. Despite its heavy burden, he couldn't just shelve it and leave it: he carried it, like an emblem, anywhere he went.

Solitude, in fact, was his identity-label, to a sounder depth than his alliteratively boyish name. Facially, he conformed to that most public role of his privacy.

Girls who otherwise might have been interested in him as a romantic prospect or as affair-fodder sensed the confirmation of his solitude that lopsided him to monolithic predictability; then instinctively, and sensibly, they dismissed any notion of however tentative a bond with him, except as only a "friend." Billy-Boy's humiliation advanced thus to a hardened pattern.

Billy-Boy's childhood could be described as "unhappy." But analysis failed to cure him. The remainder of his life was so molded to fixity, flexibility's parole was futile. He'd remain a "loner." He hadn't touched the pit's bottom, as yet, of loneliness's extremity. Time would facilitate this motion's melancholy goal.

The day gaily belonged to spring. Billy-Boy got momentum into his stride. He walked briskly on the park's side of sprightly oak. Green blossoms showered on him with the fluff of pillow-feathers.

Soon came a slight resumptive of self-pity. Isabel was wheeling a baby carriage, her older little boy keeping pace alongside.

Billy-Boy rapidly shifted his direction. But he'd been sighted by loved eyes prosaically unloving.

Distance couldn't blunt her shout. "Come over," the voice beckoned, like a bomb's casual descent.

Weeks of agony waited to follow this one confrontation. Billy-Boy quickly escaped, running headlong into his own embarrassment, that wore Isabel's staring face.

He moved to another apartment, at the contrary end of this city's populous persecution. Emptiness he needed, not such a sad fullness.

Lacking its solaces, Love was for Billy-Boy the one be-all for life's full bag of drama. Love's inner soul was romantic, and its outer body consisted of sensation's bond of clinched embrace. He sought love at dancing halls, dinner parties, cocktail parties, art gallery openings, the deep-groined vault of gray mausoleum-like museums, casual park pick-ups, theatre or concert-hall intermissions, late-night bohemian bacchanals, the magic of momentary meetings, contrived offhand introductions; and by any legal method, however it made dignity sag under the embarrassment of need's clumsy gigantism. Sometimes he'd light upon a sex affair, or a fumbling chaste flirtation: but these were armored with an impersonal character, a stylistic mechanical formalism of nondescript consequence. His solitude remained evenly in place, like a coolly combed head of hair unruffled by a pretentiously endearing wind.

Unexpectedly, a girl named Sue fell for him. All Billy-Boy had to do was reciprocate, and he'd rid himself of solitude's oafish virginity.

He tried to be impressed by her most attractive qualities; but with all the good will in the world, Billy-Boy was not smitten; he contrived to deify her charms, but only succeeded in observing their multiple imperfections. He suffered: his Solitude was immaculately out of reach: even to a girl who in turn suffered in not bridging it to hers, allying two banks in an arc of love's throbbing flow.

Sue wept; at the other end of this telephone hook-up, Billy-Boy responded with all the aloof indifference of an inaccessible mountain peak. Their end had come. Sobbing her life to the winds, Sue replaced the receiver, gently closing out Billy-Boy from hope's dearness and the dream's farewell promise.

Billy-Boy was free; costing the token tithe of pain, his solitude was unscathed; it could resume its tragic career, in its slow gradual road to misery. The threat of being detoured by Sue had been averted. Solitude's interior star would now sing its destined dirge, a solo mournful to the heavens. How agreeable was self-administered sadness! Billy-Boy's warmth was most pleasantly chilled. Autumnally, the splendor of gilt foliage thickened his flaming veins with a wild outpour of grief. (In the true world, Spring was spinning a hazy beam to scaffold July's majestic height.)

Sue was invited to dinner by some friends. Isabel and her husband were co-guests. This is how Sue, jilted only recently by Billy-Boy, met Isabel, who six years ago was for Billy-Boy the one sorrowful love in his life, the central jewel in solitude's sterling work of craftsmanship. Having rejected him, Isabel was thus ably qualified (once Sue had confided in her) to advise Sue how to go about winning Billy-Boy. Her role as an amateur psychologist would now serve Cupid's solemn mission, to relieve Billy-Boy of his gloomy robes of bachelorhood, and assist Sue to reverse her recent forlorn misfortune.

"He *ought* to get married: he's over thirty now, and he just mopes most of the time. (That's the report I get about him: we still have some acquaintances in common.) He's between jobs, and is lazy about getting ahead. He's a brooding introvert. The other day I was going by the park with my children. He was around the corner, I saw him between tree trunks. I did what was only natural. I called out to him, because six years were passed, he had time to get over me and not be so emotional. But then, of all things crazy to imagine: Lingering love gave him a cowardly fit, he vanished deliberately out of sight! It's obvious that he still hasn't grown up. There's only one way for him to mature: he needs someone like you. This is where you come in, to round out his complete personality. The way he's been going is waste, ruin, tragedy. Sue, together we must save him! He's worth our combined effort. If you seduce him into loving you, he'll get over that obsession about having a lonely complex. The trouble is, he *suspects* any romantic interest in him; he thinks he's so inferior, that he couldn't possibly be loved! So if he *is* loved, he regards it as an intrusion on the solitude he holds so dearly to, like a lifebelt in an alien sea. The time he and I went together, I learned a lot about him. I didn't choose to apply it for my personal advantage in forming an alliance with him, but now it's for you to inherit the benefits! But first, assure me that you really sincerely want him!"

"I do, believe me! — provided my case isn't absolutely hopeless! The way you described him bothers me — convince me not to doubt! — can he possibly change?"

"Only if *you* stick fast with real insistence on getting him. *He's* so defeatist, *you* mustn't be so, by giving up too early or on some easy note of discouragement. You've got to *work* to win this sticky character, this tricky, slippery guy with the built-in self-sadness system! What a wild customer, if you can haul him up!"

"All right, you sold me. What's the first step? I guess I'll have to phone him."

"No. The trick is to force him into phoning *you*."

"But how? He seemed so cold to me. He wanted no part of love. He was pretty definite about it."

"There are ways. Just wait. Come to dinner tomorrow. By then, I'll have an infallible plan. Foolproof, you'll see!"

"You *are* a dear. Never could I repay you — never!"

"Don't try — it's no sacrifice. I'd be a very happy woman to see you two merge together: *he*'d benefit, and you'd be an incomparable pair. I have an inspired intuition that it's true! This project so excites me, I'm wet! If we can only pull this wonderful thing off! That's what creativity means!"

"Sorry, I'm still disturbed by one thing: If he thinks himself so unworthy of being loved, mustn't he think me even *more* unworthy, to be the fool to take the pain to love him? If he turned me down before, how am I any different now that he shouldn't spurn me again? — I know it sounds distressing."

"Your outlook is wrong — get rid of that pessimism! Now, here's our address: seven-thirty tomorrow night. Just trust in the constructive ability of my plan!"

"But Isabel — he doesn't even care for me physically! I'm not his type! I have no appeal for him!"

"*Force* yourself to take a more positive attitude. You think that by being negative, you're being realistic! You fool, Sue — I'm sick!"

"I just couldn't stand being hurt a second time — it would be so many times worse! Oh, I'm sorry you're angry! I submit to your counsel. I'm in your hands: Direct me!"

"But smile, silly! Lift up that droop on your pathetic face — you look so dubious, I'm afraid to operate!"

To conceal the woeful cast of a face with out-of-control features, Sue placed that face inside the sloped hollow of Isabel's shoulder. Hidden abashed in smother, she embraced this person who still possessed the long-lost dark Heart of fragile Billy-Boy. That heart scorned by one, desired by the other. Perhaps a transfusion, a transference, would lodge that wrested prize in the ample nest of Sue's tender but spurned bosom.

There, the heart would be tended to so delicately, nurtured at the fount of affection's deep solicitude, that it would grow content in the mating sanctuary of delight's permanent address! Yet Sue felt ugly, in those neurotic pools of eyes behind which, in a swamp, was the abandoned hut of Billy-Boy's self-critical soul. Sue's stunt — her dedication, in fact — was to explore the sullen wilderness there, and discover some civilized outlet for the purity crippled in repression. Sue would open up his song of loneliness, and graft it melting onto hers. Their tears will waft them to the open transport of a union. Signed in rhapsody by their attending angel!

The following night, Isabel presided as a female sage. After dinner, her husband left the room so her talk with Sue would nest securely in that frankness afforded only by privacy. Billy-Boy's character was analyzed wide open.

An outspoken intimacy fell upon the two women. Billy-Boy's heart was openly transferred from the knowing bosom of the one (ending six years of quite ignored residence) to the trembling, unconfident, eagerly rent-free breast of the new nominee landlady. By instilling hope in her disciple, Isabel had doubled the force of Sue's love, whose resurrection made Easter's Ascension seem like a short jump infinitely below the gothic rafter in divinity's steeple.

Never had Billy-Boy been loved so. It even pierced his oblivion. Though he was now at the other end of their city, Sue's passion charged almost to his ears. The vibration whirred so hard, the defense alarm clanged like a lunatic. A general conscription was called, as Solitude's manpower was recruited from reserves of a slumberingly standing army. Bugles blared out the creeping closer of danger's crawling demon. Not the welcome Isabel, but the dirty daring of an infidel.

"So I'll phone him myself," volunteered Isabel, disclosing her cunning solution. "I'll invite him to forget me, and then be my friend. He'll visit me platonically, and I'll plant seeds with your name on them, in that weedy garden he calls his heart. From me to you will go his displaced love. He won't wait, but rush out of my house and phone you alone with secret trembling. You can expect a proposal, once the decent interval passes. My life's great thrill will come to fruit! Sue, you happy bride already! Kiss me, your smart savior!" They embraced violently. Their plot would have no trouble succeeding. The air stirred, to the twin throb of the bleating feminine heart. Billy-Boy's fate had been rectified. The guarantee was as dandy as a lace bonnet. And not so quaintly outmoded, either.

No sooner had the telephone been installed in his new apartment, but it rang promptly for Billy-Boy. He alertly pounced on it: the call, a most radical factor, altered his life. Love's own voice was saying, "Let's be friends."

"Isabel, will you renounce your husband?"

"Silly boy! Of course I love him! Come right over for a drink. I have some news to tell you."

"What news?"

"Not now — come!"

"But the subway would take an hour! But you want to see me! Say no more. I can understand. I care for you enormously! Be still till I arrive."

Billy-Boy suspected that Isabel had fallen tired of her husband; that belatedly, it had wisely dawned on her to heed True Love. What a joy was that subway ride! He had won a passive triumph after all! Happiness rode on deception's flying horse. Illusion's wings felt so solid, that by sensation's law they *must* be true!

Like a homeward hero returning from a Victory of State, Billy-Boy flew up the stoop to buzz open the door to claim outfrustrated Love. But only Isabel's husband answered. After reciprocal introduction, Billy-Boy was ushered in — by the very man he would ideally design to cuckold! Isabel was still busy with the children.

The husband and he made "conversation." This polite murder of awkward time forestalled the dishonesty of sincerity. The visitor's sole goal was to take possession of a love withheld to the exile of six years of suffered isolation. After all that, he finally had the right to be impatient. Imprisoned to interminable patience and the tragic suspension of hope for so long, now he longed for outright release. To slake thirst, and fling aside torment, at the bold, raped immediacy to force open Isabel's lips! Even to the husband's view: for one must lose to let the newcomer win. And the newcomer had been first, before. Now he arrived to find what had only been lost. To restore the world's balance, and even out time's odds in the jilt of delay. Prime's former season was summoned from the dead. Ripeness earns a second chance. Let jubilation escort it home.

This conspicuous pause bulged in an agony of bigness: Isabel's awaited appearance had not materialized to release the instant. The husband's dull presence became opaque. A transcendant hush looked past him. Billy-Boy slighted this overcome usurper's immaterial existence.

(The slight was noticed and stored away for a future flare of resentment. The husband suspected an unconventional tension, and shrewdly guessed its cause. But he feigned innocence, with a business speculator's guile.)

Now Billy-Boy must succeed his successor, to wrench the stolen prize of vengeance from the smug possession of its legal thief. Excusing himself, the husband left Billy-Boy to contemplate in expert solitude the restoration of justice in the scales of divine hunger's metaphysics. The next tableau called for Isabel as an original substitute for anticipation's flickering projection of an ideal picture. The re-assertion of reality's sceptre, not its impressive shadow. To solidify the emergent dream, and be love's individual symbol. In this mental way, Billy-Boy spent emotional minutes regarding Isabel at the shrine of portentous image.

"But I'm thinking of *Sue*; For*get* me; don't ever hold out hope again. Really, you're so immature! It's in*credible* that you don't appreciate her! She's not really bad-looking, in fact she's a dear! You'd find her more adorable with the years. Really, stop crying! You're a grown man!

"Oh, stop that now! You look so miserable — and all for me?! I tell you, only *Sue* can console you. She's worth ten me's. I can't rival her little finger even. My husband and I are well matched (all our friends tell us that); but *you* and *Sue*!: an un*beat*able pair! You don't know what's good for you! She's a marvel! *Phone* her; — you're too upset. Here, use *this* handkerchief now. This is the most unmasculine exhibition I've ever seen! But don't worry, Sue will never know: it's only *our* secret.

"Here's her number — should I dial it for you? Your fingers look too helpless to do *anything*! Oh, come, don't start that sobbing again! Your breast is heaving like a hurricane! This is too comical! Oh, ha, it's ludicrous! Ah — .

Isabel was stifled with laughter. The hysterical peals rose to mockery's shrill emulation. Mortified, Billy-Boy waited for her heaving to subside. But *his* sides heaved, letting his sobs ease with spasmodic control.

"Yes Sue, I really *would* like to see you. Yes, I *want* to. I've just been speaking to Isabel. She's fond of you, she's a good friend. She was just praising you. No, I'm not there now. I'm in a phone booth. Sure, I want to visit you. Get ready — I'm coming over now. Not enough notice?! For*get* your hair and your bath. I'm not interested in them. I got to see *you*."

They became engaged. Once things had begun to get rolling, Isabel shrewdly left town, having arranged to have her husband's vacation take place then. It was a critical point in the game. Her absence would force a singleminded independence on the genuineness of Billy-Boy's affection for Sue, unaided by Isabel as a scheming prop. Billy-Boy fell back on himself — and forward onto Sue. Habit had substituted Sue, assisted by pleasure, for Isabel, in love's interchangeably romantic plasticity. Sue even *dressed* like Isabel, and did her hair the same way. And Billy-Boy, at first, *wanted* to be fooled. Only self-deception blocked the violent entry of some irrational act.

Isabel's perfume lingered on Sue's person. Sue was all of Isabel that he could have.

Being obedient to Isabel, he was able to possess her in his eyes-shut embrace of her otherwise unattractive intermediary. It was as directly far as he could get with Isabel, by carrying out her summons to its utmost letter. Kissing her delegate meant being warmed remotely by the real thing. For a poet at heart, that would *almost* suffice. There was a superficial benefit, as well: the curse of physical abstinence had been lifted. (But on this point, the spirit also cashed in:) It made vivid the Isabel he idolized. Indulging his carnal sense cleaned a purer clarity for love's lofty abstraction of Isabel. Purged was the worshipper, as the shrine glowed more heavenly.

Sue was stoical, in fortitude against knowledge. Sensing her secondary role, she restrained despair and played a waiting game: in time, Billy-Boy was hoped to identify, then substitute, the symbol for the thing it symbolized. The symbol would *become* the Isabel who, being unattainable, would dwindle to a fluttered vague dimness: she'd merge with the Great Memory, and be in particular forgotten. Sue it was who would remain, as the emblem or trophy turned concrete. Or else, as the soiled oasis; the shallow dregs of consolation's worn-through mirage.

Isabel's husband had to return to work. With him and their little boys, Isabel came back home. Billy-Boy lost no time in phoning. "I want to submit my progress-report to you," he whined aggressively. "I've been making headway with Sue, you'll be glad to know. Why haven't you communicated with us? We're officially engaged, I can tell you. Didn't our letters get forwarded to you? You place yourself out of reach of our gratitude. That's unfair, for someone who was so responsible. Can you get away from the children, and meet us for a reunion? That wasn't graceful, to do a disappearing act. We owe you so much, it's a duty you shouldn't want to escape from. We would have tracked you down!"

"Yes, you 'owe me so much'! — but do you owe me this threat as well?" Isabel retorted like a roused prey. "That's what it sounds like, with your voice in that ugly tone. All right. I'm sorry, then. But I want to see the both of you *together*. And come *here*, where I can control it. Now, down to cases. Are you serious about getting married?"

"Deathly. There's no question of disappointing you."

"That's nice. But for her own sake?"

"Of course. Sue's the only girl I ever loved."

"Don't be funny, it's rude. Don't tamper with emotions; they're too delicate for your gross trifling. I'd hate you if you hurt her."

"Then you won't hate me. I'm bound, the issue is settled."

"Did you fix a date?"

"Sure, but it's indefinite."

"I'm not in the mood for your humor. Will you both come to dinner tomorrow night?"

"How can you be refused? We've taken your word *before*."

"I told you, stop being cynical. Then I'll expect you at eight o'clock. I'll be glad to see you both. Till then, give my love to Sue."

"But not to me, eh?"

Isabel said goodby for politeness, to seem gradual about hanging up. She became worried, and regretted her interference. It had been no little passing whim in his phone voice, but some stark defiance that transgressed civility and suggested an animal baring fang with raised claw. A survival of the jungle primitive was behind his witty banter. Its foreboding had a grim chill.

Much more tangibly derived was the uncertainty that *Sue* was subjected to. Matters had become unpleasant. Billy-Boy had treated her unkindly. A subtle malice, like a kind of slimy ooze, had seeped out, or trickled forth, from some of his ambivalent "cracks." He hadn't paid her a single respectful love-tribute at whose core was devotion's eloquent courtship. His cavalier dismissal of her human status was cruel to the edge of monotony. Pretense at being engaged had been laughed away. Only his sexual pleasure had been unfaked. No, that was wrong — nothing else had been faked, either. Not the slightest hint of romance, except in irony's form of manifest insult. Sue was no Isabel-substitute. That rang clear. The indignity! Her starved dignity would need to be re-asserted, not fed with irony's rotten crust! Rebellion swelled up with bristling burrs, in her chest of despised femininity that had been debased to a cesspool for lust's casual inspection. Decency was on demand by her outraged personal humanity. Billy-Boy would have to supply it, or Isabel atone.

"Come along, don't get difficult. I love you, so let's go. Isabel expects us both. My reputation isn't sneaky. She won't like it, if you don't show up too."

"*She* not like it! I don't mean to sabotage your infatuation, but what about caring how *I* feel?"

"Look, I *know* how you feel. Meanwhile, I happen to be concentrating on her just now."

"What for? To drag her into adultery — isn't that what you're using me for?"

Billy-Boy kicked Sue swiftly on the shinbone; a display of electric sparks umbrella'ed from the pain. Sue submitted, as her principles were gagged numb.

They arrived, like an ordinary, close couple. Isabel received them guardedly. Her husband suppressed annoyance. He was fed up with Isabel's glamorous role of deceit and intrigue. He resented being left out, and yet wanted to keep his nose clean. Sue was sullen and subdued. A blow-up was brewing in her, but no advance rumbles betrayed it, except the discontent that was clearly exposed. The eating had begun. Billy-Boy's eyes were bright, glowering with mirth or mischief. Isabel studied his face with furtive glances. She detected in it a desperation, a defiance, a hatred, and an insolent daredevil cockiness. She foresaw the possibility of physical danger. Billy-Boy was a bad loser: and he had lost *her*. Vanity first might chafe, but then the protest would be blown to a storm's vehemence. She must apply her power tactfully, to keep Billy-Boy in hand. She must outplay the wrath eruptive in his spirit of cutthroat revolt. She must contain this venom, keep the aggression from spreading its sour spew of pus along this path strewn with other involved lives. She must regulate, conserve, defend.

Coffee was concluded. Sue's bitterness discharged the first volley. Strident with wounded ingratitude, she let go on Isabel a nasty catapult of accusation. The husband was amused, and grateful: his wife's interference, or "assistance," was construed in the light of a punishable offense: the others would do the incriminating for him; he would sit back, in silent righteousness, to observe her destruction; she'd be put in her place, repent, and be contrite. She'd be a sweet wife, and learn submission. (And not dictate when their vacations were to take place. And not make him amicable to unruly guests chosen in her own machinations.)

Billy-Boy gallantly defended Isabel's honor with such a rude crack, Sue recoiled like a snake semi-sliced with a hacker. Then, for further instinctual preservation, she ducked in retreat behind a timely barrage of tears. She was drenched sopping dry, taking desolate refuge behind the barrier of grief's lonely deluge. The storm pattered out her dirge.

Sue was out of it for a while. Isabel scolded Billy-Boy for his vicious assault on Sue. He protested that he had punished Sue for attacking Isabel. The hostess held up a hand, and requested peace. This was reasonable, for those strained circumstances. The husband was pleased, and smug.

Billy-Boy was cordially hated from three sides. Sue felt betrayed by her lover and her helper. Isabel felt ganged up on; her husband had assented, while the couple she had experimented with were popping shots at her. Bad feelings had infested the dinner. First appetite then digestion, were poorly provided for, in violation of harmonious hygiene. Rancor and recrimination abounded.

That husband enjoyed silent immunity. He had his spokesmen. He was a tacit partner in the persecution ring that had Isabel in a shuffling trap. She was angry and scared. She had contrived a mating bridge between lonely hearts; but it snapped back with recoiling springs, sprung cables, elastic girders, to react on its surprised but kindly intentioned engineer. The project had collapsed; the blueprint had miscalculated, with an architect's fantasy. And what right had her husband, to join the jeering conspiracy?

She had match-made, by rubbing a combustible couple together; the conflagration had caught fire, to scorch the igniter. The husband wasn't even singed, but he would fan the blaze. Inflamed passions easily take perverse turns. Or bake some worse burns. Isabel was a martyr, a stake consumed to ash. Her plan had shed only heat, but little light.

An hour after dinner, the blacklash of misfired purpose was still tearing spiteful gashes in the bitten-down, chewed-up pulp of Isabel's battered pride. Four people were glued together. They remained at table; the table united their discord in a central square of cloth-covered wooden neutrality. Wine fed further flares to common dissension. Aggravation grumbled like a hound injured by rebuke. A sprite bellowing curses had the run of the room. Misshapen Evil crept in to have a look. Insult brooded; its tongue spilled out of its mouth like a boiling pot of poison. Forces were at work; supernatural smiths hammered weapons for doom's last ditch. Wicked colors stultified the light. Four souls stuck it out. The ceiling crumbled, and hissing smoke entered the room. A black cloud with ugly contours scraped the quartet. It was not laden with cherub-strung harps and pleasure's sonorous instruments. Strife chased the tail of Disorder; while Anarchy, indolently lounging, ate lizards by the gulpful. Only the husband wasn't keenly suffering. But even on *his* brow, tranquility's sweat refused to streak. Monsters were being spawned left and right, with no respect to pedigree, precedence, or natural law. They took over, while human perspective receded with safe faintness. Roars and hallucinations danced in mathematical chorus, heedless of orthodox phenomena. Revelation struck the four principal figures — but the bolt rebounded, to drive a spike through the Devil's gaping foot. He retaliated by crucifying the cosmos, including measureless eons of space. Results are delayed, by several light years.

But the husband swore by nothing but realism. Imagination had taken the upper hand, so he retired in good order, with unruffled poise and a smirk of pity for unruly children, from the wild upheaval in the room. The embattled trio were left to concentrate their turbulent dissipation.

Repressions were flung aside, as having no place in the proceedings. Sue's target, in abundant glee, was Isabel. Billy-Boy chose the same victim, and was ready to resort to violence as the appropriate technique. Ganged up on, Isabel consulted her wits, but they were out of order. Disloyalty surrounded her, even from herself. Control and assurance had run astray, leaving her in bare distress. What reason could she argue with? The arena was not mental. Logic would not halt gladiators on the circling dust. The used plates on the dinner table could not reflect a wholesome scene. Emotion's naked body, bruised with dripping glands, was obscenely on view. The cups and silverware had a dull luster. Isabel gambled a leaping step.

She blustered into the air, piercingly: "Get married, both of you!" she commanded, resorting to authority's ruse, hoping to recall the habit of obedience in her one-time wards now posing as graduate opponents in combative play. Rays of grudge replied; and dissent's barbed wire, behind which hostility's hardware of snouts was poked with unblinking clanks. Isabel reached for a fork, but was intercepted by a counterthrust. A loving hand molested her fundamental right of motion, and was intent on inhibiting other freedoms as well. Six repressed years clamped down.

Her wrist whitened in Billy-Boy's grip; to this bone-breaking pressure, he added severe corkscrew twists to vary the harmonic dissonance in pain's trills, runs, trebles, and rife muted effects: she herself was the vocalist, and in tune with the instruments she deafened the hall with a memorable scream, operatically among the higher registers. This retrieved her husband, who heeded the call and came racing in. He broke the marauder's grip and shoved him flying to a corner, where a bystanding lamp flickered, fell, but played down the drama by not breaking in the thunderous crash. All those involved were stunned; momentarily, arrested motion produced the momentous apparition of a pause. Indrawn breaths poured themselves out, to mingle balanced components in the air's stricken flow. The moving film was stilled to a solitary photograph. The grouping of the figures centered on a dynamically offset composition, full of the pomp of pose in the quick of heat, caught in the supreme moment of unconsciousness. The snapshot stirred; then sequence, regaining lifelike speed, overtook the arty hesitancy.

Sue's revenge on both Billy-Boy and Isabel was being carried out by themselves on each other as though by mutual defeat, in deference to her armless wish. Seeing her passive will granted by her victims in pendulum orgy of roughhouse affliction (assisted by the husband's intervention as a countervailing measure), Sue fluctuated between those two polar guilts of Grief and Relief in doses of alternating potency or in opposing currents of resisted emotional completeness. This conflict drew her in, and sprayed her with diffused mysticism. Her simplicity was colored in complicated tonalities. She'd be immersed in a bath, splash around a bit to remove the external coatings and foreign coloration, and get out of the tub as a woman again, her skin rippling with consistent pores. But now, agonized ecstasy quite wore her apart.

The husband took over. It was his house. Isabel froze to a corner, shrunken and broken up. To re-establish order where riot had roosted, the husband banished that pair ludicrously mismatched by his fool of a wife. They stumbled out, in dragging disarray. The husband beamed. Victory was his, over the bohemian insurrection; his sensible mind had prevailed, as the final word in an undefined dispute. He was the master. Isabel nursed her wrist. She appealed for his forgiveness. An erotic impulse surged and tingled in him. He seduced his wife, forgetting that he was her husband. The pleasure on this particular occasion exceeded the usual and hurtled past the ordinary. Her dangling wrist introduced a kind of fetish. But it was the unsettling disturbance, that little local riotous turmoil he had just stamped out, so upsetting to regularity, which had raised his sexual flame to its relishing zest of delight. He was the strong man, to protect his wife.

He had rescued her, and proved supremacy. Now she must request, not demand. He, it was he, who was the man.

While the peacemaker exulted and resumed command over a household exorcised from spells of perilous ordeal, the estranged but bound couple whom he had deported to an ignominious exile floundered in midnight anonymity in the dark city's barren streets. Their state was not tidy. Demoralized with the tipsy syrup of corruption, they wandered with no fixed goal. Gruff and grouchy, Billy-Boy made an indecent proposition, repugnant to Sue's dishonored virtue. She had already been more than sufficiently compromised. They embarked on a scolding session, until Billy-Boy tried to force the argument with such strongarm tactics as that from which Isabel was only now recovering (following a marital bout of sorts and kinds). Sue was manhandled, pummeled about, given ferocious wallops, in his writhing grip. In reflex, she kicked his shin; the jolt echoed to his coils; his flailing hold slackened, letting her slip away in an awful coupling of terror tangled with remorse. Her wounds bore bruised nerves. Love had been trampled underfoot, as a creature too lowly to be revived. Pain was compelling perfect sense. Like a torpedo, realization ripped its trail loose under the canopy of collapsing sails. It resolved her, like an oracle. No more would she submit her sordid, morbid vulnerability to a madman's whim. She was quits of the whole deal. Anguish and shock had curtailed her career as a dupe. Some other man would find her attractive — a man gentle, kind and normal. She would pretend love, and live out the cheat convincingly. The acting would turn it true; a sounder foundation would uphold it. Not a remarkable fate, but better than being cudgeled in a brutish honesty of passion to Billy-Boy's exciting range of anti-institutional strangles. What was he snorting rebellion against? Isabel had made her aversion clear. Sue would carry her compassion elsewhere; she'd clear a path for a fresher victim to volunteer. Or for Isabel to be crushed, in case Billy-Boy's business there has an account of unsated vengeance, from an appetite too conscientious to be replete. Isabel had a husband to protect her from undesired love that was too stubborn to die. Sue would seek one too, for shelter from exploitation and cruelty; and for values on a more affirmative scale, which experience would construct a rationale for, in her course of growing together with him. Any dance would yield dozens of prospects. Instinct would pluck the most likely candidate.

For forever, Sue stepped down from his life. Isabel, as well, was given the privilege of never hearing from her any more. The grotesque triangle was stripped of a corner. Disaster had rubbed away *Sue's* angle, leaving one corner empty, of that odd triangle of contrary wills. One knot had come apart: the interlocking was unraveled by this notch. Like a worm truncated by a third, the organism might coil itself to some strange endurance, in its twisting life left. With one corner eliminated, two still stood as the rushing tournament narrowed: One avoiding all contest, the other to push aggression beyond limits tolerable to society's tribunal of conservative decorum. An arrow guides this one-sided clash. The reluctance of the one is countered by increased violence on Billy-Boy's propelled part, as the loser forging rugged compensation on an oppressed victor.

He loves her. Impossible to moderate what can't be helped, either in fury or extent. Love rejected becomes hate — big, bitter, and complete. It's so excruciating, desperation's rule of all-out war, without recourse to pity, is invoked. Restrictions relaxed. Anything goes, when belligerence motivates anarchy to get going. He'll raid her house, ravish her by force. So what if it's anti-social? Such scruples don't deter true individualism. What's the prospect, from here? Anger versus defense, with panic thrown in to the latter. Husband away working all day: field is clear for rough maneuvering. Victim ought to cringe. She's lost that initiative she once enjoyed by virtue of domination as Cupid's agent. She's so scared of publicity, she fails to ask for police protection. Target easy, must be toyed with first. Set sights, employ power, inflict maximum suffering. No dainty concessions made by war. The conditions are too special, the delights too cruel.

Billy-Boy stalks, with rashness nobly proportioned. Enemy too frightened to inform husband. Stalker lurks in alley, peers in at screen, spies at street angles. Free all day to harass her gradually: between jobs, drawing government compensation. Put it to good use. Unified purpose, not squandered in dreaming. Action, to test results. Enemy knows she's trapped. Barricades herself in; her kids weep: it's summer, they want to go out to play. Billy-Boy would hold them for ransom. He has unlimited funds of immorality to draw from.

Billy-Boy total barbarian? Not one civilized spot left on his inner surface, where humane appeal might softly blandish this decent good man gone criminally astray? Open to whisper of love's quiet reason, cooling rampage of love's sour fever? He's on a haunting vigil outside Isabel's prison. A reluctantly bereft ghost, he's a reincarnated plague, a moaning idol of evil grief. A gruesome mask, to kindle demonic rituals. Spell hovers over tense Isabel. In her, a civilized anxiety in fright against archetype savage. Deep fear of basic primitive: In self, or externalized. Billy-Boy becomes figure, myth — representing dark forces. Oh, eliminate him! Husband, husband, why can't I tell you?

"Don't worry. I have my own hunches. I can smell a rat when he leaves his dirty scent. I'll take care of him. I'll make sure he won't bother you any more. Leave it to your husband. I know what's up."

Her husband was too reliable not to suspect foul play. Tenderly, but firmly, he questioned her. Like a dentist extracting a wisdom tooth, he extracted her difficult truth. Bloody root and all. Billy-Boy was on the loose. Have to pin him down, not easy to handle. Can't placate an unreasoning man with reasoning means. Fight him on his own irrational ground. Tame a savage beast — not by music, either. Deal him straight, man to man. First enlist some trusty friends — plain, solid, strong men, upstanding in this neighborhood. Fellows who not only can tell what's right, but go out and *fight* for it.

These uncomplaining citizens of convention's unofficial army help a husband to set an ambush trap to catch a maniac who's hot bent on raping a helpless wife. They get him, too. Rough him up in a simple, straightforward manner, to teach him to associate punishment with an intention that's plainly wrong. Then a little more, too, by knocking him out of commission, reduce the potency of his threat. Now wife and kiddies need not fear, but go out to shop or play without the least unpleasant second thought. Normal human rights, set back at liberty, and ahead to progress.

The culprit was really done in. Out. His body a pulp, and his head squashed of thought. Some bones misdirected from natural course. He's in sad shape, a sorry specimen.

It's early morning. Garbage collectors on their routes of mercy. Angels of sanitation.

They sweep up Billy-Boy, send for an ambulance, and watch that human refuge be carted away to the nursely attendance at a hospital sanctuary. By the capable professional skills of whose practitioners he'll be set going on the recovery shift. To be dumped out on the conveyer belt looking like an artificially new model for second-hand consumption. That's lovable Billy-Boy, in his process of bony rehabilitation, skull and all. Just a few carved interior corrections.

Convalescence needs comforting. Visions of Isabel penetrate his medicinal stupor. She floats by, regroups, filters in shades, is formed anew, reverses direction, appearing simultaneously from many places, in a multi-spectacle, like a pageantry of clouds in richly shifted contour. She's his visiting angel, companion in constancy. He, the connoisseur of solitude in that black art's most dissipated refinements, assimilates dreams of Isabel for his huge mental sky's flux of weather. He revives, he's well again approximately. He's released from the merciful hospital. It cured him of being beaten up. He *looks* all right. But what's inside?

He packs up Isabel in his bulky luggage of material imagery, and sets delicate foot on the humming city street. He's free to decide: should he seek a new city, or keep living here in his apartment? His first timid reflex advised in a stern old man's tone, "Leave! It's no good for you here." But his own voice got the last word: "Don't go away! *Stay*, while Isabel is so conveniently here."

But his anger's insane pulse has died. He wouldn't actually accost Isabel again, or stalk her purposefully. A memory clicked, warning him not to.

He develops his grand aptitude for dreams. Sitting on a park bench, he meditates. He hasn't gone home yet. His luggage is beside him. He has the faculty of depicting Isabel "visually" in poses of stupendous immodesty; the cunning vixen has enthralled him. Rapturously, he gazes through his haze.

Dusk swoops down, closing the park. He's turned out at the gate.

The subway home. Everything as he left it. Small apartment, untidy. His. No concealed spy. Enchanted by his ribald visions of Isabel, he surrenders himself to a coarse indulgence: the grandeurs of infantile self-abuse, undertaken with rigor and disapproval. Isabel is "there," like a succubus. Silken veils slip away, her thighs shake their smooth undulations, a dazzling creamy thing to behold. Suddenly she admonishes him, snapping a stern finger and lisping some slippery words on a tempting, tiny tongue, to the total effect of: "You adorable naughty!" He sobs with joy and fatigue. The room compresses them both tight together. His coyly bold mistress, whose charms have no sum of calculation except in the strict rule of infinity (whose code is yet mortally undeciphered), distracts him incessantly. (From what? From not thinking about her.) She casts a seductive benediction on him. She soothes him into the beautific surf of foamy calm. She bends over him, magic dropping from her breasts like phials of perfumed potion. They kiss an eternity, as the clock averts its handless face.

Clutching at his animal root, or its tattered stub, its weary stump, he's wafted aloft on slumber's steed, and set down in a gorgeous palace. Here repose languors, clad skimpily.

He's granted an audience with Queen Isabel, in a chamber deeply recessed, hidden in a maze of erotic corridors. There she is, on a stunning throne. Kneeling on knees of crunched bone to be blessed by this haughty regal apparition — this real, prepossessing beauty — he sinks through a trap door disguised among the gold mosaic tiles that embroider the majestic floor. His fall continues into a far depth. Snugly settled inside earth, he's walled in by a sealed shelter. But the dungeon has holes for breath. Seemingly buried there, he yet possesses all comforts and necessities for life's gay round of amusement, though restricted by his *solitary* captivity. He's even equipped with the latest spiritual gadgets. He lacks nothing, except company. Empirically, he's quite alone.

But contemplation has other ideas. Embalmed in the mysticism of meditation, he conjures Isabel's shade: she joins their underground love nest. Now he has her: she's trapped! They'll die or live *together*. She's *here*, with *him*! Love's prisoner, forever.

Only one qualm remains: She's a goddess, and he's only mortal. But Union *thrives* on inequality. Only miracles (whose age is over) can quite sever them. So Billy-Boy has won his prize. She's the most shapely Solitude he ever had.

What Marvin Carries

Marvin was always afraid of losing things, so he packed them together in a big black bag. He was *still* afraid of losing things, so much so that he didn't trust the big black bag, despite it being sealed tight and containing all those things so organizationally at once.

So he put the big black bag into a larger valise. He still feared, so he stuck the valise into a suitcase and locked the suitcase. All that luggage should afford him the sense of protection. But his insecurity prevented that. For, what container should he wrap his *insecurity* in? None, so it wrapped *him* up. It carries him, he's conveyed, he's all the things he fears to lose.

The Imperishable Container of All Current Pasts

I discover, in my girl, layers and layers of mineral deposits, archaeological strata from her encounters with previous men. These physically encumber my right of entry, and I ask her why she collects such outworn trophies. She sighs, and says, "I venerate the past. It has such masculine endurance."

"All fine and well," I agree, "but it impedes me. See, I'm left in the cold. How can I force my way in?" "Push harder," she suggests. But ah, so many things in the way! They thwart my active principle, and I say, "I'll remain outside, where the space is cleared of insurmountable obstacles." "Very well," she agrees, and extracts from her shrine a sample of the accumulated debris, which she examines with both hands. "That was Harry," she says, sighing with fond remembrance. How loyal she is to the ghastly vigor of traditional emblems kept forever in her museum of private erotica! Yet, at all hours, she's open to the public. The crowd is uncontrolable, and traffic regulations must be put into effect. Coming and going pedestrians stumble upon the remnants of their timeless ancestors, in her legend of impure, but popular, precedence.

The clutter doesn't discourage visitors. They leave their calling cards, and are filed in that amazing preservative. She's a conservatory, where the past bulges with immense lingerings. Additions are daily recorded, to stagger an impotent future. The world overfills itself, and teems with fertile overgrowth. She's due for an internal cleansing, to sweep clear the dated and admit the endless present. Let her restore her storage to the flow of successive newness. Then movement is possible, and a vital avenue of penetration.

"Try again," she implores. I strain, and then plunge into the dizzy totality of historical disorder; it's like building a housing project on a monumental cemetery whose inhabitants, according to the latest fossil explorations, belong bonily to each epoch of retreating phases raging to the evolutionary source itself, when living forms, squirming out of mud, oozed at the sight of my girl and first settled into her ample beginnings, which were to accommodate, in her mania for collecting, all subsequent species.

I'm the latest, but by no means the last. She ages only into an enlarged youth: the capacious wholeness of her widening warehouse is that interior female to unlimited containment. Nothing, once in, goes out whole again; and what remains is for the ages.

One day, my girl started bleeding at a place upon which I had sexual designs. In order to exact poetic justice, I then so beat her as to make her bleed in areas outside of the erotic zone — wherever those might be found. Thus, I neutralized the sex drive, and brutality proved to be my tranquil compensation. When the blood-letting had terminated, I was properly appeased, so much so that sleep found me a not difficult customer. Meanwhile, my pleasant victim whined so softly, that I was carefully undisturbed. Her caution was thus wisely at the disposal of an unconscious desire to survive. Which proves that she's too selfish to love me in the ultimately self-destructive sense. This, in turn, justifies the beatings I'm forced to administer on her all-absorbing body. Her soul, I can't get at; psychological warfare is one of my weakest points of attack. Therefore, I merely abuse her in the physical sense, as a direct expression of my means of honesty. I'm admired by my girl for being free of sneaky devices. If it's contact she wants, where can she find a dealer less apt to be deterred by scruples of the slim skin?

Just when I caught a cold, my girl sprayed a blunt portion of perfume on each and every zone of that topographically mapped principality of her primarily erotic republic. (So I wasn't provoked, my nostrils being stuffed up.)

She didn't know I couldn't breathe. "Can you scent a message?" she requested. "Not I," I replied, letting innocence be stupidity's tactful diplomat.

"Can't you whiff my signal?" she asked, while hay fever pollens used my nose as a rush hour subway station. "No, why?" I said, letting naivete act as a spokesman for innocence, who was already engaged on another wire.

"Can you sniff what I have to send?" she implied. The meaning failed to reach me, as well as those deliberate fumes. Ignorance had been delegated by stupidity, innocence, and naivete to be the practical administrator of their fouled-up functions. I'm wearing perfume," she declared.

"I don't see it," I answered, "can you show me where?"

"It's here, simple," she pointed out, discarding her clothes to permit clarity a finer show of brevity.

Not even asthma could make me allergic to my tactile formation of enlightenment. Substituting touch for smell's unruly sense, I wound up with the same goal.

Lugubriosity

I

(Stage is bathed in faded light.)

When did you die?

Last year, around May. When did *you* die?

Just the other day. Tuesday, I think.

No *wonder* you look so fresh and preserved!

Not for long. Soon I'll be developing that ghostly pallor.

Yes but it will *become* you most appropriately, considering where we are.

Oh, are you always looking on the bright side of things?

Sure. Since there's no sun here, I've got to make my own *artificial* one.

But there's a *worried* expression on your face.

Oh, that's because I forgot to turn the light off before I died.

What light?

The electric bulb in the bedroom. I'm compulsively fussy, because every time I switch off a light I cut down on my electricity bill.

(Aside:) He doesn't know, even now, that he can't take 'it' with him! *(Aloud:)* But surely a doctor or a relative must have switched it off by now, or else a landlord will have done it for you?

I'd be most obliged to the one who *did* do it, *if* he did it, but I have no way of telling, because there's no postal delivery of letters to be received here, and the telephone is blank, it never seems to work.

Yes, we *are* cut off. I feel *out* of things now. I just don't seem to be able to keep up with things like I used to.

But that's hardly *your* fault, since you can't help it.

You're pardoning me on the basis of fatalism, but I myself believe in free will.

Believe in it if you want, but it'll do you no good here.

Well, then it's an *abstract* belief, or a principle. Not all my ideas are for expedience.

Anyway, somebody must surely have shut it off by now.

Shut what off?

The light. — Don't you remember?

No. Illuminate me.

II

(Darkened stage.)

We're in the dark.

(Boastfully:) Not with *my* knowledge.

Why? What is it that you know?

Everything — you name it.

Where have you left your modesty?

Modesty is only typical of *life*. When I died, I left it behind.

Is there anything *else* you forgot to bring here?

My wife. She's remarried recently.

How do you know? We receive no news.

Intuition tells me.

And I guess you knew her long enough to make an educated prediction about her?

III

(Neutral, or dead, stage.)

Haven't you got any life left in your bones?

Life!? What bones?!

Those things inside, that keep your skin pinned together.

Skin!? Do you see any skin?

No, but I don't see God either, and I take *Him* on faith.

(Aside:) That's the only way you *can* take Him. *(Aloud:)* Have you only become naive *since* you died, or were you that way before?

I had a lot of practice being naive in life, because my naivety was up against a whole wordly *world*, which helped to bring it out by the emphasis of contrast. But *here*, where there's no *world* as a background for my naivety, my naivety is pale to vanishing, like white on white.

(Scornfully:) I never thought of death's atmosphere as being particularly naive.

Well, it's not *worldly*, is it?

No.

So you agree with me?

Why not? If our *bodies* are in the same fix, let our minds be as well.

Bodies! Did you mention bodies?

Why, is that a sin?

Mentioning them isn't, but *they* are sin.

Sin-ce when?

Since birth. But not now, because we don't have any (body).

(Scanning himself with head lowered. Bewildered, lost tone:) But these are my *feet*, here are my *hands*.

Never mind that. *(Emphatically:)* Did you *die*, or *not*?

I *died* all right.

I don't care whether you died *all right* or *all wrong*. *(Patiently:)* You *died*, and you're *dead*?

That's right.

(Aside:) There's nothing right about it. It's terrible, if you ask me. *(Aloud:)* Then your body's *useless*! You might as well not have it!

Then what am I *doing* with it, then?

That's *your* business. You carted your luggage here, that's why.

But you seem to think it's excess baggage.
Only because you brought it to the wrong place.
But I took a one-way, not a round-trip, ticket.
Of *course!* What do you *expect?* A *miracle?*

IV

(A totally dead stage.)

(Looking bored:) In death, there's lots of time on my hands.
Then here's soap and water: go wash your hands!
Then I might disappear *altogether!*
Then stop complaining about time.
Oh, it's not time *itself* that I mind: it's just that there's so *much* of it!
It's just your ennui: you're not *active* enough.
But what is there to *do* here?
I don't know. Death is an idle industry.
Plenty of leisure —
But no leisure *activity.*
Oh, we'll rot.
We already *did* that. How do you think we *got* here?
Oh, stop harping back! You're always harping back!
(Offended:) Who's *harping?!* *(Indignantly:)* I'm not an angel in heaven!
(Ignoring that:) But you're not content with your current fate!
What's so *current* about my fate? It looks endless.
Yes. We may not have been immortal, but we sure are *eternal!*
You're always looking at things from the broad, *general* point of view.
Why not? It's *serene* that way.
You're just too lazy to go in for *details.*
Details!? Can you point out one *detail here?*
You — you're a detail.
Me!? I don't *exist!*
Oh, don't be modest.
But it's *true.*

All right. Have it your own way.
It's not my way — I didn't *choose* it: it *is*.
You mean it's unavoidable?
Inevitable!
Eternal, as well?
All that.
Then you're not needed. Go back to sleep.

V

(*Aftermath.*)

Oh, but it's so *sterile* to be dead!
Good! That means we won't catch cold! Goodbye!

The Room as my Outward: Me as the Room's Inward

Bottled paper, cartons of running water, boxes of human interest, vats of invisible pins, cans of cleanly laundered textiles, envelopes of monumental balls, and other well-assorted receptacles, littered the cluttered warehouse of treasury-repository, a windowed room with walls between; said windows vacantly staring in on the assembly of misformed objects ill-fitted by motley shells. Somewhere among all this stock, a mirror commented vertically on the scattered proceedings of this interior wealth of still life. From object to object crept a progression of dust, to color uniformly grey this indescribable variety. Intervals of unkempt space thus alleviated the monotonously irregular solidity. The clock's hour of night or day made only the most elementary difference. This kingdom of matter (ranged in slovenly gradations) invited that most human of diseases, Sloth. I personified this sordid vice, for this room was occupied by me in a term of residence. Never had nature and surroundings enjoyed a snugger fit. All that the room was, was but the outward of me; such was the suitability of environment to man.

There was no room for my bed at the horizontal rate of expansion, so it stood tilting vertically upwards at the acute angle of discomfort, creating stoical difficulty for the intended union of sleep with the sleeper: this made my insomnia legitimate by propping it with immediate cause;

wakefulness was prolonged in one continuous dreary spell.

When summer sang its lyrical tune (as a favor for spring's promise to itself), I let in the generous outdoors by opening the combined enormity of my windows. The wind blew the dust about. Astray in disorder rippled my papers. Stale untidiness was provided with a whiff of fresh multiplication, while chaos kept up its honest appearance. I was so tired, death yawned with boredom waiting for life's painful slow dullness to complete its midway phase on the uneven descent of a rocket's vital efforts to consume the clowning of its described orbit on the turnings dictated by a cycle. But air was invigorating, and I was tormented by an ache of health. Even a career, in a profession accredited by society, was not beyond the upsurge of my momentary resolution. But soon, so exemplary an intention subsided most dismally, and with a thud I declined to the shallow depths where torpor sustained me with its mud, as vegetables subsist on their diet of foul and consistent ooze.

The door knocked, and Joe came by. Joe's my friend who always tries to reform me. With his misguided goodwill, and his misplaced common sense, he's sure a foil to my intelligent negation of life's well-meant futilities.

"Spruce up, Ira," he calls, a drop from the ocean of his good nature; "this mess is no way to live; it's indecent, and shows no self-respect for yourself."

"Oh Joe, go 'way," I say, shrugging to confirm my point. "It's useless," I added, a phrase from which affirmation was gloomed out in advance. "Try!" Joe pleaded. "No," I moaned, an effortless dirge.

"Oh Ira," Joe said, in tears: "your ability makes a graver disappointment in that your dormant talents sulk in the corruption of their latent forces and the putrefaction of what was once so glowing in promise: what waste," he wailed, his voice dropping beads of oil in oozing scales from pores of populous tragedy. "Grip yourself; be a new man," he counselled, applying wisdom where result stood in an arid festering of its own sterility. "It's hopeless," I appealed, soothing Joe with gentle doses from my limitless fund of apathy. But they were blows — heavy, relentless, crushing — on his hand of proffered kindness, the palm extended, warped now in the frustration of its tenderness. Weeping in the overflowing of compassion, Joe acted a passive Christ for my benefit. I had fallen, so he submitted to a mental crucifixion on some suburban telephone pole, exposed to the predatory nibbling by hawks and passing crows. Nor did I board the ark to salvation, graced as I was by not a tithe of faith in Joe's meddling in my spirit nestling in the sunken harbor of its disgrace, caught conservatively by an anchor's rotting permanence. "Here's a dollar," Joe said, flapping it on a floating current. Then he ducked out, having cursed me with the force-feeding of that green mercenary gift.

Barely has my loneliness resumed possession of me when a second visitor rustles her skirt across the threshold. She's Janet, a pleasant sort of girl were it not for the accidental aberration that's bound her attachment to me by an irrational jolt of bourgeois logic. Her father doesn't consider me eligible; her rebellion against parental firmness thrust her lax choice to my favor, in ties of what devout romantics call love. So now I'm seized on fixed waves of sizzle down to the plunging nest where my embraced corpse must lodge, doing its dance like a doll jerked on puppet spasms to simulate the unvarying pattern known as pleasure. And these were the heights life was devised for!

Our performance had dried itself out, and the distaste of my lapsed appetite now hustled her in clothes and out my very private door, leaving me the soiled peace for my thoughts to coagulate. For recreation, I seized a book. I read some disjointed pages to separate plot from sense and isolate both in a barren tide of mystery outside the choice ken of my selective void known as incuriosity. Boredom gripped me, and bore me aloft as its most reliable child. I emitted so cave-like a yawn, my mouth held open house to entertain some vagrant germs then loitering in my room like tramps of no fixed abode and even less driving ambition. The germs set up a colony down my facial channels, peppering my lungs with potions of poison. I voided my disapproval with a testy cough, but by now the germs were solidly entrenched as guests of no uncertain leave. To warm themselves, they blocked each nostril against the annoying intrusion of draughts. Snug in their fortifications, they dug in, snugly ballasted off for my cold's interior duration. Nor were they rustled by my slightest sneeze; and like vampires, they drank intoxicating draughts from the pitched tent of my fever, in whose consoling warmth they sprawled like drunken dissolutes, tanned by a Miami-manufactured sun in shades of rejoicing purple. As they thrived, I weakened, materially all but defeated. Thus was an official nurse called in, accompanied by an architect. And my room was remade as a hospital ward, disinfected with limp whiteness. My objects were shrunken — all those boxes and bottles and vials, tubes, and cartons — to create space for my recuperation. The dust was carted away, and hygiene installed as a function of architectural rehabilitation, to which I, reclining, was a victim faint with transparent mortality. The windows admitted what sky the city was permitted by real estate hawks. In that sky entered a sun. As I hallucinated, I read much scriptural wisdom in the sun's rotund face. Such wisdom was facetiously misapplied, in my case.

As I was taxed back to health, the nurse lost her undertaker complexion, to be taken in marriage as life's bright wife when spotted wearing only nature's cosmetic as a glossy powder that disguised the artifice under which her identity labored with puffed contrivings. Curing me with healing herbs and restorative balms, she ascended to angelic divinity, leaving an autographed halo behind as evidence of a reward neatly earned. The architect was gone, so my room reverted to normal, a peg for confusion's hat and a night's merciful lodging as an inn for wearied disorder to drop dead with sleep. Now was my rut made refamiliar, and identity restored for recognition at once to identify. And I was old Ira, digging a trench for the gay burial of youth's dwindling memory. Achievement was at hand: room and I blended, and distinction evaporated between the self I was and the room in which that self could view its surroundings. My soul and the room's soul joined mutual factors of nonentity, toward what end only inertia would solve, combating mortal mobility with a leading struggle.

What Martin Did About Not Liking his Name

Martin, you look excited, but with unpleasant results.

I have a perturbed announcement to make.

Rid your system of it: Like a cancer ball that the surgeons lift bodily from our cut-open house of stomach juices.

What I have to tell is not as disgusting as the comparison you applied to it. It's simply that I hate being Martin, though I wish personally to go on living. I wish Martin were someone else, even though I had to go nameless for it. Somehow, Martin doesn't describe me, and doesn't even begin to do me the justice of my full self-expression. Can you understand that I'm much more than 'Martin' would imply?

But 'Martin' is only the sum associative force of all your attributes. 'Martin' means different things, depending on which person it labels. There are Martins in this world who are completely different from you. Why use your name as your scapegoat for your general dissatisfaction with your particular abhored life which you must always tediously lead? Your discontent is not a *nominal* matter, but is in the manner of a discord between you and your very life. Your having been named 'Edward' could not have averted this basic disagreeable condition. So give up blaming your name. Try to repair what's *really* wrong.

My spirit is afflicted with malaise. What deeds must I alter, in personality correction, character rehabilitation, identity therapy, to be a person improved over what 'Martin' has come to signify?

Irving is my own name, so I'm hardly in a position to advise you.

I can't be reconciled to my 'Martin' me. After death, I hope to be born again as a girl named Janet.

I wish you success and an early marriage in your next metamorphosis. But do you expect your soul to be the same?

'Martin' *is* my soul. So, emphatically, no.

I thought your *body* was named Martin.

Martin is my characteristic facial feature, reflecting my Martinian soul.

Then you're Martin through and through?

Such is what it seems I am.

Then I'm correct in addressing you 'Martin'?

Yes, that's my local address, which I carry with me, like a turtle with its house on its back.

Then you ought to feel at home, being Martin.

It's my most incurable state of being.

Then you must learn to *live* with it.

Why can't I quietly live it *down*?

That would be self-defeating.

But mortification is good for the humility.

Too much of it despoils the pride.

By definition, I'm very *unproud* to be *Martin*.

How you do castigate, and persecute, your good name!

It's not an honorary title like 'Lord' or 'Duke.' Nor does it even identify my profession.

Yet you profess to be at odds with all that Martin is?

I'm determined to depart from that impediment of an appendage. Yet how it clings, and I'm called by it, barefaced, to my shame, by friend and foe, who have my name in common as an insult to term me by, slurring my reputation and consigning me to the appellation of my infamy. Martin is my disease. Were I to wear a normal suit of health, then 'Martin' would be disused, like the defunct name of a newly coined street. Destiny hounds every man; and for a nemesis, *I* have a name. Like a leper's spots, or a zebra's stripes, or an orator's distinguishing voice, or the mole on a French mistress, or the scar on a wanted criminal's face, or a birthmark that satisfies the morgue's autopsical morbidity, or the telltale colors easily spotted by birdwatchers as characteristic of that species of wingdom be it jay, robin, hawk, or a painted kite. Or an author's style. My name is a dead giveaway for me. It adds not an iota to our vast historical body of multi-classified occult sciences that drill a hole through real appearances and concrete exteriors to reduce the core to a matter of the utmost metaphysics and ultimate consideration, the legend and myth of spiritual entity, on a footing of the absolute, the pure soul of essence. I declare myself beyond Martin.

Well, Martin, thanks for saying so. I'm no more than Irving, but for me it suffices. As Irving I exist. Death will confer namelessness upon me. That's a type of immortality despicable for any ego to contemplate, any normal, self-respecting ego-consciousness worthy of its own integrity. That's why I make much of being Irving *now*, while the joyride lasts of having the self for a property under the stamp of a name as part of its equipment. I don't wish to *transcend* 'Irving': I wish to bring it out with full power. Is a name a handy labor-saving device, bandied about with promiscuous circulation as practically a public ownership? I value mine. 'Irving' goes beyond appearances, and certifies the apparent in its inmost potential. In all justice, I wear my name proudly. Yours is like a fallen flag, like a slattern's tattered depravity of a skirt slipped down to the dishonored mast's ugly ankle bone. Thus drags 'Martin' to a hideous abuse.

While 'Irving' dignifies as it signifies?

I keep my name up, and keep myself up to it. Like a gardener caring for his flowers, tendering them with gentle love's skillful fingers, so that their species will go unsullied.

You wax sentimental, in your botanical fashion, with a dash of inaccuracy to further soil your unrooted premise and sag it to seed in your groundless argument of a mythic garden plot. I got your *nominal* drift, but certainly your reference of words and terms were straying weeds to the wind. I got the impression that 'Irving' means a lot to you.

It does, for I'm *it*.

You'd defend it as the vocal of your own self, evocative of all that your life may invoke to your property-protective mind of proprietorial propriety to the letter of your nominative spirit?

As is proper. Nor is my name a mere prop. My name has become me.

You *look* like Irving; and you *are*!

I don't need your mocking. For you've betrayed the legacy in *your* name. You've let yourself down, and made 'Martin' muddy.

'Martin' muddied me at birth, when I was christened it!

What a blatantly transparent excuse! *You* are the degradation of 'Martin,' who otherwise would have remained neutral and left it for you to prove your worth on its own intrinsic terms. You're a disgrace to whatever 'Martin' could have been, in the signal failure you've made of yourself in bungling 'Martin's opportunity. We've defined, finally, what 'Martin' is.

I reject your definition, as unkind, inaccurate, assassinative, unfair, and highly unflattering. I pronounce 'Martin' to be what I *wish* to be; and from now on, will embark on a dream life, of grandeur and ideals, that uphold necessary illusions that restore pride which life's accomplishments fall short of in the right and entitlement to qualities confirmed by attainment.

Am I below *esteeming* you? — or is that too great or soon a privilege?

I'll allow you that, in time. I'll bestow. Irving is as much below Martin, as Martin is above Irving. That's the scale of my hierarchy.

We're not exactly peers?

Hardly. That's my point.

Pardon my denseness.

The Monday Rhetoric of the Love Club

The members of the Love Club congregate. First it used to be called the Male Club, that being the sex of all of its members. They would tell each other tales about their women, so love became the prime topic of conversation. That's how the name changed.

At each session, a different member relates an adventure. It could be pure fantasy, the mere reporting of a romantic image. Literal coarseness, in general, is discouraged. The tendency is to poeticize love, to rarify its distilled essence. A standard of sensitivity protects the exclusiveness of the club.

A code of regulations constitutes the rules of discipline. Each speaker is granted a courteous asylum against listener interruption. Thus the patient components of the audience are themselves secured, for protocol will protect each speaker when his turn comes. The solidarity of the group is the best assurance as to the sanctity of the individual, so long as he remains a part of the group. Monday night is their meeting time, fresh after the material compiled in an erotic weekend. No wives or girlfriends are permitted to attend; women are barred, the better to be talked about. Behind their backsides, much may be revealed.

Anonymity clads the identity of each member. Some know others in the business community or as private friends; but in the sacred clubroom, they're as if masked. A pledge of secrecy and confidence, bound by initiation rites, is never violated, or the member would be expelled.

Enforcement is rigidly kept strict, and freedom is banned as being ultra lax.

There's a secretary there, to collect minutes. The chairman observes democratic procedure; and the president presides, the principal officer in the ranks of staff maintenance of order. In case of a tie, votes are decisive. This purges the atmosphere of a foul taint of politics. Honesty is conducted, on the honor plan. This system is aboveboard, and plainly open. Periodically, it's inspected for flaws.

The members are of all ages, a joint nonarithmetical brotherhood oblivious to time differences. Some members have just raised their first pubic hair, while others can't even raise their member any more. From infancy to senility, inclusive, the Love Club is well stocked with American males. What they have in common is the love of women: which, ironically, is the source of what's *uncommon*. They deviate into particular cases and examples of individual specific uniqueness. When such experiences are *told*, they generally belong to the club at large, as common property. Thus, when each member speaks, he shares what happened to him with his fellows, and the whole assembly undergoes an enrichment, an expansion of its intricate totality. What one speaker says is, such is the unity of the club, magnified indefinitely to astounding infinitudes of depth, such are the multiple variations throughout the magnitudes of an extensive organization. Membership is partially unlimited, subject to due restrictions. The moderator beats his gavel, the meeting is called to order. The minutes from the last session are briefly given, as a spur to continuity: sequences must serve to connect these successive Mondays. Last week, the topic had been the loneliness and indecisiveness of a kiss. The discussion afterward, with its uninhibited release of questions and answers, had wound up in an agreement that the least a kiss can do is to have a girl dangling at the other end; otherwise, the raw and refined material is not there to work with. Hearty laughter had approved of this resolution, whereupon beers and cheers were served up. A spirit of unfeigned mirth had prevailed at the evening's successful termination. Comradeship was plentiful and was generously handed around in a flowing contagion of distribution. Now it's tonight, and a hush greets the speaker. The lights are dimmed, to control mood. Only he who has the floor is standing, on the raised slope of a platform. After an introductory cough (as an inducement of formality), he reveals the course of an affair of the heart: how it began and ended with only himself. A girl had participated, as well. Here's a tape recording, giving his exact inflections:

"I gave myself a kiss, as an act of betrothal. It didn't work, though, because a girl wasn't present to consummate it. I paged her, yelling her name, which floated into the endless wind, without dying out. 'Myself alone,' I said, 'will never do.' This seemed philosophical at first, until practicality used it to its own end. Feeling exploited, and without tangible reward, I gave myself flirtatious airs, and wooed a one-time woman on a sound basis aboard a floating bed, where, back and forth, we swayed to the tides of motion, without quite moving an inch. 'It was fun,' she declared, after it became convenient for her own body to pour speech upon her tiny tongue. Overcome, I fell in love. I was the heart of animated passion, and in a tropical frenzy my ardor was thrust without mercy into the snatch of her sweat. All this was to the good. We even smiled, after first thinking about it. Proving, upon reflection, that even we were also human, and agonizingly so. When it was over, and the romance soured, we became nostalgia's property, and have our memories to thank."

A polite splattering of well-intentioned applause acknowledges the speaker's efforts at communicating a message. He blushes, and then comes the question period. He parries each thrust, and is allowed to escape unwounded. Suddenly, a swelling wave of boredom rises, and crashes on the speaker's head. Mercifully, the meeting is adjourned, and the members retire home early. An epidemic of yawns sweeps over them, and other marked symptoms that betray an evident lack of enthusiasm. As Mondays go, this night was not especially memorable, except as a peculiar specimen of dullness. Next week had better revive a lagging interest, or the club might be faced with an absentee panic. Good attendance was necessary for morale. The trouble seemed to be that the past had spoiled the present, with a bolder tradition of speeches. Newness got successively paler, in comparison with precedence. Should shock effects and standard-debasing sensationalism be carted out, and resorted to as popular stimulants? How revolting to the tenets of good taste and a superior measure of breeding! Compromises were in their very nature abject.

The newest of all their Mondays arrived, up to date. It was the latest current Monday they had ever known.

In keeping with the rules of continuity, the speaker for the evening retained kisses and loneliness as a subject bound to the last lecture. The talk he'd deliver, however, conspicuously lacked a woman as an actual recipient of his well-developed lust. It was a shocking omission.

The moral seemed to be that lips were insufficient, by themselves, as carnal objects of love. Desire is very exacting, in its enormous greediness.

"I had a kiss to spend, and bought a pair of lips. (Not mine, because I'm not for sale. Only now and then.) With those hired lips, whether rented or purchased, which I merely owned or leased, I squeezed out perfection into my kiss, until, as modesty withdrew, lust called in the extravagant body, with its poison terrors gleaming from the criminal dark, but only her lips were there, and intolerable emptiness below. What savage music, and I moaned. Oh, I groaned. And only lips, for spend, or hire. The tiny puritan lips, those chaste emblems of virginity and trembling mock adventures of adolescence, so puny in the size of my passion, and the depth of my thrust. Ah, my seed. Where is your fertilizing mother, the wicked measure of my pleasure? Hidden, flirtatiously concealed, lost in the stroke of absence, where darkness and light don't mix. There I can't see her, and yet, gigantic imagination creates her monstrously complete form, while my emotion sags and delivers, free from its obsession. What have I wrought? And only lips began, where sharply sin shall climax. And guilt frowns, the mouth hideous with blood."

When the speaker had concluded, silence stirred its trembling vibrations in waves of soundlessness within the hall's four broad walls. Collectively, the audience shook its one multiheaded head, as a gesture of mass dissent. What did it all mean? That a kiss wasn't enough? Any fool knew that!

Then arguments heated up, and fumes of cigars poured forth. Scattered groups conducted informal debates on ambiguous topics, based on the uncertain value of the kiss. A kiss had a decorative utility, but not a meat-and-potatoes role, maintained some die-hearts. Women needed a little more substance, seemed to be the consensus; and men themselves found finer joy in blunter instruments than the lips sported on their barbaric faces, under which hair grew if not shaved. Kids can kiss, but true adults try their lick below, where the game assumed big-league proportions, at mature risks. Each member of the Love Club privately bestowed on his own tool a heartfelt blessing, with fondest wishes for a continued uplift of fortune, an extension of its spotted career. Each tool responded with a glow of joy, in a true magnetic current.

Thus the members were united in a general swelling. The hour struck late, so they said goodnight, adding, "It was swell." They went home under a heady steam of stimulation. Their wives or girlfriends received a pleasant surprise, but soon found out that a kiss was not the end it was the means for. Grunts and pants ended the evening.

Passion weakened into a week. Time so turned that another Monday came pop out into the present, giving a rounded approximation of its next appearance, propped on a newly erected reality to release the power of its potential in pulsating clarity. The scheduled speaker had prepared an amusing talk, the narration of an endless kiss. It was to be a long and complicated speech, in which a third party was to be introduced, as an addition to the usual first-person male and his girlfriend. Cobwebs were cleaned away from concentration, for this mental obstacle endurance hurdle marathon, told as a secondhand sporting event in verbal images. The subject was a kiss protracted to an unusual length, and its morbid consequences. The tale begins in the hospital, where the speaker and his girlfriend are held together by lips that can't be tugged apart, a kiss that physicians are trying to sever. An old friend of the speaker calls up on the telephone to find out what happened; he offers useless advice at the beginning, until the speaker is forced to explain, under physical difficulty, how he allowed his girlfriend to gain so close an advance on his affections. The effect is highly comical.

The audience suspends breath. Smiles light up the darkness, in spurts of gaudy imagination. The situation is so improbable that realism takes an enforced holiday, and only what remains is described. It taxes credulity, at marvelous interest rate. The coin of attention, then, is promptly paid.

"I felt at loose ends so I looked for a kiss. Such was my innocent intention.

"Loneliness drove me on, in my pursuit of a kiss. I craved its essential glories of contact.

"My search for a kiss ended, but success was too final. I found one, with a suitable girl attached. Trouble was, she stayed attached. That's what brought me to the hospital, stuck to the girl by our lips, and my next problem is to talk over the telephone, where my friend is waiting at the other end of the wire. That's decent of him, but my lips have to talk sideways, with my girl hanging on desperately to every word as though it were the product of her own gluey mouth, grown indistinguishable from mine. Is she eavesdropping, or am I? Hold on — here's my friend's free tripping voice coming over.

" 'Kisses are meant to be enjoyed,' my friend philosophized. I was answering him from the Incurable Ward, where my girlfriend and I, by spending the night together, were making all sorts of rules helpless, as well as difficult to obey. 'Kissing I know about,' I tried to say. The operator interrupted. She wanted another dime in her box, or else a big nickel. My friend accommodated, falling for her, and we kept on going. 'Tell me your kissing history,' he begged. 'I see you're stuck on the subject,' I said, 'but if it's curious, this is up to date: *My Last Big Kiss*.' Then the operator hushed, and began listening. Her silence seemed like a big woman. So to my collective audience, including a participant where the words issued, I recited, on the top of my wavering breath, to the depth of my lingering death:

" 'Kissing always passionately involves me, and it's hard to get a word in edgewise. Once in the middle of a kiss my partner stole my mouth but I was keeping hers in security, so we kissed and made up. It took a long time. I began with three cavities, and ended with false teeth. The only thing we ate was a tongue sandwich, washed down with nice hot saliva. Thanks to my mask, nothing grotesque was born. Were we in love? No, but we gave lip service to it.

" 'The fun stopped when her gums had their period. I got drunk being a vampire, but the Red Cross pump-leeched a free donation off me, which broke my girl's heart when I went into circulation. Just one last farewell kiss stood in the way. It's still going on, and we've been transferred to an oxygen tent. Breath gets scarce, and they've grafted our lungs together. With our dying breath, we may vow love. At this very moment, our kiss is beginning to waver. The lips are ready to come off. Flesh has begun to convert to spirit.'

" 'Hello, are you still there?' I asked the telephone. 'Of course I am,' my friend answered, 'and I want you to stop kissing right now. It's ruining your health, not to mention other things. Now come off it.' So he hung up, but I was still hung up over my kiss. 'Gosh, you're awfully kissable,' I told my twin. 'I can't help it,' she answered, and kept on kissing me. 'God, I'm losing my manhood,' I tried to say, but was too kissed to say it. How that girl can kiss! The operator must be jealous by now. But the phone was disconnected, and a technician is applying oxygen to it. Could she have fainted? Meanwhile, my girl is pressed close. I'm about to commit myself: but only for a cure. I'll make a miracle-working statement, and the results should release us, since consequences are affected sentimentally by motions of the heart, even if feigned, and love locks any key. Or unkeys the door to any lock. Or, at any rate, is the first step to divorce by mutual consent, and through it even the longest kiss undergoes severance, terminating the lips. Here we go, I'll try. Not to be tied down, Liberty, protect me: Speed my words, and urge your flighty miracle!

" 'All right, I love you,' I admitted. We grew healthy again; in record time; startling the doctors. The oxygen box opened up, the hospital door opened up, and we were expelled from both. We walked, a few inches apart, down a public street. We each tilted our heads toward the outside, for a little private independence, including separate breathing. 'Who can tell the kisser from the kissed?' we both were caught saying at the very same time. So here we were being simultaneous again. Fearing that she and I would get mutually married by that method, I made a hurried excuse and slipped away, running as fast as my pants could carry me — in hot pursuit. Although I dodged, it very naturally caught up. 'No!' I said, prepared to attend my death alive. It attached itself to me, and held me tight in its impassioned grip, until the girl came up from behind to join us. The kiss was sort of our pimp, but how amorous! Although already uniting us, it was intent on remaining. It exacted toll tax from us both, so its internal revenue blew up, and we were wet and soaking all over. This dried up our romance, and without stopping to get married, we underwent a lifelong separation, equivalent, in any man's language, to a divorce. During its duration, we abstained from all kissing, internal, external, or even eternal, as the case may be. I had to pay her alimony — kisses — on the installment plan. My lips are rubbed thin, from barrages of lipstick and blood, and the impassioned persistence of an enemy's front teeth. The pressure is off, but her memory whimpers up close. Her scented breath still lingers to mine, and our front skulls merge, the face pressed against a face, brief love's head-on affront. She's amputated off, torn violently; that operation has imposed on me my permanent loss; but the imprint of our tender joining is stamped onto our spirits. Love's portal is at the lips, and the depth of passion is prolonged in a kiss. So pucker up tonight, friends; the lips make the first big impression, and limping lust brings up the supreme rear. With so great a frontal assault, so well supported from behind, we have impotence shipped; attack, my stalwarts! on to the enemy's breach. Admit the lasting impress of a kiss, and boldly we're backed up in big behind. Grind on, men."

Voluminous applause filled the hall. Gala curtain calls implored the speaker to come forward, with the conquering mien of a prince. How proudly he received this ovation!

So grandly exposed, however, he was riddled by some slight criticism. The presence in the story of his "friend," on the telephone, was deemed unnecessary, as not contributing to the action; this superfluous character had operated only as a distraction, and interfered with interest in the kiss, that interminable kiss that had been so binding for the two participants. But at large, the story was vigorously praised, and received glowing tribute. The immensity of the success was undeniable. How many smiles testified to this!

How fabulous that Monday, so glittering its crown! It deserved fame that endured in the annals of the Love Club.

Then a dreary week followed, the invariable letdown. The next scheduled speaker cursed his luck, to succeed so unqualified a success and be a minor sequence in the wake of an eventful landmark. It defied all competition, so he changed the subject entirely, as an evasion of inevitable comparison. He stood up briskly, and made a brisk delivery. It was short, and to the point; in its way, it did admirably, on its own merit. Nor was the applause stinting, at the end. Here it was:

"The body without the girl, I thought, fell short of the ideal. It was hers, her body all right, but she certainly was somewhere else, and was not enjoying it. It seemed strange without her, and wholly unreal. Like a tranquilizer which a corpse imbibes, to escape nervousness. When I finally woke up, after not sleeping all night, only the girl was there, but her body was withdrawn. 'Which one do you like?' she asked. I was too tired to answer."

"A nice fable," said a nondetractor, during the session of general commentary. The slight sermon was bandied about in a round of pros and cons, evoking aimless discussion and generating a scattered chorus of mild debate. It was an "off" Monday, in a sedate, relaxed atmosphere. By no stretch of the term might it be called unpleasant. No explosions, no shouts, but gentlemanly discourse. Gradually the evening waned, and the members voted to go home. Not even a snore of dissent was heard in all the assembly. It was an interval for tiding over, to recuperate from last week's enormous blast; rarely can a blowout be repeated, to shake the foundations of a small week; time must restore the blood pressure, and revive the sleeping sperm. All in nature's rhythm, the tempo of the human mating instinct. Moderation blessed its divided ends, with patched-up intermediary means. Ah, generous tranquillity, the breath of soft delight!

As usual in the process of subdivided time, another Monday proceeded to arrive. Its existence couldn't be mistaken, nor its veracity be disputed. All civilized men were in agreement on this point, in a world grown speedily uniform. Swiftly the news spread, and the acceptable standard of Monday was confirmed at every hand, and held in prevailing currency. It was authentic, raised eminently above the authority of mere rumor. The consent was universal, so Monday seated itself on its legal throne, to rule as king for a day, in the regal sanctuary of certainty. Its overthrow by Tuesday could only be proclaimed by an act of the future; but time was conservative, as yet.

Careful to establish continuity, the new lecturer was to maintain ties with the last sermon by referring to erotically induced tiredness, and the loneliness that love can carnally furnish, to augment a psychic solitude. A joint isolation connected the partners in the foul deed of love; the lust that bound them broke them apart, sent them spinning into separation. Contact was forbidden to the soul, though thrown like a bone momentarily in grant to the body. This was the depressing theme; all in a setting of physical exhaustion, the narrator's heat-lost saturation which his cunning mate foiled with the wiles of the bed. It was told in a rich poetic style, in a rather stately majesty of English. It commanded a vast dignity, in such formal cadences that greater stature was accorded to the listeners, to make them worthy of so sonorous a sermon. The Love Club's haughty members were now an exalted brotherhood, privileged in exclusive snobbery to be the proud audience to whom were addressed these finely intimate words sprinkled in the splendor of defeated sex:

"When I finish off my woman — it never fails — a relaxed feeling overtakes me. I gently employ this incentive as a ruse with which to woo sleep. When the prelude of the first dream raises its curtain, a hand from the live world, belonging to the mate at my side, pulls the theater down and restores the staleness that had eased my retirement. I turn to her, and ask 'What?' 'Again,' she commands, while my flattened vigor sighs from its deflated pump of emptiness. 'I can't,' I calmly shout. She protests with open cruelty. Mildly violent, I hurt her. So agreeable a sensation promotes her fiendish gratitude, and we converse through love. I throb with more brutality, which she, in her passivity, drinks in. Our unity breaks, in its brittle components of separate division. Her last thought is that she must rest, spanned by our mile's distance. 'Lost!' I complain, and in the solid yard of myself share what room remains with the spaces of loneliness. Let her invade that stony retreat. She'll not, while an inching light gropes deeply into morning's kingdom."

Thus ended the speech, a recital of some of the problems connected with mature love. The Club members drew from their own experience to puzzle out knowingly the universal sum from the speaker's assortment of meaning-driven words, so relevant to the plight and dilemma of each listener. A respectful silence ensued, instead of a volley of questions. Thought moved in the masculine air, between the ceiling and the seated heads. No drink was served, in respect for this somber spell of contemplation, the strenuous leisure of minds at work. Nor was the evening dissipated by another note, until a unanimous motion broke up the session by voting that each and sundry should go home.

Next Monday was now, and a new speaker addresses the group. In love, or its act, is the word-laden mind part of bodily substance, or apart, divided by deed? Is behavior deflated by an inflated mentality of words? Instead of resorting to a first-person method, the deliverer of the speech filled in the shadow of his theme by this ambiguous dialogue, airing the faintness incorporeally phantomed by two indistinct voices:

" 'I don't want to end something I can't start,' said the reluctant sexual partner. 'Well then,' said his or her nonmate, 'bring your wares elsewhere.' 'Will you be there?' 'I probably will or won't.' 'Can you make up your mind?' 'It's not my mind, it's my body.' 'Please don't act so fresh.' 'It's not action, it's only talk.' 'Yes, but dangerous talk.' 'Are you always so word conscious?' 'No, but my body is.' "

This was greeted with confusion. What had the dialogue conveyed, if not a mixed intent? Would the author kindly decipher, and unearth the well-concealed message? He defended himself by appealing to humor, and invoking its inexact code, wherein precision was not accurately defined. "It means what you think it means," he confided; and the audience was restless, starved for some respite from doubt.

They grumbled; nor was their dissatisfaction appeased, by any turn or trick. The lecturer became deservedly unpopular, and a bill to oust him from membership in the cult was defeated, despite its justice, by a constitutional clause against unsportsmanlike haste in matters of communicable misunderstanding. Thus the motion was desisted from, and good standing in closed ranks, to his great relief, was retained by so ungifted a speaker, who had composed a dialogue so vaguely blurred, so repellent to the good form of easily imagined simplicity, free from that thief of comprehension, ironic subtlety, with its deforming nuances that cripple sense. The villain of this composition was hooted off the rostrum; seeking anonymity among his hostile fellows, he was jostled by the mob, and was a bit roughly handled for not telling a tale straight and spinning a good yarn. How costly was this lesson to his self-esteem! He renounced intellect, and conformed to the current depravity of taste.

The next topic was declared: eyes and women; love's eye-route to its more rooted base, the end sighted by way of the means. The speaker was announced.

"A girl in the full glory of her lipstick gave me a half-surrendering emotional wink, bathing me momentarily in a costly cascade of the most inspired department-store mascara. Reduced to naked eyes, though, she was forced to flee, in shame for her expensively protected modesty, which had been squandered, in a single orgy of dissipation, on worthless me."

By appealing more directly to the senses, and letting the abstractions go hang, this narrator earned a rousing reception, which favorably compared with the ignominy of the previous week's refinement of foolish failure. Outcries of tribute escorted him back to his seat; then there was a hush, and critically the listeners wondered what the theme had been. What, obviously, was the upshot? That cosmetics give women confidence? Nonsense! But why think? Weekends with their hectic schedules of pleasure, transferred sinners, their faculties exhausted, into Monday nighters exposed to varied irregularities of formal verbal trumpetings; and most meanings were hideously complex. Storytelling is a simple art, theoretically; but in practice, the audience is damned.

A new Monday followed, having waited out the week. Officially, the subject, pending development, was love via the sight: How do the eyes reduce the distance between men and women; how does the effect alter the cause, and open the eyes? The listeners sat back, and began to see, while the speaker, squinting hazily, sputtered out:

"One day I caught a cold in my eye, and the doctor recommended winking. I left his office, and strolled down the street. A woman came from the other direction. (She usually does.) I winked, and she took it personally. Catching my infection, she applied the similar remedy, having been a home nurse. We stopped and communicated by wink signals. This entangled our eyelashes, like the horns of two fighting elks. We sought a marriage counselor. Bearing the important honesty of his trade, he demanded to review our license. 'Can't we improvise?' I asked him. 'You mean you're single?' He clipped us apart with one of his legal scissors. The swollen pain gave us the blindness that love requires. 'Are we divorced, or annulled?' the woman promptly inquired. Holding my eyelids steady so as not to wink, I managed one of those difficult smiles which emergency brings into our life. 'I can't see straight,' I informed her, 'but just how pretty are you — are you, for example, ideal?' Modesty blushed from her primrose lips — I detected this from my sense of hearing, since my eyes were undergoing private mental surgery. Her silence was so sexy, I immediately fell in lust. I leaped out of my skin, while unbuttoning every inch of clothing all the way. She couldn't help but notice, and asked for alimony. This crushed my purity, and wounded my thrift. Smiling somewhere between her teeth, she told me that nothing was free."

A wise roar of laughter spread out. Yes, women were that way, all right. Eyes were dangerous instruments, but physical possession had marital implications or blundered into monetary commitments. Women, no sooner seen but desired, set up a social price in return for their dear favors. Pleasure is the most costly commodity.

The Love Club met without reference to season, though members vacationed for summer trips or were otherwise absent due to the severity of winter colds. Meetings were never postponed in case of sparse attendance. Love's business was year-round, without letup. The complications were endless.

The Club was located in the center of town. For all but suburbanite commuters, it was conveniently accessible. Membership conferred prestige, and a conspicuous network of secrecy gave off intimations of a hidden glamor redolent of a magical cult of the exclusive. Dues were collected to keep the organization going. Extensions were planned, lobbyists were hired, and the society held ambitions to expand until its growth commended it as a political bloc. Love would become a power, and its issues would be discussed as national problems, with international repercussions. Was not love every ounce as important as war? Didn't commerce flow through it, and wasn't the economy, in part, based on it?

Love flowered to ramifications on a scale eminently universal, and even sent out cosmic offshoots beyond the perimeter of the known. Metaphysically, love had its ultimate roots in God; man, its by-product, was considered its key exponent; and women shared in the considerable glory, as a generous concession by men when sparks of divine weakness strengthened their resolve. Love was on the map to stay, and no life was said to be complete without partaking in its restorative, generative, and purgative effects. Though primitive, love's customs permeated to the intricacies of civilization. Even laws were established, and works of art arduously constructed, to honor its reign and sway over man's immense emotions. Love's place on the map of the world was here permanently to stay, unless dislodged by agents of the diabolical, in which case, hell surely would be unloosed. Such theology was under the jurisdiction of the Love Club. The occult and the practical alike constituted its unflagging duties, its crusade to affix love on an exalted sphere, despite fornication's undenied place on the face of the world's realism. The Love Club dealt with dreams, not only such carnal deliriums as effaced the image of its purity. Wasn't love, all in all, everything? Then to be obsessed by it was only rational, even in such a moderate scheme as entailed the percentage of all. Love was a full phenomenon, as its enthusiastic addicts would flock to testify, on oath of the painful truth. Those who were devoted to love, joined the Love Club; but they must be men.

Last Monday's topic showed how a visual impediment, or infirmity, led nearly to so binding an entanglement that loss of bachelor status, and of money itself, was dangerously close to sight, with its blinding penalties. A new Monday had arrived, bringing forth a fresh speaker, vigorous and virile. He began with the eyes, and worked his way down to the groin level, where love erects its bridge to bind two shores. Here's how he proceeded:

"After eating too many carrots, I began to see too much. Logic afforded the first solution: to close my eyes. But I'm not self-sufficient, so I asked a friend to help. He blindly came to my rescue, but succeeded only in closing his own, which left me completely in the dark. Coming to my sense (and having gotten rid of my friend, that useless nuisance), I began to see visions, concrete dreams with true appearances, reality dressed as image. This was so alarming that for my next meal I avoided carrots altogether, and was struck with vitamin deficiency. I appealed to a doctor, who merely shook his head sadly, and grinned out loud. The nerve!

"But I didn't stay indignant for long, as my body commanded me to lead it, the blood warming to the occasion and, keeping the right muscles in mind, circulating with decorum. To prove my stamina, and abet my flow, I arranged a vital date inside my girlfriend, whose clothing she had had the tact to take off. There I struggled against invisible odds, shaking with frenzy. In the end, I suppose, she won."

Chuckles approved this rowdy tale, this bawdy yarn of fun. Rows of teeth shone in the luminous Monday meeting hall, relit once the speech was done. However, there were some adverse comments. The presence of the "friend," in the first paragraph, seemed superfluous to the story: even his uselessness hadn't substantially contributed to the action, which should be keen and swift, an inexorable passage through a narrative retailing of events and culminating in the climactic orgasm with which the brief piece ended. But what has love to do with literary criticism? It should be guaranteed immunity, as a thing apart. Words were but words; sensation could actually be felt, and the flesh was easily sensitive to touch. Had the hero of the tale resorted to carrot-eating again, to give his sight a brilliant luminosity? Or was love but an act of darkness, a blind groping for an essentially evil contact? Was night its daily province, while owls witnessed from the unshaded window? Or isn't sex a sunny act, a pre-star feast? The subject was likely to be continued. Lights dimmed, until Monday was renewed again, allowing for a lapse of a week's interval, along the orderly chart of measured time. How well punctuated in even strokes were these periodical durations! The precision was mathematical, on astronomy's cadenced authority, in beats of yearly eternities. How fatal was the next Monday, and historically appropriate!

Amid fanfare came in the predestined day. The meeting was called to order at the usual time in the evening, a program undeviated from. Striving for continuity, the speaker wore spectacles. He wanted to prove an old adage, to wit, the blindness, proverbially, of love, trite as it may seem. Can love operate without sight, and ply its unseen functions, with mechanical imprecision, in the utmost blackness of the night, which not the slightest star or starriest bulb can, by illuminating, alleviate? The answer was in his story, which he entitled, *Bright Proof of Love's Blindness*. The audience settled back, in postures eager for enlightment. Would they see the point?

"One albino, who had weak eyes, married another albino, who had weak eyes. Even in the dark, unlike owls, they had great trouble seeing. They tried to have conjugal relations of the legal bed. But neither could locate where, in each other. They tried to find their matching parts together, but lacked even instinctual vision. Thus, even physically, love is blind."

Discrimination being ugly, no one laughed: an albino was in attendance who would wear a pink blush of offense. Not one clap was heard, in deference to the wounded feelings of a minority member, since the Love Club was democratically nondenominational, operating on a policy of liberal antiprejudice, founded on the broad principles of desegregation. Out of delicacy and tact, no mention was made of the story, nor was a single glance directed at the nonplussed white head of youthful embarrassment. Is it a crime to be white? The pulse of one man's shame vibrated among his red-blooded fellows, to spoil the assembly for that evening. In collective guilt, those sturdy brothers went home: in their bedrooms, the light went on, to locate the vital parts of girlfriends or wives. Why take a chance, and risk total darkness?

This was their identification with the unfortunate albino. Nor could they trust their eyes. Deep inside, they were assured of final contact, the dreamy touch. There, the feel found a close heaven with bliss for they had been securely met.

Once out, they became puritanical. It came to seem that to abstain was to reduce the stain, and that to strain for restraint, even under pain, was a discipline nobility couldn't afford to disdain. For a brief fashion, a vogue of platonic romanticism sprang up; they would look a girl's character up and down, and fall in virtue with her. Platonic orgies were held, virtuous revels; chivalry came in style again.

Holding hands was considered slightly scandalous, even under Victorian standards. The body was unmentionable; love meant the duty to suffer, an opportunity to mortify the passions it set aflame. Love imposed a rigorous ideal of frustration, and one must be austerely miserable, stoically deprived of the darling illusionary fruits of gratification. Desire would have to be crushed, and agony inserted in its stead. This code of conduct seemed like fun; the members of the Love Club revolted against pleasure's tyranny, and unyoked themselves of bondage to sensual indulgence. They were liberated from being men, to become freely either gods or fools, in their experimental wisdom. Sex was completely taboo, a primitive crime against civilization. It was so foul that even in hell its immorality was legion; only the lowest fiends, lost immortally, could creep in vile appetite to a burning deed that couldn't cool off their ardor; what they committed in the name of love thrust holiness back billions of years, to a pre-evolutionary level; it was evil pollution that they were spreading: would the contagion catch on to the innocent animals, and depopulate the fields of paradise forever? Thank God for God, who'd call a sin black; if religion is the price of redemption, why, it's a cheap bargain, at that. Piety was all the rage to a fanatical extreme beyond the Greek pagan ideal of moderation. And lust was a worse abomination than murder in the range of man's diabolical capacity. Conscience was on the upswing, while guilt was depravity's barometer, a sure giveaway. Love underwent a new definition.

Women were changed, too. They were like dummies, not real or alive. As idols without hair on their flesh, and without flesh on their frame, they were lifted into pure inaccessibility and idealized beyond the remotely pallid circumference of nature. Only a bloodless form was worthy of love, a well-censored transcendence that perfectly obeyed the rigid denials implicit in the severities of puritanical strictness. Indications of a lewd bestiality were held against a woman's virtue; for a woman to seem human was a resounding vice — an incredible offense against even the least requirements of decency: an absolute outrage that no relative spark of leniency would ever condone. So next Monday's speaker fell in love with a dummy, who "lived" (if that's the word) in a department store. What happened in due course of that ill-fated romance, which consumed more than five years of patient pining and melancholy yearning, is the subject of that discourse, or confession, which he delivered in so self-pitying a manner that the audience was basked in tears, drenched in pathetic water streaming from their ducts. The hall was choked with sentimentality while reason fled. Never was woman so glorified on a papier-mâché pedestal; this saga of doomed love had a generous effect on the nobler emotions. How true to life it was, not a painted stage for the histrionic paintings of an ideal: the speaker was revealed as very alive, compared with the object of his fancy, the image most real to the sentiments that fluttered in his heart, like soft-feathered birds restless in a cage of rusty wire and spaces of sacred air:

"I flirted with a window dummy. She was nude but frigid. The night watchman wasn't looking. But I couldn't get in the window. I stood with a moon on me. The night was hot and warm. I put on my favorite wink. She appeared unmoved. But I am not a mannequin, and I felt the cold rejection. A policeman briefly interrupted us. Five years later I returned. Jail had mellowed me. But she wasn't in the window. Whoever had her, I hoped that at least she had clothes on. In her place was an article of empty furniture. Behind me, a lamppost glared down: a false but constant moon.

"The even-tempered sun replaced the hostile scene. The gay sidewalk was spanking with beams. Shadows and their substance walked the human pavement. The bark of a dog, like a cough approved by the doctor, fell on lighthearted ears. Each iron building, square like a lawyer, dry with practical years, kept insisting it was a tree. Our city April, like a burst of natural birth inside a cage, could point to a rare sparrow and to a smile carefully disposed behind someone's teeth. Not even a dirty flower; not even a stubborn rainbow.

"The season slowly improved and grew fat with its fame. Benches were reserved months in advance; and the park seemed a great display of all that weather. The shadow-frowning trees, reflecting office windows, looked sadly mismatched in their zoo, and naked without a nest. Cooing couples, in withered puffery like pigeons, soiled the forbidden grass.

"I balanced a sneeze from my nose and returned it to the distracted pollen. The stores were boasting their sales. Seeking my dummy, I moved like a regretful shopper. Every window echoed another.

"Memories of bars lengthened the waning shadows. Jail had played corruption in me and staggered my sense to be amazed. I calmly found her again. Time, like a solid wedge, forced our hearts apart. In the window, where she wore silks, the early and empty moon made a slow mockery, showing her fashionable enlargement of status against my own frame, reduced from pulse to wire, where nostalgia, decayed like a pigeon, kept its lonely cage. The bloated moon fell upon her face, and the reflection wiped away her character. As a cloud escorted the moon from the scene, my love was only a blur of blankness."

The Love Club was a smudge of sobs, a broken weaving of tears, a weeping moan; its members, in a unison of compassion, cried copiously, melting hardness with liquid groans genuinely heartfelt, not dissembled or counterfeit. What rapport of story with audience: the communication had been total, a mood multiplied without loss from one mind to all. It provoked the comment, "One touch of love makes the whole world mannequin," which was not unaccompanied by some tear-stained smile, though hardly of the jovial kind. It was a moving occasion.

Next Monday was to be a joint performance, a dual effort, instead of the usual solo stint. It would be a lightning dialogue, in which the entertainers would alternate line by line, in witty retort, each completing what the other had added, in turn, and being extended in united progression. Frankly, the subject was sex, with allied pathways of gender in its undiluted admixture. It was really to be an intellectual treat, the likes of which were rare as the earth was presently shaped. All members were sure to attend, with minimal absenteeism, so fine a show had been publicized. To miss it would be a disgrace; the Love Club was in full session on a grand occasion. It was becoming increasingly memorable, even before the performers had gone through their stunt. Expectation throbbed, like a humming hive of electricity. What magnetism cruised the air, in buzzing glows and other vibrant overtones! A yawn would have been blasphemous, and the culprit bodily ejected from the thronged room. Now was the stage lit, and from either corner of that dramatic curtain emerged one half of this frenzied dialogue. A colorful brilliancy marked this spectacle for the unforgetting envy of all posterity. The triumph of the twentieth century was announced!

Attention was undivided, in a concentrated ray of focus.

The atmosphere was indeed tense. Grown men were prepared to faint in the heat of the suspense.

Now had all relativity vanished in the clean sway of the Absolute!

One performer was distinguished from his partner (referred to as B) by being called A. The other, known as B, could be told apart from *his* partner by the latter's nominal name of anonymity. A. Each was different from the other in the same similar way; they shared this difference as what they most mutually had in common. By common form of precedence, A spoke first, B followed, and so on — but A ended, bringing the cycle back to its original conclusion. A stood at one side, B on the other. They would double in and by opposite polarity multiply one indefinitely. Between them was a link of infinity, a bond for their joint participation. Two would become one, as a limitless factor. Was eternity listening?

A: Why do you chase the girls?
B: Well, aren't they good to squeeze?

A: Has your answer turned girlish with a question?
B: Is flesh understood to be sensually sexy?
A: Yes, passion's modest sheet sheet clothing.
B: A kiss bridges girl — and boy — opposite banks.
A: Love is lust's inhibited dream.
B: Drives are repressed into romance.
A: Orgasms follow, but they don't lead.
B: Ah, how empty is pleasure's core!
A: Arms embrace living ghosts . . .
B: Within sensation's anarchy . . .
A: Death blindly throbs with birth.
B: Pimp us gently together, God.
A: Your children are twinned by their intimacy.
B: Nature owns a growing profit,
A: Converts us to business ends
B: Whose occupation is to meet.
A: Ah, delirium, protect me,
B: The skin's tyranny is hard and deep.
A: Or softly frozen over with warmth.
B: Hold me, the coming's so good,
A: As energies overrun me, and I'm gone,
B: One man, a medium of mankind,
A: Ancestored by the ancestors to be.

Never had an ovation so stirred an excited pulse as was that of the rank-and-file mob which constituted membership in the Love Club. The applause lasted a conservative fifteen minutes, or twenty at a radical guess. What had just been heard was called the finest catechism in the history of ultrareligious profanity, by a pair of eloquent laymen. Outside of proper church Mass, it was the most provocative secular invocation to God that the Almighty had yet ignored from His out-of-hearing height. Mysticism was allied to sex, and they romped together in holy heartiness and a righteous license of an exalted and profane bliss. God benefited mightily from this, and His kingdom was augmented by enriched properties. His capitalistic monopoly was appalling.

A week created another Monday, but the speaker was embittered with age. In grumbling mock despair, he reviewed how his life fluctuated from hate to its alternative, love. The pendulum, even now, swung him from one to the other with its retrospective regularity. Was he bowed with heavy regrets? How did he look back; and when breath takes its final leave, driven from his wind-dry lungs, on what mood will he be perched? In a croaking voice, he stoops back into the dim land of recall. Life is exhumed on the visible intellect of his tongue. On wings of hate and love, his past rises on its low informative flight. What will his gnarled years reveal, remote from hopes of his frail youth? Mentally what will he conclude?

"As I sat waiting to be loved, my life fled by. When I had amassed an age totaling forty, I sat waiting to be loved. When I was seventy-five, I gave up. My earlier failures had been enthusiastic, with plenty of gay despair. Love would always come. I sat, secure and comfortable, waiting for it.

"Hate came at an early age. My clearest memories command it. Rage was close to nobility, and I hated with great dignity. Then the hate went away, exhausted in the fury of its objects. What replaced it I had hoped would be complacency. Now, I'm old. There's no use.

"I remember my early love. Equal to a flower she was. A silly comparison, and as always I lost. A habit, compiled as lifetime.

"Would hate outlast love, in my graveward direction? I have entertained both, and with politeness they have ignored me.

"Perhaps hate achieved my greater aggression, and the passive passion for soft love used up all the patience I had. Now, I can rage."

The audience didn't stir. Is that what their senior member had forecast? The cult of failure and a creed of pessimism had been preached. This sullen message would be rejected by the wholesome taste with aims of aspiration. But does love breed hate? How does frustration heap revenge on a despised cause? One must psychologically deliberate. On what process are emotions transformed, in the wild seasons of their sequence? Can love be stored up? Or does hate wait, like death, to terminate (or pass on, in grim relay) this cycle of roughly flayed edges that flap with vague momentum? In short, where does love lead on its uneven journey along the mind's jagging wilderness? Must even love's essence alter its time-ridden nature? A new Monday would solve the riddle, or increase it. The speaker, a psychiatrist, hacked out an abstract entry into this diseased problem of emotion. Can he chart the route of man's earth?

"Love spoils other emotions, like a king greedily eating his mirror. Whoever we love is destroyed, if not slaughtered, by our love's self-devouring excess, until love corruptly flees from its object, and the beloved, left free, becomes herself in a fit of person. Then the love we had, like a passion all fatal, kills the reflection of its own death, and dies mortally affected. One by one, the sunrise of other emotions resumes, especially that ignored one, hate."

"Oh," said the members of the Love Club, suitably enlightened. But what was love? The speaker had omitted its definition, though treating its symptoms with skimpily prescribed remedies. Which are: "Don't bother." His diagnosis was a masterpiece of professional negligence. So his heedings were soundly ignored by the lay public. They'd carry on in the usual way.

Love could be very simple. Advice is out of place. Just mount the girl, and —

But why were there wars? Only an army officer could explain that and the Club boasted one in its membership file. He was summoned forth and told to pretend to be Mars, the war god who finds time out to probe inside the love goddess, Venus. Then love's relation to other forms of violence, such as hate, murder, and war, might be clarified, and peace reap profit. Why did men kill? Why, too, did they fornicate? Is one's love-mate also one's hate-mate? — they'd tie up, in a stalemate. In his identity of war and love, the officer of arms places his imagination on the crucial territory, that battle of conflict, deploying his forces in an offensive thrust, while contriving on all available fronts, with the material at hand, to speed lovingly the attack, and converge on love's death.

"Being born, Venus discarded her half shell and turned to love. Strange, she picked me. As Mars, I showed her a good time, until her crippled husband wove a brilliant net. What was left? I warred. Now, only the hydrogen can do, anything less fails to be sufficient. You see what love leads to? As a mature adult, my instinct melted into my reason, I've run out of excuses. Blood wants blood, that's all. Ruin all creation. Created, then destroyed. Because whatever is built up can be torn down. Because the new replaces the old. I fail to explain. Yet the deed explains all; hostility, hatred, converts love from what it was to what it's meant to be, wants to be intended for. My logic can be faulted, but I record, and what happens is so. Bad energy in the air endangers future babies, because bombs are no longer only immediate, but eat up the time to come. Is this right? I'm not empowered to answer, but wish Venus would return. With her, a couch and a bed foiled the hour of sleep, and surely the aching moment was golden. I explain what I am: war. But what is war? Ask Jupiter, he's the boss. I go crazy if I think. I only itch to fire, to squeeze the gun. Mankind is enemy. I urge to destroy, and live my happy game a long life. But Venus, she's gone. She would replace war, or abet it. Thinking is not my game, but I get a commission for death. I lack good words, but a world of men reads the clarity of eloquent persuasion into my fiery expression. I'm appealing, I know. Just one Venus, but bring her back. Only return her. I sell all my triumph, and add any bonus, to clash into her arms again. Where all violence melts, and war is softened, a gentle pressure exploding its gun. Meanwhile, I'm a bomb, and am afraid to blow her up. The girl is old now, that proud queen, ruler of wombs for future warriors. War and love. That's my game."

He was in civilian clothes, the officer, but his rank was colonel, or, rumor had it, general. In stiff, rather martial bearing, he left the platform, leading first with a portly belly and trailing behind with his white, well-trained hair. Would Venus, should she return, feel anew the same old love for him? She'd be a hag herself, now.

And where is she, along with all former love? Time's most tragic victim is said to be love. The following Monday would contain a dirge or mourning for the past, a keening wail; the speaker, all alone, would bemoan what he'd lost, tortured by insubstantial memory. Who can but pity his outcast state? All jocular gaiety had abandoned the Love Club; it was a trying period.

Now Monday was here, and a pall of gloom heavily saddened the atmosphere with depressed melancholy. A man so old he was bent, yet not far removed from youth, barely past his teens, came upon the stage. He looked morosely at the audience, and inflicted his sympathy on them. At the proper time, he spoke:

"I've lived almost exclusively in the past, so far, despite my well-diminished future. Whenever anything happened in the past, I generally call it a memory. However, I've already forgotten it. Which adds a nostalgic dimension, and sweetens the mystery. Not that I care. But I'm loyal, you know?

"As I recall youth, generously dipped in pain, a live woman, colored by herself, steps forward, enhancing her slow substance. Into my arms, as it were. But those cold arms, securing her embrace, belong not to me, but, through prolonged amputation, to an almost impersonal past, in which I was my own relative, distantly related to myself as I am today. A blood relative, as it were, from my mother's excellent stock. How I envy him. No wonder my pain is unbearable. Absolutely. Of course. Now, *that* me really had something. He had her. And I, I have it. What? The memory, well removed, that's what. At most a dim consolation. Frightful yet natural. How inferior we are today. How short is death, and how intimate. A wonder it doesn't shut me off altogether. From some woman, embraced by arms I no longer know, or even claim to own. We are poor now. The poor cousin to the past. Gaining scraps. What a delicate nutrition I have. And how well fed formerly. As I said, I live foreshadowed in an ever rounded memory, in whose pure sunny serenity I quite dismally fade. And not fast enough, either. I should go, at once, poof! Then where will *she* be? In another's memory? I can't take the chance. So I love, and belong to her. As the arms enfold. And I am my former flesh, just now panicking in warmth, on her shattering entrance. Surely it can never live. Once is ever too many, a happening so rare that memory deepens, staggers, and refuses to believe itself. I call it to reality, quite detached from it. There always was a her. Of that I'm sure. Convinced, bridged over the sea of doubt, into the assurance of now. This is a bitter faith. But keeping me alive, it secures for me a lasting function. I operate, and am. And guard my memory, though I am frail and open, sickened by elements. Weaker, as a vessel, than the memory it contains. I'm poorly reduced, like the porter to a former rich man, who used to be himself. What a comedown. No honor. Where's my pride? In those arms, there. Where once such an embrace occurred. Unforgettable. In fact there she is now. The very woman. And I, I'm the embrace. I do it by memory. Without arms. With a vigor, a strength, that knocks now through itself, smashes past the past, and carries her raping into now, ravished by hands that molest, where formerly they were wanted. By force, squeezing the desperate intensity, instead of the old comfort, the invited and accomplished deed."

The Love Club was silent, and sad. Ends are less fun than beginnings, and it hated to leave on that note. A free-for-all talkathon commenced, and conversation issued from every quarter. The time heralded another Monday out, in a short distance. Love, that inexhaustible topic, was discussed. Love was there to endure, handed from man to man, each of whom prized his own tool. The absent women were everywhere.

FABLES AT LIFE'S EXPENSE

To James Ruoff and Brian Swann. Though each has in different ways helped my life substantially, I like them both anyway as people in their own right.

The human voice is my favorite instrument.
—Marvin Cohen

TRUTH, TIME, AND THE INCONVENIENCE OF LIVING

delplessly one

Delp was only one person. All the other people in the world combined to outnumber him by a decisive majority. His numerical inferiority gave him an individual-complex. "What I lack in quantity," he resolved in gruesome grim determination, "I'll make up in that *other* value: but what is it?

Off he went, searching for it. It led him through interminable compromises.

knowing your place and being humble in it

There are so many more things that you are not, than there are the things that you are. Think of all that you are not. They include negative and positive possibilities. In other words, everything—except you. Whatever is left, is you. Left over—from what? From the All that is not you.

And the tiny you that *is*: is in a tiny *time*, too. Of all the time spanning before you, spanning after you—the tiny trail of time *not* included, is *your* time. The time you have, and the you that you are: that's all. That's all for *you*. You are as tiny as what you have. *Outside* of that—don't you wish you were *there*?

psychology, semantics, philosophy—something

By definition, a good person is anyone I like. His goodness is in the likeness of my liking him, like an old portrait capturing the likeness of the one who posed. My liking a person makes him worthy of my liking him, and his goodness rises to the occasion in the fitness of my likely creation. You're good because I like you. I like you because you're good. I like you because I like you. You're likeable because you're good. You're good, I like you. Otherwise, what am I wasting my time for?

(The above is a contribution to philosophy. Whatever it lacks in itself, may be remedied by a brilliant reader reading it erratically / creatively ((redoing it by so reading)). By itself it falls. Readers need to co-operate. Please apply.)

a re-examination of "bad" and "good"

I'm a lot of "bad" things—opportunist, social climber, semi-alcoholic, sponge, scrounge, flatterer, "operator" and some other similarly unflattering things to be.

Yet, that's me (seen in a bad light).

Well, I'll train the *good* light on me. As its rays play on me, I'm seen much more becomingly.

Ah, *that's* me, too. As seen by an advantageous light, by whose favoring rays I appear rather splendid. Ah, fine. I *need* to be that way. Makes up for the *other* way, you know. Lots to make up for. And lots to do the making up—by necessity.

I'm redeemed—by good traits.

Redeemed *for* bad traits.

It's an even-up trade of traits, good for bad.

In the trait trade, my assets balance my liabilities: I'm barely solvent.
Ah, "good"; "bad."
That's a morality issue.
Morals. What are they?
That leads us to . . .
Ethics!
(Branch of Philosophy.)
And Philosophy leads . . .
I don't know. (. . . But wisely, anyhow.)

mental adjustments

Sex is a partial solution to the answers of life. There *is* no life. There are only answers. Where does *man* stand? He's an answer—one of them. But to what? Find the questions suitable to man as an answer. If you can't, then find *some* questions, and alter man so that man will be a suitable answer to them. Make things fit, *somehow*.

neuter ideas culminating in sex

When my girlfriend gets an idea, her breast heaves. When her first idea's logical companion next occurs to her (the neat sequence of antithesis), her other breast also heaves. (She's very maternal toward ideas.)

Should a third and a fourth idea join the first two, my girl's upper legs start wriggling to the rhythm. A fifth idea, and *I'm* soon involved, stuck in the radiant center where her ideas spread outward. This metaphysical marriage of our minds finds the concrete correlative for any disembodied idea: we work hard to make ideas *matter*.

a dialogue limited to what's inside of life. anything else gets no treatment, here.

The reward of youth is sex: the penalty of age is death.
What did youth do to deserve its reward?
Getting born.
What did age to merit its penalty?
Growing old.
How could youth help or prevent its birth and young state? How could age help or prevent its acquiring the later state?
Neither could help or prevent itself. No blaming, no faulting, upon them.
But within life, do actions count?
Yes, but only *within* it.
What's outside it?
What's not in it.
What's not in it?
The unaccountable. Ignore them. They're inconsequential.
Should I study what's inside life?
Confine yourself to that, it's still plenty.
And when I exhaust it?
Then you can see your way clear to other matters. Not *till* then, though.

crystalizing the raw

The dream materialized. Love answered. A particular replacing a general. The fortunate experience corresponding to the hungry desire. Reaching out and touching—not just reaching out. The solidly representative symbolic set. The work, concretizing all that floating mental material. The special abstraction of so much thinking. Localizing the everywhere.

a deadly merger by a strenuous stealth of degrees

When my girlfriend was born, the midwife discovered a tiny slip of paper sticking out of her sexual slot. On it, in discreetly typewritten script, was my full prophetic name, in which not a single letter was misspelled. This was fate's way of showing its hand and arranging a gradual introduction to me which eventually the girlfriend consummated, once growth had escorted her past the age of consent. We met at the bus station, and sealed our embrace with a kiss. The public wore a hushed tone.

I walk alone, but instead of shoes I wear beds, flat beds on my feet. She's always on one at a time, lying in wait for the next step. We're not so intimate that we can afford a double bed yet. So we alternate, and as my legs scrape together in the act of passing, the friction generates the mild electric current between us.

At night, we wait for the other bed to fall. But she's straight-laced, and as yet our merger has been momentarily delayed. If nothing else, our long-term engagement has stimulated in us the single virtue of Patience. Moderately sized, our Patience is finite, so we learn to share it, daily rationing it all a little at a time. When the supply is exhausted, we undergo a blood transfusion pumped from our separate wells. On the basis of this exchange program, we realize how the other half lives. This mutual process of discovery gradually invades the remaining privacy, until we're two beds whose springs, like antlers' horns, are intertwisted on one and the same person, until the scorched mattresses stop thumping. On that signal, we retreat into our separate stratospheres of independence.

Where, sucking on the brittle bones of pride, we stay thus a-stuck apart, waiting for Death to chew away the leather. Death is a corporate entity. We plan to become twins, once we go. Thus dissembled under the same single identity, we'll ride the stallion of Eternity, a pair of equal jockeys.

how impatience perpetuates its round scheme

I fell in love with her before waiting for the relationship to develop. She considered my action rash, precipitous, premature--and unfair, in that I had decided matters for us both presumptuously, before she had fair time to develop an equal share. She punished me by hurting me in my most vulnerable place—my love. The brutal weapon she used was unrequital.

"That'll teach you to be impatient," she moralized. I was being taught by the pain method. I was impatient to learn its lesson. I had lost her, in exchange for learning patience. Patience hardly compensated. This was an unfair trade. How could I apply my patience, if it was already too late for my patience to win her back? The patience proved useless. Impatiently, I abandoned it. I resumed my previous impatience. But I had no-one or thing to be impatient *for*.

Impatient without a cause, I couldn't even uselessly squander it. The girl has unavailably disappeared. My impatience was as useless as my patience. Worthless—with no object in my mind.

I could try religion, work, art, something—but what?

Now I'm impatient for its *own* sake. I gain nothing by it. All it brings me is dissatisfaction. When the dissatisfaction proves too much, it's relieved by discontent. Neither assuages my impatience. My impatience is searching for a worthy object.

I've met a new girl, and impatiently seek her love at a rapid rate. This impatience scares her off. I have my impatience left but no her.

a man's defiant pledge of resistance

The heart is a silly fool, sentimental to a fault. Its worst allergy is love; girls are the notorious carriers, and like ragweed and other noxious pollen-spreaders, must be dearly avoided, deceitfully dodged, arduously spurned, adroitly overlooked, and tantalizingly ignored. Even then, they constitute a danger, a major impediment to health, a disease to well-being. Pleasure is their pimp, and comes with many recommendations; he's sly, and subtle. Everything conspires; even society: an institutional romance-pusher, the peddler of pairs, as opposed to single solitude. Marriage is so bureaucratically official, it's the native harbor and refuge for man-security-minded women, whose bosoms and thighs bulge to passionately pursue their panting and sorely-tempted prey. The heart is between the legs, where the view, though foul, is reproductive at long range; and the wearers of bathing suits are but a single remove from the arching purity of nakedness. Of cure there is none, remedies are unfashionable, antidotes are killjoys. Then submit? No. We have our pride.

thought only accepts impermanent feelings, being unequipped to consider anything permanent. only finite subject matter, then, is meat for consciousness.

If I'm always desperate, then I'm never desperate;
if I'm always happy, then I'm never happy.

a positive victim of group negation

"That girl's beauty is nothing but a facial accident!" I disparaged, to a company of my chosen friends, at a place of public assemblage. It was outdoors, so we were accorded a fine view of the weather. It was unusually seasonal for the time of year, so we were dressed accordingly. As yet, daylight still ruled.

We all looked at her. She was sitting, by herself, pretending to notice a book, of which, at the time, she was illiterate. Behind her, a public trunk of a tree reared its tall branches. It was decidedly in a park. A blushing bench was the object on which she sat. My group were all men; as such, her presence made an impression on our awareness, in no uncertain sense. "Her beauty was a facial accident," I repeated; we stared at her, yards away.

One of our number rose, to accost her. He'd sink a line in, with witty bait; would she bite?

Enviously, we watched him operate. It afforded us much relief to see him return, defeated. His dejection honored us, by signaling his failure.

Then another of us tried. He received the same treatment, to our silent delight. But would the next one succeed?

One by one, the hopeful approach and the dismal return was our uniform fate, until I alone had not ventured that formula. "You go," they said, so I trembled, abiding my despair. I left them, walking straight at her. "I expected you," she said, having counted us: "You remained, as the last. Why were you so cowardly? Did you expect rejection?"

"I didn't dare to alter my usual lack of confidence, in your exceptional case," I remarked, in an ornate flourish of gallantry. "Well, I like you best," she decided, eyeing me. "Then may I ask you for a date?" I replied, aware of heaven within reach. "I'd be insulted if you didn't," she said tremorously. But before the conversation could proceed further, with its enchanted promise of great romantic reward, my eliminated competitors decided to ruin my chance. They ran at us, and pushed me away. "We can't tolerate a successful rival," they apologized; "so we must deprive you of your gain." They hauled me with them, leaving that facial accident to the isolated spectacle of her own beauty, emanating from herself. "You've been cruel," I told them. "It was our misery, against your happiness," they explained: "and as our numbers were superior, we felt it was just to reverse it: your loss is our relief, and we maintain this fraternal equality, at your pain. The individual must be sacrificed to the group."

So I quit them, turned in my membership card, and became a free agent, unaffiliated to some restricting sect. They released me, with cordial reluctance. "Godspeed," they wished, rather contrite. I was blocks away from the park; I sped back.

The bench was vacant. "Where's she gone?" I wondered. The lampposts were aglow, for it was night. Now I was alone, but without the consolation of belonging. She, who had benefitted from that facial accident, was no more. Nocturnal winds had scattered that improbable being, the rich progenitor of so multiple a desire. I wandered; and as the minutes purchased midnight, I missed my whole life, missing her. The loss soared, and claimed an empty moon.

how not to need love

We all know that love rules the world. But do we do anything about it?

No. We sigh, we kiss, we hold hands in the dark park at night, and invent new dreams for the moon to shine on. We rarify our language, and search the sky for soul and beauty.

Hours and hours of time are thus consumed. By the time we snap out of it, half or three quarters of life has flown out the window.

The only cure is discipline. One must practice hard at being alone.

First, you feel yourself up and down. Make quite sure that it's you. Don't rely on the mirror, but on your own sense of feeling.

Then, look at the wall. Make sure it's blank. Then, feel yourself, and feel the wall. Know the difference.

Stay there. Don't move.

Unless somebody knocks, you have been alone.

a sobering encounter that left its mark

I walked into a semi-restaurant to order coffee and a buttered roll. I saw this other man order exactly the same thing. And when *I* paid, I saw that *he* handed in the same denomination bill, so I looked again, I looked hard, and there he was, he was me. I wasn't fooled. It was too real to believe in mirrors, at that rate. I went over, antagonistically, to greet him. He deigned to condescend to do the honor, but only out of a sense of obligation in keeping with the sonorous demands of an occasion so unprecedented that its complete avoidance of familiarity necessitated an improvised, but severe, code of formality. "You do repeat me!" I chastized. He was sternly unamused, in his stiff duplication of me. He presented a prim figure as an intimate critical device, to make me look bad. "If you *must* emulate," I went on, "then kindly *improve* on me. That way, you'd at least serve my image, rather than damage my character." This subtlety had no effect on him: his resistance blocked it. I went on being him: but the distance had increased.

how to outthink a wall

If my head bumped into the wall, my head, which is *much* more intelligent, would give, would bend inward; and the wall, so much *less* intelligent, would be the same as before, unchanged: not even dented.

Therefore the conclusion is obvious: Intelligence is soft, brittle, delicate, fragile.

Its opposite is *thickness*: obduracy, opacity, heaviness, dullness, impenetrability, coarseness, insensitivity.

That's my scientific report. It was intelligently inspired by the pain received by a blow in the head caused by the bumping of said head by me against a tough wall which, in itself, came out undamaged, though my head was much the worse in wear and tear for that unpremeditated encounter. My head was sensitive, the wall was not. Human beings are still ahead, being weaker. Their frailty makes them meeker. They'll have all the earth to inherit.

Gross clod of wall, beware! My head will ignore you: and stoically deal you no revenge. Cunning passivity is wiser, to unlearn foolish aggression. The smack of impact is but a memory now: retreating into inert forgetfulness.

I'll avoid you, wall, and steer shy; I'll clear my head of you, when the buzz settles down. (Though your existence will be the same as before.)

When I become oblivious of you, I'll rival *your* oblivion to *me*. Only then will I have overtaken your wall-like quality: and add you to me.

As for me, I'm already added to you. If you only but knew it! Then, how far would my ringing still ache in your spirit's aural region?

But you possess no soul! My sponge-like soul soaked you in. Something there is in me, which disliked a wall. Your wall-like being is in me, it's set itself up: it divides us twain, ever again.

That barrier parts us separate. On *my* side, all is me. How I long to know what's behind *yours*! More of you?

Wall, wall, keep to yourself. To avoid colliding head-on, I've absorbed you. I've assimilated your poison. You were tough, but that's past. You were hard, but that's *my* strength, now.

Well, I've outthought you. That's all I'm good for. Objects get in the way, or they're used. I make headway.

a daring experiment in defiance of gravity

To test the law of gravity (which I'm always suspicious of, being a lawbreaker), I applied it in reverse to a commonplace act: eating. Here's how. I lay down on a table on my stomach, it was a high table; then I wriggled forward till my whole torso was dangling down, head bottom, to the very floor. Flat *on* the table stretched out was that half of me from feet to groin, at the horizontal. From groin to head (bottommost) made a vertical from the edge of the table. That was my experimental position.

On the floor along with my head was a bowl of food, and a plate of more food. I fed morsels of food with my dangling hands into my dangling mouth. Here was gravity's real test.

Most people eat upright so that the food that enters their mouth can travel down through the neck into the stomach, where digestion and assimilation wait to put their processes to work.

But I was defying the law of gravity by daring the food to travel upward from mouth to neck to stomach. My whole body would know the result, soon.

The result was that the food had nowhere to go, it never moved from settling in the mouth: it *refused* to travel upward—a refusal prompted and instructed by the orthodox dictates of the law of gravity.

My mouth was *bursting* with an accumulation of food that never left the mouth. That wouldn't do, it was intolerable. Gravity would *have* to be obeyed. Starvation, with its deficiency of nourishment, would follow upon the breaking of the law.

So I righted myself upright from my right-angles position, and became a normal man. I was left with a lot of swallowing to do, and I did it. Regularity welcomed me back to my commonplace.

I placed the unfinished bowl and plate on the table, which I sat on, with this time my *feet* dangling down, instead of my head. I easily ate the remainder of both bowl and plate. It all went down well. My body and gravity had come to an understanding.

the human table

Sometimes I use my lap as a human table. This is necessary when tea is served on a saucer but nothing else, with the cup fitted in the saucer, but precariously heaped to the top with tea. (Fulfilling the what-for in the design of the cup.)

The saucer is a kind of junior table for the cup. (The cup is a kind of primary table for the tea. But can a vessel be a table for what it contains? Or is that too much of a contradiction? I'm not eligible to answer this question, having never been either tea, cup, or saucer, or any combination of those three, in any order whatever. So I'm unqualified to speak on the matter, or on any other matter, except on the matter touching what I am, it being my being a human person, which is all I was ever destined to be, and all I ever managed to realize.)

Back to the pre-digression, and then to travel straight from it. The saucer, it was written, is a kind of junior table for the cup (which itself is a kind of primary table for the tea contained in it). But the saucer is unstable unless set somewhere; while the cup of tea is also unstable so long as its own table (the saucer) is. That's where my lap comes in, as a reserve stability agent (or, as said before, human table). If the tea isn't served on a real furniture table (generally of wood material, including "legs" that usually number four) then the human lap is pressed into service, and is fabricated to be improvised as a sort of artificial table. (But since when is the human body "artificial"? Certainly I wear no artificial limbs, they're my own. In fact, they're as natural as nature can be, since nature made them. *I* surely didn't make them. I—all of me—*was* made. That's what being natural consists in. So I'm a *natural* table, not an artificial one. These distinctions are not hair-splitting. They're *essential* distinctions. We'd be lost, without them.)

To go back to the substance that preceded the latest digression (determined not to be waylaid into still another tempting digression, and thus be seduced from the narrow narrative path which, taken straitly, would lead logically somewhere by virtue of itself or else virtually falter in its own purpose, end, and aim, meanly demeaning thereby its own means, by which is meant . . .)

So in the absence of a real manufactured table, I sit forward on the upholstered armchair, and rest on my lap the saucer-held, tea-filled cup. My torso tilted stiff; my upper legs absolutely horizontal, parallel to the floor and the ceiling, from pelvis to knees; my lower legs vertical, from knees to feet. Obviously (it goes without saying) my knees are bent. Bending is done by knees thousands of times before the total death of the whole person for whom the knees serve as parts. Much hinges on this function of the knees. But enough on that subject, whose obviousness is usually beneath the mentioning would derive, as a physically mentalized act. Sometimes knees are above the head. It often happens to ladies who are being ravished in bed. Such indecent behavior, so as to be unobserved, is done in retired private quarters. Romantic images by the participants euphemize the sordid deed. The function of fantasy is often to exalt.

To go back behind this latest digression and recover the rather rambling theme. To recapitulate, before, in despair, I capitulate altogether.

The tea is in the cup. (Still somehow hot, just poured from that procelain teapot where it was brewed in recently boiling water.) The cup is on the saucer. The saucer is on my lap, for want of a real table. My lap is on my upper legs and loins, which, in turn, are on the armchair. The armchair is on the rug. The rug is on the floor. Is the floor the final, all-containing table—the "table-of-contents" to begin and end the whole book? No, the floor is on something. That something is on something else. And that something else is on the earth. But where is the earth on? What table holds the orbiting earth? Magnetic space? And what's the table for that?

All will slip off the table, when the tablecloth is pulled. When the body dies, the table is turned on physical life, for the individual lodged within. Is there a tablet of laws on such a turned table? This is a tale or fable, insecurely set upon a table. All that's "on" is precarious. We use the term "based on". On what, ultimately, does all rest? The discourse on tables comes to perch upon metaphysics. Metaphysics is perched upon a set of premises.

On what, ultimately, is all laid? I'd like to lay my weary mind to rest. I'd like to allay my tedium; to lay a lady; to get laid.

The table is laid, for tea. The tea stuff is laden on it, consisting of saucer, cup, and tea, and little silver spoon. The table is my own lap. My lap may commit a lapse, if unsteadily it lets the tea stuff slip off. I drink the tea while it's hot. Tea is over. I stop my lap by standing up from the chair, ending the improvised "table". The empty cup, the saucer, the spoon, spill off by my act of standing, for the table is taken away from under them, and they don't even have a leg to stand on, so they fall on the floor, or on the rug. This was a lapse in decorum. I kneed my lap, strait. Straightened, it was a lapse. The hostess bends down to retrieve the fallen service. I bend down to retrieve the hostess; to resume my service. Tea is over. We fornicate on the rug, through rips in our body where the clothes are worn through. A fitting ending to a tea. A table to uphold it all. A table to grunt, and bear the weight.

I couldn't bear the wait, from tea to that. My hostess bears my weight, weighted down with my wait. We bear the bearing instruments, unartificial. We make nature, after tea was made. For that we're made.

Our laps are pressed into service, but not for tea. We don't kneed laps for tea-posture now. Our knees are freed. We weigh down heavy. We wear out the human race, as the table groans with our pounding. O Table, can you bear us? And bear too, on you successively from superficials deep down, the rug, the floor, the earth that spins, and the spin that spaces off? What's at the bottom, of this table business?

I now put a ceiling on my flawed talk of floors, and box the room in, with hinged doors. The tableau is based on what table? O Table of rectitude, uphold us!

soup spilled vs the monumentality of the can

Soup, which is food boiled down to its liquid form, is wasteful when served in a plate as flat as the contemporaries of the man who discovered America considered the round globe to be. If this frustration isn't sufficient, then use a flat spoon to convey the said soup to the mouth, portal of hunger's methodical murder. The end product of this futiley ineffective attempt at nourishment may be defined as that state whereby the soup is now in a *spilled* form. The consumption of that soup may be psychologically said to be hindered, or, to apply a human emotion, frustrated. To avoid this self-defeating cycle, this process conducive to the humiliation of its victim, it is recommended that the enduring edibility of foods in a *solid* form be resorted to, staving off that state of emergency known to sociologists by the term of starvation.

Since *canned* food is food in its most solidified form as a fact of observable exterior, this is logically the antidote to the liquid weakness of soup spilled from a platter. What *harder*, more durable condition can food be heir to, than that of a symmetrically metal can, whose lack of fragility has toughened the fortitude of those who occupy themselves in that department of domestic utility known by all as a kitchen? By comparison, spilled soup is as soft as air and even less valuable, since its properties do not include such air-like elements as the lungs see fit to breathe.

Few things are as negligible to usage as that form of liquid waste recognized by mankind as soup in its spilled shape. The loss of thrift is amazing. Nor is any useful aesthetic function thereby served. The perishable contents of fallen soup may be proverbially surmised.

As a solution, cans are less perishable and may last a long time. As kinetic examples of sculpture, they contribute to hopeful perspectives of art. For art's excellence has been predicated on its *enduring* character. Cans automatically fit this description, and as such are self-evident works of intrinsically built-in art. No paper-printed novel can afford to compete with them, in this respect.

Yet a paradox is hereby contained. If the can is the cure of the problem necessitated by the flat feebleness of soup already fallen, what if theoretically the can is said to *contain* soup? The most authentically contrived Wisdom as a mature testimony to experience would bristle at this challenge to world-based Logic, that power of man's thought whereby the irrelevant is effectually eliminated from the abstract popularization of practicality-purified essences.

Even philosophers would be stifled by the attempt to reconcile the "blessedness" of cans per se with the inferior moral structure of soup whose outstanding property is its ability to *spill* when placed on top of a flat plate or directed to the mouth by the transitional inadequacy of an equally flat spoon. As for practical homekeepers, they are equally incompetent to cope with this eternal contradiction of qualities which speculation teaches us to regard as incompatible. Yet, there *are* cans of soup.

Endnote: In England, cans are called "tins". Yet the above essay, once this difference of nomenclature is reconciled, may be fruitfully read in England as serviceable to the typical English concern for frugal maintenance of economical reduction of basic essences to their most functionally sensible applicability, a no-nonsense mentality worthy of a nation that produced Carroll and Lear to uphold the starchily stiff virtues of directness of procedure and an undistracted attentiveness to the object or task at hand, whether it be to found an empire, change cans to soup, or fitfully avoid the absurd.

England has proved itself most worthy of its well-deserved reputation as a nation so formidable that spilled soup can pre-exist in its ready-made canned state of embryonic potentiality to fulfill its ultimately spilled fate. Englishmen hate "can't", detest hypocrisy as a necessarily evil virtue. Their "tins" are solidly made. But even their polite upbringing and refined bunch of exquisitely polished manners, those sterling products of a code of definitive gentlemanliness as a habit institutionalized by tradition, cannot prevent them from spilling soup on their rounded laps, thus reducing a commercially nutritious liquid to its least useful approximation of usability, if the aforementioned soup had been served on a flat plate and taken in transit to a waiting mouth by means of an equally flat spoon. "Spilling" observed its inevitable course, thus vindicating the English obsession for suitability, regulated by a well-rounded respect for what, after all, can only be "proper". (Hence the word, "propriety," which the conventional Englishman is certain to include in the workable vocabulary he employs on social occasions.)

A "tin" (as the English refer to a can), is a solidly hard substance, despite its frequently paper label. That the soft weakness of soup may exist inside a durably structured container such as a "tin" or can, is an insane metaphysical notion, though a distinctively plain concretion of physical likelihood, viewed by material standards. Irony is an English invention. Thus it is just, fitting, and eminently proper that iron should have gone into the manufacture of that ironic object. That would iron out the difficulty: but a flat can would find it humanly impossible to contain even flat soup. Round soup is another problem.

Suffering from ontological deficiency?
Don't do nothing — take Vitamin Be!

the mind searches for being—but finds the mind

I'm trying with my *mind* to understand what being is. And that's impossible: Wrong instrument.

Then *how* can I understand what being is? Impossible. Being is not understandable. Being *is.* Understanding follows lamely behind, inadequate before the "object."

Being is not an *object*, to be seen or understood. It's beyond objectifying. It's not the mind's toy or game.

Yet the mind doesn't give up. It invents new "means," to corner its prey, to track down, to hound out.

The wrong pursuer. The mind can't pursue. It takes traces of what *just was.* It's always on the spot, but too late—the spot is gone.

where does truth lie?

Ah, the truth, what a thing it is! I sacrifice so much for it, with people: I forego, for truth's sake, discretion, loyalty, diplomacy, tact, polite manners, elegance, grace, poise, balance, good taste, conformity, image-role, fashionableness, polish, confidences, promises, ambition, consistency, identity, clarity, comprehensibleness, good will, hypocrisy, and lots of other things—amass sacrifice, at truth's altar. God! is truth worth it? I *hope* it is. It *better* be, in fact.

A lie is the truth in masquerade. But the truth may be a *lie* in masquerade, too. In what direction does the truth lie? It lies in *many* directions, I think. Even now, the truth is lying—somewhere. The truth is *always* lying. Its life is hard, but it doesn't take it lying down—for the truth lies straight ahead —it lies just out of sight. And so, it's changing, in motion. To catch itself lying.

Goodbye, gentle truth. Time for someone *else* to take up your cause. Me, I'm headed for fiction—your other self.

the art of seeming

How much of being rubs off into *seeming*?

Not much. Often, seeming is independent of *being*. A famous man of the time in the public eye may indeed be idolized, and often is, for what is only apparent, not transparent, and smacks essentially of solid *appearance*, unrelated to what internally is actual. Indeed, the inside may be inconsequential, irrelevant, or even harmful, to the external "image". The cultivation of what *appears*—deliberately designed deception—is often what's behind the making of a public figure. What counts, what pays off, is charm, radiation, effect, personal magnetism, some sort of sex appeal, or appeal to the maternal, or appeal to the infantile, or appeal to the insecure, or appeal to the ambitious, or appeal to the vicarious, or appeal to the power-frustrated, or appeal to the forbidden. We react to what *seems*: that's all we have to go by, or all we want to go by, for we enjoy being deceived, duped, "taken for a ride". The deep, persuasive voice of that magnificent specimen of a successful political statesman amply disguises the rot and hypocrisy, the chicanery and charlatanism, beneath. Those rolling tones *sound* benign: that's all that counts. You're given the feeling that he'd protect you personally: he's a benevolently firm father figure, or so he postures as such, making a convincing gesture, which we bite and fall for. Then we're in his net, and vote him back into office, despite his record (well concealed) of having acted effectively against anything that would have truly benefitted us, or *for* anything that keeps us mired in detriment. How susceptible we are, to what *seems*; and very easily seduced.

Will you now offer a *feminine* illustration of the same point?

That universally acclaimed celebrity is falsely padded up front with an artificial brassiere prodded to look natural in propped circumstance. But duping the public even worse is the frank and open hoax of her voice. It's a palpable fraud, its tremors are all uneven. Yet she's far-sung for all her recorded songs: she's not unsung, as a singing hit. Her fans and supporters adore the deception. How splendid to be victimized by her.

They passionately patronize in the mob frenzy of autograph-hounding hysteria! They've given her fame, and riches: And they've received the special bonus, the too-good-to-be-true privilege: her scorn and contempt for them. What a deliriously one-sided relationship! It's the ecstasy that masochism is enthralled of, and made of! It's *genuine* to be so dazzlingly beguiled! It's at the magic root of art: the agreed-upon convention of a willing fiction, suspension of incredulity, the artful mistaking of shade for substance, that fabulously holds us spellbound, in the swoon of enchantment. How drab the *truth* would be, were it allowed loose! No, it's safely secreted, so that it won't spoil the joy we're paying, paying, paying for: with our heart, our soul, our culture, our money, our all. Her manager cultivated her calculated "show": She's in *show*-business. And what shows is showy: it *shouldn't* reveal essence. Showiness for show's sake: the genuine article.

the mind swells with imagination, then evacuates with tedium. boredom, inanity, and other objects of mental emptiness, described drearily here.

The book my friend is reading in the library is only imagined. But surely isn't he sitting on a real library chair? Or is the chair air-owned, by imagination? But here, unmistakably, is the library? This obvious public book-lined interior? This atmosphere credits itself to authenticity, no?

But the library is in his mind. And so is everything else. There's nothing that isn't. A psychopath? Not far from it. Poor tool and fool of delusions, as though the entire globe of the earth, teeming with continents and major cities, waterways and races of so-called people, were just a private image to play with, his personal possession. Maybe he's luckier than most. He can have fun, that way. Who's a fool? Excessive rational sanity can be very confining and so limiting that the person obsessed by it can dwindle into a narrow freak, complete with all of a half of one dimension and casting no shadow, and partaking nothing of the sun. My multifold friend.

At last, the mind had nothing more to offer. This was bound to happen. The emptiness was now perfect. To trifle with the time, my friend began to yawn. This proved he was alive, doing something. Why he stopped, I don't know. He gets awfully inconsistent. I left the room, and came back. My friend had a closed book in front of him. He looked like he was thinking. "Being deceptive again," I thought. Out loud, I voiced, "What have you been up to, all the while? Eternity can't wait forever, you know." "I've been active, after my fashion," protested my friend. "Then list your recent behavior." "That's simple enough," said my friend: "it's a deal."

"To begin, I yawned so vigorously that the jaw snapped, proving how destructive *ennui* can be. A lucky stroke, actually: for now at least I had some pain with which to occupy my leisure time.

"Yes, I was idle no longer; but then, to my dismay, the pain stopped, leaving my soul completely empty: and in two minutes *ennui* had filled it entirely.

"I decided to become hungry. But the food had no taste, and my stomach welcomed it indifferently.

"So I picked up a book. I read the first word: 'The'. Then I felt saturated. Too much culture in one day, I decided, would be harmful. But I tried to digest what I *had* read: I meditated on the word 'The'."

"Can you produce a statement beginning with that interesting word?" I challenged. "By all means. I have had adequate preparation." And so he recited, in sing-song inventiveness, like an incantation by a beat beatnik priest commemorating the last day on earth for the stricken brethren of his marijuana-wasted, novocaine-declining, barbiturate-ravished, and Christ-hounded congregation, wailing a sad dirge shrouded in the black tears of farewell:

"The weather keeps on occurring. The apparel industry both anticipates and lags. We wear according to sex and size, age and occupation. Hot wrestles with cold, wet with dry, dark with light. These playthings amuse the sense, but ultimately depress. The total of variety is, again, boredom."

1. does seeing consume? we'll see.

2. how deep does seeing go? we'll see that, deeply.

The more you see in another, the less there is.

You mean, as I see him, I'm consuming what he is, and if my seeing continues, gradually there'll come to be nothing to remain of him, for I've seen it all?

Yes, but deep down, he has an unfathomable mystery. So you'll never use him *all* up, in your act of depth perception.

If I smell the fragrance of the lovely lilac in its early prime, would there still be enough of its perfume left over for a new smeller of the same bush in the Botanical Gardens?

Horticulturally? Yes. A flower *retains* its perfume as we smell it, till it withers, at a later time, independent of how intensely we've smelled it, or how long we've been bending over smelling it. It'll wilt at its own time.

And with a person, I can observe him, understand him, but he'll still go on being himself undiminished?

Maybe. How deep is he?

I observed him for a long time. Deep down, I found him rather shallow.

Maybe you only *saw* him superficially.

You're insulting my penetrating powers of perception. I plumbed him, deeply.

But his very *depths* were shallow?

I probed so deeply, that his superficiality showed itself to be amazingly constant, with a durable consistency.

How did *he* find your findings?

Insulting. He *prides* himself on being *deeply* complex—inscrutable, in fact. I pierced his "mystery," to the core, and exposed it as a fraud.

Didn't he want to slap you? Or avoid being seen by you again?

He made it clear that further contact between him and me was on his part unwelcome, on my part forbidden.

By *him*, forbidden?

Yes. He rejects me. I've lost a friend.

Do you mourn, grieve?

I haven't lost *much*. A *shallow* loss, I'd say.

But still—he was a close personal friend! Then he's uniquely irreplaceable.

I miss him.

Deeply?

Yes, deeply.

You deeply miss a shallow man?

Yes. *I'm* deep, you see.

what is the real, really?

In the early birth of the world, sometime in a former age, there were indeed real things. So many real things existed, reality was formed, on an organized basis. Its proponents worked realistically to this end, and found reward. But when their work was ended, things were no longer real. Only formulations and patterns were, the thoughts and meditations of such. The removal from real things had begun.

Today, meanings are notoriously elastic, and may be stretched to mean anything. Just short of nothing. We debate what is real, and only the debate is real, but not the subjects discussed. And not the things the subjects are about. We have evaded the simple, and built layers of length confounded against absolute elements. Indeed, the real is remote.

How may we re-attain it? Is there magic to enter the real, or merely fundamental simplicity? Of what is a real thing constituted, and by what may we recognize it, as against the sheen of appearance? And when real things are mixed, is it wise to distinguish? Or does wisdom avoid the real?

The real, the real is childish. Is it really so? Yes.

And in the adult world, reality rears its ugly head. Nothing real is left.

Old age, maturity gone to rot, returns to feeble semblances of the real, reverts to foolish sight, a dimming vision of a young and dancing real.

The real, the real. If only I had you once more, I would not be writing this. Instead, I would be rejoicing at you. The lovely image of the real. The real itself, mirror-source of the image. The true real, a real devoid of world, empty in the fullness of itself. That real for which we laboriously compensate, piling on. The nature of the real. A real thing, burning in unreality.

reality and the universe: a legal partnership

The universe is the dictionary of reality.
Then what's the encyclopedia of reality?
The universe is *that*, as well.
What's the something of reality that the universe is *not*?
The universe is the *everything* of reality.
And does reality agree?
It has no choice.
Why not?
It's made a deal with the universe.
Advantageous to both?
Sure. Reality's no sucker. It knows a good thing when it sees one.
That's why its reputation is universal?
Sure *is*.

how momentarily time almost drowned

Dublin Bay is the source of time's disappearance. Let's fish it out quick, since no place else can continue without time to stride through.

Time comes out dripping wet from Dublin Bay. By the time it dries, the other places are allowed to move.

the past has been, and always is.

I *am* my past: it continues to have been done.

All that I was, I'm still responsible for being.

All that I ever did, I support by my present being.

Yet I vary off, veer off. Burdened by my past, responsible for it, yet I spontaneously fly off into a new path of choice. Unprecedented emergencies, unexpected modes, unpredictable ventures, surprising projections occur: in spite of all that past, which can't *entirely* pin me down.

No confining the future into astrological determinations, predetermined configurations, confirmations of chartedness. We violate the openness of the future, at our own impoverishment. We can't regulate what's to be, on what's been's basis. We can't—though often we try to—domesticate the wild unknown of the future into a tame pattern of presecurity. We seek assurance, against the frightening novelty of what's to be.

the significance of change

The house is falling down. Here are the things in it that can be itemized as falling down. One: The law of gravity. Two: Everything that weighs anything. Three: Everything else, too. Other than that, the house is quiet.

The house is being repaired. But in such a way, it can never be a house again.

statement by a time-dweller

Time? I don't know what it is. However, I'd be a fool not to let it *act* on me. After all, I'm *in* it, in some way.

The past? The future? They're both in my present—which moves. I have states of consciousness, in succession, one after another, always. Each moment brings a new rearrangement of parts of my past, with intentions and tendencies toward an unknown future.

If I knew what time is and how it does what it does, I'd understand myself better, and also understand an opera, a symphony, a poem, a play, a novel better.

All that moves, moves with time. I'm in it, but I can't see me in it. I see only disconnected tableaus, not vital sequences and transitions. I see no temporal structure of my mind and feelings. I'm cut off, from the true me.

I'll die not having seen. I'll die having had many not-put-together awarenesses—I'll die in my own clutter.

It makes no sense—yet, better to be than not to have been. At least I existed; but so too did everything else. It's no special distinction, to have existed. But at the least, it was *something*. And there was nothing else ever being me, but myself. It was a unique experience.

wise counsel to the employer

I hired somebody to sleep for me, once, when I was too busy to do my own sleeping. I snatched him from the ranks of the unemployed, and others as well, equally shiftless; thus, I was able to sleep by snatches, relays, and shifts—through the proxy of the peculiar "industry" of those men. However, I ultimately got tired of that set-up—*strenuously* tired, in fact. I fell asleep on my own. I woke up, felt better, or better enough to fire my employees for sleeping on their job. "That's what we were hired for," they objected. But I fell back asleep, deaf to their indignation. They disappeared. Sleep compels so many things to disappear: consciousness not the least. I'm too sleeping to be busy. So I'll hire others to be busy *for* me—letting me get on with the job of my sleeping. Of course, I can't keep watch on them, that way. They may easily shirk, to take advantage. Hired help can't be trusted. "Do it yourself," I always maintained. But only one thing at a time. If I sleep, work is suspended. If I work, sleep is suspended.

When there's a *simultaneous* necessity for them, I must hire, since I cannot split into two people like that old one-celled amoeba. I admit to not having *tried* lately. But there's plenty of people to *help* me split, and be the other half. People help each other, what else are they for? "The division of labor" was a good invention. To get varied things done, in industry's hum.

several eventful men

A man with the best intentions was nevertheless unable to help himself. The court helped him, with a fifty dollar fine.

A man found out he was sleepy. By the time he found out, he was awake a minute.

A man, by the time he finished eating, found out, too late, that he wasn't hungry.

A man pursued happiness. It was one of his rights.

A man collected dollar bills. He had to work for them, though.

A man developed a habit. By then, it was too late to break it.

"if"-created adjustments

What would you do if time went on strike?

I'd just have to make space work overtime.

What would you do if *space* went on strike?

Then I'd just have to make more room for time.

How much more room?

As much as space would allow.

space, and other places

There was no sense in walking without a purpose, so we set a destination, with the help of one of those upside-down maps that are so careful to avoid being dogmatic in pointing out any direction.

Then where did you go?

Somewhere else, at the same time.

At what point did you avoid confusion?

Equally, at none.

By then—

By then, it was all beyond recovery. Where we were, became the place to be. Anywhere else would be away from that, and left there. So, we stayed. Much later—but that's another story—we moved.

why trouble is unavoidable

Troubles besiege me. To avoid them, I go to all lengths. That spells out further trouble, in the end.

I hid my head under my cover, ducking deep under, burrowing my way in, to leave trouble outside on top. I'm almost smothered, deep down in there. What do I find? Cosiness? Comfort? Warmth? The womb-like lullaby? A snug, secure, serene haven? Wrong. I find *trouble*.

Because trouble is wherever I rest my head. But I don't "rest" my head *anywhere*. My head is too restless for that.

Till my last "resting" place, I find trouble. Wherever my head is (and not only that, but *whenever*), there's trouble. It's built in. It goes with my head. I can't head it off. It precedes me, far ahead.

I lamely limp behind. Little troubles dance around my feet. Like tugboats, they escort my deep ocean liner into trouble's rough ocean.

impractical advice to meet every occasion

Never commit suicide when the water is icy. You'll merely cut yourself.

Kiss briefly, if at all. Otherwise, you might enjoy yourself.

When smiling, keep a mirror handy. It might remind you how funny things are.

If you ever get short of money, remember that life is essentially mystical.

The harder you pray, the more a mountain remains where it is.

Try to be sleeping when you dream.

When you get drunk, remember that life is short and you'll soon be sober.

Grow old, if at all, reluctantly.

If you're young, don't brag. You were just lucky to get off to a late start.

If you can't achieve sanity, then resign yourself to mere happiness.

If your arm hurts you, try to think how nice the other arm feels by comparison. If that arm also hurts, then you ought to see a doctor.

Every day, practice something.

When you get perfect, stop.

the luminous leftover

The light that was left over from yesterday is nowhere to be seen outside the eye's mind. This light is beautiful, divine—but dull. And it's all too private—for private consumption. But it's never consumed. It's inside me forever—this light from yesterday; and it's busy lighting up all the new things I'm only just now undergoing. Without it, I'm quite blind.

eyes, and the rest

To see something steady *and* to see it whole? No, it's one or the other. You see a part of something steady, but not all of it whole. Or, you forego seeing a part of it steady, in order to see the whole thing whole.

After that act of seeing is over, you wash your eyes and put them to sleep. Your body follows. The eyes have it, first. Then your whole being.

Your eyes are first to wake, then all of you does. You follow your eyes out of bed. You keep following them, legs and all.

The eyes are kept in the head, for protective reasons. The eyes *act* as the head—for visionary reasons.

Follow your eyes about. Follow, till they're dead. Just then, *you* are, too.

No eyes are survived very long by their remaining followers. Blindness is not for wading—it's for drowning in.

"Give me light!" when we die, the plea, ignored—by darkness. Darkness? That's another thing. We need new eyes, for that.

PROPHETIC PARANOIA

THE TRANSFORMING TRAVELER'S RADICAL EFFECT ON THE INHABITANTS OF A TOWN HE'S DRASTICALLY VISITED

I'm from a totally different town.

"Different" is relative. Different from *what*? From this town I've just come to.

I've been here for somewhat of a short while. A *minute* while, by eternity's incomparable comparison, to put it briefly and squeeze it into a beginningless and endless scale.

It's funny what's been happening. Hence this tale which by spurts I'm starting off toward elaborating.

The town I came from, where for years I worked to save money and then quit, didn't one bit even begin to prepare me toward what I'm finding out in this town I've come to for vacation, life, and adventure, and the calculated accidents of discovery. Which leads me to what's happening, of an unusual character, that I'm about to reveal:

I'm the town stranger. They haven't had a visitor in a whole generation. First I was a curiosity piece, and any street I roamed or bench I sat on, the townsfolk followed and there congregated, as though hours and days weren't enough to exhaust or even satisfy the insatiable curiosity that the entire town (though it wasn't suspicion or paranoia— simply the uncharted open innocence of curiosity itself) entertained concerning me, my person, and my actions, including anything that emerged as speech. I was the moving focal center. Observed, followed, relentlessly studied. But not with hostility. Just increasing interest, as though through me, or in me, each native would locate his utmost personal salvation or come across the sole goal of his whole undefined life in its blurry wanderings through all its living stages.

I was *it*. I basked in their attention, as their unremitting object for scholarship or mulling to dwell ever on. I never felt this way, having been ignored in my home town, so it was as new for me as it was for them— though I had the *receiving* side, and they the pondering one. It went on like this, and gradually I could see what the next development was, startling and disconcerting as it was.

I was being imitated. I was everyone's model. The inflections of my accent (native to where I came from) were quickly picked up by those who patiently listened. My gait of walk, as I bent my knees in the rhythm of making my legs propel me, was now everyone's new acquisition as their walking style, in mass emulation. Then the tailors made clothes to resemble mine: overnight, the fashion changed, uniformly to all the men: they took me for their model, and from that I could only take amazement.

Even little children wore miniature suits of clothes cut and designed after the ones I wore. And the women, as well, purchased dress suits exactly, though femininely, along my lines.

My thought patterns, as revealed through casual discourse and repeated conversations on different subjects, were *also* taken on by my emulators. A total transformation was going on, to the specifications of my own image, the whole town through. What should I make of all this? I was bewildered, but unthreatened, for I divined no bad intention in their becoming replicas of me, in my finding myself duplicated all over as though spontaneously reproduced to full scale by some astounding machine that was a human and accurate advance on the pale paper mimeograph. I felt central, like a king, or patriarch who's the proto- or archetype of his loyal and devoted subjects. Should I regard this new town as my kingdom? This was a power temptation. Even the mayor had changed into an aping image of me; and my likeness was pasted all over the ruling municipal council's elders who governed, and stamped on every high official. Here was an ideal exploiter's opportunity; how far was it foreseen that I "take advantage?" My life had pounced upon a glorious promise, after the drab, undistinguished career I had led in my unappreciating birthplace. Traveling would be more than broadening: it would be my making. It was all being set up. It was falling to place before me, or rising. My host citizens were cooperating, to a most flattering extent, in perching me on a seat of indisputable eminence, privilege, authority, dominance, conspicuousness, and distinction. "Some have greatness *thrust* upon them," once wrote Francis Bacon. Wasn't he meaning me, and now I was here? I wouldn't deny my fate, that was being so lavished on me, through so profuse an "offering." Why resist hospitality? I'd be a docile guest, and go along. It was a *unique* brand of hospitality, conferred solely upon me. I would graciously consent, and be led by it.

So in soon time, the town was transformed by the visitor, done over to all the details of the "image" his existence visited upon them. It was *my* town, by adoptation. Each inhabitant was a conscientious version of me, so far as he was capable, and to his most studious extent. Even the buildings became altered. Some were less suitable, some more, to me who ruled. I was the rod and rule of measure, all things and beings conforming to my magnetic example that radiated a uniformity principle through the town. All were guided by what was appropriate to me. My own lead was passive; their emulation was fanatical, exacting, active, painstaking, worshipful. Harm would come of this, I knew.

In time, the natives were restless. Obsessed with me throughout, they had so thoroughly absorbed what I was, in all my manifest essence, that where could they go from there, in pursuing their cult?

Beginning in dribs and drabs, but soon steadily, they embarked on a mass exodus, a pilgrimage, in immigration, to the town I had come from: assuming that all my revered magic was the product of my native place. Now they trooped to the *source*, itself: having gone through its *product*, me, and exhausted my personal powers of transforming them.

They reasoned—my "hosts"—that if they were derivative of me, I in turn had been derivative of my home town. They had assimilated me as *secondary* source, and consumed my powers of influencing them. Now they would go to *my* primary origin, to make it *theirs*. They took all their household effects, and abandoned forever their birthplace—for the first time, in each case. None had ever traveled before. Now the whole town was migrating, to *my* town. Leaving me here, in my new adopted town. They reversed *my* path; and soon, with the exodus complete, I was the only person dwelling in this ghost town. It was eerie, naturally. I had been so celebrated before, and imitated into glory. Now I was abandoned. But I'd stay here. I'd never return to the place that had caused me to be idolized in *this* place. I'd make my home here till death. I'd take up permanent "exile" here.

For back there, where I came from, I'd only be one of many, lost in the populous native throng. Here, I was *someone*. I was *the* one, the supreme visiting celebrity. I was still *the* one: the unique resident. It was a come-down. My hero's laurels were done, and my distinction eaten-through, like a down-at-the-heels, battered outfit of worn-out clothes I should have long discarded. I reigned yet: the monarch of all I surveyed, in my desolate museum honoring me. I strode about, with a king's step. Who was to dispute my pride? I had full right here as the reigning resident. I had emptied out a town, and filled it up myself.

PURSUED LIKE A CRIMINAL

If there are no police watching out for me, but I apprehend police everywhere, then my incidence of paranoia is at its zenith.

If there are police everywhere trying to track me down, and I'm blissfully unsuspecting of the danger in an innocent unguarded oblivion, then my paranoia is nil. It's as equally unrealistic as in the case preceding, though at the pole opposite.

If there are a few police who are searching for me, and I know exactly how many, and how close they are to finding me, then I'm neither oblivious nor paranoiac, but acutely attuned to the unfortunate reality of my actual predicament.

What constitutes the true danger of being caught? What constitutes the imaginary persecution mania of apprehensions unfounded in real life? What constitutes a true appraisal of exactly what's happening, and the likely forecast of its outcome?

Is the world only a dream? In that case, police are dream figures. Then I'm being stalked, as in a dream.

Hounded down, unearthed, brought to justice.

They're coming to get me!

But for what? I did nothing!

I'm a fugitive, I flee. But they're surrounding me, they're hemming me in.

I'll escape!

But how?

I'll *leave* the dream.

And enter what world?

HIDING IN THE VOID FROM IMAGINARY ASSAILANTS AS THE BEST PLACE TO AVOID THEM

A man afflicted by paranoia knew that the whole world was gaining on him. The manhunt was on, he was being tracked down. In cities and towns, in the country, in the remotest spots—everywhere *they were after him.* Endless flight would exhaust him, slow him down, make him an easily-found prey. He had to find out the right place to hide, take provisions for his remaining lifetime there, and steel himself in. Where would no-one think of pursuing him? If he tried to take refuge in a stranger's house or barn or warehouse or office building, he'd be detected, spied on, and "turned in," for everyone is his enemy and all enemies inform. Even his friends would turn spy on him; but his paranoia had alienated the last of his friends, so no worry on *that* score. Where should his hiding place be? The ideal hiding place for the frantically paranoiac gentleman? In a flash, an inspiration paid him a visit and revealed that no-one would *think* of stalking him in the *Void.*

He thanked the Messenger for that timeliest assistance, and took his ready-packed possessions, effects, and condensed provisions with him in each tensened arm and made straight for the Void, to turn aside at no detour. He arrived, and is still hiding there. His paranoia is being cured, for no-one has gone after him for the years he's been there. He's ready to return to his human race in the world with his paranoia soon healed. That's his intention. But the Void is not easy to exit from. In fact, he's cooped up in there forever. The moral is that the escape remedy becomes itself the foremost trap. That's regrettably so. So avoid paranoia. Avoid voids. Resort to *other* recourses in desperate measure, that admit of a return when the cure beckons. Leave open the survival hope. Your anxiety may be *temporary* now. So hide in a *temporary* place. (However seemingly unsafe, at the time.)

THE ACCURATE REALISTIC TRUTH OF PROPHETIC PARANOIA

I had to learn to hurt.

Why?

Because I'm always so afraid of *being* hurt. I'm so vulnerable I've become armed, I'm an ever-bristling armory, an arsenal of anticipation and alertness, which is at contrary odds with the actual size of the objective threat stemming from outside, which is small enough not to justify the paranoia of my armed alarm.

This harm is imaginary that you apprehend?

It is an enlarged neurosis of the anxiety gland.

You would wage reprisal in retaliation against what never offended?

That's how inflamed is my organ of persecution mania. So I'm always ready to requite the delusionary damager, pay him back in unkind cut for what he's still yet to do to me, and never would do, but now *he's* injured by *my* instigation; and so I bring about, by first warding it off when it wasn't there, the blow I had feared from him.

That's a self-destructive anti-social cycle you've built around yourself, like a circular fence that contains a captive unicorn and bars him from congress with other creatures. Is this your iron-bound habit set in, too rigid to break? It's a disaster that cuts you off from the easy current of a normal life. Are your ways so hardened that not even a psychiatrist with a good curing record could restore the sanity of your health and alleviate your grimly set suspicion of all your fellow men who certainly don't conspire to plot against you? Or has your disease progressed past mending—straining you to discomfort with a constant phobia? Are you alien to ease forever, except in the swollen refuge of solitude? Crippled emotionally, and pain for each drawn mental breath poisoned by the world? Your condition is pitied. But you stir up tension against others, and bring bad feelings about. By seeking threat in others, you threaten them. For their sake, you'd be put out of the way; for you obstruct the roads of graceful human intercourse by misplacing the assumed tact of conventional trust in the honorable disposition of good will. Essentially, you breed malevolence, by suspecting it. Society regards you as a danger: since you're a breeder of danger, by falsely seeing its persistent delusion. You impair the flow of good intentions. As an enemy to peace in its daily functions, you're a disrupter that people should get rid of. You've brought all this about yourself. You worked very hard, and became an evil self-prophet. And you've caused your worst prophecy to come true: you've created antagonism to you in your fellow men. The consequence will be just: bitterly poetic, apt, as effect matches cause in symmetrical equality, and retribution obeys the harmony of balance. You've wrought your nemesis: now be devoured by it.

You've pronounced my doom.

You made it: and even sentenced your*self*. You've independently gone about your fate: constructing it: but it's become destructive. And so you pay: by fairly assuming the burden of the penalty, as your own work you've striven for all your life. You've worked in the dark: now, you see the light: an unfriendly one, glowering gloom on all your prospects. A self-made destiny: poison meted in for all doled out. And distribution poises judgment on the verdict of impartiality: much to your doom. I would give you pity: but you've denied pity from other people, so as to distrust them undisturbed, in a purely contaminating reproach. Paranoia is an offense: so your stand is indefensible: you must be put down, taken out of the way: brought to your place: which ought to be solitary, out of harm's way: for your own sake, but more, for that of others. They haven't deserved you: so you deserve being denied them. The welfare of the most, being at stake, calls for you to be sacrificed. The world is trouble enough, without you adding to it. So your subtraction is all to the good, on the whole. And the elimination of your paranoiac element would help to clear the air: sullied already, as it is.

Is that a hint I should die?

Live alone in exile remote, in solitary banishment. Then the public bad that's in you would be dead, posing no trouble or problem to your fellow men. A hermit in isolation can do no harm. That's the sentence I pass on you: on behalf of all. Getting you out of our way cuts us off from the obnoxious source itself. We're rid of the pestilence, when *you're* removed, though as yourself you live. We place an embargo of quarantine on you, and impose your leave at once. Away. Haste your obedience. You survive; but we survive you. Paranoia is a social disease. So quit this society, at once.

I accuse you of plotting to kick me out, I nurse the suspicion of your conspiring to make me evacuate. My paranoia has proven correct. So it's accurate, not neurotic. It's so realistic, that it's no longer paranoia. And so I'm cured. I face a realistic situation.

Yes, it's very real, and you realize it. Out you go.

But I'm cured. There's no danger in my remaining. Please give me a reprieve.

No. It became realistic because you caused it to be so. The imaginary harm you suspected has turned out to be true, by the strength of your delusions. The fair consequence is to evict you, from mankind. You made the truth, on which the case for your banishment is justified. So go.

I'll stay, till you force me.

So force is required. I'll go out for reinforcements, to help me oust you.

A plot against me! An actually self-confessed conspiracy.

A plot first conceived by you. With your inconceivable delusion.

You make me responsible?

Take the full blame. You've architected what's now being completed by my engineering. The start you made will mean the end of you, for us. A process of your devising, now full circle comes home. What you wrought is unacceptable? Not to your taste? Be your fault's victim. Wait, till I recruit your social enemies, which you schemed, though you dislike the shape it's inevitably had to take. And it's too late for you to regret. You can't retreat. Your fate is made.

I can't retract, when society *will* overwhelm me. I knew it all along! It's come to be. I'm right.

It's a consolation of your making. You trained the world, to unmake you as its participant. A well-done act of success! Though it took time.

I'm a prophet of my own doom. But first I was doomed to prophesy. I was innocently not responsible for that!

Way back, we're all innocent. We can't help how we first contrived to ruin ourselves. Regrettably, you were moved. Then *you* did the moving. Now, forcibly, you're being removed. At a further remove from that first movement. Society takes the last move. This movement will dispose of you. For good.

Not for *my* good. But for all peoples.

We've now entered politics. Politically, you're a nuisance. You've compelled us to vote for the removal of your menace, which includes you too. You're now a political exile. Some barren island, denominated by no name of a country, due to its being uninhabited, will be the arena where your meditations can pace back and forth, wondering why you had to be so suspicious, instead of trusting all your fellow men. You won't figure it out. The answer will not come. But there you'll be. Till you'll suspect *yourself* of hatching a vile plot. And it'll turn out true. For you will plot.

And the plot will work. And you *will* be dead. For things can come to be, whose seeds grew up in a festered mind. Our fate is part will. The will works its disease in on the turning of events. Fatally, in your case.

A PERSONALITY CONFESSION

What I wanted most was power over people: to get them to do what I want, to have them in my power, to be on top. But I had no power to persuade them to be in my power, so I tried to develop talents, such as physical attractiveness and more money. I failed to develop these means of power; leading to frustration and the need to compensate for all my failings and littleness, my unconvincingness when it comes to exercising any power over people. I tried personality defects like sadism, but potential victims resisted and I failed. I felt a growing futility, which I tried to arrest, but it grew into helplessness, which put a stop to my power drive. Then, I made helplessness a virtue.

I traded on my helplessness, and people fell into my power by trying to protect, help, care for me. So I had hit on a method toward my original goal, by the process of having failed in more aggressive, direct, and obvious methods toward that goal. Failure had found out a solution—in fact, *was* the solution. This reversed my fall which had hit the bottom in total abjection; I exploited people's good-natured compassion and generosity toward a downtrodden underdog; and had them in my power. I wouldn't let go. My helplessness was brutally directed. I drew upon it, ruthlessly.

REWARDING CONSOLATIONS IN MAKING THE ABSOLUTE HIT OF A UNANIMOUS BAD IMPRESSION

I hope I make a good impression on you.

You've already begun by making a bad one.

How contrary to my confessed intentions! I must reverse my initial bad impression on you. What don't you like about me so far?

Your eagerness to make a good impression on me. It's so craven and dependent of you. Whereas if you didn't care, I would respect you more. You've made me suspicious that you're lowly and lack confidence for being considered worthy, and have inferiority worries, so you're anxious to please, to reassure yourself on the count that after all you're not so bad. But why should *I* be the source of your reassurance? You've come a-begging to me.

True, my position is a supplicating one, in soliciting your approval. Despite my efforts, you're shrewdly unflattered to have me seek your good will. So I'm belittled worse than when I began, and by gambling have only succeeded in further debasing myself, by incurring your disdain, and submitting to your contempt. My inferiority worry has intensified, to an anxiety level. Only one way is open for recouping my self-esteem, or enough self-esteem so that I haven't been reduced agonizingly beyond an intolerable limit: and that is, to regard *you* as inferior, and your opinion of me deluded. Then I'd regain self-respect, by discounting your low estimate of me and nullifying its blow. May I have your permission to, at your expense, artificially bolster, pamper, humor, baby, and nurse my little ego? It wouldn't cost *you* anything, except momentary damage to your own pride. But by your sacrifice, I'd be benefitting enormously. May I, please?

No. I won't concede. You're so unworthy, that I won't help you feel worthier at my permitted expense. If that would make you feel worse, it's not my concern, and my compassion is not sympathetic to you. To conclude: You've made a very bad impression on me. So I've taken your measure accurately. You *ought* to feel what you *are*: inferior. So I won't discourage it. You're *right* to feel what you *are*: inferior. Congratulations on the accuracy of your insight. How well you know yourself! Don't ever change your view. Your worthlessness should remain permanent, so that your low estimate of yourself will be undyingly correct. You've just gained immortal knowledge. At the cost of some minor pride. It's a good trade. Keep it up—I mean down. I've contributed to your immortalization by concurring on, and confirming, your low state. May your knowledge never top it, but keep it par, matching your lowliness of being with *its* lowliness of opinion. Then your equilibrium is an honest one, and an expert balance has been reached between being and thought. Let *that* be your source of pride, secretly maintained, despite outwardly making a bad impression wherever you go. Your state of harmony between inward and outward depreciation is rare, and conducive to nobility. Don't be dismayed by all your inevitable detractors: they're not detracting: they're declaring you as you are. They share, universally, in the splendid precision of your vision. That's your place in society: well earned, and well deserved. Continue to be "worthy" of it. You *are* as you seem: appearances are not deceiving in your case. Live down to it, always: so that your identity, as such, shall not perish. And you shall be known. This is my prophecy. You're worthy of your bad impression: and have become equal to your truth. Preserve this social standing, and distinguished inner view. You're a marvelous rarity. You make such a bad impression on me, I feel humble, and unworthy of it. I'm in awe. You leave me, at the end, speechless. How have you managed? It's a wonder! I must proclaim it. Most bad impressions are only mortal. But yours is a beauty. An outstanding marvel, a masterpiece, pure. I admire you, for leaving an *absolute* bad impression. It's ultimately *most* impressive! You're supreme! It elevates you, far superior to those on whom you have succeeded in making this bad impression. We're mean, by comparison, and infinitely lowly. You're a myth, and we its observers.

A MISTAKE, DUE TO OVERPRESUMING, WHICH HAS PLUNGED INTO THE CROWNING EMBARRASSMENT THAT GUARANTEES A LIFE-LONG HUMILITY

Your smile, when it favored me and directed itself at me, or addressed me selectively as apparently being worthy of the strenuous spontaneity that muscled in on your face as its beaming feature. Your smile signaled that, as its recipient, I was flattered. And I needn't even *feel* flattered: the smile *conferred* flattery on me. It *raped* flattery *into* me. It deluged my unworthiness with the unaccountable beneficence of its approving aspect that endowed me with an unearned grace, a blessing gratuitously showered from the charitable munificence of capriciously irresponsible generosity. No, your smile is what I've never deserved. Is that why, to my astonishing fortune, it just happened to be awarded to *me*? Unfairness rules the world; inequity throws all balances at odds, and, as precisely wasn't my due and I had no right to expect it, my luck, thanks to you, shot up astoundingly with that smile you conferred on me, like a medal pinned on my breast in awesome ceremony by the greatest self-proclaimed General of all time. What! You mean the smile wasn't intended for *me*?! Oh, my mistake is building itself an unliveable-down embarrassment that I shall never get over, what presumption, arrogance, and audacity I unwittingly displayed, daring to believe that *your* smile, from your *own* face, would so condescendingly refer itself to the immensely undeserving object that I am; making the most incongruous assumption in the absurd annals of vanity. Let me be contemptible and ridiculous. I *had* hoped for, even solicited, I'm afraid, that fabulous smile. This lesson is blushing bubbles from me. Never again will I call for the furious distortion your face must make, in livid contortion, to convert itself into the humanity of a smile. My vainglory was incredible. It's like asking the sun to read me a prayer in its husky biblical voice, as a special concession, to me exclusively, an ungranted privilege which quite properly will remain ungranted. I should restrain my star-fishing ardor, and settle for infinitely less than a private, personal miracle you can't really afford to donate. Scarcity, not having something, is the source of stinginess. The justice of your withholding is precise, and fair. I was denied what wasn't yours to give. Can I complain of being cheated, when my claim was false? I presumed on your humanity. Pardon me for the liberty.

A STREET, AND HOW TO GET THERE

Hydrania Street is one of the places east of somewhere. I'm not even sure what *country* it's located in. (If you're ignorant of information, then a vague reliance on *relativity* is attempted, but doesn't get very far in the solid direction of fact.)

On the map, Hydrania Street is nowhere, much less than a mere dot. However, don't let *that* discourage you. Maps are only material objects, anyway. After all, what is the map? It won't even give you the time of the day! It's just a little crossword puzzle pretending to be geographic. For *real* geography, *travel*. Get on a bus, train, car, boat, plane, and go. When you'll arrive, you'll be there.

But if you want to go to Hydrania Street, let your travel agent, me, arrange it. I charge a prohibitive fee, due to the complicated skein of difficulty to unravel in directing you, and booking your passage, including accommodations, to this Hydrania Street, which, were it to be an animal, the animal would be a unicorn, due to its mythical existence rather than strictly factual one. For timetables, schedules, facilities, and other tourist data, if you can't afford my services (no one can—not even a corporation), consult the privacy of your own imagination, which will conduct you there on a guided tour, from one end of Hydrania Street to the other (and back again, if your energy or curiosity still hold up).

Hydrania Street. Once you're there, you never forget it—once you're there, you're *always* there (which is a great assistance to memory).

"Always?! Never to get away?"

"Never! You're stuck there!"

"But how did I ever get here?"

"You got here *wanting* to."

"But most of what I want never turns out. Why did *this*?"

"Just because it did. *Live* with it. In it. Of it. By it. For it. To it. Never, alas, from it. You're there. Hydrania Street."

"*This* is Hydrania Street? *This*?"

"Because it's not more, you're here, forever, pinched in. The only more you'll get is of *this.* The *undesired* more. The punishment for having desired *only* this."

THE CITY ASSIMILATES GEORGE, AFTER A TUSSLE

I

George was tired of his city. But he lived in it! How to get rid of it? For himself to go away from it, to leave it by moving, was made impossible by his laziness. Only one solution remained: George would have to persuade the *city* to leave, despite its heavy railroad station and other immovable fixtures. The weight of its central business buildings (moored fast into hard rock deep down) was enough to remove hope and substitute tears. But George wouldn't give up.

He contemplated a landslide, to induce the city to give way. Then he had to give it up, since a landslide has overtones of a sweeping political election of so one-sided a contest that it simply wouldn't be fair. George had to give the city a fighting chance. George would *play fair,* to win; any other method was intolerable to the fastidious, lofty organ cathedraled in his pealing Dignity.

Why not an earthquake, to submerge the city? Or a volcano to erupt lava on it? These crossed George's mind. Idle musings! The unthreatened city continued as before: hardly suspecting its citizen's plot of total removal. Vain plot, as yet: he hadn't any.

Oblivious to its danger, ignoring George's mind, the city increased in substance. George's mind, conversely, increased in vapor. The rich richer, the poor poorer. The city more cityfied; with George not even certified. He shrunk. The city grew.

"This city is spreading thicker around me. It's hemming me in. I'm getting lost here. Everywhere, solid edifices, whose bulk is so durable that even the morning or evening shadows cast by them are of sturdier dimension than my own feeble braining in the flimsy cross-hatchery of thought. This city won't move; but nor will I. Who will outlast? I'll stick firmly. Let the city subside.

"How? That's too practical: defeating me. By *dreams* I may win. I'll resort to *fantasy*. Against the city's *reality*. Unequal weapons! Which will prevail? Let's see."

II

The city stayed right where it was. So did George with equal stubbornness. Little did the city realize it was locked in stalemate, pitted desperately against its would-be-ouster's obdurate, relentlessly insisting patience. "I won't leave," George reasoned. "As the city and I can't get along nor long remain together, *one* of us has got to go. And it won't be me! I won't give an inch! Let the *city* relent! Now it's *its* move. I'm firm!"

So stoutly maintained George. He kept on living in the city. The city was staying right where it was, but spreading all around into the suburbs. Its center (downtown core or nucleus) dug imperishable roots that tradition was steadfastly reinforcing the longer the city endured against the might of George's feeble wish that it would all just blow away. George was losing out, in his secret "campaign" to get rid of his metropolitan enemy. He would have to resort to a desperate measure; else give up, and suffer in private his pride's humiliation. The city wouldn't budge. This was getting increasingly evident.

III

George surveyed the city, to weigh his slim human chances against all that concrete, plaster, wood, steel, iron, metal, glass, stone, all this articulated material which architectural engineering and city planning had staked so stickingly to pierce the earth's foresty mound that formed the original site. George began calculating the numerous skyscrapers. They were enormous! Like those mastodons of gigantic prehistory, those titanic beasts of monumental obesity, behemoths of might. George had the slip of the ghost of a chance! He might push and pull at night, but not even a sleeping truck could be moved. And all those squatting warehouses! The freight yards! The crowded parking lots! How could a whole city be moved, by one man alone!? George most decidedly must have had to be insane, to have even thought of it! He would have to *imagine* winning, or forgo the *real* pleasure. This city wasn't meant to be pushed around! Its indomitable structures! Like the Municipal Building, the Court of Justice, and City Hall! Like the vast supermarkets. The teeming outlet stores and produce centers, the shopping complexes, the traffic labyrinths, the mechanical factories, the coal chutes, the electrical transformatories, the prisons themselves, not to mention the outlying residential districts where resided a heavy race of people with their heavy television sets, pianos, and refrigerators. And all those branch libraries with their staggering rows of books, stack by stack! And the maternity wards! The athletic stadia! The racing track, and stables of thoroughbreds. The trees, weighted down with heavy rain, soaked solid to the bone. The lengthy cemeteries, as far as the eye could see, ponderous with mausoleums and heavy tombstones. The ironworks. The lumberyards. The rock quarries. The zoos with their heavy bars and heavier animals. It would prove too much for George, unarmed, unaided, to effect the removal of all this. Only in his *mind* could it happen. There alone, could this wholesale event transpire: a city leaving its premises, mayor and aldermen and all, lock stock and barrel, all the jailbirds and all the police; peaceful citizenry too, going away *en masse*, in full force. So that George would have the place all to himself. Have what? All would be vacated, there would be nothing left; the migrating evacuation would be so complete that nothing but George would be seen for miles around, otherwise just horizons in their empty chorus, distant hills, and the abandoned shore. Even the port would disappear! Nothing would *implement* George's survival. Devoid of instruments, of utensils, of things, what could George all alone do, or even be? Had he desired this?! It would be bad for him. Let him reconsider, at somber leisure. He should deliberate this further. Oscar Wilde said the real tragedy to life was to get what you wanted. How foolish of George to want what he wanted. A fully-stocked city was *good* for him. It would serve his needs, *provide* him with things. Yet his wish opposed it, his caprice wished it away, for himself alone to remain. Let him take stock. Quiet. The city's buzz is stilled, its manufacturing subdued. George is at work in his mind. What will it yield?

IV

"Being an art lover, I think of the heavy statuary in the heavy museum laden to the gills with treasures of priceless value. It's in the heart of the city. I change my mind about wanting the city to go. My desire is reversed, and now I *want* it to stay. This is my deepest heart's wish. I'm sitting down in my apartment. Now I'm getting up to go out and look around. I want to survey all my properties, to make sure they're all still there. I'd miss anything missing. I want everything in place. It's all mine."

This was George's determinate rationalization. He grew deeply in love with the bulky city. He lightly longs daily for what ever outweighs him. He cruises the city regularly, before and after his regular job in one of its big offices. He has a heavy crush on his belov'd city. The girders and beams go up, of new tools and scaffolding by demolishing crews whose steel helmets peer out of window frames and other skeletal spaces. Bulk goes up. George roots for it. He's a friend of contracting firms. The city grows dense. The population swarms. George warms to this. "Let it remain!" he declares. The king gets obeyed. He ordains what cannot help but be. His fantasy *is* reality. The city is his brain. He wears it under his consenting head. He approves. "Let it be. It can stay." It does.

"The city is solid with me. It must be. Right here. Neither I nor it shall move. We'll have a good time, while the same place is together, it and me. Only by death shall *I* be removed: but locally to be incarcerated. There'll be no leavetaking. Departures are forbidden. Our lots are thrown in, we lie where our bed is made, it's here. One place, a city and me. Only time differs. The place is alike, unvaried. It likes me, I like it. The city is for me, a man. The world gave me to it. We do nicely coincide. This solves my rebellious problem, I'm at peace. I'm one piece, a part of this whole. This whole sweet city. In me. My light burden. My heavy duty."

End of George, lost somewhere in the city. The *city* is well located, but George is vague around there. Other Georges surround him. One city binds them all.

City, city. George changed his mind, just for you. He had to. *You* wouldn't adjust. It was up to him, and *he* did. Now he's blended in, not singled out. He's lost from focus. He's found *you*.

INCREASED UNEMPLOYMENT THAT FINALLY REACHES THE PHILOSOPHICAL STAGE

A man was arrested for unemployment. While in jail, he filled out an application form, and sent it in to a prospective employer. The answer came back that because of his jail record, it was not the company's policy to hire him. This additional unemployment, to the regret of the warden, for whom the man had been on model behavior, increased the prison sentence, and automatically made him undesirable for civilian employment. This, coupled with the prisoner's record of poverty, classified him as a social outcast, which in turn imposed another severe penalty. Under heavy guard, the man was removed to an unescapable chamber. There, in the eyes of the law, his unemployment reached the incurable stage, and he was retried and given a life sentence, with an additional half a life tagged on to punish him for being so hardened. By now a confirmed public enemy, he has, in mere self defense, taken to philosophy. Philosophy, on examining his record, has approved wholeheartedly, recommending him especially for his virtue of reflective idleness, which, in time of habit, has thrown his mind into a frenzy of thought. Since he receives no wages, death expects to find him philosophizing in jail, and by removing him will in no way interfere with his hard-won poverty. Philosophy, his sponsor, expects no profit. Publicity is notoriously absent in this case.

PROTECTED BY JUSTICE

He was arrested for marrying without a license. Another charge levied against him by the traffic marshal was, I'm afraid, drunken marrying. He opened his breath to produce a smell, but just then a sober wind blew, and the cop came down with the flu. This postponed the trial.

His wife waited immediately outside wedlock, while a very deliberate jury, whose verdict took years to mellow, examined her finger for evidence of a wedding ring. They tried her much-preserved virginity, but found it wanting.

Bored of jail, he bought a mail order law course, and defended his case. Finally he had to saw his way out, but since the bars were made of wood, already rotten, on the honor system, he barely managed to escape freedom.

An autopsy rendered a decision of old age. His corpse was in no mood to protest, so he calmly accepted the penalty. Was there a widow?

His burial proved nothing. Police are still awaiting a clue.

NOT GETTING IT

I said to him (looking him in the eye), *"Pass some money."*
Oh. And how did he answer that?
He said, *"Parsimony*? It's the only thing I can offer you."
Not very much.
No. A generous deficiency.
You mean a deficiency in generosity.
To a fault.

ART, KING OF WASTE

ART, KING OF WASTE

Art is a product of man's extravagance. Beyond the economic call of duty, man hurls forth the wares of his abundance. Gothic curves, monstrous gargoyles, superfluous sonnets, delicately embroidered plays, repetition stocked epics, concerti for the chattering piano, character weighted novels, mobile dances, joy's delirium of shapes, form's apocalyptic ecstasy, the artifacts that punctuate time, the monumental wooing of unyielding metaphysics by stunning postures of aesthetics. Art is totally unnecessary. But it wills the dictum of its own ways. Its calling is to have a say. Sculpture outweighs man, and ancient temples shun ruin with a venerable resident spirit. Art ghosts our corridors, and deep museums exhale purity. Squadrons of mere dust can't annihilate a worm-proof library. Art keeps out intruders, and permits a cult of the initiates. Only those susceptible may apply.

PICASSO BECOMES FOLDED AWAY IN SPACE UNTIL HIS DISAPPEARANCE IS SCATTERED INTO THE VISUAL ROUND EVERYWHERE FLAT UNFOLDING FORMS OF ALL THE NOTHINGS

Picasso got to the point where he was unable to see anything flat anymore. So he drove to an eye specialist, in a real car, a distance of over one hundred miles across actual country—simply by visualizing it. He was at home during the whole journey—though he allowed it to take place without inconveniencing himself to get up from his chair, which was being sat continually on by his very old body on top of which were eyes that had lost the ability even to conceive of flatness. Space gave him a medal for the way he invaded it all at once, simply without bothering to shift his view. His senile lazy decline into an assault on space from all sides: and space could only be flattered for such singular attention. The man was artistically an Einstein; silhouettes collapsed at his sigh, and facades were eaten away; veneers lost their mask-like quality, and deception had to hide. Illusion turned honest, for once, and was arrested on the spot. Picasso will die in a flat box. The eyes have jumped away already, and go between things: like flies in and around everything. Visuality has had her virginity penetrated—and her roaming bridegroom still has his bachelor cunning. Sight blushes, for her shame. The rape is on permanent view. The stages slip by slowly; this performing exhibitionist is Art; life retreats to a safe remove while the spectacle keeps on happening, with dice-like combinations from eyes endless in their motion, firmly shifting at every turn, yielding a corridor behind each tableau, and the corridor renews itself, emptying time of that human parasite: Impatience.

THE PAINTER AND HIS SUBJECT CONSTITUTE ART ONGOING

A painter suffers stagefright in front of his model. He kneels to apologize. She becomes an abstract model. He paints his real memory of her. It's so three-dimensional, she's reincarnated as a sculptural study of herself. But he still isn't satisfied. Only when they lived happily ever after since becoming married, is he convinced that she's no ordinary painting, even in the abstract sense. His art career thrives on their happy union. Love blends them to the absolute of oneness. They're so close together that three dimensions are superfluous to express it. Probably a single line will do.

AN ICY AESTHETIC MERGER

"Architecture is frozen music," said John Ruskin or some other famous man.

He was challenged to prove it. So he went to an Islamic country of Mohammedanism, during a severe wintry season. A native architect was building something tall and slender on an ancient mosque, which, though religious, was caked with icicles. Ruskin asked him what his composition was. In good English vocables, the architect musically intonated his creation as "My minaret in G".

"I thought *Paderewski* did that," Ruskin retorted, like a skeptical westerner. This chilling rebuff made the architect sing a song of building construction, but the notes froze, turning into the building that the song was about. A sacred building. You had to remove your shoes to ascend its scales, toward an overhead harmony. The Creator links the arts.

Ruskin went home, but no one believed him. In western skepticism things stood divided, as before.

HIS READING TASTE A MATTER OF WHAT HE LIKES. HOW HE RECTIFIES A READING MISTAKE BY ERADICATING WHAT HE'S JUST READ WHEN HE REALIZES TOO LATE HE'S NOT LIKED IT.

Do you like spy stories?

No.

Why?

Because I don't read them. I only like what I read.

But what if you read something and you *don't* like it?

Then I stop reading it.

But what if you don't stop *quick* enough?

Then when I *do* stop, I carefully undo all the reading I've just done, by reading that passage backwards, till it slides right out of my system. Then I'm cleansed of it; and look forward to some *good* reading, next time.

VERBAL OUTCRY OF PROTEST AGAINST PICTURES AND FILMS THAT VISUALLY POLLUTE THE PURE PRINTED TEXT OF BOOKS

Book illustrations bully your imagination.

What should I do? Scissor them out of the book?

No, there might be text on the other side. Paint over the illustrations with a thick layer of opaque black oil.

But what if, before I've done that, I've already glimpsed the illustrations in my careless ignorance, so that, even after the page pictures are blacked out in oil, my mind keeps reproducing them in pure pictorial recall?

Then tear those images out of your mind, or black them over, or block them out. Obstruct them, before they usurp or displace or eclipse or replace the pure verbal type text itself.

Yes, but I have another worry.

What's that?

What if I've already seen the movie version of the book? Then my attempts to follow the printed words with obedient projections of my own images in conceptual corresponding loyalty to the literary sentences in close fidelity, will be contaminated by vulgar remembrances of passages of the film that obtrusively substitute for my pure images plucked from straight reading. How can I disremember a technicolor film, or even a black and white one, which colors and prejudices my reading judgment and verbal comprehension?

The answer is, make sure not to have seen the film in the first place. Then your book interpretation will be unsullied.

But what if it's too late already not to have first seen that damn film? It's *already* a mistake of the past. Once seen, then, how unseen? It's already pre-tarnished my reading of the original book. When innocence falls, how can the fall be undone?

By unrecollecting. Selective oblivion. By a "control-only" memory.

But my past is indiscriminately adulterated by the compound mixture of all that's been. The film having been seen, the book illustrations having been once noticed, they're mine in eternal totality, to plague any subsequent reading of the virginal text, and bias each word. There's no redemption to blot out the crime's consequence.

The solution is never to have been born.

Too late. *That* matter's been committed, too. Not even *death* can erase one's birth.

Then we're pitifully helpless. I see no recourse.

O vile world.

O compromising one. What words can protect words, from the infamy of pictures?

THE SINGER WHO LOST HER SHAPE

She's so thin, that her mirror has almost no work to do, and remains on holiday even when she casts herself in front of it. Her mirror is envied by other people's mirrors for its soft job; its loafing is especially conspicious, even flamboyant, not to mention ostentatious, when the thin figure of its mistress is being imaged: the reflection consists of two rays!

Why does she even look into the mirror, if that's all the returns she gets from it?

She has to be reassured.

On what count?

On, counting herself, that there includes one image reflected back. For she doubts if she's all there.

Plenty of reason. Why doesn't she eat more?

The food is heavier than herself: she can barely budge it.

Can't she be fed by an assistant?

No, people are *revolted* by her thin looks. They wouldn't go near.

She must be too skinny to boast much sex appeal.

She's never been married, but she's only a young lady, and *extremely* attractive!

That contradicts her revolting appearance that you only just mentioned; what charm *does* she have?

A voice of pure melody: it's even musical.

But has she the strength to use it?

The chords are vocal. And what a tune!

Arias as from the opera?

Haunting! As though a total orchestra were instrumentally rallying her forth! And the whole cast of a chorus to background her feature solo strength in swelling anthem and tonal immensitude massively contrapuntal to her astrally inspired virtuosity!

She sounds like a star.

A *star* sounds like *her*!

What's her occupation?

She's a singer.

Yet she's thin?

You can hardly see her, unless you happen to *be* her.

Then she's nearsighted?

Close-up, she is. She has no perspective on distance.

Nor could *distance* involve *her* in its *own* scheme of perspective, whether aerial or lineal or even distorted.

You're right. She'd be out of sight.

Yet how far can she fling her voice?

Past the sound barrier. Breaking the window panes of remotely far-flung cities in a mountain range that spans several continents. Her supersonic power physically outcapacities an entire air fleet of modern jet planes streamlined by the latest engines. The source, or origin, of her voice is a military secret. Even her whisper would drill a hole through both of the listener's ears, two holes meeting in the central skull, containing enough vibrations to echo out a generation along the wave lengths that time conducts. I want to pay a tribute to her voice. It's prodigious!

You've convinced me. When can I hear her?

Right now, she's invisible. So she can't be located.

Not even by her sound?

She's silent. So she's in hiding.

Oh. That's carrying incognito too far. Why doesn't she present herself? The *real* reason?

Yes.

She's shy. She doesn't want people to laugh at her being underweight.

That's quite understandable. But meanwhile, people are being deprived of her great voice.

She must *eat* more! *That's* the solution!

I admire your determination. But how can we enforce our resolution on her, seeing that she's not even here, or there, or anywhere!? Where to find her?

Before finding her, we must find a *way* of finding her.

But what way will that be?

We'll just follow the road she took on her road to disappearance.

That's not easy to do, for she was too light to make footprints.

Any *other* procedure, to track her down, and give us a clue to her whereabouts?

All *previous* methods have not only been tried, but have been found wanting. So far, we've failed.

What *new* slant can you suggest?

Let's seek her out through the murmurs of *rumor*. Often, that's a reliable social compass.

Should we tune in on the gossip circuit?

Especially in musical circles, where singers and musicians are sure to flock. The concoction of a malicious scandal involving her might bring to bear such intuition—unerring, inadvertent, and uncanny—on the part of the instigator, that a valuable clue, as byproduct, might be tossed off, on the careless wings of accident, for our detection to pick up. So we seize on what our intellect can complete: and directly we'll be led, to her.

A choice discovery! *Now* what?

Then we'll force feed her, so she'll gain weight; and be less shy; and oblige us, from the miraculous fund of her talent. Songs will be wafted all day at us. We'll drown in their mellifluous sweetness. An audio paradise, for our drifting amusement, waking in lovely slumber.

THE HURRY-UP WAY TO GO ABOUT FALLING BACK

I feel important when I get mail.

I feel important when I receive a telephone call. I answer it so immediately that my caller hadn't even begun dialing yet for my phone to begin ringing. Expectation is a way of speeding up a desired event. I make actual what needs to be anticipated, so my joy comes true.

You make prematurity your asset.

Will does it.

For me, talking on the telephone is too immediate a contact.

What exhilarates me is finding a letter in my mailbox. There I am, ripping open the envelope, and reading with pleasure a friendly communication, before my tardy correspondent had even posted the epistle, or yet written it. Yet, it's all there, unfolded, before me. The handwriting is unmistakable. I mail it back to him to prove what he has written. It startles him, for it contains the very ideas he had *meant* to write! And the style is all his own, irrefutable. So I enclose a scribbled note that says: "No need to apologize: you really *did* write this." Then he replies asking me why I haven't answered. I claim he owes me a letter. And the mail flies thick between us, and mouths parched for stamp-licked spittle.

For such an old-fashioned way of keeping in touch, do you use clairvoyance?

Yes, forecasting something makes it easier to plan.

By your keeping ahead, how can he keep up?

He's got to, for our friendship has a rapid tempo.

But not so swift as *mine*, by way of electronic telephone. There's no day's delay between *my* communicant and me, when phone to phone the conversation rages. Our voices are hooked up. It's instant, the give and take, and flares on fuel of its own manufacture.

That's too modern, I like the sullen delay of anticipation.

And I the sudden call, abrupt wires tingling, with an urgent pre-reply.

You're too hasty. How can you contemplate a relationship so instantaneously based that rapidity hastily outspeeds itself on the swift wings of device?

There's no time to contemplate it; what I do is consummate it. The message is already crackling.

Really? That's quicker than eye can behold.

Even quicker. The other party doesn't know.

When are they to find out?

When I choose to betray how I outwit by calculated predicting.

It seems more like a contest than a communication.

Competition stimulates contact, gives it an edge, rubs some vibration into what would otherwise be a casual relation.

Why pep up what would be *natural*, and artifically heighten its tone?

Because you're not sitting back, you're *creating*.

Oh. That *is* radical.

The pitch of acceleration is on us these days.

It's so glittering, and leaves me so uneasy.

Nerves between people are frayed with excitement.

They bounce, they buzz, they peal. My ears ring, I'm alarmed with exhaustion. Is there no way out?

It's what comes with living in the city. For a remedy, move to the country.

No, my roots are in concrete. Thus is my urbanization based.

When will peace find me?

When the world slows down. We're so frenetic, thought has no room to rove.

I wish vitality weren't so important.

So do I.

It points a relentless stress in needle-like movements. There's no breaking away. Motion has confused itself to a tumultuous strife. It makes *peace* so precious.

But *action* is what moves me.
Because you're the world's toy. Your life is at the mercy of forces.
Which forces?
Tugging ones. They split you, and rail you apart.
It gets me down.
By fighting it, you increase it.
If resistance is futile, should I try renunciation?
Submit. Be passive to what assails you.
What good would that do me?
None. But it restricts energy-loss.
What does that solve?
Nothing. Just an economy measure.
Oh. Then why live at all?
It keeps death from being too previous, and puts it more ripely in its place.
Is earth the passive goal I'm striving for?
Yes, in your whizzing path to glory.
By the minute, I feel sour.
Then fill up, for your sweet hour.
Oh, perished by dusk is dawn's dear flower.
Why fight?
What should I yield to?
A grand, and all-encompassing, despair.

A SPEECH GIVEN AT A HALLOWEEN PARTY

This is a halloween party, so I'll talk about it. The party is the thing, not what brought it about. I'm glad there's this party, but I don't care what the historical origin of halloween is. We have this party, the pretext is the holiday, but it doesn't matter what the source of this traditional holiday is, so long as the holiday serves to justify making a party.

If I play the radio or television or record player, I can get the benefit I want without having to pay, in return, the service of understanding how the gadget works electronically mechanically. Same with driving a car. You just have to know how to operate it safely and effectively: no need to know how it's all put together inside.

Also, people can go ahead and make love without having to know what biological dynamics are interpersonally being operative. You can eat, or breathe, or sleep, without having to know the biological operative dynamics inside.

You can be in Rome staring up at a ceiling where there's a famous mural up there, without having to see the scaffolding that had allowed the famous painter to be suspended securely high enough up near the ceiling to work well and easily on the painting. The scaffolding came down once the painting was completed. And the *painter* came down even before the *scaffolding*. So we don't see the traces of his being perched up there in his crow's nest. All we see is the result—the tourist payoff. We don't even see any traces of his original sketching-in that he did preliminary to his building up the work with his gradual finishing touches of brush strokes to give us the final outcome. And we certainly can't see *him*, in his original costume, in the funny dress they had those days.

All we have is the painting—the finished painting. All that went into it disappeared: the *process* has evaporated, the *product* remains. It's called a *finished product*.

Part of having the finished product is being unbound to the necessity of questioning the origin or process that culminated in the product. What we *have*, suffices. Our product here is the collective one—a party.

Did it take a famous Italian ceiling painting to bring home to us that we needn't examine the tradition behind this halloween party? Yes, thanks to me.

PLATO UNRECOGNIZABLE, BEING EXTINCT. ONCE DISTINCT, HE'S GONE, ALAS, PLATONIC

I once adored a certain Greek philosopher, but from a distance. It was strictly platonic.

Who was he? Aristotle?

He was *called* Aristotle. But all the writing ever attributed to him was really secretly written by Plato.

Why was Plato using Aristotle for a pseudonym?

To divide up Plato's own body of work into two schisms: that attributed to Plato for author, and that under *Aristotle's* name.

Then Plato covered a huge range.

He was myriad-minded, to do two different people's lifetime work-outposts from two opposed world-views, all in one by his own divided self.

Then Plato was a *double*-genius, if you add Aristotle's to his?

Sure. A *triple*-genius, if you add Socrates as well.

I admire him—but Platonically.

He's too long remotely dead to have sex with. *All* our generation can only have a platonic relationship with him.

But not all of *his* generation did.

No, he had some intimate scandals, involving his own person in directly sexual inflammation with some obscene lovers, in the most purely absolute carnality.

Then he defied his own name!

He *himself* was hardly Platonic. Freud was no Freudian, Marx no Marxist, Darwin no Darwinian. *History* confers reputations, which apply to subsequent scholars and disciples; to the follower, not to the original.

Does history contort?

By definition. Who knows the original Plato? We see him dimly, not in his full sun's glare; but darkly, reflectively, as shadows, in the cave. The first Plato's true inner existence had no platonic essence. The abstraction, or absolute, of Platonic essence, came later: our legacy's consolation.

Will that happen to me too?

If tradition's river floats your surviving reputation. Otherwise, on oblivion's shore you drift.

I'd like to be continuously resurrected by a succeeding continuity of generational translations, interpretations, an evolving legend altered age by age according to that age; shiftingly, in fits and contorted faces, to endure across time, in a protean succession of survivals. On this chain of transformations, posterity may keep me bobbing alive.

Unrecognizable from you as original.

As I am now?

Yes. You're you now. You haven't been handed over to history's re-creation chamber, to be fit meat for the feat of myth, in the convoluted intestinal absorptions by mankind's later aging body.

Sounds unappetizing.

Death is another name, for posthumous fame.

WHAT'S WRONG WITH DEATH'S APPETITE THESE DAYS?

Death has been complaining. It seems that Death hasn't been getting enough nourishment lately. "It"'s been getting plenty of men and women, all right, "it"'s been having no trouble getting quantity. (So far as quantity goes, "it"'s been getting more than ever before.) It's just that the *quality* of the food has been insufficient. Death is fed up dining on inferior quality, and wants a few gourmet meals and has the excellent taste to miss them in "its" current fare. If "it" had been less well-bred, "it" wouldn't know the difference. "It" compares new meals with a high standard of tradition. "It"'s cursing whoever chefs are responsible, who haven't kept up their trade. Meals aren't the same anymore.

I'm a Research Bureau, and Death has employed me to uncover why. I hope my services will be of use. Death is *not* the customer to let down, if I value continuing in business, which I surely do, having a family to support and a high mode of life to keep up, in my customary wealth.

Death a customer? No, a *client*. But why quibble about terms? I've been commissioned to do a job, or more than my reputation will suffer should I fail that client or customer. I'll go about it thoroughly. If Death isn't satisfied, "he" may have my head. And as I value my life, I aim to keep my head on. Survival is nothing to blame me for. It's *everyone's* goal.

Before I go any further, I owe some sort of explanation here, which I propose to deliver now, rather than running up a debt.

When I mention men and women served dead up for Death to eat, I'm referring to *literary* characters, not people in "real life."

And suddenly the mystery is solved. Or so it seems, in my expert and practiced eye.

You see, though there's been plenty of fiction going on lately, and the more or less "tragic" characters are killed off in the end through the mercilessness of all their authors, Death isn't being given enough of a feast for the quite obvious reason that the characters' lives weren't rich and meaningful and happy enough to constitute some really solid nourishment for Death to dine on.

It used to be that great kings or princes, like Hector or Hamlet, or Oedipus or Agamemnon or other Europeans or Asiatics, died great deaths to bear the weight of truly noble, lordly, magnificent, and majestic lives. So when Death claimed them, the food was superb. Those very meals lavished on Death cultivated a connoisseurship of the art and science of food, and an everlasting fastidiousness, in that ever-privileged diner. What meager fare has been served "him" lately! Recent stories, plays, and novels offer rather thin stuff, compared to those elegant repasts of yesteryear.

When Don Quixote died, when Falstaff died, the former had been bone-thin, the latter gross-fat. Both had been seasoned as characters and delectably served up with sauce. Their taste treats were enthralling!

The authors of Falstaff and Quixote had developed those two morsels just ripe for oven, frying pan, broiler, or spit. They were *rich in substance*! They weren't half-baked or carelessly overdone.

I reported my findings to Death, with the following recommendation: That authors make *major* characters, and build them up, and provide a truly rich background of real strong life, life felt to the bone, for Death to balance a good meal off of. Death is wasting away, practically starving, of literary malnutrition. Rescue "him", authors! Create sufficient life!

THE LETHAL POWER OF POETRY

I was once a writer of poems.

I'm not blaming you. Meanwhile, continue your confession.

Conviction, passion, spirit, and intellect went into them.

All that is lovely. But I hope you used *words*, as well? The words were wrought with the care of a fastidious craftsman. I even had to mangle some, and wring and rend, in order to wreak my point. Style was my arch ecstasy of deliberation.

Did you turn out some good stuff?

Not good merely, but blessed with originality. Lesser poets hung on derivatively, and did me the fawning discourtesy to emulate.

How did they come across your poems? You must have been published?

Yes, in literary magazines of limited circulation. *So* limited, that only pretentious aesthetes or highbrow intellectuals that dabble in symbolmongery and value criticism above what's only originally created, read them, and never the common plain folk that make up the massive *normal* belt of our society.

I see.

Anyway, I wanted to reach a wider audience.

With what? Your esoteric poems?

Yes, I wanted a broad, popular appeal to be the fate of my poems, so that they wouldn't be only the precious property of the few.

How benevolently generous on your part!

Why *not* be protective and paternal toward my own poems?

I can't fault a logic based on such instinctive possessiveness.

That's shrewd of you to back down, before I would open fire.

Let's not bicker. We're here in order for you to tell me something.

I'm glad your priorities are so primary.

Proceed.

I determined to impose my poems on the people.

How?

I took my most difficult poems to the printing press, and had millions of copies made of each. Then I rented out an airplane, took the copies up with me, and flew over the heart of the most vulgar, culture-hating metropolis possible, that lowbrow, mindless principality, Philistinelphia. In that city, the only reference ever made to "arts" is "the art of commerce."

But didn't it profane your poems to be flown over a city totally devoted to business and practical occupations such as industry and trade? Your poems would have been met with the chilliest indifference, or the most raucous opposition! What *was* your purpose, then?

It was the diabolical one of forcing poetry onto the populace. I dropped my millions and millions of copies down from a bottom hatch, and they floated like a lot of verbal parachutes, obscuring the sun and filling out the whole sky like an endless cover, as down they fluttered, casting closer and closer shadows on that ugly city. I dive-bombed more and more poems. What a spectacle! Those uniform rectangles of white, serenely descending. Down below, all work was stopped. An emergency was declared. The city was caught unprepared. My raid was like a blind rape: the poems gutted the vitals of the city. They rained on railway stations, bus depots, factory warehouse districts, shipping docks, advertising communities, factory residential lots, humming beehives of a chronically employed city. Executives and workers alike were exposed to the sudden bombardment, and stunned into submission. For the shock had penetrated even to the illiterate heart of the city! And the results would have to be stupendous!

Could you picture the scene for me?

There were all my poem-missiles, skipping and jumping in the air, blocking out the sky's ordinary blue. It was eleven o'clock on a

Wednesday morning, when work is going full-blast and the full employment force is proceeding uninterrupted, on operations regulated to the maximum routine. A slavish efficiency was hum-drumming at a production overtime rate, and the downtown financial profits netted on secretarial computors were in astronomically high gear, leaving the economy in a healthy condition.

What a time to drop poems!

Each office was innocent, as the corruptive pestilence descended. Sales were at an all-time peak, and happy customers were buying, at an unprecedented rate of consumption. The stock market burned with glee, as corporations prospered indeed.

And how was business doing?

Quite well.

What happened?

The poems fell.

Adding gravity to the situation?

No, because the gravity was being used up in falling.

Yes, yet buoyed up by a merry lightness?

Although the poems had considerable weight, and would weigh heavily on the intellect.

Was a levity delaying their descent?

Only gradually, till the city became smothered with them. Every house and office and factory owned dozens of my poems, a captive audience held inescapably to them. I was being *read*, by the *mass*!

How did it feel?

Popular. I was liberated from the tiny intellectual quarterly. *Now*, I was being solidly circulated! My poems would weigh down hard and cause a dent.

On what?

On the pulpy mass mind. And I would be the contemporary myth. My songs belonged to the common people. Philistinelphia was glutting itself on my intellectual fare. I had manufactured a need for beauty, verbally clad. A big demand went up, for aesthetic truth.

What a marvelous missionary you were, in your crusade to inflict culture on the people!

I was a super-salesman! My sales campaign worked. Even the infant memory was spoon-fed with my poems. Gifted kids could recite by rote the magic potions of my inspired lyrics. And my works were the adult legacy of the city fathers, the sober-minded citizens whose respectability would now solemnly advocate, endorse, underwrite, and wholeheartedly sponsor my rhymes and dissonances for rhapsodical community consumption. However, work slacked off. Business declined. My poems had drugged industriousness into a stupor. Incentive was now barren of practical gain, money was inconsequential, since the sole value of life, the one excuse for living, was the study, appreciation, and delight that my poems could constantly afford. The rabble were drunk with my gift of sensitivity; but, irresponsibly, I had undermined the competitive society, emasculated the virile dragon of enterprise, and brought all of capitalism to a slump in the area and dominion of my poems' activation. What a blight on the market I was, though an aesthetic saviour!

What a revolutionary effect your poems had!

Insurrectionary, yes. Poetry has usurped the prosaic system of hard, simple materialism. I had committed the most glorious of crimes, with audacious privilege.

And what is Philistinelphia *today* called?

Aestheticville. And my lines are being read and recited in each of this diminishing town's remaining ivory towers. For those are the only buildings left; all industrial and commercial and residential buildings have long been razed. For the town, materially, is dead.

You called it a city before; why a town now?

Alas, it's a village, a hamlet. Soon, it's nothing, or a fossilled morgue for belated archaeology. First the people went on relief, but they starved anyway, for their unemployment compensation doles ran out, and the municipal coffers were drained as dry as the mounds and heaps of piled-up bones which poetry has wrought. Business-wise, it was soon a ghost-town. One by one, everyone is dying. All my poetry-lovers.

Then poetry *does* corrupt the people?

Only their bodies. Which soon turn into corpses, so it doesn't matter. But poetry *uplifts* the mind. Into a rare, giddy, lightheaded ecstasy: which precedes dying on a weeklong empty stomach. Poetry *does* nourish the *soul*. But that's all.

A sad tale. But why don't you write poetry any more?

My muse is silent, in memory of Philistinelphia's staunch bohemians and their heroic conversion from work to mind. To do them honor, my muse is stilled, and her harpstrings plucked out. Poetry is an intoxicant: and may devastate a community.

Have you any guilt? What responsibility do you bear? Or do you deem yourself a saviour?

Guilt is irrelevant to what I've achieved, and brought to pass. I haven't ravaged, but I've *built*.

How do you justify what you've done? And abstain from the stain of guilt?

Poems are as immortal as the soul. The *good* ones, that is. On wings of eternal verse, atonement soars.

Is that your practical solution?

No, my ideal one.

THE AVANT-GARDE

Interviewed in his reluctant hour of death, at bedside, by sub-editor of obscure but current literary magazine whose exclusiveness is based on enduring the smallest purchasing circulation in captivity.

I, who invented the avant-garde, now must recline on my bed of declining age and read how others are abusing my great discovery and violating the inspired genius of its founding.

What did you have in mind when you invented the avant-garde?

The avant-garde.

Are you—or rather were you—indebted to previous artistic—

No. I did it without current aid or past assistance. It suddenly occurred to me one day.

What did?

The avant-garde.

And once it was invented, did you sell rights, shares, concessions, privileges, apportionments, licenses, permissions, and other things of that nature to the practitioners of the arts, like sculptors, painters, novelists, poets, composers, architects, choreographers, and similar such creative people?

Yes, therefore the whole movement got started.

And what did the critics have to say about it?

The reactionary ones reviewed it unfavorably. The intelligent ones gave their uncritical admiration to it. For that reason, I hate conservatists, and adore radical thinking, which butters my own bread for me and keeps the pie heating up in the oven.

Were you just speaking metaphorically?

After a manner of speaking, yes.

And this new movement—what name did you give it?

The avant-garde.

But isn't that French?

Yes, but why not? The French have culture, too.

Where else did it take root?

In London and New York, as well as elsewhere in the world.

How cosmopolitan! No wonder the avant-garde has a sophisticated air!

Of course! I, its founder, am *very* worldly.

No wonder this unmistakable universal flavor is so pungent about you! But now that you are very old, are you afraid of dying?

Not so long as I'm assured my movement will go on living.

What is the longevity of the avant-garde?

An *indefinite* longevity. It can go on forever.

But wouldn't it then become outmoded, and live beyond its time?

I don't care! I want what I invented to be eternal!

I see. Well, what led you to invent the avant-garde?

Hunch, instinct, intuition, brilliant insight, divination, instantaneous foresight, applied prophecy, a gleam of analytical illumination, an inspired totality of concept, and weary saturated disgust with the then-current modes of art and literature.

Which were what?

I'm trying to forget!

Of course. Did you patent your invention?

There were no patent rights then to protect it. It was stolen and pirated at random; and grossly imitated, plagiarized and copied shamelessly with acknowledgement and credit withheld from the stricken author. I was sick for a month with despair and grief—my property was being ravaged!

But now do the historians acknowledge your paternity of this thriving, pervasive, vigorous offspring, and acclaim the sovereignty of its legitimacy?

Yes, they seconded what I fecunded.

Oh yes! It's all the rage today. Your brainchild has become fashionable in the foremost as well as secondary salons, literary circles, art hangouts, studio parties, gallery openings, and other uncommercially promotional exponents of what you alone have propagated. In fact, there are countless derivative propagators of what you first invented.

And what was that?

The avant-garde.

Oh yes. It's my proudest creation. I have innumerable followers.

But isn't the movement getting out of hand?

No. It was intended to be big, and to expand, in fact, with time. There's no size-limitation to the avant-garde. Some day it will take over the world.

Is that a threat?

No, it's a boast!

Oh, really?

Its reality is confirmed by history, science, fact, informed opinion, consumer and marketing research, mathematical logic, mysticism—both theological and paganistic, sociology, exacting laboratory experimentation, legislative acts, executive edicts, judiciary deliberation, pragmatic verification, popular demand, documentary evidence, and other factors that convince all doubt aside, without enlisting that sweeping impassioned fervor of dogmatic certitude! It can't be denied—the avant-garde is here to stay!

But in time, won't it become the rear-garde if it doesn't change?

Oh, don't talk to me about change—I'm sick of hearing about *change!*

But wasn't your invention based on the precept of change?

At the time, yes. I remember now. It was, at the time, yes.

And now that's not true any more?

No! It's the duty of the avant-garde to hold the fort, to resist being invaded by new things from outside, to consolidate what it's already gained, to conserve and maintain, to be steeled off from external alteration by insidious infiltrations and radical influences, to be self-perpetuating in homage to the original prototype which is the archetype of its ever-sameness.

Where are the threats coming from?

Everywhere.

But isn't your fame still sung? At old-fashioned cocktail parties, at banquets for aging artists, at Academy presentations to senile novelists, at poetry conventions for old-timers, wherever the veteran award-winners and eminent men of letters gather as venerable idols for an adoring but decimated public of dotards that are dying out from the drowsy seniority that weighs down their years in drooping pursuit of their belated graves?

Exactly! And who's to blame? The young! What I invented isn't good enough for them! Ingrates! How *dare* they improvise and originate on their own? Who gave them such permission? They're undoing all my work, they're the cause of my undoing. I've already had at least eighty strokes—that would have finished off any less vigorous campaigner. But I hang on! The avant-garde is here to stay. While I'm still around, it'll never be done!

But do you accept your defeat?

Never! You! What does your magazine stand for? Is it pro or con?

It's definitely for the avant-garde.

Ah! That's me!

But I mean today's avant-garde.

But it's my invention!

Well, perhaps they were influenced by you, but ventured off into a new direction; perhaps they do acknowledge their debt to you; and admit to the inspiring example you set.

Those dogs! My weapon was the New, and they've snatched it out of my hands. Now they use it to their own devices! Once it was I who shocked. Now *I* am shocked! For *them*, I sacrificed my life?

You're sentimentalizing yourself with gross liberty! You were dedicated; what more reward do you want? What you produced will be preserved—in libraries, galleries, museums, concert halls, all the cultural strongholds. Doesn't that satisfy you?

Ah, pity and gratitude have fled. My generation's virtues have never been renewed. Instead, hordes of monstrosities are here, fickle vogues in the name of the New, gimmicks of giddy falsity, unalterable detours—and there's no returning to me, with my genuine sanctity. The standard I set is violated past redeeming! Alas, my movement collapses.

What movement?

The avant-garde.

Yes. My sympathies. Can't waste time on you. Got to cover what's really happening.

THE LAST POSTSCRIPT

I am now a very old man. It is hard to hold a pen. Yet these thoughts I must write. I can no longer be patient enough to cope with the tangled operations on a typewriter. Then why cannot I *dictate* my thoughts, to keep my hands still? Because my thoughts and their expression depend on my being solitary at the time. Otherwise I merely chat, and hold a "conversation."

The pen quivers in my grip. But *it* doesn't mind, so why should *I* mind?

Of course, the sum of my years entitles me to claim that I have been through "a lot." It's true, I have been *through* it. What remains on me, besides the wrinkled memories inside?

My housekeeper takes every opportunity to remind me "to rest." She hisses this fierce command. She has authority behind her, by no less an expert in the wisdom of delaying health's decadence than that final arbiter, "the doctor."

I've rested myself restless. I've kept my bed company. I've slept when sleep was no longer necessary. I've worn out my need for rest. So I plunge into action, by taking up this pen.

Good, but what have I to say? Is "Nothing" the answer I now give to my former, former years that devoted relentless energy to curiosity, search, lust, fatigue, and recuperation? Often intense, those experiences were. I alternated between boredom and resuming interest.

"Meaningful", "significant": that's what different people would be to me at different times, and different pursuits I would take up, passions that would be so keenly obsessive: yearnings to travel, problems in work, difficult women: I was taken up with all these. And intellectual issues I went into. All those things that "meant" so much to me. Even matters of pride and survival. Jobs, money, companionship. The intricate choreography of a fully-cast social life. And other exciting absorptions. The enthusiasm of following the seasonal fortunes of your favorite sporting teams. And the news of the world: politics, progress, international friction, economic crises, humanity's plight—all symptoms of communal unrest.

My life traveled among "events"—personal mainly, my own involved participations; but some, as well, related, more remotely, to the fellow members of my race. (I belong, by birth, to a fellowship of men. Whatever is mortally human, touches on me: so deeply, in fact, I'm scarred all over.)

Now I sit here, old. (The chair is only a quarter of my age.) Writing without knowing why. Puzzling what to say, or why the compulsion to say anything. The housekeeper frowns on what she calls my "scribbling." If I do this once a month, she derides it for breaking in on what must be the even tenor of my "rest." My housekeeper believes that inactivity ought to prepare my respects for the honor of "death." She wants my life to die, to make it that easier for my body to follow the transition by itself dying. She's very considerate to my future corpse—*that's* her master, and *I'm* in the way!

All right, I've vented my spleen against her. Poor thing, she's not a young child herself any more. But she commits the sin of going against my wishes. Which are what? To be allowed to stir, to shake my pen, to eke out some small words on a few trifling sheets of paper. "Why" I do this—with open furtiveness, with defiant secretiveness—eludes my (I have enough years to claim senility) "comprehension." Did I ever know why I ever did *any* thing?

I did manage to convey that I underwent "events," "interests," "pursuits," "involvements," necessary for pride, pleasure, or survival. But were these things that absorbed me: were they *distractions*—or were they the things to be distracted *from*?

Age is supposed to ripen wisdom. It merely lessens activity. (Including what we call mental activity.) As my housekeeper would characteristically remind anyone weak enough to listen to her, it's a time "to rest."

But rest from *what*? I marvel at my endurance—since I'm supposed to be feeble—in pursuing this problem, which thanklessly offers no solution. Or none yet, while actively I bend my beating brow in hunting around an imaginary bush.

Oh dear me. Will death find all my affairs unanswered? I must try to tidy up, and *conclude* something. I don't want *this* session of scribbling (which has advanced far—thank God my housekeeper hasn't peeked in) to go in vain, like most other endeavors I was crazy enough to scheme, hope, plan, initiate, and tear away on.

I *did* achieve some things in life. I sustained some deep relationships with women and friends, I reaped certain honorary fruits from my vocation, and earned several sorts of rewards along my concentrated paths. I had happy moments, and periods of great joy. I would be ungrateful to life's spontaneous privilege to say that I lived it out in vain. What I lacked was some consistent sort of goal. And by "lacked" I mean "missed"—*sorely* missed.

Moments of elevation, elation; of disgust, revulsion; of everything emotional that ever happened—what's the design they helped to form a pattern of? Or am I reading in a gratuitous demand? Do I still impose youthful ideals on the planlessness of what no order can be found in? Has my heart's bent been so determined in its rigid course, that it's not learned to desist, this late, in the fixed craving for an "aim"? Or has my goal already been overtaken, arrived at long ago, and so mastered, assimilated, incorporated, that it has lost outside validity in the ghost-haunted wanderings of my distractedness? Silence: there's no answer.

I'm not glad that I'm old. My future is almost microscopic to behold.

Where was I? Oh yes. If life is a first-class education, what was taught that I learned? If a science is an organized body of knowledge, then my life has no right to be called a science. Then what was it—an industry, an art, a metaphysical illusion, a mystic experience—what have I harvested?

My housekeeper was right. I'm fermented to a froth, because I neglected the rule that I must always rest. Why do I violate such sage advice?

She's seen me! She comes in—

LOVE LETTERS

AN ENCOUNTER CONSUMMATED BY THE JOYOUS CONCORD OF A SEPARATION

What a coincidence, that we should have met!

Unless pre-arranged, *all* meetings are to some extent coincidental.

How pedantic! As for me, I'm spontaneously happy to see you again.

And I too. Enough of these preliminaries.

Preliminaries to *what*?

Why, let's enjoy our meeting.

Naturally, and to that we shake welcome hands, my friend.

Gorgeous. I'm stunned with delight.

Don't outdo it. Your company has become tedious.

On that note, let's part, biding our next coincidence.

I'd tolerate only a coincidence as our next basis of meeting. I don't pursue you actively out of my way, you bore!

Your reflections act adversely upon my regard for you.

That's excellent, if it discourages you from seeking an eager coincidence again. Another meeting with you would incur my distaste.

Then deliberately, and not by coincidence, let's be bent upon avoiding it.

Good day, and bad coincidence to you, you leper!

Coincidentally, I concur, in assessing *you* that way.

I boil with impatience to be parted from you.

Your feelings are generously reciprocated. Let that be the last cue for our simultaneous mutual interaction. No news from you would only be too welcome.

How *identically* I share your views.

HOW I LEARNED TO BE TOO PROUD, TOO HONORABLY PRINCIPLED, TO STOOP TO NAME-DROPPING AS A DEVICE TO WIN THE LOVE OF A BEAUTIFUL GIRL

I dropped the name of a famous person, in order to impress a pretty girl, since *I* had no fame to attract her with, and she was insufficiently attracted to me as merely a person in my own right and a male suitor for the favors she presumably had to give.

She was indifferent to me as a man. She was likely to show no romantic interest in me (which is the sublimation of sexual response or some other potent but subtly combined chemical compound of spiritual affinity) unless I artifically induced one in her, by such a ploy as name-dropping, which by inference intimates that I'm intimate mates with somebody she regards as famous. Then she'll have to think highly of me, since the renown and glamor of the famous name rubs somehow off on me and reflects the glory of my equality—through intimate friendship—to the person of the famous name. This is supposed to elevate me, in the girl's eye, to the stature of the person of the famous name. As a reward, I get my kiss from her, followed hopefully by the total gratification of lust and love, which includes lifelong marriage as bodily and soulful inseparables. So I had great incentive to namedrop, for the prize would be this beautiful girl, who would grow a sudden love for me or a poignantly gradual one in a sensational suspense of sentimental rapture with a romantically dizzying culmination.

That's sufficient motivation, isn't it?, for me to stoop to the heights of namedropping. Thus, that name I did drop.

"Who's he?" she asked—supremely unimpressed. "But, but, surely you must know him, or rather, have heard of him."

"Never heard of him."

In a frenzy I muttered, "He's the best-known poet by critical acclaim of all of West Sixty Fourth Street from Broadway to West End Avenue on both sides of the street." Even to that last-ditch attempt inspired by the futility of desperation, she was imperturbably cold—unmoved. I had lost. To confirm my loss and make it deathlessly official, she carelessly shrugged her infinitely desirable shoulders tightly clad in a tempting little blouse, and disdainfully shrouded my annihilation with the final distance of "So what?" The corpse of my recent love was shrouded over in mockery and humiliation. From then on, I resolved that it would be a dishonorable principle to name-drop: by chagrin, I learned to be above such a low tactic, such a cheap, stooping trick. My pride recoiled from it. Name-dropping was beneath me—when in vain.

THE FEMALE EXHIBIT IN FRONT OF A MALE MIRROR

A male mirror, tall and erect, became sexually stimulated by a pretty girl's antics in front of him. She kept looking into him, coy, flirting, coquettish. (She was innocent of his being a *male* mirror capable of being aroused. She assumed he was merely a neuter *thing*, an object for her vanity's scrupulous self-examinations in preparing herself for a public appearance when she must look at her best to enchant a larger choice of males.)

Unknown to her, she was tormenting him. Why was he a mirror?, or why did his spirit take such a flat, mercurial, glittering, and—on the face of it—promiscuous form?

It happened this way: This was his punishment for a previous existence as an unscrupulous philanderer, rake, Don Juan, and seducer. It was moral retribution, to imprison him within a mirror's frame where he'd be at the mercy of any and sundry who used him. For he still felt lust. His tool, however, was flattened to the point of invisibility. But he was vulnerable, susceptible, as ever, as notoriously before, to those peculiar charms which women even unconsciously wield.

He desired Dora and wished to possess her, naturally. But in his present guise, he wore an impotent incarnation. This rendered him powerless, despite her astonishing appeal.

By now he couldn't take it any more, and was desperate. Dora was adorable. But what could he do?

She simpered, she gazed, glanced, peeped, minced, it was atrocious. He suffered his arousement in his stoical profession of silence, for his identity was that of a mirror, and she was using him in kind: in unkind kind: he couldn't resist her; but was stuck to what he was.

Dora had deep, plump curves everywhere. Suddenly, the mirror burst free. As though by impulse, he had wrenched loose, and reassumed the semblance of a man. He artfully "took" her. She was gratified. After all, she was a narcissist.

A LOVE-LETTER SEQUENCE

the solemn and soulful letter of deep gravity

I don't want to devour you. I want you to be as much as you want to be. I would stand by and gaze with awe and admiration, but I wouldn't prevent or interfere. Why should I prevent and interfere, when I have so much of my own being to be into more being? More power to you. I'm big enough not to be threatened or intimidated by what you're becoming. Can you stand me as well—or will you later? I used to see people as threats, but I don't see you as a threat. I'm undaunted. You also?

If you're understood, you still can function, and operate. You would just have to get used to being understood. Being understood need not be an impediment.

Besides, there's so much of you I don't know, and things of you I can never know. You're inviolate; I will not violate.

*

I see in you the confirmation of my being. But you're another, not me. You're a definite other, you in partidular, no other. That which you are is a confirmation of me. It's especially valuable to me because of that scarcity: I'm not confirmed in that way by any other. I could go through life lacking that special confirmation: but it would be a lack.

Am I not the confirmation of you?

a quick letter to cement a link

I'm in a big hurry so I'm writing a fast letter just to say that I'm in a big hurry, which I hope will excuse this fast letter, which I'm writing anyway just to tell you that I'm in a big rush, so I just have time to get this letter off before I rapidly have to be on my way toward where I'm going so fast: Which is nowhere, but with haste.

To reverse the process, read this slowly, till it comes to a full halt. Then, just as slowly, stop.

A letter written fast but read slow is thus a well-balanced letter, on the whole. Dashed off at first hastily, then read by the recipient with all due deliberation, the rate and pace tend to average out between sender and receiver in the transmission being rounded off and complete. A letter is a two-way process: giving and getting. The giver and the getter are not only in different situations as regard to this letter—they're different anyway, from each other, in themselves. This letter was hardly needed to prove *that*.

What *did* it prove, then? Transparently, nothing too apparent. But still, it lived its life, utilizing two people in the process. *Some* letters aren't even *written*. This one got off the ground, and linked two heads with the same words. It served as a go-between. The heads were already linked before the letter, and will be linked after the letter. The link survives the letter. Will the heads survive the link?

the letter that just won't do

This letter is a poor shadow of the motive that impelled it. But products often but feebly represent what they're the products of. Witness *this* poor fellow: he limps to you. No, he hardly "embodied forth." Let this creature dribble to his close, then.

"Pity me," he requests, his dying request. But scorned he should be, or slighted. An unrepresentative letter! Removed from office, he ought to be, following his lame commission that so ill-served me, his sender. With the authority invested in me, I terminate him, *now*.

His dying squawk: "Your orders were unclear."

the phone-substitutional letter

Being forbidden from phoning you for a few days, which is a tough constraint, gets "sneaked around" by way of the *letter*, which had not been expressly prohibited. Thus, as far as your strict order goes: my disobedience is by the *letter*, if not by the spirit.

(Poem for the occasion, of uneven lines ironed out by rhyme:)

Letters reach where phones fear to tread.
The phone is incommunicado; but the letter gets read.

a letter that barely brushes against you

I send you this letter "just because." Its arrival is a slight brush of contact. Included in that marginal contact is the time the letter took between its writing and its reception. That little bit of time, being abstract, fled. The letter remains, tangible, and frail.

a letter with something disguised as nothing

I'm letting the saying of nothing ease this letter of weighty content to lighten the poor postman's unknowing burden.

A MOVIE IS FOR HOLDING HANDS?

There we were, sitting alongside each other in the dark of the movie theatre. The screen was flickering with the projected cinematic images. Sometimes it would flash bright, other times all the light would drain out, but mostly different parts of the screen got lit up with shifting intensities and subtly modulated obscurities. All of us who are not blind know the experience, so I can cut the description out right here.

As for the seating arrangements: I was on Martha's right, she was on my left. We were seated in the middle aisle half way back from the screen to the back of the movie hall. Straight ahead was the screen. We were at a direct angle, for a central fullness of vision.

All the time, I was aware of her. We had only just met a few hours ago: properly introduced in a legitimate "mutual friend" situation, not a degrading "pick-up." So our "romance" had started off on strict, not tawdry, footing. My awareness was soaked with love. Lust also bloated me. I dared to assume she felt the same things. This "daring to assume" was part of my mood. I didn't want to wait. I wanted it all to come to an immediate head. I was stealthily impetuous. My goal was to clinch our hearts together, this very evening, on our first day of meeting. It would prove the intensity. I flung prudence to the wind, headlong, in reckless confidence; cunning, deliberate, calculating. My immediate short-range goal, to implement my "long"-range goal, was to engage our hands in a holding fest; tender, but erotic.

Stealthily, I took up the armrest between us with my entire left arm, hogging it. But demurely, her right hand was clasped in her own chaste and pure left one, on their own mutual lap. How I yearned, for that golden lap!

Furtively (yet deliberately) I set out to test and provoke her reactions. I leaned my left shoulder against her right one, while pretending to bear my full central weight on a symmetrical spinal posture sitting. Would she respond?

She remained neutral, upright. Feigning not to commit herself, as yet.

Subtly, I had communicated my "interest." In a broad but hedging hint. I had wanted a sharp, instantaneous, positive answer: an embrace right there. It hadn't been delivered. I was held short.

I'd send more "advance" message. Martha would be a hypocrite to ignore it. She'd pour out warmth, on my re-assuring her.

I increased the "pressure." I leaned the whole left side of my body to poach on her seating territory in willful trespassing: I was "out of line." A challenging encroaching. The ball was in her court. Your move, Martha.

It was positive: though backward. She accepted my searching hand, and held it in hers. But she remained rigid (or rather, casually stiff) in her torso verticality and her neck alignment. Her head wasn't tilting, but erect.

Martha held her place, neither budging nor giving an inch. The leaning was all my own. I was an inclined plane. She was directly vertical.

I went out on a limb, out on a tangent. Our hands, though, were clasped: my left in her right: or her right in my left. Slightly on her side of the armrest.

For half an hour I had been thus concentrated. I had forgotten all about what the screen was constantly showing in motion. But *Martha* was partially attentive. She had less a film *over* her eyes, more *in* her eyes. I felt, thereby, neglected.

I had made a "pass," but its intended emotional impact had been diverted or blunted, neutralized somewhat, by her lukewarm acceptance. This infuriated me, and increased my love.

My elbow was on the armrest. The movie palace was plunged in darkness, then suddenly sprung the light: the film was over! The chandeliers were on. The stage curtain closed. The theatre was to empty itself, of its audience.

We got up, not holding hands, and one by one made our way to the aisle. Now we were side by side again, about to march out of the theatre. I offered a new test, proffering my hand. I had made the wrong move, by being on the wrong side of her *free* hand. I was on the side of her hand being busy in holding her purse.

I got on the *other* side of her, as we passed into the public street through the cinema door marked expediently "Exit." I was now on the side of her *free* hand. I was walking her home, for she lived only nine blocks from the cinema, and the weather was fine.

But I felt suddenly inhibited. My hand felt foolish dangling. Nor did *she* take the initiative, by grasping it.

Suddenly I lurched out, and grabbed hers. But this was an abrupt, awkward move. It startled her. She dropped her purse.

She bent down to pick it up, but so did I. We were both squatting down, near a streetlamp, and I was afforded an immodest view of her thighs and lower haunches, I'm afraid. I was frenzied with the paralysis of lust civilly inhibited. This was no caveman situation. Restraint ached me. I desired Martha. She gave no sign. *She* picked up the handbag, before *I* could. We walked on, not holding hands. Perhaps significantly, she had transferred the handbag to her hand on the side of her adjacent to *my* inclining one. A deliberate non-invitation?

Spurning, refusal. I felt rejected. I was in the throes of self-consciousness, very badly. Conversation was ineffectual, sporadic, perfunctory. I was doing badly. Martha would not be mine.

I would give up, maybe? Too late to save face. I had failed. Plain and obvious, to us both.

We walked home mostly silently and with no hand-holding. I began to panic, anew, wondering what would happen when we reached her door. Should I try to kiss her? That would be to risk a fatal rejection. It would be too conclusive, an ignominious climax. I was acutely embarrassed.

We came to the entrance of her apartment building. I stiffly held myself apart. I sputtered out a good-night. She echoed it in her higher-sounding voice, but dead. She turned her back, and unlocked the entrance door. I made no move, but stood flatfooted.

Now the door was closed and her form absent. She was making her way alone up the elevator, or staircase, I couldn't see. The night was late. I was alone.

What movie had we seen?

I wasted a movie experience. I *could* have seen it.

Where attention is placed. And to what effect. That's what life (actively speaking, the active life) is about, in wisdom.

Ah, but the *inner* life. I had all my loneliness for cultivating it. It redeems all "failure."

ARGUMENTS WITH IRENE. THEY GIVE DEATH MY FORM, AND MY LIFE SETTLES IN IT.

I

Irene and I were at argument. We had only just met, and already our argument routine was well established. This was one thing we were good at, arguing. It's what kept us together. We were paired off perfectly by the argumentative bond, ideally suited as mates in that neglected art which historically carried such conjugal tradition behind it. Our voices clashed at just the domestic duet pitch that shrilled out discord to smash the window pane of language division. Smoldering, hot, heavy, we played devisive variety on any tonal length, down the argumentative scale to color the gamut with the full palette. We were at each other's throats, verbally, that rung of inspired enmity. Our clashing swore a fury that poured exasperated venom down an erotic funneling that never got past the mouth. We really meant it, too, but could never fall into sex's circuit of exhaustion. No vent to relieve us, so we squeezed more fatigue from argument's flying purple, in wilder peals of hatred's high abandonment that tore through extremes. It was our growing force of need. We loved to argue. Love could gnaw on no other channel but argument true and pure, and how we would soar, tried blue and sore to the unendurable, and then more. On that we stood loyal and secure. Betrayal was impossible with another arguing partner, for our match had perfected the art, and perfection raged to renew its standard perpetually. *More* shining bouts, in sure delirium's swoon, a rancor never paralleled by other shouters ever; and we grew gravely dependent, she on me, I on her, in swollen spirals of completion that kept hysteria raging tightly contained in the hoarse and tense bottleneck that pent-in our gush from the mounting backflow of its frantic release. Crescendo developed a gigantic obesity of glandular containment, in the hectic renewal of arrested accumulation bloating itself staggeringly. No escape to slide into, so we plunged into the regressive freedom of falling back on the wizardry and artistry of argument, reduced to a fine art as our sole outlet. This clinched our relationship, cut off from saner choice. Together, in one perfectly mismatched voice, we traded discord for the harmony of horror: and kept our arguing up.

Wow, we flew at it, fast and furious. "Irene, you're wrong!" I found myself immediately saying no sooner had we already met. We had met at a party where for an hour we talked after being formally introduced. Then I offered to take her home. I escorted her to the subway, it was after midnight already, I said "Invite me up to where you live," she said no, only to the door; I countered with "Then let's go to *my* place," she said no she's not a whore; it made me angry, I swore, and flew into her: "Who's accusing you?!" Then she snarled and talked back, till the subway screeched up at her stop. I said, not willing to relinquish her for the evening, "Let's go into a coffee shop where we can continue shouting at a table till the manager comes over with his stained apron and with the power invested in him by proprietory right or delegated to him therefrom, he kicks us out with official finality, after making us pay. So we'll have *him* to be mad at, not just ourselves. We need to recruit scapegoats from outside to divert from each other some of our excess hostility. We're snarling, so let's import victims in common, to give our rage a united front." But Irene disagreed, and we waged our argument anew, with a new theme to lend it fresh fire. We had a running argument, non-stop, but it gathered fresh fuel along the sameness of its way to break up our bitter constancy with a diversity of material to keep it flaring. Our recriminations gained head. We became more and more adept at it, as love's immediate substitute or infernal sublimation or fur-flying compensation which would preclude and frustrate lust; since our *arguments* were lusty enough, so why resort to lust itself when already we perverted it in fine explosive fury? Positive feelings were trained into distortion. Only negative feelings were left. These we nurtured with all the wounded tenderness from our hurt and rampant hearts. Thus we were embroiled, embattled. It was too much, yet too little, so it soon impelled us into habit's iron tyranny; tugged and compelled, we left all mercy behind and flung ourselves rabidly into mutual and cutting slaughter. It couldn't be stopped; its nature was of prolonged duration of indefinite antagonism. We rushed in readily for the kill, with eager confrontation: but were evenly matched, and no one had the edge: the contest was doomed *endless*, from the start. There were no betting odds; the tussle was balanced like a dream; verbally with no holds barred. But the coffee shop was abandoned of other customers at the lateness of the hour, and the serving man was deaf or he chose to ignore our squabbling; for three hours, till four in the morning, we fought on—*gaining* energy, not losing it. The game had our enthusiasm; we were never peaked, but enjoyment sustained itself to a total malice of delight. We were right for each other. The normal tenderness of couples would now be too tame for us; exhilaration had spoiled us for the usual love blending. Hate fascinated deeper than pale love. What a horrid lesson to learn.

We were still sitting there at a table in the dimly lit place. A puddle of spilled coffee was between us, as we still faced each other over the table top. It was our first night of knowing each other: not lovingly, but too critically; banter toppled wit into malice, and we slashed to draw blood. This raw feast on each other's ego-vulnerable flesh was rapidly corrupting our palate. There was no civil tongue left in our head. We were now infant savages; with more regressing ahead.

We tore in, for the forestalled kill; but our impasse kept up a steady stalemate. Evil fires emitted from hate. The sharpened teeth were whet for further gnashing; it was a bond between us, fate's dirty-work. How tepid to have *friends*, how innocuous and banal, once exposed to the brutal consolations of our primitively mutual abuse. Other relationships would be insipid, vapid. We lived *strong*, in each other; in destruction's life-giving vigor. And so, innocently, we arrived at harm, in our daggering exchange that settled our taste on confirmed maladdiction; it was impossible to turn away; punishment was our craving, in all morbidity's power, at each other's tearing hands: an intimacy deeper than sex, and most primitively appealing. We were stuck in this: and struggled not to loosen it, but to prod on excess' limit on an uncurbed terror market, employing tongues, not bodies. Our language gained color, with racy vernacular, spiced with spikes. Irene became essential. I couldn't do without her spite. All love's potential was at hate's disposal in a gruesome pack of reinforcement. We were paired off, with no respite. And danger was our safety.

The coffee shop showed no sign of closing. We looked at the window where there was a note hanging. It said in crude hand, "Open all night." But this was ridiculous. Frankly, I was worn out. Sullenly, it occurred to me what an impossible situation we had become trapped by. I felt conciliatory. My organs were inflamed by arguing; how good it would be to make love, and get all the spleen out of us. I begged Irene, but she said no. But two blocks away was her apartment! Could she not put me up for the night—or the morning anyway, for it was well into Saturday, which meant we were off from work on a holiday weekend, she from her typing office, I from college teaching. She was a prude, all right. But a genius at argument, in devout over-compensation. I could sleep on her couch in another room, I pleaded, feeling weak and appeasing. Still no. True to her bitchery, she had no mercy whatever, and wouldn't concede a point, due to a solemn pride grown rigid as a nail. Why had I picked *her*? I turned soft. I declared, "I love you." "Weakling!" she replied. Frailty, thy name is *not* woman. Hardness would be more accurately descriptive, in this case. I was sexually hooked on her, couldn't let go: my masochism came purring out; putting a foul smirk on her sadism's coarse face. I was falling, and couldn't stop. I hung on to her. Haughtily, *she* held on too. Our descent was hell-bound. No fairer direction had the daring and insincerity to suggest itself. My life had fallen upon error, and I couldn't get out; nor did I wish to, tightened erotically on it, fastened grimly on it, in spiritual suicide. Perverse sex was behind this all, restrained. I had stumbled upon a wrong, with helpless tenacity; the error had made a goal of itself, in all my longing. It had reared itself as a virtue. Our relationship was set. Nothing but to complete it, in its destiny-beset course. "Well, I'm in for it now," I thought. Did I hear an "amen" being sighed from above?—or from Irene's side of the table? "I love you," I repeated. "You're a fraud, a cheat," came back at me: her voice: not a woman's gentle music, but the organ peal of the woman I adored, declaring my undoing. I was caught. I would *hate* to escape: I'm fascinated by my doom. I'll give in, with manly opposition. I'll fight, and be amorously defeated. Let Irene stamp on me; her triumph is *my* victory, anyway, and I hoped for her gloating to begin. But first she must earn it.

That was our first night together. It was given to memory as a souvenir. Memory mounted it. Now it's enshrined, immortal.

Every night after that, I saw her, and at the time of writing this we regularly see each other nightly, it's going on, seemingly forever. We're "going steady", with nightly dates. Our social life is confined to each other, primarily. We gain a lot, by always losing. A psychologist would call our relationship "destructive." He's right, though clinical. We're mutually destructive.

I teach history courses in a university, unmarried and past thirty, living alone, with slim prospects joylessly narrowed down to bleak. Irene is a typist in some corporation office with considerable managerial responsibility as well, being the bossy type. She types less, and bosses more. She has the temperament for that.

Our relationship is "platonic." We're severely abstinent, fidgety. This is abnormal, unhealthy. Irene lives by herself. What does she want out of life? To bicker with me? Not even a family? We're both lonely souls. Our circumstances are constricted, we're settling for low ideals. What's wrong with us? It's all so pathetic. What's more, it can't be helped. We're victimized by forces. Pity us. Where can we get pity? She gives me none, I have none for her. We feed off each other, vulturesquely. We've perverted the soul. We've repressed what detracts from our "dispute of long standing": we don't know what it's about, this tyrannical dispute, this tirade-toller. It's about everything, no less? Or about us? It doesn't matter. We're both repressed. Our servility is abject, to our irrational chains. We drag each other down; and as for stopping it, we're under no external guidance. We confound each other like buzzards, swooping to the kill. Pick, pick, pick, claw, claw, claw. It's just not decent. Our souls are ruined. We've stripped each other of dignity, and see the worst in each other, magnified bold. We'll die that way, clutching on, scratching while clinging, biting. A more enjoyable embrace is not for us: we won't let ourselves.

What's going to happen to us? We're poor, huddled things.

We've been driven wretched. No respite, for a rest. We're worn out fighting, but revive instantly to fiercer fighting. No let-up. We're at each other's service in the loosened instinct of suicide. Our love is buried in this. Can love be so indirect? Certainly! Look at us!

II

A year has gone by. We're dying at each other's hands. Or rather tongues. We never touch, in the flesh.

"No, you *don't* love me!" insists Irene. "Then what do I feel?" I maintain. "You're only infatuated," she specifies, in her unfeminine precise fatuous pedantic corrective but punitive tortureincisionism of precision that curdles my blood. "I loathe you," I declare weakly. "How nice that you're honest," she retorts. We're sitting, late one night, over table at dinner she's given me at her apartment. "You're quite taxing," she reminds. "*You're* no daisy, either," I thrust, in meek reprisal. It's an unending circle. We've been in a rut. All the openings have closed. Our monotonous tune carries on, as variety slumps. I'm feeling pretty much despair. Irene continues:

"I've said this before, Jake, that you're imagining love for me when all you have is a futile little crush on me that I'll never requite, since I'm your superior. If I'm arrogant, it's because I'm sincere. You can *thank* me, at least."

I gave in, and thanked her: a thankless admission. She always wins; but she never finishes me off lethally. She stings me but keeps me alive to work off her malice, her harpy vindictiveness, against, for all the days of our future. I'm kept for that service, made nice use of.

"You're jealous!", she unsubtly accuses one day. "Of who?!" I challenge. "You hate me!" she says in provocative spite. "You're right!" I agree. And thus we go round again. It's now another year gone, we're two years at each other, and a life ahead for more in reserve. We test death prematurely, in life. Death reacts positively, but keeps putting us off. It gives us no mercy. Who do we fall back on? Each other. Well, that's been normal for some time. A routine has become tradition. And that's our sacred religion! We can't break faith.

Nor can we lose face. We have our pride to keep up. We've grown pig-headed, and stubborn. We're in collusion, our collision; sworn to a conspiracy, in vowed double plague. We're good at cooperating, by practice of opposing. It's grueling, monotonous. Determined vanity is at stake. We protect it, and how! By nursing destruction, our gentle art. Resolved by no conclusion. Suspended on the hook of torture. Our virtue is consistency, which we share equally, but at a heaven-dealt expense, on pain of hell's strife tossed up here. Couldn't we resolve this issue? It's burning. No, that's not the point. We're instruments to suffer by, I stung by her, she by me, in perpetuity. This is no fun, and I wish for intervention. But God won't dare tackle Irene, she's too fierce. So the status quo resumes, true to the nature of any status quo worth its own salt, and productive of our tears. What's *our* bond productive of? Deterioration, but slow.

This is not leading to anything positive; but having set in, it's too late to alter. The ride rides us, and we're two parts of one ridden life. The parts refuse to snap off. They're barnacles on a rock that's slowly consuming them with a toxic acid stored up by centuries for this patient wearing away. "Stop!", I scream, "I've had it!" True to what in kindness I call her nature Miss Deadly resorts to her gift for taunting, which wicked cunning has highly polished. She's had me to practice on, I'm never unavailable. In her life, I'm her one standard constant: on me she relies, and I reward her trust. I'm her victim clamoring for more. "Dig it in," I ask. She obliges. She does me a favor, by not spoiling me. I can rely on her. Irene is my dream-girl. But in the nightmare mold, and totally dependable, I can count on it. I wish I can ride my mare at night. She frigidly spurns this proposal as rash. I'm overbold. I must curb my amorous tendencies, they disturb her. I *want* too much, that's my trouble. I need some mortifying, and she's there for that. She'll chastize me over and over again. I still won't see the light, so she'll repeat the dose. I mustn't take it lightly. The bad she's doing is for my own good. She's taking trouble over me, to try to purify my education. Some day I'll learn, if not too late. Meanwhile, some harm must befall me, that's fate. It's her responsibility to impose it on me. I must pardon her rigor. Administratively, she's thorough; especially on my punitive occasions. Can't I take it like a man, and not holler? She doubts I'm a man. No, she won't let me prove it, she offers no test for my manhood, her body is off-limits. I must wake up to this repeated fact. She'll drill me on it, with a whip's hand. She'll flagellate, if my lust persists. It's a demon I must control. She'll assist me in that. She's a stickler for duty. She's very good about discipline: mine.

That's the gist of how she treats me. I can't complain, for I seek it out. I need it badly. I'm badly off if I don't have it. It's a little like narcotic addiction. If I'm helpless, then Irene is to help me in that capacity; my helplessness is encouraged by her, and rewarded. Her message is being driven home, by the gradual route. She's slowly uprooting me, and planting me in *her* soil, where I'm sure to get soiled, as I need to be. She's my guardian angel, at war on welfare. The object is to destroy me. But to take my whole life doing it. She's pacing it on a long-drawn-out plan, to the tune of all my years. It was a costly adventure, meeting her. But why should I regret it? I've learned to accept my fate, the hard way.

III

Time has gone by, let's say another year. The sameness goes on. But unpleasant news is due me, in this form: Irene has taken on a lover. She changes apartments, moves in with him. I'm alone on the outside, but I must always visit them. Then they require that *I* move in, and sleep on a spare bed in the parlor room. So I leave my apartment, and go join them. Irene has suddenly become physical; only not with me. First I'm stunned. And now jealousy has entered me, chronic, in disease form. So I'm a secondary citizen, in that three-person little household. The lover is an idler with an income. He does very little. He saves his energy up. Then when Irene returns from work (where she's now a promoted executive), the lover-host (whose guest I am on a no-rent basis) knows how to put his energy to work. He and Irene "retire" to the bedroom. I can slightly hear them, but it's enough. Thus has been introduced this foul, unwelcome change in the much-disputed romance I've been conducting with my dear and fickle Irene; it was hell before, but worse now. I'm so sad, it's despondent. I'm put to scorn by lover and Irene, who have paired against me. How did I get into this? I seem to *court* destruction. I picked the right one in Irene, who's led me to *this*. Of *course* I hate her lover. Now my hatred is split. Formerly it all went against Irene. She must divide it with her lover now, each taking half. They've come to expect it, and I give. I give *generously* of my hatred. What *else* have I? Look at me! My circumstance is contemptible. Of whose making is it? Irene helped, and so did my innocence. Now there's this lover. With *him*, there are no exchanged words. He grins silently, and ignores me insolently. With *Irene*, there are more words; as always. We're established on argument, as from the beginning. *This* lives the same, through all this new change. *Before* the lover, was misery. In the *new* regime, there's *also* misery; a little different, but much the same, as well. Irene played me unfair. I resent what she's done. But I *must* live here. I can't be without her.

The radical introduction of the lover into the endless argumentative rounds with Irene has become, with another year, familiar. It hasn't affected my work as a college instructor. I take the subway to the college at the other end of the city, and make my students appreciate history. They like it, and me. Some of my girl students flirt with me. But I'm so indifferent to them! The reason is that they're not hateable. Irene has a talent for being hated. It absorbs so much hatred, that my love has been compounded in as well. We now argue *violently*—but it never comes to blows. Her lover hears us, unconcerned. He knows all is well—for him.

No, my life is *not* a tragedy. I would be a tragic failure if I had had nobler qualities to begin with, and had a tragic downfall, a misfortune in the curse of reversal. I wasn't built of such stuff for my plunge to seem distressing. But I've *always* been prone to become what I've become with Irene. I have the nature of a slave? No heroism in that. Nor comedy either. Pathos, maybe. Or who cares? My role is for certain, I'm sure about it. I'm Irene's creature, full of hate and argument, and perverse love. My ambition's horizon has closed in; I've accepted my fate. The *lover* fits in, too. How many men know their place? What would life have been, without Irene? Life *is* Irene. Hardly delightful. But does necessity ever consider delight? Necessity is concerned with essence. I am what I am. And if I'm not, Irene is there. She's my reminder. I argue, I resist, I concede, I relent. She wins, I lose; and the argument grows. Life is different, depending on what person you are. Being Jake, I know *my* life; with Irene there, persuasively enforcing it, with her irresistible hold on my will, her definite control over me. I love it, I hate it. The "lover" looks on and smiles. He's in on this, he understands. He's about to *marry* Irene, who always gets her way. They bid me to stay. Of *course* I will. I can be their history instructor. There's always a place for me, they're so generous. Now my love for Irene includes love for her lover too, her groom-to-be. I have hate and love enough, for both of them. Thus, I have a balanced emotional economy. I'm comfortable, I'm secure, within. My world has narrowed to what it is, which is the external of me. I'm fine. I don't complain; I argue and lose. I was cut out for this; and I've cut out all else: thus purifying my simplicity, the oneness of me with my condition. By accident, life endowed me Irene: I've taken her to my heart, made the most of her, by reducing me to my least. And the least, I live on: sufficient, habitual, at the true level of my merits, having no further deserving. Is it really me, I am? I'm no one else. If I need confirmation, I go to Irene, who's always handy. By her I'm reassured. I argue and give in. I lose; am I a saint? No, a loser by vehement arguing. I know myself; content with my lot. Irene has carved out my life. I'm living my truth. My truth is for Irene to say. She's not shy, she says it. I resist, but the truth takes hold, as sworn by her. She defines me, to what I am. Confined I am, by her; and our arguments grow less. I concord. Life is evening out. I have no will. The years are passing. My will's rein is in Irene's hand. She tugs, I obey. I'm less than a man. I'm under control. She's expecting a baby. I'll be the uncle. It'll call me uncle. That's a *further* role, for me. Life goes on expanding. With time running out, it's a dramatic race. With the only life I have, why not serve Irene with it? I hear no dissenting voice. I hear *Irene's* voice. "Jake, you're wrong. Can't you get *anything* straight?" I'm humiliated. It's dear to my ears. Arguments can't go on indefinitely. *Someone's* will must snap. Mine is her's in her command. It's as it *should* be. She's made it so, and what she's forged is mine to take. *I'm* forged, by her, as I am. What else am I. I *could* have been different. Irene eliminated that difference. She let me come out as I'm beheld, at a certain form. I'm held to it. It's mine, being me. My sole identity is owed to Irene. I haven't been able to thank her yet. I'll find a way, one day. I *owe* her this thanks. Love and hate are in it. What form will it take?

A BROWN SEQUENCE

brown's unanswering telephone trouble

Brown telephoned Martha, who was out, so her phone never answered itself, in spite of the insistent signal. This spelled out discouragement to Brown, who owned a loneliness he didn't need just by being independently bodied. The inaccessibility of Martha forced Brown back on his own resources, his own native resources, which crumbled under the extra weight, thanks to Martha neglecting her share. To have to put up with his self's company was poisonous to Brown, who pseudo-promptly phoned an acquaintance, Lemon, whose phone however *Mrs.* Lemon answered, in an inquiring voice, which had Brown identifying himself on the stuttering defensive. No, they were busy, Brown was superfluous, in time they would contact him, but not now. So Brown found himself superficially rejected, let out in the open cold, forced back again upon his own company by default of being elsewhere desirable by opportunity of invitation. But there was still hope. Enough time had been used up to make it wise or expedient to take one more try on the often used but little availing telephone number of Martha, perhaps returned from her distant mystery that kept her phone being unanswered when Brown had last tried it with ever forlorn result. Life was active with loneliness, and it kept him busy.

martha judges brown by how he seems

Brown struck Martha as seeming to look quite well; and really inside he felt horrendous. Martha said, "You look healthy. You seem happy. You're in good form, nothing's wrong."

But Brown knew contrariwise, for so his feelings could well inform him that things inside stood the reverse from what Martha claimed to detect from the appearances that Brown gave off in spite of the state he was truly in.

Brown corrected Martha, and attempted this explanation: "The way anyone looked reflected not his current state at the time of looking, but his state of two weeks ago, that being the time gap between the way someone is and the later delayed way he accordingly seems. Two weeks ago I felt well. But I didn't look it: I seemed miserable. The miserable way I seemed was the delayed outward reaction to the miserable way I *was* two weeks previous to that. And so a man is always at odds with himself, for never at the same time does he look the way he is: except by accident or the rare intensity of impulse."

Martha accepted this lesson. "I still think you look quite well," she said. "And that's how I must react to you. How you are will gradually catch up. Given enough time, I'm always right."

martha's untimely rejection

In his troubled state, having been early defeated by the world and been dealt deeper into the debt of disaster, Brown reached out with desperate recourse to Martha. He needed her to blot out those ills by stamping her bright presence on his strife-ridden life.

Why was her reply so stubbornly negative? It kept him still in the thrust of solitude. His need grew worse, for life cast him thicker into the pit, which the world had mercilessly dug. His ardent desperation made him further unattractive, repulsively bitter, as he condemned her for not accepting him in his hour of peril. "I hate to fill your need." Martha was open with him: "Men I feel romantic for and give myself to in the sheer and liberal way are those who can get along nicely without me. I admire their strength, sexually even. I sigh and throb, in the presence of their independence."

Brown resented this brutality, his love for her turning into surly distress, and given a sentimental sanctity to play the hurt partner. "Oh, stop pouting," she declared: "You're a child. I can't love you."

"It would do me so much good," he pleaded: "You see what afflictions I'm in, the world brooding my life into a million bruised particles of sensitivity. Is *this* the time to reject me? It's ideally so ripe, right now, that you should return my love, now that my love craves you." And so he begged. But a beggar was distasteful to Martha. If he moved her at all, it was to a perverse response. His heart was so full, she *had* to refuse it.

how mozart was vindicated as brown's invader, and to this day is still the beneficiary of brown's opulently-lavished hospitality

Brown felt the music coming over him. He was being lost to it, and he had half a second to reflect (before "going under" to the numbing anaesthesia of Mozart's melodic strains) on his own personal self-consciousness from his continuous introspective flux which was about to be suspended by interruption.

He caught a last glimpse of himself, in the egoistic preoccupations of his indwelling vanity that specializes on the problem of social identity; then the Mozart swept him over, and he drowned.

Brown was not being Brown, but was Mozart now.

His ears pierced his mind, and the flow took its circuit.

In the trance he gave himself to the composer, and was being commanded by every note, without the slightest resistance from Brown the personal man.

Mozart was inhabiting him. Why should Brown charge rent? He wasn't in the real estate business, nor had he sunk so low as to become a slum landlord. So Mozart, the transient, enjoyed temporary free lodgings in the abode of Brown's ear-tuned body, while the music still held sway.

It was not in a concert hall, but was coming from a record player in Brown's living room. The recording had been made in Vienna, but purchased in America in the form of a record album with a cover. The body or spirit of the music was residing through Brown like a current. He was under its spell, and Mozart had him pulsating like a sensitive sponge to an electronic musical cell that had stuck inside. Mozart had Brown reeling, like a confident boxing champion toying with an inadequate challenger to prolong a bout whose outcome was a long-foregone conclusion, just to work up some healthy sweat. It was no contest. Mozart had Brown spinning. The genius dictated the recipient's every response, even from a couple of centuries' authority, thanks to the recording machine and the household record player that put Vienna's orchestra in Brown's Mozart-throbbing living room that shook and rocked to a dead composer's orchestrated and instrumentalized ideas. It was happening, and heard. Brown was no longer Brown, during the duration, for he had suspended personal operation, on an involuntary basis, for the Mozart was now in his bones, stemming from the congested ear canal. The lesson by the master was being undergone, in a bout of musical appreciation; no getting away from it; Mozart was letting Brown have it, full blast, in too thorough a dose to permit Brown an inch of consciousness on his own. This involuntary concentration was Brown's act of homage, while absorption by the live lesser man in the dead and greater Austrian erected a profound bond that cut out time and made the blending pure.

But it came to an end, just like a surgical operation, and the anaesthetic had worn off, permitting Brown to mix the exiting echoing Mozart with the return to personal consciousness along the past jungle of Brown's untamed life, though traveled and partly charted by the explorative indweller. He recognized the recent insertion of the Mozart piece, to the exclusion of anything else, in his now-liberated soul. Brown was his own, now, and what had Mozart been doing there? What license had the latter to invade the former with so constant an overpowering? Now that Brown had regained sovereignty over the person of his own psyche, he'd institute investigations and a fact-finding research commission into Mozart's unchecked overrunning of the private tract of Brown's vulnerable territory. It had resulted in Brown being lost. His defenses had been down; luckily Mozart had meant no malice, so that Brown found himself whole and unharmed, upon the resumption of his control at the helm of his destiny. But he must make provident provisions to ensure against an unguarded defense in case a truly *dangerous* invader were to catch him off guard. Mozart had done him no harm; there was no marijuana secretly inserted in Mozart's musical chords, or any other illicit contraband illegally imported, that would have gotten Brown in trouble with the customs authority or rendered him the victim to the stealth of the Trojan Horse with his borders infiltrated in pernicious penetration. Mozart might even have improved him. But that had been an off chance.

Brown had been lucky to escape not merely lightly, but with a cultural gain to show for that narrow escape. The germ of Mozart injected in him was a benign one; a culture had been taken, and a bill of health granted. Mozart shrilled and whistled in the echoes of Brown, still, and the unscathed absorber of that fine material was the better for it, taking all in all. Brown had been a taker of risks, however inadvertently, and to this happy conclusion. However faintly, Mozart breathed in him. This Brown regally permitted, like a prince affording his kingdom's hospitality to a forlorn visiting genius who's granted the alms of a permanent stay, upon vouchsafed behavior constituting no determined peril to the home that now welcomes a distinguished guest. Thus Brown bade Mozart to stay; and charity was acceptable to the footloose dead wanderer. The terms were hardly degrading; and Mozart had a new refuge, to haven his eternity in. Brown would do; chalk up another, to the growing list.

brown can't stop

Brown was engaged in an arduous task. He kept at it, resisting fatigue, in sustained endurance. A bystander observed him and marveled that Brown had not long ago succumbed to such prolonged exertions; this laborious trial would have worn out even a fresh replacement; how had Brown maintained the energy?

"I'm not the slightest bit tired," Brown answered the amazed bystander, "and I credit this marathon exploit to a natural cause in due modesty, rather than attribute my powers to the occult workings of a miracle."

"Then please explain it scientifically," the bystander begged, while Brown kept up without pause his lengthy feat.

"I can work uninterrupted because I still have my baby energy, from which I draw a continual replenishment, that keeps me going non-stop."

The bystander then asked what Brown meant by "baby energy," a term the former admitted to never having heard before. At this point, on cue, Brown took pains to define or describe this astounding source:

Keeping on working, all in his strenuous stride, the ever-active Brown revealed the anyway open secret: "As a baby, by taking extra naps I kept storing up energy in an energy bank that gave me a large reserve for my later age, which is now. I accumulated, in other words, a surplus, like stored-away fat inside an eskimo's reindeer-belly. Now I draw upon the credit of those former naps, and cash it in, that gives me something extra in reserve when so my task requires, as in the present case. That ought to clear up the mystery. I slumbered my infancy in excess, now convertible to these timely work-energy outbursts that laugh away what normally is fatigue's onslaught. This paces me well for the long run, and in relentless ease I persevere at will. Goals come up to me, in time, I needn't pursue them, since patience is my gainful gait and nature throws in its effortless aid. Each stroke moves in time to an unseen, finely-manipulated rhythm. My articulations devolve from an outer grace."

"But when will your baby-energy fund become exhausted?" the bystander had to ask.

"I slept *so* much as a baby, that the reserve energy it stored away will *never* be depleted," Brown vigorously assured his awed admirer. Meanwhile Brown was going ahead, unabated, with the task at hand, applying himself with unflagging heat and undiminished ardor. The bystander got tired of watching: it wore him out.

So the bystander left. But now a new bystander approached. Another inquisitive audience? Brown worked on, as before. At his disposal was energy by the abundance, the yield of his sleeping infancy. Brown prepared to answer "Baby energy" to the new bystander's amazement, which was sure to turn querulous. That too was part of the process. The perpetual energy dynamo that Brown had become had its conspicuous and social responsibilities, and "baby energy" would suffice as the standard answer in stock, for predictably all the questions were the same, bystander by bystander, in an ever-standing sequence of monotony. It had become automatic. It was all so mechanically inevitable. Brown yearned to break up the process, or cut it short; but he had forgotten to wake up when critically still in his infancy yet, and now was forced to pay for such early sloth with unremitting industriousness that lasted into an endless bore, with no end in sight yet. But all work and all motion would have to stop, and this reflection had to console Brown who otherwise was so occupied that nothing could slow him down. He's still at it, and must be left to his work, for he wears reporters out whose observations for recording fall short of their subject's steady pace. Bystander replaces bystander, and still it's the same Brown whom each one observes and finally tires of. He goes on, on as before, while historians are newly recruited to be his next observers, while humanity reproduces. When will the end be, of Brown's eternal industry, until the subject is exhausted of interest, and though Brown plies on, one day he'll toil alone, with no one to notice. Other feats compel us. Brown's reality will then be actively his, but passive and still for anyone else. Even that will happen, in time.

THE INCONVENIENCE OF LIVING & OTHER ACTS OF FOLLY

To Lou Asekoff, who, though he's from Boston, really belongs to the whole world; which, were it wider, then thus much wider would his belonging's empire expand, to the very utmost universal limit, confining his wings' extent and his soul's outer barrier, which had its humble start in mere Boston.

PART ONE: AN AMICABLE SOLUTION

An Amicable Solution *(Peace over Beastliness)*

A crocodile and a hippopotamus met one dark afternoon on the muddy bank of an uncertain river. They looked each other balefully in the eye, under lids scaly with protective leather. This confrontation was timeless, for time had no meaning for either of those hidebound animals. The hippopotamus confused the crocodile for a snake. The crocodile confused the hippopotamus for an elephant that likes to travel light and so has deposited its trunk with an immovable porter. These confusions grew out of ignorance, and simply added to what they grew out of. "Good-by to your fat and thick ugliness," assured the crocodile, casting a cordial look upon the mud-baked hulk and graceless bulk of the bulging, blunt, and brutish hippopotamus. The hippopotamus was not a beast to take an insult lightly. (Not for nothing does it weigh a useless ton.) "Farewell, you sea snake stuck to a dried-up river hole with nothing slimy to slither on," wished the unpleasant hippopotamus. On that unfriendly note, those decided enemies parted, having outdone man in wisdom: war and bloodshed had not been resorted to.

How the Precious Human Instrument of Truth Failed to Survive in the Crude Accidents of Evolution

An evolutionary professor took a trip to the zoo to see who was extinct already. The animals had to line up, and a roll call was called. The surviving species were fit enough to shout "Here!" when the name of their type was called. Each survivor was able to mate and continue the respective race of his persuasion and belonging.

However, one species was dying, and its sole representative felt weak enough to have lost all the vigor it never even had. The inspector-professor, a professed zoological expert, was at a loss what to do. "Where could a suitable mate be obtained?" the analysis specified, dying out in a trail of diagnosis.

All the other zoos in the world were contacted, and the call went through into the heart of every jungle where the species in question, failing and feeble, had ever habituated. Specialists of the species, and other noted authorities in the field of that and related species, were called upon to tackle this problem and contribute however remote a key to the dim likelihood of a solution. Hope and optimism were far apart, as despair grew fat on the insoluble. The sole survivor of the species was barely extant, and too wan to have the vigor to couple, even should the miracle of a mate be produced. His prime was far past: and even *then*, he had been sedentary to celibacy, combining the abstemiousnesses of the scholar, the hermit, and the prude.

The professor was determined, against these odds, never to lose heart and give up. Even if a synthetic and artificial mate had to be devised, from a combination of nearby species, and endowed with enough sex appeal to stimulate the flagging reproductory member of the delicately venerable male survivor. It would have to be a fragile pairing: prompted, propped, and cued like a pair of fledgling actors in their summer-stock debut, stumbling on the boards.

Chemists and biologists worked overtime in relays on the project, and finally fabricated the facsimile of an approximate mate for the collapsing male survivor. She was endowed with genuine glands ripped off and grafted on from squealing slaughtered females of neighboring races allied in species to be kinfolk. However, not the slightest suspicion of incest had the fantasy to be entertained. All was in readiness, for the critical moment, when the artificial female and the ancient male would be caged in the same cage together, with aphrodisiac lighting effects and organic hormone food as stimulants. (Pornographic literature was barred, due to illiteracy.)

Scientific specialists from every animal-minded country in the known universe were flown in, shipped in, and carried in, so that the honor of their presence at this historic occasion would testify to the importance of so crucial an event in the life line of this particular variety of the animal kingdom. No sensationalist gimmick would slur the vitality of a race trying to continue itself, against the twin impediments of age and artificiality. Nature sent all its Gods to report back what happened. Notice was attracted, and a vibration of attendant attentions.

At first, the artificial female circled the antiquated male, to try to rouse the latter's incipient lust. Insipidly. Not a sip.

Next, she pounced on him, squatted on him, rubbed against him, sprayed her smell on him; and still, the indifference of impotence was his only response. She almost lost heart. But the scientists rallied her to persevere against the formidable obstacle of his stubborn, apathetic male unwillingness. A battle against futility was raged bitterly.

He fell asleep. The female was angry. It was an insult to her attractiveness.

She beckoned to the original evolutionary professor who had first concerned himself with this whole business and stirred publicity from elsewhere. She motioned that he enter the cage. And so the human obeyed. He stepped over the sleeping, senile survivor to an almost extinct race. The female excited the human, and in full view they had to couple. The result was a monstrosity, born on the spot. It began a new race, uglier than any previous: half-human, half-artificial, and beastly to contemplate.

A dangerous limit had been tempted. The line was drawn; the fates overreached.

Nature recoiled. It recalled its ambassador Gods, and broke off diplomatic relations with not only all *animal* races, but especially the *human* one, beside. "No freaks" was its policy. (Its constitution had forbidden miracles on anti-religious grounds.)

Birds were allowed to multiply, and fishes to generate, and Nature was generous with insects as well. Of course, all plant life continued. But mammals had to die, to purge the evolutionary process of that horrid attempt to resuscitate that one unfortunate species. The artificial female, so miserably contrived, was kept as a token display in the Museum of Horror. The professor and that sole surviving male were blotted out and extinct through the black bludgeon of death. Along with the human race, the other scientists were consumed, too. They had overstepped the bounds of curiosity, and for this forbidden blunder and occult taboo, were punished with blank minds incapable of pursuing the phantom of truth. And that was how truth died: Man alone had fueled it.

It had come to the end of the line. For minds had run out. Nothing remained, capable of animating that sacred abstraction in the multiplicity of worldly replicas. The extinction of truth to its reduced versions in huge hunks of act, uncommented on, perpetually unanalyzed, never doped out, yielding neither theory, nor research, nor observation. Nature was devoid of its scribe; and without record, unreported, lived only in deed. Dumb time had to do all the articulating. It merely rambled on, and babbled at Eternity. No cerebral inhibition, no verbal waste of interference, nor those high human crimes, speculation, contemplating, discussion, and education. Evolution, in the raw, plunged amorally on.

The Eaten Bananas' Revolt, and How Their Newly Devoid Gorger Becomes Transfigured

(Characters:
Two normal, un-unusual men:
But the first speaker has a fat paunch.)

I have a passion for bananas—I eat them by the dozen.
How monkey-like. Why?

It's a current obsession, till I get it out of my system.

Looks like you get them *into* your system.

Yes, that's how I get them out of my system.

How systematic.

What's systematic?

You and bananas.

What's the relationship?

Whereas *they're* eaten by *you, you* eat *them.*

The mystery is peeled away.

And stomached uneasily in *you,* I'm afraid.

Why?

You have dozens of unvomited bananas in you.

(*Defensively; on his dignity:*) Why not?! They *like* being unvomited.

So you dictatorially assume! Why not let them take a vote?

According to the democratic system?

Yes, let them get out, of your democratic system.

Into what? Anarchy? They're better off (*patting own stomach proudly, proprietorally:*) here.

(*Non-banana character disappears. Invisible bananas take his place, in remaining banana character:*)

(*From inside his stomach:*) Let us out! What do you think we are? Sardines!?

Who are you? (*Bending ear close to own stomach, which bulges:*) Aren't you part of my corporation?

We're incorporated in your corpulence.

(*Yelling down so that his own stomach cavity can hear him:*) Then how far assimilated are you?

Indigestibly.

Where do you want to go?

Out.

Front or back?

Either, but quick.

(*Sadly, to audience:*) The day has come when a man isn't even the master of his own bananas! They may be peeled and eaten; but they demand a voice! How far can self-determination go, in the *body politic*? What's good for bananas may oppose man's own interest. And I'm bigger, federally, than the bulge of bananas that prod my belly to protest. Unity means one state. What I eat enlarges me. Territorially, real estate must be respected: and *property* is no mean thing. Whatever is lodged within, must pay rent. The law is on the landlord's side, however the tenant may squawk. As an imperialist, I expand within my rights, and my bananas are blessed to be internally colonized by me. I divested them of their close-fitting jackets and precariousness to outside perils. But who'll peel *me* off of them? Let them enjoy their new homeland, their tropical coziness my capacious stomach provides. In a house is where *I* reside; but *bananas* are sheltered in *me*, their *human* house. My benevolence exercises a protectorate, for their snug security. Only that is why I had to eat them.

(At this confession or declaration, as by a signal, the bananas revolt. The character's gestures and features must mime this out. His stomach is writhing, as he lurches unsteadily, in truly physical nausea. Then, naked of their skins but otherwise whole, white, and entire, bananas begin jumping out of his mouth. [A stage illusion or tiny-seeming actors must work out this desired effect.] The bananas war-dance around their former consumer, and in common voice, whooping spritely, demand their independence. Their gorger submits, and they gleefully bounce off the stage, joyous with liberty, into the waiting wings. The character has lost his paunch, and is now very slim.)

(Admiring himself, casting mincing glances down, like a narcissistic homosexual:) I *knew* I should have dieted! What a wonderful result! *(He wiggles off. He's lost his bananas, is light-headed about it. Clasps hands ecstatically:)* Oh, all those nasty bananas! They just ravished me! Now that I'm raped, my beauty is regained, and my true shape has appeared forever! *(Slithers off, with a final half-dance, and a conspiratorial wave to the shocked audience. Curtain blushes its embarrassment down, while the audience gasps to hide its hush, or sniggers in nervous fits.)*

A Perfectly Horrible Tale, in Its Awful Truth

I was nursing a favorite tic on my face, which was breeding more of its kind and building up a nest jutting out as an independent organic unit from the mainland of my face proper. It reached the point where it ought to be pared or pruned: purged away: surgically sliced off. So I lay my face down on its unaffected side on an operating table, exposing for the surgeon's scalpel the side afflicted with this diseased tropical adjunct. But the presiding doctor took exception to the act of beginning by delaying it. There was a political peeve he had first to vent, brought to a boil by the boil-like obtrusion that I displayed as a sacrificial offer to his medicinal artistry as a cutter-out of poisonous overgrowths canceriously censurable as injurious to the corporate health body politic. He told his crew to withhold their tools till the matter of a political issue should first settle its doctrine off physical limits. The debonair doctrinaire doctor putting scruples ahead of scalpels. When my anesthesia wore off, I would hear his protest.

It did, and sluggishly I revived. "Is it out now?" I asked. "No, we let it be," said the head surgeon, "till is ironed out a political objection we have to put." "I thought this would simply be a physical matter," said I, annoyed that here I was awake with the operation still to be gone through again—by "again" meaning my being put into artificial sleep for immunity to what consciousness would have to bear under the burden of pain as an alternative otherwise. "No, we doctors have principles and beliefs; we're not mere performers." "What offense have I given your mental set?" I asked, perturbed to the bone of my innocence. The doctors sighed collectively: a fine bit of teamwork.

So far as I can make out, the objection had this official explanation: I was accused of imperialism. I had colonized an outlying facial district beyond the borders of my face proper, and was dictating its extermination without conceding to its noble resolve of becoming self-determining. It wanted its own form of government alien to mine; it was vulnerable, unprotected; unable to defend itself. I was about to declare a brutal act of aggression, before it could complete its formation into sover-eignty: proposing to wipe it off the face of my earth—or the earth of my face. This was imperialistic expansion and a ruthless brand of presumption. True, it might constitute a danger to my national mainland. But it had self-sufficiently built its own borders and virtually cut off communication with the personality of me on my side of the boundary. A border dispute had arisen by my instigation—I would be held responsible. Who was I to interfere with another's affairs?

A moral restraint would be imposed on me. My self-interests mustn't undermine others'. A bully is deprived of his powers of intimidation, in this age of liberal enlightenment. The doctors respect the right of my cyst to grow.

I was harangued with repetitional slogans, as the doctor-spokesman admonished me, threatened chastisement. Ethical principles were rudimentary, and were spelled out. The world was now free. This applied to such things as my facial growth. It had its own destiny to pursue, its nature to realize, unimpeded. I must let other powers be, however puny. It had its right to self-determination; I was obliged to restrain fire and let the division be in peace. To ravage a soil settled by others, to plunder and rape their land and denude their life resources, would be unwarranted belligerence on my part. The doctors would hold their hand from assisting my aggression in an evil pact of alliance. The colony of tics now had its own capital, with a working constitution. Let it be, however too-close-for-comfort to my national security across the border. I must respect the right of others to set themselves up. The doctors personally would guarantee the sovereignty of the new government of that overt dropsical tumor that had taken root from my native soil. The doctors declared themselves for universal peace: meaning, piece by piece, and piecemeal, the right to secede by one piece from another was protected under world constitution. As conscientious objectors with a governing body of power, they declared illegal any operation upon my facial tumor of tics either in their hospital or any other hospital whatever: and would not revoke their decision, for they were the final board of arbitration.

"But this is pathological, on the face of it," I protested. Overruled. "I might *die* of this colony that has derived its parasitical subsistence from my own raw material," I wept, officially. The doctors' mind had been made up. Though sympathetic, they had signed my death warrant. There was no further board I could lodge a protest with. And to take matters into my own hands and lacerate or lance my malignant jutting neighbor from the rooted confines of my offended flesh, in the privacy of my own kitchen with the butchery of my own stainless-steel, oven-antisepticked knife, would be a punishable criminal act, flagrantly at odds with the law handed down to me by this body of over-principled surgeons. I was no governor or guardian of a self-proclaimed unit. On authority, I was stripped of certain "self-evident" concerns. Legally, my face was no longer my own.

"But, Doctor," I moaned, "can't I even be cured of my own cancer?" "Not," I was answered, "when it violates the cancer's new-fledged nationality with territorial aggression by a big power over a little one." "But it may prove fatal!" I whined, "and then wouldn't the colony also die, since it maintains itself at the expense of my own bordering tissue?" This was a sore point. The doctors held a conference and formed a committee to report their findings after exhaustive research. Meanwhile the life was ebbing out of me. I was still on the operating theater in a patient's uniform. My life was at stake on the mainland, which I identified as me. On the face of it, the small, spawning colony was maintaining a precarious existence on its own. But it was multiplying at a robust rate. Would *it* take *me* over? That, on the face of it, was my fear. It had been granted diplomatic immunity from my delegation of chiselers who backed out from doing the job on a doctrinaire rule of pacifism. But these tics were my undoing, in their convulsive overbreeding that sapped my living vitals out in across-the-border parasitism. I was a political victim of my time. My face was being eaten up. The doctors, in whose expensively trained, precision-honed hands my very fate lay, were slowly still deliberating, with no decision yet to reverse their original, seemingly lethal one that sentenced me on their idle cooperation to a lingering death. My life was in their skilled but inactive hands. My tics were multiplying by the spasm. In their thriving, I could only reverse their bursts in my own weakening. My fragility started toward the bone.

My position was helpless, positively. It was a very negative situation. I lay there dying. The nurses, in kindly fits of compassion, sprayed my tic colony with sterilizer gas to cut down the reproduction rate. For those merciful pains, they were dismissed from employment on the grounds of "interference" by an indignant doctor-bureaucrat-spokesman for the detaining committee. My last line of assistance from distress thus being removed, I lay crippled of authority. My will was futilely devoid of motor means. I'm feebler with the pallor. A shadow steals across.

I lay fidgetly still. My tics are defacing me. My body is sending up reserves of corpuscles; but I'm being eaten up. My vital matter is being wasted and consumed by *enemy* warfare. I wish to point this out. But the rot has spread to my mouth: I'm speechless. My tongue is being dissolved: decay, cellular disintegration, is organically rife, on my facial mainland. A pestilence is sweeping its warring tides over my slowly shrouded resistance. I'm about to die by political cause. How will the doctors justify this neglect while I wither, a prey to what they protected from me? They had taken sides, and chosen to protect the lesser from the greater. The greater is now being chewed away. Upon the death of the greater, can the lesser survive? No, tics don't thrive, even in their awful independence, when the organic sleeping master ceases on the whole to be. I accuse these doctors of murder, stupidity, negligence, craven omission. How will they answer this charge?—which I can't deliver. I'm dumb, the damage is being done. I have but half a face. With what will I have left, to face my Maker? Modern medicine is my undoer—the political staying of its hand from ministering to my rooted disease, from plucking the evil matter out. I'm under physical corruption, and mentally soon begin to rot.

The protest seeps out of me, and I give in. My brain nerves stop functioning. I give vegetable permission to the doctors to continue their willful negligence. It's like signing my own demise on the dotted line, by passive consent. The prevailing political muddle doomed me. Persecuted by an age, it's for all time. Cut off by a historical phase, I retreat from history. There's no redress, for *this* injury, till death can reverse itself, and the victim come alive to vindictively prosecute his cause and seek reparations for ill done in his time and to his former bodily self. Obviously, reality won't permit this. So I stick to death with a civil tongue; an unaccusing victim. Ages have passed, where are those doctors? What state is the world in? I don't know. Revenge issues from no grave. Justice miscarried has no overturning. Fatality knows no loophole, for legal satisfaction. Victims remain in extremity. Only when in health could they have vigorously enforced their grievance. Cut off underground, they find revolt impossible, and wrongs unrectified. Retribution has no effectual plea, or voice in the matter. Life only is grounds for complaint; case dismissed and file made inactive, once life's cause is rubbed out however wrongly. Morality can only proceed from vitality. Thus I rest dissatisfied. I can air no ghost to represent my resentments. Unspoken, I'm permanently wronged. Preserved as an injured party by the grave, that's my final state. In that the case unsatisfactorily rests. The wrong done to me lives forever. Its remedy, alas, is dead.

The Collector's Aspiration Toward the Selfless Collective

Should I collect wives on the divorce plan, or children on the matrimony plan, or money on the miser plan (plus compounded investments wisely gilded on schemes of sure-fire speculation), or jobs on the quitting trail, or friends on the pumping up of gregarious loneliness, or articles obscenely laden with sexual fetish, or conquests on a deliberate campaign of eroticism, or spoons I've stirred coffee or tea with (stolen goods, hence illegal), or doctor bills, or quart bottles of all my urinatings from this day forward, or sales receipts from innumerable purchasings, or plucked hair from my belly, or newspapers saved with daily regularity so that old ones go brown or yellow and crinkle at cracked edges, or specimens of handwriting, or my observations in some notebook or journal, or cigarette butts or box tops or funny inventive names or telephone numbers or concrete memories or certified hallucinations or dusty book jackets or black dirt scraped from between the toes or wax excretions in the spiraled chambers of the ear or mucous mementos of the nose or contraceptives bearing dry flakes of moist use or facial wrinkles etched by age's delineating industry or photographs stored away in the eye's retina: —what may my hoarding compile, for fascination, ownership or baubles of minor distraction? Expense is limited; principally, I can afford almost nothing, unless it's an open free public thing, like a museum's permanent exhibit or flowers ceremonious to spring's generous shower of philanthropy lavished by God for the people's pleasure. Air, sunshine and a view of the sea—that's what I need.

But when I *get* them, do I *have* them? What testimony have I as proof of this life I've been living? Had I been an emperor, I would have hoarded kingdoms, taking dynasties away in my ruthless expansion. My naked body is only the *start* of things: I want to move outward, and take over.

I take off *my* shoes, *my* socks; I put on *my* pajamas; after brushing *my* teeth, I lie down on *my* bed, enter *my* sleep, have *my* dream. I'm possessive at the elementary level; let me carry my studies further.

My friend throws a dance party. The lights are dim for romance.

I meet one special dreamy girl. We sigh, hold hands and embark on a mutual course of reciprocal love. "I'm yours," she says. "You're mine," I say.

Now, I own a *soul*. I've caught up with the mythical legend of Mephistopheles. I'm empowered over this girl. In my hands has been placed, on trust, that key to poetic drama: the heart.

"You have my heart," she says. "So I do," I say, caressing it gently.

I gloat: It's *mine*.

One day, she says, "I'm leaving you. We must part forever."

"Come back," I plead. Too late. She's gone. The night is black and windy.

Leaves float down from empty trees. What I had, I lost. Do I now *mourn* or *grieve*? What tear is this I weep?

The vacancy in my heart. The moaning of my ghostly agony.

I call up to God. "I'm a bankrupt miser," I declare.

Lonely. I don't *have* her.

I *own* no one.

What's left? This shell of desire—me.

"I *want* her," I weep.

The world's gift in reply is: "No."

I drop dead, and only slowly revive.

What have I to acquire? What collection can console my greed?

I'd turn religious, if I thought God could be had.

My hands are open at the palms. Air drops down between my fingers.

I've been trapped: the world wants *me*, I declare.

Why struggle, if I'm only caught? I'm a minor part in a collection outside my ken. My acquisitive mania is solved: But *Whose* acquisition I am: This fills my days with wondering.

Years ago, I wrote that. Since then I sought to be owned, as a small piece in a vaster structure, a minor brick in a cosmic edifice. Mystically, I strove to be a component somewhere. The years rolled away, and today I'm brought no closer to my goal of being a greater whole's humble part. My sacrificial role of subordination has not been hired by an enclosing corporation.

What articles to clutter my cabinets' gaping accommodations? If I'm not *owned* at large (the waiting tired me out till expectation wavered and the self-abnegating ideal reverted back to the egotistic self-center), then let *me* be sun to some selected satellites. I urgently want to have. Only that would answer me what I am. Without having, Being has nothing to support, becomes insupportable, and floats loose from its moorings, an unsupported vagrant unbearably devoid of bearings or ballast.

I acquired a wife, and have children. We have an apartment with four rooms. We pay rent, but the furniture is all ours. Our wardrobe is full of clothing we paid for. The television set is ours, owned outright. And a patch of lawn is ours, thrown in by lease in the landlord's generosity. We intend to plant flowers there. (Not vegetables: a supermarket neighbors us quite strategically.) We bought toys to give the children, who soon outgrew them and wanted more advanced toys, which in turn they'll lose or destroy. Then they'll outgrow *us*, and marry out of our lives.

I have a job, in an office: I sit down at *my* desk, and in the drawers are *my* implements as a responsible functionary clerk with a department supervisory to and by myself: the drawers contain these tools of my sedentary trade: rubber bands, paper clips, pens, forms, stationery, stamps, carbons, envelopes, seals, memos, pads, files, notes, figures, accounts, stumps of salary checks, erasers, contracts, projects, manuals, references, paraphernalia of drearydom. (And *I'm* part of *other* lists in this bureaucratic hierarchy. I'm a digit figuring in a minor way in administrative tabulations and executive substructure. A dispensable cog in a set-up organizationally aloof from my soul's personal agitation.)

I'd rather do without the contents of my desk, its burdens of official miscellany and ritualistic utility. But I've got to stick to my post, though its obligations are hateful in my wage servility to them, and the money is real in every Friday's check: its power to purchase is an economic guarantee.

Monday to Friday, from nine to five, I must be there. I have to work, to support my family. I leave *my* family at home and take *my* train to work. *My* office building is tall and dull. *My* boss is remote and strict. *My* floor is functional and streamlined. *My* office is mine: abhorrent and familiar. *My* secretary is shared by colleagues from other departments who jokingly refer to her nifty legs and gloat with insinuendos of "possessing" that fictional dull girlish creature who happens to be quite married and certainly is the mistress of none of them—those bluffing, blustering, hustling bustlers with the gruff guffaws and their boom-or-bust go-ahead guff of industrious stuff and the guts not to muff it in their puffing rut.

My working day is a semi-productive service to the tyrant clock for ends of commercially gained profit by paid industry for my corporate employers in the line of big business, to keep my family going and myself as well who must be fed pure in return for being fed up with the disagreeable commitments of this routine of clerical work. I feed *myself* by putting *my* (paid for) food into *my* mouth between one and two, for that's *my* lunch hour. Then there's *my* coffee break, later in the afternoon. What's *mine* is tried and true. And found wanting.

My. Me. Mine. I. Us. Our. We. Ours.

No getting out of that. As I have and had, I'm me. I possess belongings; I belong to a family; to a larger corporation; to our living race of universal humanity, its organic tissue of cultures, that derive from all the dead.

I'm one of all who are dead and not. I'm placed, among them.

What I have belongs to me. But I belong to all, passing through family and business office to the outer world. I'm in everything; everything came from things that are lost: I'm in them, too.

What, in fact, is *not* me? I'm everywhere, in all the dead and living, all things that ever were, or are.

And those are my extensions. You see, I'm well-connected. *So* well-connected, where do *I* end, and everything else begin; or *I* begin, and all else end? With my skin's barrier? At the surface level, of clothes and hair, of shoes and face?

My family, my job, stretch outward, from me. My empire is an endless collection. I own all that owns me. We're stuck.

In a lump? But of separable parts. This, and that. Him, and her. An infinite sum's tiny separate cells, of self and stuff; cabbages, kings and cabinets.

Wholly of parts. My hands and legs are parts of me. My wife and children are parts of us. I'm part of "my" corporation. I'm history's part. I'm a part of space. I'm part of all. All is an almighty whole. It's an all-encompassing whole. It's wholly there. It's all so holy. It's a big, filled hole.

The Blood of a Dentist

My dentist pulls my tooth out a little bit at a time, on the installment plan. After years, as the root gives way, I catch up on my pain, and with the final faint, I'm all through paying. For a tip, I leave the dentist my tooth. If he continues torturing it, I privately don't care.

With the extra hole in my head (which I don't need) I rattle my brains about, adding more bite to my thoughts, and sharper ventilation. Now I'm all set.

When attacked by a steak, I chew with such vigor, my digestion is often caught by surprise. My wit is that way too. Its victims let blood, yet the sting isn't felt till years afterward.

My tongue is forked, due to an operation, and resembles a dragon or devil. The peppery words, like minor darts, spray invisible venom, which matures to a slow aging of vengeance, like the patience of a prisoner abiding his lengthy term. This serves malice, with superprofessional dispatch.

If a careless enemy ventures near my trap, I contain him in clean glass, so that his agony can be self-observed. I always donate his bones to society.

To murder beauty, I seduce their hair off women, and plant a garden of weeds on the accessible baldness. This striking note of glamour, I suppose, adds zest to the gossip columns. A photograph throws each rape to the most critical public eye. Honesty is everywhere.

Dogs and innocent cats, I let alone. Their very lack of humanity dis-candidates them from my multiple animosity. People, their hearts yet warm and bare, tempt my deepest research.

A crippled bird staggers through the air. One feather less, and his death falls earthward. The moon casts an evil beam. And I, promoting sin in my humble way, watch the cruel winds reach Halloween. The holiday plays its triumph. I relax, within lurking distance of my friendly obituary column. A smile, lacking the tooth the dentist pulled, crawls over my face like an incomplete insect. I write my sister a poison-pen letter. I sign it with a few anonymous kisses, and let the hair dry.

The ocean is extravagant. Like a sea dentist, I pull tears from my friends, to fill a fishbowl where the scrawny fish puff desperately for air. How nice to swim in a den of tears! For iniquity, I visit my tavern. The drunk bartender, verging on collapse, is my dentist himself. "Don't hyde, Mr. Jekyll," I yell. This abruptly puts him to sleep.

To amuse my raging tooth, I recall that ancient root. How nagging. My pain is loyal to me, like a dead lover whispering from her grave. I tap the tooth where it isn't, and grab hold of my dentist's leg. To ease the tickle, I remove the shoe. Then, by short jerks, I tug him wholesale out of my mouth, and swing him against the chandelier, while he drips from his foul bath of saliva. "How nice for you to have arrived!" I find myself telling him.

His life, right now, is so close to death, I can barely tell the difference. Neither can he.

Each time I burp, he winces ever so slightly. Like an immigrant in America, he is being assimilated. It takes time, and I start him through the elementary grade. His graduation is expected to take place through my bowels. To celebrate, I'll splash some perfume over his corpse. Life is chemical, and the body delights in this.

Paul's Surmised Demise and Relocated Deification

I

The ceaseless activity of the mind, which Paul called "flux," took away his interest from the world of outside matter. His friends, relatives, and colleagues worried for his sanity. They liked him well enough to care. His mind was inverting itself, and spells of unrelieved introspection reinforced his increasing remoteness from the day-by-day world. Those who knew him were alarmed at how lost he looked; as though the outside of his face was in the wrong direction and turned vacant; while the *inverse* of that blank mask got all the play and life, hidden inside.

It was morbid, unhealthy; it became the self-imposed duty of the likers of Paul to "help" him snap out of it. A trance was like a cancer: unless quickly arrested, isolated, and removed, it was likely to develop into dangerous, often lethal, stealth: at a certain point, outside help would be futile, at advanced malignity. Paul was approaching this state, it seemed. What he needed was a jolt, to wake him up. His friends rallied to the alarm.

II

The "Save Paul" campaign was in full blast. A national fund-raising organization was institutionalized out of literally nothing, as a nonprofit charity (contributions tax-exempt) for the worthy cause. Benefit performances by entertainers, musicians, and artists raked in much philanthropic revenue for the Paul Fund. However, the charity workers absconded with the proceeds of the donations, leaving Paul poverty-crippled, while his inward-dwelling absence from worldly affairs prevented the whole fiasco from registering on his sealed-off consciousness.

External sensations, which are a total assault for sane people, were reduced to a faint trickle that negligibly seeped in, for the Paul who was now receding from earth's shore into the lost, uninhabitable ocean where the vacillating hermitage of a washed-away incommunicado-bound self wailed the ever piercing dirge of solitude's rolling waste. He was too far out for people to go out after him: at first they waded, but then the breakers growled a foamy warning to keep safe. High and dry, Paul drowned in a million vacuum-suction pockets of the ocean's oasis-filled desert. He was out of sight. To locate him meant being Paul himself: which would have meant nonrecognition. So the crusade to rescue Paul gradually folded up. The world was told it would have to do without him, and make suitable accommodations. The world took it all in its stride, and overlooked him. To overlook someone who is absent anyway is as easy as nature. So Paul was hardly missed.

III

"Where's Paul?" was heard less and less. The police had been notified, and Paul had become a file case, in the Missing Persons Bureau. Cobwebs were spun over his index card, indicating the lack of an active search. His relatives, friends, and colleagues were rounded up, and told by the presiding detective that it was now legal for them to give up, so far as hope went for Paul's eventual discovery. "Now go home," admonished the detective, and the knowers of Paul dispersed, following this heartless news. The clock traveled timeward, and two years passed. By then, Paul was roundly forgotten. "Who?" would have been the reply, had his name been brought up. But remote were the chances of the name of Paul ever sounding again, unless it pertained to someone else, it being a common name, still fresh from its Biblical ancestry.

IV

One day, a rumor started that Paul had gone underground. Then began a big Paul Revival, which became a faddish cult, whose members were mostly the weird-of-mind or the vacuous young, or else those acquaintances of Paul's former days, who now put forth their claim to having known personally that legendary and disputed hero himself. Skeptics cynically protested that the *real* Paul had not been Paul at all, but someone else. These scoffers were themselves derided and offered pious rebuttal. The Paul-lovers took their hero seriously. His myth became it crusading reality.

V

The Paul Cult had spread into an organized religion. The devout testified, and swore to pious miracles performed by the Pauls of their vision when self-induced trances invited divine and occult visitations. The older religions protested, especially Protestant clergymen whose faith was stung with insult by implications of this new surge. Episcopal ministers joined indignant Catholic priests to boycott the new movement with a series of protest riots along conservative lines. Paul was called an imposter, and roundly cursed. Neutral agnostics called the whole thing a broad hoax, and poked loads of fun at the riotous dissensions. Such tumults were expensive to God's dignity; apostles mourned, while disbelievers rejoiced. The world was embroiled in a theological war, with disputing factions at crucial loggerheads in a strife of faith. It was now being whispered that Paul was a disrupting devil. Since his spurious rise to fame, see how troubled are men's principles, that had been dormant before. Paul had disturbed the peace; the blame would rest on his disciples. The world was in an uproar. Man's belief was brought into fundamental question. Religious scholars now heard their voice being heard, for the first time. Religious interest enjoyed a spectacular boost. Wave after wave of anarchy was spread by it. What had Paul wrought? Appaulingly much. Chaos threatened the known globe, and Noah's Ark made ready to evacuate, on the flood of all this controversy. Every participle of faith was now under dispute. Religion, as an actuality, was thrust into public recognition, on an equal par with such things as science and law. Like sports, art, and culture, it had come into its own. It rivaled business as an obsession. The *root* of religion was now considered Paul. Investigations were made into his origin, and institutions of inquiry were set up, with vast funds for research. Paul had even preceded mystery, said chronology experts. History was revised, pending the latest findings. Paul was being preached from every pulpit, as a Gospel-unto-Himself. Had he *ever* existed? Only sacrilege could carve that question. An inquisition rounded up cynics for a wholescale persecution. To be in awe of God was being enforced. God's new name was Paul; and a whole Myth Foundation was erected to uncover His identity. Had he ever been born? Had he never so much as died? Scholars pored into this. Even alchemy was enlisted, torn away from its obsolescence, to probe and crack the mystery. Churches were the sole preoccupations of architects, and chapels were the only other buildings going up. A wave of piety swept the planetary system. Paul was not known. But worshipped.

VI

The rage died down. Paul was posthumously crucified by proxy. That paralleled a previous martyrdom, and allowed for the cyclical nature of archetypes. Civilization made new strides. Paul was now an ancient folk hero, but more often quaintly despised as an antiquity too venerable to be disposed of. He was evaporated into Legend's miasmic Limbo, and assigned an indefinite perch among the fading fossils of archaeological predetermination, doomed to rust in a never-attended archives of undefined deities that the Faith Volcano had vomited into eruption for a certain spell and then had died down. Paul was undergoing periodic transformations in the capricious metamorphosis of popular imagery. When last heard of, Paul was an untouchable sacred cow in a society of bees, where he enjoyed a certain tribal distinction conferred on a distinct outsider. What will the Paul cycle next pursue? There's so much time left. Man is impatient, and needs new fashions. Harvey has become the latest rage. Paul is in eclipse. He had his day, had he ever known it.

The Underdog Minority of a Queue's Singular Majority

A queue is the lowest common denomination of a social unit. I'm queuing up for a certain bus. I'm the first on line. (I'm also the last, as well as all those inbetween; so you see, I bear a certain responsibility for my supremely patient constituency.) I began this long vigil around November. Now that I'm thawing, I reckon spring to be my deliverer.

What of that damned bus? Was it rechanneled to a different route, without public notification?

I stubbornly wait for it. Having already waited *this* long, I have a certain stake in this.

Has this stop been disbandoned? But the *sign* is still up. And I've been brought up to believe in signs.

No *other* bus stops here; but *their* destinations don't concern me. I remain, fixed and adamant, in my steadfast confidence that the bus *I* specialize in—that most particular of all buses—will come along, as though its schedule had been routinely fastened to with the promptitude of a public-minded vehicle. Time (out of sympathy, no doubt) has now stopped scorning me, and taken *my* side in this tussle.

Across the street, a building is torn down. When I *began* my queuing, it was entered in and exited from (by the door, of course) with a certain frequent regularity.

While waiting for my bus, I've seen the political atmosphere change. Under all these topical mutations, the weather has remained variably at odds with my distress or convenience. It's been a dependable bitch—fickle, but abiding.

It's a two-way street I'm waiting at. Thus my monotony is diverted by both directions at once—and equally in vain. Who needs such symmetry?

Pretty girls promenade on the sidewalk. Their high heels beat a stacatto rhythm.

I would chase them; but I wouldn't take the risk of missing my bus. So I forgo romance, with its wayward distractions.

Near this desolate bus sign, there's a haberdashery store. Clearly through the window, the proprietor has been noticing me.

He interrupts business, out of pity. He goes up to me. "I've been noticing you," he begins. "You're waiting a long time. Your faith in public transportation is touching. You stick to your post, with duty or like a mission. You'd be the ideal shop clerk—selling my goods behind the counter. I *need* someone with your low metabolism. You're hired: begin work at once."

I turned down the offer, saying that I had a bus to catch. Though he didn't argue, he *did* call me a sucker. Now he spies on my waiting. He's a nuisance.

On the beat, there's a regular policeman. He passed me so often, that now we're on the familiar terms of nodding. This gives me a glow of seeming to be protected. Who knows when I may need the law's friendly support?

The bus is due, any minute now. And *has* been, for the last six months.

Once it arrives, I'll get on. No sense waiting for another; my motto is grab opportunity the minute it pulls up; no telling *when*, or *if*, this sly thing will dare approach again.

Group Thinking's Fashion in Motion; My Individuality, Never Catching up, Remaining Far Ahead. The Compass Will Point to Where I Haven't Strayed. *That* Will Be the Direction, Soon

I wasn't prepared for the mass awareness that suddenly took place. The most recent one had been three months before, and infected all the people at once in a mental contagion of the populace.

Some ideas, that start out quite modestly, without any presumptions, suddenly find themselves galloping into proportions of an epidemic landslide; and can't be arrested till all the conformity-brains carry them fashionably in their vogue at once.

However, *I'm* always slow off the mark. What's simultaneous for others is in my case retarded into the backwards of delay. When I finally catch on, the rage has already died down. By then, something new is in the air: that I'm ill-prepared for.

My slowness equips me as an eccentric and provides my tardy excuse. The fashionable conformist people consider me a cretin. This makes *them* look good. At my expense as a fool.

To be behind in *clothing* fashions is not such a crime, since everyone knows that clothing is more superficial than ideas. The *real* conformists value idea-conformity as much more deeper the real thing than mere clothes or hair style or popular songs or where the smart ones go on their holiday or the latest sports team to be on the bandwagon of, or such immaterial matters as taste in art or music or what novel "everyone" is reading.

Today, everyone was electrified by the most radical of political convictions, which spread like the proverbial wildfire to inflame the dull, dry timber in everybody's sawdust-crinkly lumberyard. It was the fashionable thing to be a flaming revolutionary and go so far as to advocate the overthrow, if that's not going too far, of the Government itself; as well as to distrust the Constitution its authority has been established on.

Three months previously, the "in" thing to do was to be so conservative as to be living reactionaries totally dead to progress.

All the liberals, then, quickly switched from that conservative rage of three months ago, to the revolutionary one of today. They wouldn't get caught between in the lurch; they were hysterical to latch on before the forerunners, pacesetters, or avant-gardists had been first, right off the mark, in the wild surge or rampage to beat the stampede by staying in front. The liberals had their minds geared to these outside fluctuations, supersensitive to the slightest turnover in wave lengths, which they anticipate and join in the bud. They're so clever! But not me, I'm dull.

So there I was. I had let my reactionaryism (now dreadfully obsolete, déclassé, outmoded) of the previous plague set in as I took it to heart, and it had hardened in my mold, for I was a sluggish type. But my swiftly flexible, durably adaptable comembers of my tribe's race were now busy protesting and demonstrating that the current Administration needed to be torn down, and the corrupt system that had fostered it must be destroyed without the slightest hesitation, since qualms or scruples were the inner psychic spies in the pay of authority's corrupt regime. Debates, deliberation, judicial soul-searching, skeptical procedure, critical disputation, were only the stalling tactics to keep off the Inevitable mired in the shackles of a scorched-earth delay. But the Day was at hand, just like the Day of Judgment, the Second Coming, Doomsday, or the End of the Earth. Those exclusively in the know, the smart ones, anticipated it with a glad hand. It isn't every day that Retribution arrives for all time.

It was only a passing fad. But I missed that one, entirely. I hadn't joined in. I was laughed at. I was still a reactionary.

Now time has gone by, the pendulum has swung. What I got stuck with in my slowness of getting off the mark, mass awareness is reapproaching. It will be resumed as the new rage soon.

I'm far ahead of the game. I'm there already. Let all the rest catch up.

While they were running around, I was staying. What foresight I had! In time I was right.

A Vulnerable Temple to Mars

An honorably traditional country has an extended history of noble warfare; therefore one of its most prominent buildings is a centrally attractive War Museum. Only pacifists consider the contents of this public building to be sinister, morbid, ugly, and dispiriting. For their opinions they risk jail sentences, public censure, and subcitizenship.

On exhibit are the army and navy uniforms from the modern present back along retrosuccessive epochs of each military and naval generation to the land's pre-national foundation as a primitively ferocious tribe of ranging warriors whose communal rites belligerently practiced pagan excursions as looters, marauders, plunderers, and savages that scalped and maimed and whose vocabulary was unburdened by the word "mercy."

These barbaric beginnings are now replaced by a supercultivated war machine civilized by the polish of the latest instruments. Such refinements speed culture along the path first dug out by ancestral rapacity. War's course has a reactionary precedence.

This republic has adopted Mars as its presiding genius. Strife is its harmony, and foreign discord quickens its unified pulse to dis-individualized solidarity. A surge of nationalism is anthemed on each tongue. Pride stirs a consensus of one people.

The collective temple is visited.

The War Museum features both domestic and enemy weapons, and boasts an outstanding collection of captured trophies and metallic mementos of lethal dastardliness. The evidence is on show of a valiant record of combat. Hall after hall echoes the thunderclap of a bloodbath. Each era fashioned a similar result, draining manpower's fodder-blossom in valleys far or plains up close.

War was this country's chronic profession. Victory was preferred, but defeat was better than peace.

But peace there would have to be, to rejoice, mourn, and prepare. To repair, to plot, and to declare.

The peace interludes were for recouping courage; stepping up recruiting tactics or inducements to allure enlisting; exchanging obsolete armaments for precision-improved ones engineered along a streamlined economy primed to pump destructive potency to a more crusading peak; revamping the officer staff according to a fair system of merit on an ascendant scale of ability; purging softly malartistic doves and hailing harsh hawk extremity; accelerating training procedure; multiplying munitions stock; rationing harmless leisure pampered by the void created by no war effort to enforce; escalating the pinch of discipline; lifting patriotic morale by factual propaganda; maintaining diplomatic severity and installing tactless ambassadors; imposing stiff demands and competitive ultimatums on offensive countries as part of a "get-tough" campaign of anti-foreign policy; domestically providing for a "peace-doesn't-pay" principle by setting up slumps and economic hard times to depress peaceful enthusiasm and create an unprofitable recession for which war is the sole solvent remedy and sovereign unemployment cure to stimulate some nasty business; rewriting history to whip up the desired outlook with scores to settle on a weighed scale of revenge; promoting the self-superiority myth (violated by natural enemies: made right by the exercise of a dire might). Peace was a great phase of war, with a depleted casualty list and a fortified manpower register. The chieftains discussed strategy, in the prestigious aura of secrecy; the fatal balance of the next tribal deaths was staked toward the ensuing justified murder on a mass selective scale honored by an international protocol and witnessed by the most talented journalists whose awe and horror are transcribed for syndicated millions to read and other millions to hear at the grey-and-white picture box with its conveniently informative magic to lull suspense and control impatient anticipation. Peace was a marvelous drawing-in of breath. The War Museum was scoured and a more imposing arrangement was devised by its slightly diabolical curator. The *last* war was given space priority in the main hall, for memories were fresh about it; even children still imagined it and played with bright toys commemorating it: camouflage-blurred tanks, leaden guerrilla troops, gleaming aircraft carriers, smoked-up bombers releasing reluctant parachuters, slinky submarines about to spring the torpedo loose like a bee poised at the sting. Wonderful diversions!—a practical education for the very young, and a booster to realistic fantasy to regulate imagination by a right and tight degree. Symbolically, the museum substituted for the actual thing, during an armistice-tedium. Treaties would be negotiated, pending the resumption of hostilities on a more liberal scale and on fresher terms, perhaps against new enemies. The future contained fascinations, barely hidden from sight. A "prophecy" wing of the War Museum speculated on the rich tidings that loudly waited for fate to explode. Live and see.

For the little girl visitors, the museum exhibited generations of war nurses: dummies bearing fashions that the ages varied. And the Home Front was represented by suitable showcases of patriotic endeavor in factories and other key places.

Aging visitors, caned and stooping, were veterans misty with nostalgia. They had performed their heroism at the front, and an amputated leg or arm would occasionally prove it, or the muted crutches worn blandly by the blind whose fingers "read" the cannon surface and the dive bomber wing. Each day was Inspiration Day, in this popular museum. The Soul of the nation resided there.

The Medal Room is like a colorful butterfly collection. Boys who wander in there come staggering out puffed high with a dream's mighty incentive. Glory's a sufficient self-reward, but a medal confirms it, glittering a conspicuous rarity; the bulging chest it's worn on owns a surface gleam beyond the interior wealth of a merely technical heart that pumps red blood to supply limbs armed in national defense. Honor earned by war swaggers a brave deed about, and girls hang on admiringly. Soldier, sailor, marine, or pilot: the ego's splendor is war's heroic gift.

Movement's City

There's a certain city that is where it is, so that, were a person to come to it, he'd have to arrive from afar; for afar is where most of the people are, it being why this city is "out of the way." Well, one day, the city got tired of waiting for people to come to it; so it put on ball bearings under its collective feet and got rolling. It simply traveled to where the people are. Its fame grew as the first of the mobile cities. Other envious cities emulated by also donning wheels. But literally, they got nowhere. This city was the first and only one to travel to people, somewhat like a huge portable bus. The people who hoped to be visited by it queued up at various stations along its rumored way. The city would come along and stop, and the passengers would get on, much to the gratification of the moving city's jolly chamber of commerce, whose fees for boarding tourists and other transient visitors kept parity with rates of residential transport. Soon, the city grew new features. Its church spiral, for example, lost its vertical quality and took a horizontal position for the sake of a streamlined effect, belonging as it did to a shifting community the constituency of whose parish had a notably vagrant turnover. Hotels in this city tended to be one big motel, since what's a city if you can't sleep in it? (Dreams must pivot on a still basis.)

Now, most cities have a *site*, such as with mountains nearby, or on a plain, or by riverbanks. Well, this city continually shifted its site, depending on where it was going at the time and also in what direction along the different ways. The city would pass many landscapes and not a few seascapes, in its versatile ability to have an unsettled location. In the city hall, the Board of Aldermen said, "This city is going places!" How right they were.

But there were some dissenters, especially among the Division of City Planners (part of any cosmopolitan bureaucracy). "We want permanent roots!" their spokesman said, "we want to *be* visited, and not abjectly have to beseech people to become our citizens by going out of our way in this relentless pursuit of, and search for, them. Besides, a city's dignity is befouled by too many transients and not enough rooted natives who may breed, and be bred by generations loyal to a family tradition of locality. Where is the sense of a *community*, if the ground is always shifting under our feet? Nor are we developing a respect for the land —for *one* land; a symptom of this is that our agricultural industry has fallen off. Our farmers feel a sense of futility; the land is slipping from under their feet, which is insecure for purposes of plowing. We're going too far with ourselves. We're not even the same nationality any more; we're just flowing through countries and discarding them, as a ship discards the waves that bounce off its prow. I say we must stop! It's time to conserve. We *must* slow down. And rebuild roots, for national identity, for cultural stability, and for our general solidity as one unified people. Otherwise, we're not goin' anywhere, by being in too many places in too short a time. I profoundly believe that we should always be in the same place. On this, I take my stand."

This dissenter was applauded at a municipal meeting; yet the city, in flux, continued to travel.

Despite such reactionary views as that projected by the travel-disparaging city planner, the city remained gathering no moss, like a brilliantly peopled stone whose rambling rolling kicked up many breeds of foreign dust and a heroic sense of homelessness. But then it happened: the citizens of the city became homesick! They were homesick for the very city they were in, merely because the city itself was not situated anywhere, in its strolling capacity to wander site in site out, bewildering the dweller with too multiple a passing sight. But, "This will pass," they said, referring to their moving brand of homesickness. On they went, this landless community whose home spread into a divergence of many wayward extensions, expanding everywhere in a homeless radiance far from that central myth known by legend to be the dream of home. It was an international city; the shops sold motley goods, even those who boasted specialties of the homegrown domestic nature; as for the "wine of the land," it just couldn't be bought. The city gradually grew to be without features, a bland assortment of nondescript internationalism ever so vaguely "modern," as a descriptive appendage. Everywhere it goes, the city changes its mayor, to suit the new climate—of opinion, as well as of weather. "Where are we?" is the most constant question asked by one citizen to another. It soon proves unanswerable.

Like the Wandering Jew, or the Man without a Country, or Odysseus straining to return to Ithaca and being buffeted by perverse Neptune in nautical distress, this city roams the world, in a weary round of roads and ways. Forward-seeking engineers have even installed sails, and the wooden bottom of a boat, so that seas may be transgressed. Not even the air is an obstacle. Aeronautical engineers have fitted the city with jet-like wings and immeasurably ample propellers, for vast mileage of cosmic flight, of such height that moonward rockets endanger national security. The proximity, during these excursions, to the sun has provided the citizens with a characteristically uniform tan. This stimulates sex appeal, and boosts the birth rate.

Should the city be so minded, it's converted with prefabrication into a roving submarine, the citizens being forehandedly equipped with facial outfits essential to breathing (globular glass masks and sturdy bubble tubes). Nests of fish are thus explored by those whose curiosity is so inclined, as well as seaweed rotting for ages on the earth's sunken bed. Science is the main item of the city's education, since field research is so accessible.

Archaeological expeditions are also invariably frequent. The city has a nose to knowledge, unearthing rough-and-ready facts with frenetic aptitude.

All the inhabitants of the city are fat. This is because they take their civic motto seriously: "Travel is broadening."

There are certain immigration quotas. Only those to whom these restrictions apply may apply. This is the most velocity-prone melting pot that has ever sizzled with various racial types. Every single citizen is a proven foreigner. And all the *other* citizens, as well, are unproven foreigners. Nevertheless, national pride continues to thrive.

Racial supremacy is their outstanding myth. This city considers itself not only as a nation (a republic), but as a distinct race in itself. Their motto in this regard is: "The race is to the swift."

So they accelerate motion. With a suffocating momentum, this mobile city races along its widening career. Only pilots or navigators are now considered for mayor. The city is roving so fast, that policemen don't even need horses or autos. Just by standing still, they're on the scent.

Hospitals accompany the rest of the city. So the bedridden go along for the ride, and are known as traveling convalescents, whose nurses and doctors maintain their infirmities on a line known as progress. Germs are swift as air, and disease progresses with keen swiftness along its mortal voyage. But its opponent, Recovery, sails on just as rapid a cycle.

This traveling city has a built-in railroad complex. All the tracks are laid out, along routes to their devised stations. Yet the bulky trains themselves are missing, the better so that this entire city will not be impeded by the extraneous weight of engines, locomotives, and puffing passenger cars.

It's hard to conduct horse races here. Since the city itself moves, how can the relative speed rates, on an interior track, of competing horses be assessed? Thus gambling is not a daily crime.

This city has a built-in historian. He charts its progress. Gradually, he's growing old. The son he's training (to replace himself with) is also aging, but at a more retarded pace, for his start in life was ever later and quite secondary in order of precedence.

The stock market, on this moving city (when seen in time's course), fluctuates. Bears and bulls seem to go through slow motion, since the city that comprises their zoo is ever on the go.

The official geographer of the city had such a protracted nervous spell that the destined result became insanity. He was driven mad by the city, and everybody was moved to tears on faces fraught with motion.

Gravity operates in a funny way on this city. Objects descend obliquely, since a horizontal propulsion serves as a lever for a sideways kick. Throw a ball up in the air: then watch it float away.

Games are dizzy on this island. Their scores are mostly improbable. Victor and defeated feel, equally, in the same boat. Democracy somewhat softens their competition.

Once, civil war gripped this city. It was torn by two rates of progress. Gradually, one rate prevailed.

Women's fashion is daily altered, or by the minute. Women are continually taking off their clothes and putting new ones on. Inbetween, men document the rhythm, or punctuate the intervals between dressing sessions, by lying on top of women's exposed nudity until spasms deplete the masculine superimposed resources. Fashion throws everyone into a continual state of excitement. Sexuality is no mean product: there's always a rush on, to the nearest fornication booth.

On the city there's one morning newspaper, and one evening (afternoon) newspaper. Their circulations spiral at quite a descent or ascent. Each boasts readership. And both are headlong in a far-sighted liberal approach, too radical to make stability certain. Their plights reflect the insecure foundations on which the city is unsurely grounded in its tendency to be so consistently in motion that even movement itself moves, as may be seen on film, where the camera imposes reels on different tracks, making the observer reel off his track and cluttering his clarity with clear-cut confusion. Art itself verges on disintegration, for too many molecules divert the compound's unity.

The citizens of the city are afflicted with moving sickness. The body politic can't even stop for the body private to vomit in peace by the roadside. The scene is cursed by a lack of fixity. Motion retards progress, stagnating in a puddle of stillness.

The old and the infirm look for peace. Where is the one immutable fixed horizon, a gauge to measure other motions by, such as the friendly old sun's? So common is movement in this city, that bowel movements observe regularity, abashed in their backwardness. The city moves, but the globe it moves on also moves. And the firmament on which the globe hangs has its own motion. The air swims in oceans of movement. Breath is devoured by lungs, and impelled forth again. This is the roundness of the roving cycle.

A flood of citizens emigrate to stiller lands. They long for one steady view of peace. Experience has taught them an aversion to change. They search for the stationary, though placid and unvital. They seek out the tree-like city that never moves.

This city makes haste. Birth outspeeds death, so the city builds upper tiers and levels to place the excess. Catacombs of underground cemeteries convey the buried, through tunnels of gloom and channels subterraneously conductive of flesh-stripping, on the same path as the hurtling live citizens themselves who pursue their commercial obsessions on vital terrain. Dead and living plunge through similar ozone, a mutual joy ride on a vehicle transporting them through rapid zones of oblivion. Boundaries and dimensions are no obstacle. Time is merely a temporal metaphor for that misplaced and rapidly-trampled-over element, space. Clocks are confounded timekeepers, in this city. Their ticking consumes our eternities.

This city mourns its excitizens, who emigrated to distant lands on passports forged by desperation and visas of surpassing tempo. Movement cancels itself by being incessantly in the same state. Thus, and ultimately, it's employed as a reactionary factor; for it stunts *true* progress, as the invariable protagonist for having things arrested to a course monotonously in motion. Motion being a phase, in the process of our steady wending into the unhurried stillness of a truth.

On mountain slopes, the city wears skis. It glides on snow toward a southern spring. It roller-skates across meadows. Its continuity is diversely unbroken.

It cruises over flowerbeds, completed above by mountainous clouds. It makes an international tour of nations. The city can't be reached; one must be reached by *it*.

You who long for this city: Wait. It comes by, prodded on by the boredom you reek for the place of your habitation, the pit of gloom where your doomed dwelling sits. In time, the city passes by: Board it.

In it, you're transferred. Transportation transports one's self to new scenes of identity. On many tides rests the motion on which existence lives at its various peril. Leaving certainty, the city is on a traveled route for suburbs of Mystery, the site destined as that one brilliant dot of blackness where the journey of a city's passage may put in at a peaceful port. Where motion has solved the sore loss of a former womb.

The city roars through space. Drunk with their dizzy flight, interchangeable citizens romp at a temporary rate. They're replaced in the course of a curving purge, and those newly born board this vessel of curiosity. Dust, kicked up behind, provides dew for the return rainbow; maps are fertilized by matter, to maturely contain the chugging of this city's motor. Such municipal purity, charged in energy's ounce of motion! A city's colossal weight, converted by winged wheels to the lightness speed spends for drawing far bounds of space dearly near, details refueling the fickle freshness of eyes sated by any slow dose of hesitating immediacy. The city's policy is a resuming state of change so multiplied, sameness roams a versatile field. Horizons are hauled inward, and no bounds may confine. No relative distance can exist as an outpost to the absolute; space is colonized for an empire, absorbed in a city's expanding fury. Infinity is next, in the imperial destination.

And is soon overtaken. Now what's expected, but eternity's conquest in consequence? First *local* time is slaughtered; *middle* time is flanked, and soon annihilated; and our city wars on death itself! Can God, with His obsolete weaponry, campaign a successful resistance? No! Time is soon dispatched, and brought to a city's mercy. And all ancient secrets are brought to their knees. Nothing remains, in the mercurial onslaught of knowledge's total penetration! What trophies soon, for the central library!

The See-Gooder

A satirist criticized humanity. His barbs were wicked and witty. He made foibles seem like vices, and his cunning craft transformed virtues into foibles. He reduced mankind to its average worst, at its mean lowliest.

Then, he himself was criticized, subject to counter-satire. His vitriolic self-defense only set off such blasts of vituperative venom in retaliation by his vindictive enemies, that now he does nothing but praise humanity and laud its graceful excellences found in each member of the population. His praise is a famous reversal.

Now, everyone likes him. He's known for having a "positive attitude," which goes well with a "constructive outlook." He's accorded much honor, and has won the respect of all.

He's quoted as saying, "Man is wonderful." This creates great rejoicing in the land.

And everyone remarks an obvious tone of happiness in this reformed man whose "no" has violently assented to "yes." Wherever good may be found, he sees it.

And where no good is, he creates it, in gracious artifice, as a generous fiction he believes in. Heaven intends to reward such fantasy.

PART TWO: THE ECHOES OF UNREQUITAL

The Echoes of Unrequital

Two people met for the first time. They parted, but only briefly.

Soon after, they met again. Before they parted *this* time, they took care to arrange an appointment. When they met the third time, then, it was deliberate on both their parts.

The meetings were now becoming pretty regular. But while one of those friends loved the other, the one loved did not also love the one who loved.

So they parted company, forever. One did all the remembering while the other did all the forgetting. Before they began, they were two. After they ended, they were three: the one who remembered, the one who was remembered, and the image of the remembered one, held in the memory of the one who remembered.

A century later, all three were dead. But two graves served for the three of them.

Eternities went by, one after another, in succession. For economy's sake, the three were now none.

Later, the none continued to diminish. It's even less than none, with increasing negation. But the three parts still seek each other, in the magnetic circuit of the dark. Lacking substance in the ultimate physical depth, they grope in the metaphysical. Their interrelationship, unresolved, craves some absolute clarity of definition.

Kathy, Both Seen and Heard. Felt, to a Consuming Degree. I'm Devoured. She Swallowed Me Deeply in. So Far in, I Know Her Own Recent Experiences, Like They Were My Own.

Kathy is so cute and large. I can swim among her furless skin. There are deep folds of warmth, packed in there.

When she speaks, Mendelssohn tumbles out of the clouds, to resume the piano that's always waiting for him: a costly pearl of a piano, specially guarded, attended by two retainer-like servants that his old family hired last century just for this occasion. The occasion arrived. The piano too: practically flew in. Installs itself, right here. Stool and all.

Kathy speaks. There's Mendelssohn, to accompany her. His hands fly and alight, fly and alight (white cuffs brilliantly gleaming from his starchy black dinner jacket), all along the black and white keyboard. It's perfect timing. Kathy's white teeth flutter, her tongue darts in and out like a dragon-turned-lizard. Her speaking is in counterpoint, as Mendelssohn sings the piano, he spanks it into song. Then, with a long wail (Kathy is left speechless, at this), it goes tumbling away—that huge, open piano. The two ancient retainers are shocked, and disappear. The stool is elsewhere.

Mendelssohn's foot is caught in the pedal bar. He slides along the bright, slick floor, with its ballroom polish. His shoes are matchless, from his expensive family, but old, like last century.

Kathy has stopped speaking. Mendelssohn has become the apparition he was before. Silence gleams audibly. It sparkles, like Kathy.

Kathy leans forward. As she kisses me, her breasts grow bulge-ier. I hug them, if I can.

I hang on. I kiss her. I'm spun deep. I'm like a dwarf. She's swallowed me. I make myself at home. Turn on the radio. Make coffee, stir it with a spoon. All, inside Kathy. Inside her. She's recently had a Mendelssohn experience. So I'm being entertained, in her musical home.

She joins me there. We make a domestic couple. She's wearing an apron string. (But where's the apron?) A bowl of flowers smells sweetly. We dance in harmonious song. Inside Kathy, Kathy and I live a great life, together.

Were We Destined to Meet? Or Was It by Accidental Chance? Our Having Met Reconstructs Our Meeting into an Inevitable Past. It Erects the Certitude of Retrospect.

It seems as though we were made for each other: but only now that we have actually met does it seem so. If we had never actually met, it would never have seemed so.

Similarly, if one had never actually been born, he would never have been, no matter how much his "being" seems so natural, inevitable, necessary, determined, real, unmistakable, definite, true, complete, and actual. For all this to seem, he first had to be born. Only much later do we accept it with "of course." "Of course" is a property of aftersight, of retrospect. Time makes a miracle commonplace, an odd chance fore-destined, an accident regular. First something must come into being, for it to "seem" right. And once right, it could "only" have been right. Only the reality of something can confirm the possibility of that thing ever emerging into the being of real. First a thing must be partly or wholly past, for it ever to be seen as in the first place "being." Its pastness is a confirmation. Till then, it almost never was.

* * * * *

We were made for each other. But we only conceive this as a result of an almost inconceivable thing: our meeting.

"Our meeting" made it all legitimate. Before that, there was absolutely nothing like it was afterward. There was not even a single clue. There was no "fate."

We met. Therefore it seems we were always fated to.

It abruptly happened. *Then*, fate took its course.

United by the Chance of Destiny

In order to be, Sid had to be born. Thus it came to be.

The star of a destiny was born with him. His true love was to be Charlotte. But the maker of the destiny omitted the guarantee of an essential factor: the maker had not arranged the preparation of the *meeting* of Sid with Charlotte: this had to be left to that nest of improbables, the vagaries of chance.

Charlotte's birth, a few years later, was attended by the reciprocal, but equally difficult, destiny: that of her true love being Sid. But again, puckishly, the maker of her destiny had made no provision for just how and when they were to meet: it would be buffeted about by the cruelty of chance.

Thus Sid and Charlotte, apart, were separately doomed to unhappy lives until the accident of their meeting. At least they were both in the same city. But so were millions of others.

Being both in the same city eased the problem considerably: eliminating a lot of extraneous searching in cities apart.

But the combination of events required to have their paths cross was a miraculous impossibility. Would their meeting *ever* come to pass?

Without Charlotte, whom he never met, Sid was sad. He grew up sad. So did Charlotte, not knowing why. She had a vague need, undefined. If she only knew—it was for Sid. She hunted around, not knowing quite for what. Her destiny was to find Sid: but it was up to her and Sid to do it. Innocent blind stumbling.

Each had come to the age of it being natural to mate. Family pressures were brought to bear on both of them, to hurry up and marry. It was past time, already. Social pressures were brought to bear too. All the people

Charlotte knew urged her to find a beau. And in Sid's social circles, likewise for him to find a girl and settle down. But destiny helped Charlotte resist, and Sid to resist; each kept himself free, for the destined meeting with the other. But the perverse flaw in their destined meeting was that destiny left it to chance. Each would scour the city. But how big that city was! And people, people, always in their way: floating between them: keeping them apart.

"You're so eligible," Sid was numerously told, "good-looking, with a good job, excellent prospects, healthy habits; but yet you're not dating any girl. Are you degenerate? What are you saving yourself for?"

"What are you saving yourself for?"—those very words—was constantly being asked of Charlotte, in the parts of the city *she* frequented. She'd hear, over and over again, versions and refrains of the following: "You're quite a young beauty. So many business executives and rising young managers would, upon exposure to you, like nothing better than to make you their Missus. You're always being asked out but you always refuse. Your restraint suspiciously smacks of the disciplined mortification and self-denial of one about to take her holy vows as an aspiring Christian nun. Yet you're no churchgoer, so why not let a little romance enter your life, with its attendant prize of sex? What are you saving yourself for? Prince Charming? A prince imprisoned in the body of a little frog or toad, for you to liberate? Are you wasting your youth over a fairy tale?"

This was the standard criticism Charlotte had everywhere to submit to. *For* what was she abstaining, from a normal woman's role?

Other women resented her. They read her solitude as an implied criticism of their own careers of promiscuity and feminine normality. Charlotte's purity was a reproach—they were laden with guilt before her immaculate example.

So life was being tough on Charlotte. Hints, broad and subtle, bombarded her with increasing dosage. But she would be led solely by her destiny—though vaguely it hadn't declared itself yet, in its clarity of a specific aim. She kept faith to it—ignoring, as best she could, the meddlesome busybodies who dared prescribe what her fate should be. She kept only an *inward* counsel: a patient devotee of an obscure spiritual destiny. One day the message would be dropped—like fruit (not too overripe?) from the bending bough. Fruition and reward. But first, patience.

Forbearance. Old-fashioned virtue. And she acquired the reputation of a prude. Tongues wagged around her—Charlotte was repressed, had had a Freudian fixation upon her own father, leading to premature sexual arrestment. Studs and bucks and rakes flocked to liberate her. But Charlotte's prim "No" had an absolute finality about it—even a cynic had to submit to it. All that beauty wasted! And not even for religion! What was the secret? Charlotte confided to no one. A big guessing game surrounded her.

Sid, in *his* parts of town, had an equal mystery's aura. It was alleged that his aloofness from sportive gaiety with women owed its reason to impotence. But how was that to be proven? Girls had fallen for Sid and tried to entice him: he remained cold. Was he a eunuch with a lacking member? Or a fornicator of men and boys belonging to his own masculine gender? Was he psychotically repressed, confounding his sexual powers in a deep emotive paralysis? He was the subject of conjecture. Rumors spun. But he confided to no friend. He had given himself to a destiny. He was heroically dedicated. In his dedication, he underwent personal sacrifice, puzzling to any outsider. To willfully deprive himself could be considered as nothing but irrational. His mystery grew to a legend. Women were moved to tempt him. In vain.

Sid was a challenge for a woman to test her beauty on; as Charlotte became the sought-after darling prize of a succession of Don Juans who in her met their first failure. The legend of Charlotte grew. It fanned out. It mingled with the brother-legend of Sid. The impenetrable city now grew smaller, to encompass their twin legends. Fate doomed them to meet. Their starved destiny stood poised and whet on their being brought together. It was coming close, to happen.

One cloud swept them up, both. It dropped them into a close embrace, dangled huddled from its fated bosom where they had been mutually enclosed. Ambassador angels swooped down from heaven, to consummate destiny's plan with all due pomp and ceremony, bearing that high official blessing that dignifies anything destined. Destiny had its triumph. Sid rejoiced, in her; Charlotte, in him. Their joint destiny had been engendered, and fulfilled. A meet theme for song. A fit toast, at their full-some feast.

Heaven's lavished its best, on these, who by circumstance discovered each other. They had to do it themselves. It's no illusion what they accomplished. Mortal credit is given them, having assisted divine destiny through self-abnegation, trial, endurance, and faith. They took destiny's part, with effort. In them, destiny rests. They act it out, in ease. They're met. They stay put. Divorce can't touch them. They're too well-joined. Sundering contents itself with more flimsy pairs. Charlotte is Sid's; Sid is Charlotte's. The chance struck. By chance in one city, destiny had her match. Destiny rounds out the pair; in sweet but permanent retirement; unobtrusive; with them: the welcome mother-in-law, or the matchmaker whose reward is a modest lodging with the couple joined.

The anti-destiny, Death, grows ominously into view. Its cloud broods the final darkness, enlarging. Its power will prove too much for marriage. "How" is by casual chance. Time aids it.

They'll die singly, not together. They had worked for constructive destiny, and brought its achievement into being. Ahead looms destruction. They borrow courage from love, to face it.

Legs; and Why Not?
(*Where They Jointly End: Where the Joining Juncture Is Enjoined to Join, Jointly Enjoyed, and Disjointly Deployed*)

My girl has *matching* legs.
Then do you set fire to them?
Well, I use them as friction, the primitive way, to ignite my *own* little

matchstick, at its combustible tip.

Is the flame safe?

Sure. It soon goes out.

Oh good. I *hate* conflagrations.

(*Interval.*)

You said your girl had thin legs?

Not the slightest. Why?

But they're like matchsticks, you said?

No. They match up, and there's a place to stick. But the matchstick is *mine*, from the friction her legs provide.

Fiction? Then you're not telling the truth.

Anyway, I sigh at the size of my girl's thighs.

Do you pant, as well?

Yes, they're nice in her pants, as well.

Oh well, that's swell.

Yes, they swell at the top: what *ends* well, *is* well.

(*Interval.*)

Are they thick and round as well?

They're not thick and round as a *well*; but by God, they really *spread* at the top!

Really! That's cheeky of her.

And when she's slapped, she turns the other cheek.

She uses her rolls of flab to enact a meek role.

What an inheritable piece of earth, she is!

Then do her legs *converge*?

Yes. Infinite parallels are a bore, so far as sex goes.

Yes. Begin two lines at a right ankle and left, till they curve high and come to a meeting point.

Otherwise, copulation doesn't have a leg to stand on.

No. It needs two, befour it lies down.

And four, two do what it has two do.

Yes. Always for an end.

Two ends, and to make them meet.

But ends were *always* meat.
But raw, till brought to the boil.
How inflammatory!
Ah! One man's meat is another man's person.
Personally, I love to fry my meat, and watch it sizzle.
Well, agreed she has stout legs?
That's a point on which I wish I were in a greater concentric harmony.
Well, *visualize* her, as *long* as it's not in the flesh.
It *is* long, that's the trouble. Tell me, do you rise to her occasion?
Occasionally, I do rise, and so disappear.
Out of sight, you go?
From the *outside* view, yes.
Oh, that *is* intimate!
When you get down to it, what else is there but intimacy?
But how do her legs keep from falling off?
I screw them down in tight.
Tight and fast?
So fast, they can't run.
But her *stockings* run.
Oh, they're off.
You mean off and running?
I barely get your meaning.
Well, legs have to end *somewhere*.
Better there, than not at all.
Of course. Unending legs would make infinity unpleasant.
Yes. Infinity should climax herself.
But then it turns finite.
Ah! It must end *somewhere*.
Yes, at the sum of all wares.
(*Interval.*)
But don't legs *begin* at the top, rather than end there?
I care about the end result, to begin with.
Then have you a theory of shapes?

Yes, I shape my theories according to the legs they measure.
Oh. Then you get down to cases.
Legs, really. Uncovered.
Why?
To bare the truth, at bottom.
To unearth your findings?
No, to find my earth, and get my barings, there.
Do you hold to what you find?
Yes, they're my corporate holdings.
Splendid. Any dividends?
Oh, diverse.
(*Interval.*)
Then without legs, women would lose a firm ass-et?
And my liquid holdings would evaporate.
So there must be a *base*.
Yes, and there for base deeds, basically, indeed.
Then we get to the bottom of it.
And hold fast.
Which way? In?
Out too. As a backward dimension, depth is thrust forward, too.
Oh. When to stop?
When the legs give way, and your tightness is eased.
Ah, that's hard.
But it turns soft soon. Fire is earth's melting point.
Ah, what a watery grave.
Not so grave: you merely come out for air.
And?
And in time—
In we go again?
Why not? Youth may be long, but virility's pause is short.
Then I should pull up short?
No, deepen your dividends.
Ah, to make those divid-ends meat!

You have far grounds for a good grounding in her.
But being grounded, how can I take flight?
Imaginatively. You soar out of your hangar.
Oh, hang her. She's boring.
No, *you* must do the boring.
And she the bearing?
If she can bear you.
But I'm *already* of age.
Then put the point of your age into the snapping cage. Thrust far, and let the bird nibble.
Why? Is it feeding time?
No. Till she be fed up.
On the *whole*, you're *right*.
No. Best to be *centered*, where the *hole* is.
Why?
To round out your trip.
Oh. How far is back again?
When fitness be no longer snug.
How lax.
Yes, she'll tear you limp from limp.
Till I be dis-membered?
Aye, and you hang out to dry.
Why, is that my ultimate fate?
Yes, when the weight has slackened.
And the tool is lackened.
And your member's ember is an ash that's blackened.
Alas.
Sure: "a lass" was involved.
To what extent?
In that she covered your in-tent.
Till it was extant?
To some extent.
And which way went?

The way weighed.
Till the rocking cradle breaks?
And the stiff joints come loose.
Ah, and what do we lose?
You lose hold.
And?
Go grip your solitude.

The Transference

On one of my infrequent journeys, I visited the business section of a city. As an abrupt storm of rain fell, I ducked into an office building where a cousin of mine worked. I found the right floor, but was impeded by a receptionist. She sat at an ample desk, but her brazen front was equal to the task. I submitted my cousin's name, but he was at a conference meeting which wasn't yet to be broken up. "Wait," smiled the receptionist, and she indicated a chair for that signal purpose. As I was in the act of sitting, I was inspired to ask what time it was, as a small concession to my mortality. The receptionist glanced at a clock, which she contained up her crotch. (She guarded it, as the most erotic secret she possessed.)

"It's 4:30," she emerged saying, and covered her legs again by draping her dress in eloquent folds about her desk-concealed knees. "Is that what the clock wanted to be by itself," I stipulated, "or did you want it to be that, in your greed to end the working day and reclaim your private life?" Her answer was evasive. She quickened to a little throb of guilt.

The inner door opened, admitting my cousin, all of him exposed to my one view. His hand gave a nervous pat on the willing back of that receptionist who kept so remarkable a place for the day's turning time. It came to me at once that those two were perhaps intimate. Afraid to betray my knowledge (garbed in the stage of assumption), I casually assumed a front of alert nonchalance. I conversed briefly with my cousin, and left. Waiting for the elevator, I heard my cousin declare (through the thin door) that he wished to wind up the receptionist's clock. "He's making time," I thought, "and two-timing his own wife." To restore a cast of mental prudence, I contemplated space: but in such infinite terms, time cycled up to sequence the association. Sexuality now claimed my attitude. Home I repaired, to furtively assail my wife, in time to the receptionist's image. How transferable, then, are women by the temporal route. One girl generates the impulse: another formally completes it. Romantic individuation was insolvent, so my fidelity was extended to the species, of whom my wife was the most handy representative and my most practiced accomplice to lust's general whim. She was my local stop; eternity was too much for one lifetime to fulfill.

Title at End of Story

Just as the soup was being poured, Mark, the comember of my club, regaled me with this confession: (We were in dinner dress, for the formal occasion, the once-a-month eating-meeting of our undefined but masculine club with no purpose or identity or basis for unity in our collective grouping: why we had been formed into this club, and how, escapes me. We were arbitrarily there, and about to eat.)

Mark's words follow, mark them: nothing concrete, just a complacent abstraction of romantic misfortune in a generalized void of detail, a vague summing, an anonymous universality: how Joan halted him in midstride and cramped momentarily his style of unruffled, even living tone, the safe comfort of his regularity; Mark being, by his account, a sedate creature soberly unremarkable, a blank. For here's how he reported (to me whom he knew only by club membership) his slipping-down off his even tenor into the Joan-jolt eventually well-recovered from in secure resumption of a dead and balanced emotional life:

"I was once normal and neutral. I wasn't especially worried; what I was doing and what I was wanting were in a state of reasonable balance, relative. I didn't desire anything with extremity and discomfort. The world was behaving pretty moderately, I didn't complain. I wasn't the intense victim of some passion or suffering. Life was playing me fair; I had equilibrium, though not ecstasy. It was satisfactory, though too dull for heaven's violence, much too mild to get a quarrelsome response from hell. Things settled evenly; life was working out. I was spared much.

"Then a friend gave a party. I was in my usual contented mood, cheerfully open, not especially happy; I was 'all right.' I met Joan, another guest at the party. I was overthrown. My calmness and peace were jolted loose; and turbulence erupted in me. My heart fell onto a wild rampage, my sanity exploded to bits. Love had entered me. I threw all my dependence on Joan, a very radical investment, a costly loss of my voluntary will. This was Joan's undoing of me, but not her fault at all. I had plunged, reckoning for bliss. Missing it, I landed in misery; devils stuck pins of despair in me; feelings raged in opposition, my poise flew away; calmness fled; agony ripped me apart with excruciation. I had taken the love-risk; and failure came at a price, with no composure to protect me. My life had entered upon evil. My love was unrequited. Requited, it would have worked out differently. It was a bad period indeed. But I've survived, for I tell about it. I'm alive, at least. I died in the heart. But my body's brain is still intact. My embittered memory kept Joan's pinch upon me. I'm numb now, and memory has taken mercy. I've endured the worst. Joan happened to me. Man is tough and resilient, but not at first. It was rough. But I've come through, I leave my ordeal with Joan behind. I'm happy to have recovered. At the time, though—desired Joan and not had; is not advisable."

Thus Mark confessed, at our club, where all the members were dining sumptuously. I was his table-neighbor on the right. He told his cyclical tale to me alone, in a low-keyed voice. Course replaced course by the waiters, and there was much wining. Mark's tale took about eight minutes to be told to me. It was completed before the middle of the first course (soup). Then I had a plan. I calculated that before dinner was over (it was a slow, luxurious, opulent repast, with a stately pace to the leisure),

Mark's tale could be told all around the whole table to all thirty of the presiding members of our once-met-a-month dining club (males only). But one by one, it would go around. Mark began it, about himself, to me on his right: an abstraction of his ill-fated passion for his Joan that interrupted his usual equilibrium for a spell of ill-starred unrequited discomfort. I'd pass it along to the neighbor on *my* right: about Mark and Joan, employing the same names of the heroes of the tale originally told by Mark, the participating narrator. Then my right-hand neighbor would whisper it to *his* right-hand neighbor, and so on, until the full circuit of the table had been one by one negotiated in the relay of this one story making its full round. It would culminate with its finally being told to the original teller himself: with what distortions accumulated on the route and round of the wine-filled way? We'll see. So I relayed it, in full, to my right-hand neighbor, telling him to pass it on in complete memory of detail so far as he was able to. The experiment was launched.

The buzzing kept moving, mouth to ear, while course replaced course in this one meal's pleasant career. Mark didn't know about this spreading. He assumed his tale, told in confidence, lodged within my locked and silent head, there to be lost and forgotten. It was, though, making the rounds. It was steadily moving from one member to the next. What was happening to it, along the way?

Stage by stage, in stations of ears, the passing tale went. Full circuit almost, now. It was being told to the member on Mark's own left. We were in the process of dessert.

The member flanking Mark on the left now tapped him on the shoulder and poured into his ear, as I leaned close to listen carefully in on, this following battered tale of collective club authorship that had originated as a frank confession to me, blandly stated and in the full trust of innocence, by Mark, unsuspecting of my prank:

"Mark and Joan screwed, then Mark got tired and they broke up."

When Mark heard this, he muttered something about oversimplification, distortion, falsification, and inaccuracy. Then he finished his dessert, as we all did. Coffee was served. The table was rousing with empty wine bottles. Thirty members helped themselves to brandy with the coffee. There was merry cheer in the room. Mark nudged me: "You didn't betray my confidence: it took its course in rumor's windy inaccuracy, repetition-contorted. I don't care. Joan is past."

He winced stoically: betraying the opposite. Joan had come back, upon his heart. He sank into half-drunken memory. The club's festivity rose, in clamor. Mark was forgotten, and Joan.

The evening closed. I went out to hail a cab, Mark at my elbow; other club members flocked out in groups also, in severals, in couples. This month's meeting had been an enjoyable dinner, and our good-bys were cordial, hearty too. Mark and I shared our cab, we lived in the same direction. "I'm calling on Joan," he said. "I've left her alone for three years. Now my anguish is revived, with the gushing memories evoked, due to tonight's playful prank you pulled on as a youthful joke. It's hurting now. I must return to her; however difficult."

"Is she still living at the same place?"

"Yes, right there down the street," as he ordered the driver to pull over to the curb. "I checked it in the phone directory. Under her husband's name, naturally. I'll wake them up out of bed probably, it's late. But drunkenness makes my responsibility light. Her husband remembers me, as his failed rival. He didn't expect to confront me, once he won her: but three years later, here I am. I'll have to ring their bell, and take the chance."

He was dislodging himself from the cab. "Won't you regret this?" I asked, guilty for my part in rousing those dead romantic embers in the cold fire grate of his drafty, disused heart. "Don't be foolhardy," I cautioned, "or rash. You might annoy them, but try not to antagonize." He was gone from the cab, and hadn't heard my last phrases of advice. The dark night scared me, for him. I asked the driver to wait, parked right there. I expected Mark back, repulsed by a surprised and unwelcoming couple, disturbed at an uncivil hour by a drink-demented caller. I waited half an hour. Still no Mark, he hadn't emerged from the residential building's doorway. The cab meter rose its fare steadily. I paid and got out, to spare my wallet any further depletion. I waited by the building entrance. Guilty, sleepy, repentent. The night deepened. I'd persist. I wouldn't go home, till I saw what fated Mark. It was my doing he was here. I'd stick it out.

In discomfort I felt an hour forcing by. Night sent its eeriest winds out to discourage me. I shook them off, eager to see Mark. For one not invited, he sure was there a long time!

I had now waited two hours, and I had to go to work in the morning! I had already invested so much emotional, compassionate, guilt-ridden, and actual clock-time on seeing through to the outcome of this, that I determined not to have it go to waste. Rather than give up, I decided to phone in "sick" in the morning to the office, so I'd have the day free to sleep off tonight's fatiguing, intriguing, mystiquing, and beleaguering effects. I huddled up by the doorway. No doorman was on duty, to suspect, to accuse me of loitering. This spared me a social disgrace, and a tag of vagrancy. Oh I was so sleepy! I examined the doorbells, the nameplates attached. There were six last names for the six apartments. I didn't know Joan's husband's last name. And I'd just barely met Mark, for this matter! It was too late to ring bells at random. I was too old to be a juvenile delinquent. I stiffened in restraint. The night air was brisk, my coat light. It was a foul season, in this somewhere world. I had a tedious night to wear out. Could I barely last it? By will, yes. Inclination, no.

I squatted down in the forehall, to doze off in some comparative warmth. My vagrancy was undisturbed, and undetected my loitering. I was no law fugitive; just a responsible carer for Mark, whom I had *caused* to be here by a "light" prank I had played. It had turned out ill-advised, as I'm finding out too late. I must pay the moral price. I must linger here, and wait.

The chilling dawn was unpleasant. Why wasn't I in my customary bed? Or, alternatively, and better yet, in my girl friend's bed? For Mark's sake, I was here. Here, here.

I learned to hate this building entrance. It became sickeningly familiar. The morning had reached the go-to-work hour. Soon I'd find out!

Some people left the building. But no Mark yet.

Here was *Mark* stepping out! Accompanied by, and with his arms around, a rather lovely girl. Was it Joan? Of course.

"Were you waiting the whole night?"

"Yes, so explain what happened."

"Joan, here, was alone in her apartment, since her husband moved out, they're separated, in twin divorce proceedings. I had awakened her, sure. But she was ever so dear to me." He glanced at Joan, and she approved, with a loving beam, of this honest revelation to me, not a friend but a fellow club member. She smiled, they both smiled. They had been blessed by fortune, by benign chance; and *my* responsibility now smiled. I had helped to be the author of their re-pairing off. We all went to a breakfast shop. Mark and Joan were grateful. It was Mark's treat, he would pay, but I only wanted coffee. I had lost a small fortune on that taxi. My remorse was absolved. They said they were in love, and would be married. I felt glad. They owed me a major debt. They invited me to the wedding. I would go, but gladly. It all turned out wonderfully. There was a magic in this circumstance-sequence of events. My contribution had been handsome. The conclusion had been unexpected, and not intended. The two lovebirds went off to their respective places of work, holding hands, thanking me. I phoned my office in a public booth, and announced being ill. I was free to go home and sleep. The angelic sleep, the sleep of the just: surprised in his innocence; pleased with his potency; untroubled by the world's chances, for once; praising of love. Of the newly known Mark, and the Joan whom he had given up, been rejected by, three years ago. He was newly in love; and she for the first time with him. I purred in envy, which I blissfully tolerated. I wouldn't grudge what I *had caused*: repeating a "secret," divulging an honest openness: I was rewarded; Mark was; and Joan. There *is* happiness. The world can surprise. Love *can* go right. Ideals can unsour; turn sweet; be true. Rarely; and prized more dearly, in the rarity. It was lovely, to have helped love; I loved it. I was on my way home in the subway, which was dirty, but my peaceful mind glided it over. It had been an eventful evening, flowing over onto today. I went to bed, and slept. I dreamed that I had married Joan; then Mark had killed me. The nightmare woke me up. A dream, only. The reality turned out better; I being less ambitious or personally covetous in *true* life, than in my dream dungeon. I was a pleasant angel. But I was jealous. Why should *Mark* get Joan? I'll go after her. I can locate the building. I'll accost her when I see her without him. I'll muscle in. I'm not through. I once meddled. Now to renew my plunge: to interfere, to take away; to molest, to undo. I felt destructive rage. I would ruin.

Post-Story Title:
Surprised in the Cupid Role; the Perverse Compulsion to Spoil It? Begrudging a Love Match "Arranged" Inadvertently by Me. Lacking the Largeness to Grant It Good Grace Free of Envy. Petty and Competitive; Compassion's Failed Nerve, in Me. I'm Small: and So Must Undermine What's Lofty, Impersonal, and True. And So to the Nasty Undoing, in Malice and Spite, of Mark-and-Joan's Love— Distasteful: for It Scores My Being Outside, and Alone.

The Cosmic Meadows That Vanished Love Was Browsing In

Said he to her: "Love itself quite gnaws at my bones." They were discreetly an inch apart on a dimly lit couch. It was their first intimate verbal exchange.

Her need to be convinced spread suspicious features over her face. Noting this, her suitor waged a hot trail of pursuit.

Their knees touched, and thousands of vibrant electric atoms flew in a sparkling dance from this furtive contact. The thigh nerves were informed by relays, until the groin center was forewarned. Then war went to peace, and peace declared war.

Feeling her hand held by his with moist throbs, she dangerously asked how far he intended to dangle his intention. Blood flashed splotches all over his face.

Relaxed in the coils of tension, he pressed his object in the grip of a hungry embrace. Desire in waves extended his will upon hers. Facially, they wore a double-faced kiss.

When the smoke of passion had lifted, the bond temporarily erected collapsed like a stood-up deck of cards. They eyed each other in the official language of strangers.

Abruptly reclothed, their bodies sent silent signals of fatigue with such receding familiarity, that soon the total global distance covered them. Separated by a polar geography, they went hunting for opposite planets.

He found one, orbiting like a top. Hers was a nebulous radiance in a field of fish-swarming stars. Solitude had made their souls solar.

PART THREE: THE DEFINITION CURE

The Book of the World—Containing All Creation in Time, without a Stitch Loose. But Who's Its Author? As a Subject, the World Very Much Cares Who Its Author Is. It Wants to Be Rendered as Itself. Was It Its Own Author? Consult the Text, and What's Behind It? A Mind. A *Man*'s Mind, or a "Mind"? Or All Minds, Combined? Or All Things, Self-Reflected?

I would like to write a book that contains literally everything. But that would be impossible, and who would publish it? So I content myself with *imagining* having written it, which really is not the same thing as trying to hold, with the help of two or three strong men, that proposed book itself.

Consider that book done. A strong table would be necessary, to bear its fullsome weight.

Now, let's consider it. What's in it?

As I said before, literally everything. Try containing in your mind the awesome, impressive, all-inclusiveness of this inconceivable abstraction, "everything." It means that nothing is missing, a negative way of saying that everything is there. The mind is overwhelmed. It complains, it speaks its mind:

"I can't handle it. 'Everything' is too unwieldy. You've got to pare it down, delete, omit, and so eliminate that at last you illuminate. Narrowing it to particulars permits manageable comprehension, maneuverable lightness: the mind can operate. I speak for *all* minds, not just me. There are human mental proportions that must be respected;

give the mind its measure; allot it a few select things at a time, otherwise its capacity is overprodigiously taxed. Even at the genius level, the mind (my species) has to discriminate, or else be inundated. Too much can be as impossible as its opposite, a dearth or lack. The *body* needs a standard comfortable room temperature; the stomach must keep up its water supply; the mind can deal with so much, but no more. Its function moderates its capacity. As I'm a mind, I suppose I must define the mind's function. That's no easy problem. Let me give it some thought."

That was my mind, speaking. It's gone off on an intellectual binge, and is examining its own reasons for being, with a self-consciousness for which it alone is so capably equipped. The mind contemplating itself is a staggering concept; the very thought of it gives me a dizzy spell. I must spin away, or undergo vertigo. The mind is a mental trap, where you can get all psychologically involved. I've got to keep my head about this, above the water-on-the-brain level. My ideas are swirling in a heady congestion. Then they settle into a lump, and sink in a bog. I must keep ahead of them, and not go under. Sanity is kept under mental lock and key. When broken into, it can so easily be swept away; ideas are insubstantial things; some say they *are* things: which is a matter of mind having the matter to master mere matter itself. And that brings me back to my book. (I'll leave my mind, for the nonce; it's trying to figure out what its function is, which is too obvious for its cerebral comprehension. It's pondering down devious channels, winding about the intricacies of a maze, where it proceeds to get lost along the way. That's my involuted brain for you—ingrown on itself, remotely wrapped up far away from the world outside, on which it had nourished.) That brings me back to my book. My book is the opposite to my mind: it's about everything, not about itself. The more profit to examine, then, my book, than my mind. The book informs, the mind boggles. The book is *about*; the mind, poor thing, *is*. By comparison my book is the *antidote* to my mind. But I need my mind to grasp it, and it can't. The *possibilities* in my book are infinite; but my mind is finitely unequal, and bungles its task. The book's potential is unrealized, thanks to my mental inadequacy. The book *could have been*;

the mind wouldn't let it: letting it down. I blame my mind; but praise my book the more.

There's my book on the table. The table is solid, for my book is endlessly heavy. The table is *so* solid, that it's without legs! It needed all the space *between* the legs to consolidate its densely massive bulk of solidity. On such a formidable base, rests my book. You can't see the covers of my book, for it's open about to the middle, with the weight thrown back on its incredibly tense spine, on which the title is printed, the same title but in different type on the cover, under its dust jacket on which the same title is printed with still a different type. (Including, in all three "cases," my name as author.) What pages is my book open to? That's too long to go into. The page numbers at the bottom of the two exposed pages each take up seven full lines of footnote-tiny type at the pages' bottoms! So why drag mathematics into it?

Obviously, it's a monster opus; not a mere "slim volume" or standard tome. "Why is the book so big?" you ask. Fool! Because of its containing everything. With such a subject, could I *possibly* be brief? My theme tends to expand; and the book with it.

Was I being arrogantly presumptuous in tackling a topic that gigantic? Guilty of *hubris*, perhaps (which is pride where humility should be)? Only a God would have undertaken what I did. Even the *Bible* is only a propaganda tract, compared to the encyclopedic ambitiousness of *my* master enterprise. Everything is contained in my book, so it's a worldly scripture; and as "everything" includes things *outside* of the world, I've produced a superworldly gospel as well, or paraworldly, or whatever transcends whatever can be transcended; a meta-complete book. Nothing is missing. Look it up.

Copies were made for all libraries and bookshops, in a limitless edition, including translation into other (therefore foreign) languages. My publisher went overboard, with his enthusiasm; to sink or swim, in his publishing venture, on the basis of my one work. (One!? One means all!)

The reviews have been very generous. *The Times Literary Supplement* (of London) and the *New York Times Book Review* gave it rave notices, totally uncritical. "Of broad dimensions" is a quote from one. "Comprehensive" is a quote from another. Other quotes by other critics: "Compendious." "Gargantuan." "Definitive." "Sweeping." "Of classical scope." "Laudably thorough." "Immodest, and therefore the more complete." "Whole. Cosmic." "He [the author—me] took a theme, and stuck to it. And did it last!" "Imperishably permanent, being the last word." "Outdoes God's Creation; and how!" "Bold in concept, majestic in execution, minutely painstaking in precision of detail, flamboyantly accurate, cosmically entire, out of this world in range; a *fabulous* creation; mirroring reality itself, which ranks as its sole (and possibly outdone) competitor." That last review thrilled me, I was flattered. It upheld, even vindicated, my career as a writer. Boast-worthy, I felt my book to be. I had extended my all-in-all theme till nothing was uncovered; and the form held up under the magnitude of the content. My book had universal structure; garrisoned, buttressed, and scaffolded by a skeletal framework of timelessly eternal dimensions of infinitely spatial scope. Then I embroidered details, lavished flourishes, indulged in decorative adornments of such lush profusion lovingly wrought, and carestakingly rendered, is it any wonder a masterpiece should result? If anything, those critics were guilty of understatement. I had built it up from nothing, this book, from the void itself; and it came out to be everything, in its myriad course of development. In the beginning was the word? And then came all the material, pouring out in a heap, mounting up in abundance? Well, in the *end* was the word: Mine.

So now I was a celebrated author. My book had really gone to town, in the girth of its prodigious proportions. It started men thinking. (Women, too.) My content had been thought-provoking, and mentally stimulating. I was interviewed on radio, television, periodicals, and newspapers. I got away by answering "Read my book" uniformly to every question, an irrefutable reply. My book had all the answers, as well as their questions. I was asked what I was worried about; and I gave this liberal reply:

"Book-burning. I'm doomed, should that happen. Let's not have intellectual suppression. Let's respect books, and keep them dry."

I was, of course, referring to my own. Lesser authors were jealous of my greater stature. They had a world of reason to be. I couldn't deny the supreme logical basis of their jealousy, those inferior souls. They had *attempted* less than me. The ambitiousness of my scale was rivalled only by the thoroughness of my success. It immeasurably satisfied me.

My book gathered up all the superlatives, which is what readers' comments became reduced to. I was boundlessly gratified by the praise thus heaped on me—via, of course, my book. But then my comedown came, my fall. Like my book falling, off its big table.

I was accused of plagiarism! Well, that's not true. I hadn't plagiarized a *work*; I had but imitated *reality*. I had, as it were, held the mirror up to nature. I had *shown* what was; set down, brought forth, revealed. Nothing was in my book that didn't have its exact counterpart in the world of things. I had given a complete catalogue of correspondences to the matter of all that was. Was that to be guilty of plagiarism? No. But my vulturesque accusers at the court trial summed up their misgivings through their prosecuting attorney, who to this effect dished out such legal maleloquence:

"The accused put down in his book everything about every subject of the world from all time in all stages of history including the future. He dealt with sociology, anthropology, mythology, criminology, philosophy, psychology, and a jolly lot of other 'ologies.' Philology too, and politics, and warfare, geography, history, mathematics, chemistry, biology, electrology, physics, technology, linguistics, literature, art, music, architecture, the performing arts, theater, rhetoric, law, propaganda, commerce, industry, advertising, marketing, sports, hygiene, medicine, bacteriology, zoology, botany, astronomy, mysticism, theology, alchemy, civics, ecology, oceanology, geology, everything, and everything again. Under his infernal scheme, nothing was discluded; he didn't *select*, he *compiled*. All the data, facts galore, scientifically organized, in his diabolical system. He plagiarized God, from the fundamentalist doctrine of God's being the original Author of all Creation. God's copyright is everywhere, in His own name. The accused has usurped God's rightful domain. Here was arrogance of audacity, all right! Let him be brought low, and punished. Give him a sentence of undoing the whole fabrication of his book bit by bit, thread by thread, till the book is undone, and rests unread. On that note, the prosecution rests. The whole book is put under protest, we detest it and the writer of it as foully copying God's universal mysterious secrets *in full.* The revelations are too open; what's revealed should be more closed. The accused lacked modesty, and was too proud. Let's bring him low, to raise God above."

But I *hadn't* set out to compete with God. Was it my fault to have outdone Him? My defense attorneys argued as best as they could, but my case was lost, and I *was* brought low. Thus ended my grandiose dream. I had carried it out, but then it was rejected, after having been fully accepted. In life, you never can tell, with its ups and downs. What a disappointment! All copies were confiscated of that controversial book, and the law burned them, all. Now no copy is extant, of what had set the world on fire; the world then set *it* on fire—and society stamped "me" out. What am I, without my work?

I had taken too much authority on myself, and had come to grief. Authority has the word "author" in it. But what are words? Make enough words, and you have a book. Make enough fire, and the book is done. The world is empty of my book. The mind alone is left. What does it say?

"I'm a mind; my owner is a man; I live in him. My man was a scribe for matter, and words were his manner. A whole manor was made from that manner, but now the house has come tumbling down, the Edifice Complex is now stumping on its truncated foundations, which once had reared proudly the manse. Pity the poor man, who tried to be an author. He eked out a volume that was bigger than all the world. Accused of vainglory, he now has nothing to show for it. Achilles's shield once had on it depicted the known world, by Vulcan the blacksmith. The man I'm a mind of made all the libraries in one book, put the whole world in it; and the book caved in, since society wouldn't let him get away with it. He's sentenced, for a sentence too many, to serve out a sentence in unwritten silence longer than his very life. This he won't outlive, alas.

"I'm his mind, and I was contemplating myself. I was wondering what my function is, to define it. I confess I don't know. I'm a mind only—not a miracle.

"The man I'm a mind of made a fabulous work, once. There's no trace of it. Will some day come when the subject of his study—the world itself, through all of time—will also vanish and leave no trace? When a *man* vanishes, there's no mental trace of himself left. Given enough *men*, and a *world* is made. If *I'm* *one* man's mind, then that's the very *world's* mind? Is there a world's mind? What a collective, general abstraction it must be! It must be a *vast* mind, at that. Imagine! Not the mind of one man, but the mind of the whole world! It defies concept, doesn't it! I can vaguely imagine it, but it must be. I wonder what it's like.

"The man I'm a mind of made a book, once. The book is gone now. The book was about everything. If the *whole world* were to make a book, one book, would it be any different than the book my owner made, the one individual man I'm a mind of?

"Unanswered questions are these. I quest on, and in vain.

"And I plug ahead. For the book made by the composite of all the world at once in all of time, would be that world's autobiography, in time. The one man I'm a mind of, being but one man and not the world himself, made a definitive *biography* of that world. Had that *world* tended to itself as a subject, it would have made the *same* book, with the exception that the author would be collective; and it would be a total *auto*biography, though containing the same words and the same things—everything. So *who* the author is, *is* important. The man I'm a mind of attempted too much; his crime was that he succeeded, entirely. The *whole world* should have done that book, of itself: then, it never would have been burned; and we'd have it yet, to this very day, and beyond today, to all of time.

"I'm one mind, in one man. I'm then finite. Enough of me, though, all others of my kind in all time, compile a thoroughgoing, lasting infinity, of eternal dimension. That would have legitimized 'our' book, and branded it safeguarded against any burning. I'll join forces with all other minds of all other men. We'll work hard together, and produce the one book, the product of our joint collaboration. The world will recognize its own portrait in it, for all of time an *authorized* portrait, of itself, official. The book will keep on being. It will *be* the world."

Thus said my mind. But I disagree. How can a book *be* the world? A book is *of* the world. Let's not carry symbology too far, nor succumb to it too literally in identifying verbal image with thing itself. Let's remember that outside there's a world. The modesty of a book is that it can *duplicate* it, but not be it. I learned this lesson the hard way. I'm chastised down to modesty. The world is too much. Even for a book.

"That's what the man I'm in says. But as his mind, I'm allowed to speak myself. He's wrong, I disagree with him. Now, he's *too* humble. The humble pie he was forced to swallow has gone to his head, poor poll. The world is on the outside. It *is* a book. There aren't enough copiers, yet. Let's bring the book about, bring it out, realize it. Let's release the book that the world is of. Let's read the world, to know its book. The mind tears between them, and makes them one."

That's what my *mind* said, not me. I'm afraid to go any further in theorizing. I'm getting confused of the difference between the world's book and the book's world. I contributed one, once. Was it a book, or was it a world? Or was it both in one? I'm going under. I can't think anymore.

"That's what the man who owns me said. I'm his mind, and I'm *supposed* to think. What I think is the world. Get the words, and make the book. Write it down."

Write *what* down? I don't understand my mind. It's beyond me. I'm losing it. I'm taking leave of it. It's on its own. May it thrive.

"The man I was a mind to has just died, or turned crazy. Now I'm only me, without him. Can I fare alone? The world is big. Where do I fit?

"The man I belonged to, I was his mind. Now I'm free of him. I can roam, impersonal. His personal identity had stamped me, before. Now, suddenly, I can just *be*. I'm not owned! It's *freed*om, for me!

"I'll do what I said. I'll join all other minds: minds free of the 'burdens' of their owners: minds impersonal, their owners being crazed or dead or both at once. When all minds get together, we *contain* the world. And where there's a world, there's a book. Just as the handkerchief of the Lord is strewn everywhere, and all things partake of Him, and every blade of the Leaves of Grass is His equal handicraft under the law: so too, everything in the world is part of a page of the endless volume that the universe constitutes. The world in time is an unending book, being ever printed, everywhere, and read, bit by bit, part by part, chapter by verse. Some *rare* people can read whole hunks; others, a line or two. The print blurs, sometimes, and the text is confused. But the body of the work is a whole, just as the universe is a sphere whose center is everywhere, anywhere local, where you happen to 'be.' The book that is the world. A fiction cosmic indeed. We needn't believe in it. But why not be entertained? What are minds for? I'm devoid of my owner; liberated to the impersonal. I'll go everywhere, see everything, in time back and forth. 'Mind,' am I? *Soul* too. I'm one soul, among many. Books confirm us. Each soul is a book. All books are one, and all souls one. I'll modestly do my part."

Everything Entered Is Exited From. Everything Begun Is—Even if Prematurely—Ended. Man's Ledger Balances Out, in the End—and in the Start; in the Out, as in the In. What's Life? What's Man? What's Time? What's Space? Where, When? How, Why? What? For Non-Answers, Consult the Text, to Follow.

Every place I've ever entered, I've always exited from—with one exception.

What's that?

The world.

Just wait.

Don't have anticipatory glee. I'll take my time, while waiting.

That's what waiting *is*—taking your time. But you can't take it *with* you, when you leave.

Leave where?

The world. You'll leave the world you entered. Everything *else* you've ever entered, you've left from. Every room you've ever been in, you first entered it, then you left it, even if by a different door from the one you entered. Every girl you've ever entered, or every time you've entered the same girl, you've gone out the very same entrance-exit you entered in. Every plane you've been in, or train, car, bus, ship—always you left. Every time you've gone up, you've returned down. In, out. The world, too.

Once I *left* from something that I never entered.

Really? What was it?

My mother. I was *born* from her, you see.

Yes, but first you entered, as your father's sperm.

But when I entered, I was unrecognizable.

You were cast in a rudimentary form. But you came out fine, at the end.

And here I am. In the world. Where in memory I've always been. My memory will betray me, when I'm not here.

And your memory's larger vessel—your life—will end simultaneously with your earth-departure.

Leaving the earth, where will I then arrive?

Nowhere, without the basic necessity—you. For anywhere you go, it must be you. When *you're* done, you don't *go.*

If I don't go, then I don't *leave.* I'll stay here on earth.

But it won't be *you.*

Who *will* it be?

No "who." No "who," at all.

But where—

—No "where"; for without your "who," all wheres wear away, and there's no where for you to peddle your wares.

I'm wary.

Wary? Being aware? It won't help.

Where will my awareness go? Aware will I be?

No-aware.

I'll wear out—or in?

You'll wear not at all; lacking "where," you'll be nothing. To *be* nothing is to *have* nothing; you'll have nothing to wear.

I'm aware of that. Let's go on to another *subject*, please.

Any subject *begun*, is always ended. Prematurely, without middle development, in many a case.

Are there more endings than beginnings?

They balance out with equal sums, at either end. There are as many endings as beginnings; as many exitings, as enterings. To begin and then to end, is a time unit—or cycle, if you wish. To enter and then to exit, is a completed act of space.

What *else* is there? You gave me only space and time. What completes the trinity?

Both find unity in man. But man's not a *separate* third from them; in him, those two find their temporal motion, and their spatial duration. In him, they rest.

Rest? What from?

Moving. Action. Enduring. Lasting. Going. Coming. The in, the out. The making, the doing, the being. Feeling, thinking. Wanting. Stopping. Starting. Ending. Beginning. Endless.

That's quite a lot to rest from. But we're wrested from it—it's wrested from us. To arrest all that—

Others continue. More "in" and "out," more "begin" and "end," by others, once we stop. And even while we're going, too.

Confusion Takes the Definition Cure. The Result Only Compounds the Confusion of Before. Words Can't Make the World Give Up Its Mystery. So I Give Up. I'm Nervous, and That Calms Me Down.

I don't know what anything is any more. Living in this world is confusing me. Despite having been warned by a relaxed friend that the need for definitions is the sign of a nervous mind, I nervously craved definitions, to put a veneer of intellectual clarity over my hugely indecisive interior.

Toward that end I consulted a dictionary-maker, for it was easy to see that the defining material was verbal, though the material *defined* was originally not. Before consulting a dictionary-maker, I had to find one. By whatever ways and means the process elaborated, I was determined to acquire definitions that would curb my nervous futility whose obscure origins were possibly cosmic in the intensity of their scope.

To my luck, the only dictionary-maker within a radius of seven thousand miles from where I lived turned out to live next door. (Hence the use of "handy" by dictionary-advertisers.)

A scruple gave me hesitation by suggesting that it would be cheating on unfair advantage to accept such good luck by stepping up next door; more character-building would have been the adversity of finding him at the opposite side of the world after a hazardous labor of heroic travel under difficulty: it would have tested my resolve to endure a stern trial in a lengthy and risky search. But I dispensed with such a scruple. It was too theoretical, when my goal lay right at hand. I had too much guilt already in the concrete, to bother to incur a tediously abstract one based on the speculative misgiving and a sheer waste of conscience. I went next door and knocked; without delay was I welcomed; he proved indeed to be a neighbor. We had chatted daily for forty years. Not till now had I known his occupation. Not till now had I needed to exploit such. He would calm me by defining things. He would give me a settled mind: based on verbal certitudes. Just in time, for my nerves were already giving out. I fainted on his couch. He revived me with brandy—*momentarily.* Could he restore my worldly balance and confidence *permanently?*—upon a stability of fixed mind? That's why I had visited him. I told him so. He looked doubtful that he would have a ready cure. I relapsed in a tormented apathy that gave him alarm. Humanitarianly, he vowed to do all he could. He would summon definitions, to succor to my ease from travail in the haunts of doubt. Such solicitude sank me into infantile protectedness. He had so much to allay—I was a mind without a center. I wanted intellectual pinnings—not the mere overlay of a borrowed religious faith or other fabricated support. I wanted deep organic therapy in the region of words and meanings. There would I find peace and content, within an active mold. The dictionary-maker would be my improvised doctor. His treatment would restore the verbal roots that had never had the security to grow, since the world had given me an uneasy state of anxiety.

Fortified by my new word confidence, I'll be able for literally the first time to meet the world head-on and actually answer back. Meaning-based words will be my reality-matching strength. The power to cope with too-real things in the world's tyranny of circumstances will be the word-endowed ritual of magic, potent to understand. I would master that which I would define. Conviction of definition would "take care" of complications—by stamping out, eliminating, ruthlessly, all complications, ambiguities, uncertainties, and complexities that defy Definition by remaining outside of its all-encompassing. I would sweep aside all obstacles or problems, crush underfoot any deterrent, armed with a barrage of Definitions to meet any "occasion." I would be ready with the "answers"—to weaken the force of any questions that dare appear. This verbally bolstered confidence will wear down reality, and my life will advance behind its weaponry of glittering words that pierce challenges with rapier definitions. The world will crumble at my feet: annihilated, held captive, by my definitions bold.

First the dictionary-maker's wife made us a meal for vigor of body. Then she and the children in attendance retired for the evening, leaving me face to face on opposite soft seats with my mentor in his library-studio. "Yes?" he queried.

"I'm all confused, so set me straight."

"Yes, you told me that. What shall I clear up, step by step? Proceed with particular words and I'll define them on the spot."

"I'm afraid to be specific, since my trouble is so general."

"A *lot* of specifics will gradually total up the whole general. And each specific is a kind of sample or example, leading *toward* the general, and temporarily *representing* that general, from a certain angle. Begin *somewhere*, at least. I can only help you by particulars: from which you'll do your own concluding, as you restore—or for the first time find—your sound mental basis within. Now, shoot."

"Tell me, doctor, what's business?"

"Business? Now let me see. It's the useful trade of time for money. That takes care of *that* business. Your next word?"

"What's money?"

"Money must be power over need. But *more* money is simply just power."

"Then I want money. But now I want to know what life is."

"In the broad sense? It's hard to define. It baffles me."

"I'll get you thrown out of your profession as dictionary-maker unless you define life."

"Don't threaten me. Let *me* scare *you*. Life? To put it one way, it's an active negation of death."

"That's not affirmative. Then define death."

"Death is the state of no life."

"That's too negative for me."

"You're not the *only* one it's negative for. What else do you want defined?"

"Everything."

"Not all at once. One at a time."

"But my time is short."

"Only eternally it is."

"What do you mean?"

"It slipped out. I don't know."

"Define what color is."

"Color? The visual alphabet."

"I'm too blind to understand."

"Then ask another. We'll skip the ones not immediately grasped. What you need is confidence through success; failure would confuse you the more."

"What seems success could be failure."

"Heed only what *seems*. Build up your strength. When you're enough strong to grapple with what *is*, then we'll advance to that deeper stage.

But not till then."

"You're gently gradual with me in my progress?"

"Yes, I lend encouragement. But is it progress?"

"It doesn't *seem* to be."

"Then maybe most likely it *is*. For seeming and being so often go as opposites."

"A new word to define?"

"I'm ready."

"Ready with what? You don't know what I'll ask you."

"Ready with the head I have. That's where the answers are."

"Since it's night, what's night?"

"I'll shed light on such a dark question."

"But that would be artificial illumination."

"That's what words are: an artificial illumination."

"Then shed your words over 'night'?"

"I would put it this way, as referring to night: 'a daily absence of day itself, for a regulated period.' "

"You better give me 'day': I might see more."

"Day?: the visible complement of night."

"That's like life and death; good and bad; night and day: you're hardly really *saying* what these things are. You use their oppositeness to get out of the hard, if not impossible, task of applying definitions that really *stick* to what they define."

"Like labels and tags and stickers . . . ?"

"Oh, like nothing. Now tell me: what is man?"

"You ask my professional opinion?"

"How would you print it in the dictionary?"

"I'd have it: 'Man: as distinguished from *woman*.' "

"Then let me put it this way: 'What's woman?' "

"That entry would be: 'Woman: a non-man. See *man*.' "

"But that's not *enough*!"

"Enough of what?"

"Of meaning."

"I *define*; I don't *mean*."

"I thought 'define' *was* to 'mean' or to 'make to mean' or to 'give meaning to.' "

"Yes, you thought that. But it's not what you thought; it's what I do."

"What you say is what you do?"

"Saying is a vocal form of doing, or oral action."

"Are you doing now, or saying?"

"Both."

"All right. Then do me a new definition."

"Doing, saying, and making."

"Making goes in with doing and saying?"

"It belongs."

"Well, you made it that way. You did it, you said it, you made it."

"And all at once, too. The time I save!"

"What do you save the time *for*?"

"For later."

"Time? What's time?"

Time is a unit in space."

"That's insufficient for my needs."

"What are your needs?"

"To *embrace* space. To *consume* time."

"I can only define. To define is a kind of interpretation, a breed of assessment. Make of it what you want. I can't live your life. I can only define."

"But you define, it would seem, inadequately."

"You're consulting me. I didn't advertise. Go elsewhere, if you're unsatisfied."

"I have no choice but to stick with you."

"Then mark my defining, refrain from complaining that it's inferior. Test me anew."

"That window trickles with light. Having been here all night, we're in for dawn. Define sky; define window."

"Sky is free real estate, providing it's high. I forgot the other."

"Window."

"That's right at hand. It's not hard: An indoor-outdoor compromise, with seeing privileges."

"Then what's the sun?"

"The ancient light source that we still tap."

"And what can a butterfly be, whose flutter glimmers with a sun's slice?"

"A paraplegic bird."

"That's too pathologically slanted. You malign it."

"Definitions have to take chances. They're abusive sometimes. They unavoidably give offense, unable to please everything; they're only verbally impersonal. The defined has no case for a law suit on grounds of defamation. Immunity is granted defining. So it carelessly slips irresponsible, at times."

"You're liable to libel, but able to slip free. Say something nice about a flower."

"It's an ornamental plant."

"But not so important as food. Then what's farming?"

"A crude method of food manufacturing. Know what the city version of a farmer is?"

"No, then let me ask."

"Though he cultivates the soil, he's uncultivated because soiled."

"Do puns enter definitions?"

"Sometimes too dominantly."

"What's God?"

"That's too high for me."

"Then what's the soul?"

"An ambassador of God."

"What are you?"

"A dictionary-maker."

"And me?"

"Confused."

"Why did I come to you?"

"Out of confusion."

"But you didn't seek me. I beseeched you.

"True."

"You didn't advertise."

"No."

"What's advertising?"

"A suggestion disguised into art."

"What do you recommend?"

"It's morning now. I suggest you give up. You haven't been helped. Words have no power to help you. You're left helpless. I can't help it."

"Then you've failed?"

"I did my best. *You* failed. You're a failure."

"Then?"

"Be one. If you are one, be one."

"But isn't that disgraceful?"

"Only if you care what people think. You can't make out reality, can you? The world is something you can't cope with, master, withstand, adjust to, or fathom. You're at a loss."

"I had sought cure in definitions."

"Words *seem* to be magic, but they're not. Only magic is magic. Words at times are instrumental."

"Is there no remedy for me?"

"None. Give up."

"Is our session over?"

"And our only one it is. There'll be no other."

"I'm miserable. I have no understanding. I'm defeated."

"You are."

"Then I've defined myself?"

"Yes."

"Then who needs you? Goodnight."

"You mean good morning."

"I mean anything. Or nothing. It's all meaningless, somehow." I shrugged. That was my silent gesture. It signified—

And I walked out, opening and closing the door myself, while he remained seated. I went next door to where I lived. And have remained nervous, ever since.

An Endless, Long, Etcetera, Lexicographer's Languish; Ending, Etcetera, in the Same Language, Etcetera

There was a lazy dictionary-maker.

Samuel Johnson? Webster? Oxford University Press? Who was he?

He's obscure now, but famous in his own day.

Oh. (*Pause.*) Why was he lazy?

He was given seven years to make a dictionary, the contract was drawn up by the publisher, and he was given a huge editorial staff of derivation-experts, grammarians, vocabularists, spelling-bees, connotation-technicians, meaning-literalists, form-stylists, synonym-semanticists, metaphor-parabolists, locution-linguasticists, and such others in verbal scholarship, a compilation of specialists renowned in the fields they covered, and he was made head editor. An exhausting project, to be undertaken with voluminous enterprise.

How did it turn out?

Lazily. They all went to sleep on the job.

Did the seven years then pass by, and the publisher clamor for the completed manuscript as per contract?

That's just what happened to those seven years. He wanted the letter of his contract strictly honored, a dictionary minutely accurate, extensively unabridged, exactingly definitive to the slightest possible syllable.

What did the dictionary-workers, or responsibly their chief editor, hand in, for an opus of the English language?

How they did languish!

In English?

Yes; theirs was the English languish.

How many pages?

Three thousand.

It sounds industrious, for languishing scholarship. A goodly tome, and heavy too. And what text, or content?

All in context.

Was the publisher content?

No. Acutely disappointed.

How so?

Well, the first listing, the very first word of the whole chronological order, from which the entire sequence depended, was of course initially "a".

Only to be expected. The logical way to begin *any* dictionary. "a: an indefinite article." Naturally, of course. Then what follows? What of all the remaining columns of listings, to fill out those three thousand lexigraphically complete pages?

Etcetera. Only that.

Etcetera?

Yes. All the other lines on that first page and on every other page the whole book through, up to and including the final page at the end, contained the same listing: "etcetera."

What an orgy of repetition!

Totally unvaried.

Dull, yet simple.

And lazy. For in what way does laziness manifest itself?

Through, by, of, and in *repetition*.

And so the same repeated word.

"Etcetera"'s all the way through?

Page after page, straight down the line.

When the publisher perused the submitted manuscript he had commissioned, didn't he, in perplexity, feel cheated?

(*With academic, corrective emphasis:*) He not only *felt* cheated: he *was* cheated.

Then the dictionary-maker and his equally lazy editorial staff—were they punished by being unpaid?

No, each was paid in millions of installments.

How fair-sporting of their hoaxed publisher! What did he give them, in what coin reward their effortless freedom from painstaking toil?

Each was given nothing to start with, and then an endless repetition of etceteras.

The table was turned on them?

Yes, the table of contents was fully overturned. And so returned, as to content reciprocal and vindictive vengeance that bruised the publisher's heart.

Did the lazy dictionary-maker continue in his unpromising career?

You mean was his lack of accomplishment further fulfilled?

Yes, did his achievement take like lines?

His laziness etcetera'd itself so far beyond repetition that the gradation into death was ever sluggishly slight.

A culmination of all his sloth.

Not a just *end*, but a just *perpetuity*.

Yes, a continuation. A linear etcetera, extended as infinitely as etcetera is capable.

And so on. Yes. And so forth.

What was he, in afterlife?

A dictionary-maker. A soft job for him, an unpaid sinecure. Industry indolently passive, to the nth degree. Etceteras rolling by, in manufactured echoes.

Can etcetera mass-produce itself?

Who's to stop its incestuous breeding?

I think people should signify what they mean. "Etcetera" sounds so vague.

Yes. If there are a string of examples, even similar in kind, differentiation should be marked in them, to tell them apart.

But the self-duplicating process of "etcetera" tends to eradicate distinctions, to lump things together, blur their identities into one general blending.

"Etcetera" is a *grouping* agent.

It sure is. Tirelessly.

Then it's socially inclined?

Yes. The lazy dictionary-maker had company. His editorial staff joined him. They're still working on their dictionary.

What a slumbering unity!

On they drone. Endlessly.

While the publisher frets?

He's *with* them, now. *His* etcetera has been *added*, to the lot.

Will one more etcetera spoil the job?

No. But it won't *finish* it, either.

What a vastly overworked vehicle, is this "etcetera"!

(*Correctively academic:*) It's an overworked *entity*. As a *vehicle*, it leads only to itself.

Perfect endlessness. But not *my* ideal of the best dictionary.

Ditto mine, neither.

Ditto?

Yes. Etcetera.

Are you etcetera-ing me?

No: first there was *me*: you're *my* etcetera.

No; I came first; followed, etcetera, by you.

You're the etcetera!

You are!

What a squabble! What will resolve it?

Nothing. Etcetera.

What's etcetera to nothing?

You mean what's nothing's etcetera?

Yes, so to speak.

The same thing. Ad infinitum.

Oh. Those Latins cursed us. They bequeathed us trouble. Ditto laziness. Ad infinitum. And etcetera: that hazy, crumbled bunch of lax meaning crushed into etcetera's pulp, ditto ad infinitum, and all the rest.

All the rest? All *what* rest?

The rest we need, once etcetera is done.

Done from what?

From imitating itself as a substitute for a catalogue of likenesses.

What is etcetera similar to?

It's *similar* to, and not only that, but *is*, *another* etcetera. Altogether.

Altogether what?

The same thing. In etcetera-form.

Etcetera has a form!?

It's formed along lumpish lines. Let's delete it.

From what?

From the whole list.

Of what?

Etceteras.

Then, lacking the list, we'll be listless.

Listen: That's good.

What's "good"?

Meaning is good.

Meaning what?

Anything, and the other etceteras.

Oh, what a lazy energy we have.

And a slack energy. And a void energy. Limp, negligible—(*Groping:*) I'm fishing for other synonyms.

(*Suddenly solving it:*) Just insert "etcetera."

(*Brightening:*) Of *course!* That will do.

The Bedtime Play

To what extent is reading aloud to send an old man to sleep a linguistic activity?

It depends on what you read to him. Trashy newspapers? Or great classics?

How can I tell? I don't *follow* the words, *uttering* them is *enough* for my salary.

As an old union member and still a socialist agitator, I'd like to know what your pay scale is.

My wage is earned only during the time he's sleeping. So I try to read boringly, in a monotonous tone of voice, droning a lullaby of endless vowels, to drowse him into slumber's rhythm. I repeat what I'm reading over and over again. My employer's only relief is to seek refuge in the sweet audible chamber of sleep. And my words tap softly on the window, to remind him gently.

Don't *you* occasionally doze off, to keep in step?

Yes, that way I'm in closer contact with my job, and participate in my boss's intention in a sympathetic union of understanding. There's an obvious bond between us.

Is your boss senile?

No, he sleeps it off.

Oh. (*Pause.*) But doesn't the job age *you*?

Old age is infectious. *His* rubs off on me. A few working hours, and years of my prime are stripped away.

(*Concerned, warning:*) You're giving too much to your work. You'd better ease off!

But there's an economic depression, and I can't find another job.

Isn't going hungry preferable to growing old too quick?

Cut out your rhetoric. Theories don't interest me.

Then will you permit a *practical* question?

Toss it, and I'll see.

Do you get paid when your boss is afflicted with *insomnia*, and finds sleep impossible?

No, then I'm reading free of charge, for I'm not doing my duty. My pay rate begins with his sleep, and ends with his waking. So it's essential I succeed, and so I seek the worst literature written, for its soporific effect. Nothing adventurous, dramatic, pulsating with excitement, intensely suspenseful, would serve my monetary purpose: such literature is a professional liability, so I shun it. If a dreary piece has survived from a long time ago (I'm limited only to modern English, with my client), I roll it out like a hot blanket, and its uniformity lures him, or absorbs his membrane, to his chosen dream's gripping change of interest, to raise his drooping submission to serenity's oblivious flight on a heavy swell of earth-like air. I'm not allowed to read incomprehensively: the words must do it, themselves.

Are your working conditions easy?

I try to shut the windows to get a smothering airlessness in the room, but this he won't approve of. He wants to be *alertly* comfortable. I must *work* for my salary, under more handicaps than advantages. He's perverse. He takes a nap before I show up on the job, to increase the exertion of my labor, if I'm to succeed. He's wide-awake when I arrive, and pep pills have boosted his stimulation to boot. He fails to go off spontaneously, I have to *seduce* him to the merits of sleep. He resists its appreciation until completely overtaken. My burden is exhausting. He's so fresh and vigorous with sleep behind him, that my art, by guile, deception, cunning, enchantment, spells, and potions — all with written matter — is to renew him numbly into being overcome. He won't permit my rattling off of multiplication tables from a mathematical text: he prefers fiction, in which he takes an active interest, until persuaded passively by my sleep-inducing act of reading. The effort is so tedious, I drone myself away, while he mocks me, and prods me awake. When I recover, I take the heaviest book, and bang him on the head. The words come down hard on him, and he's spun out. But I'm penalized for such violence, and deprived of an hour's pay. But I've weakened him, and he's a readier prey.

Your description has made me sleepy. (*Begins to droop off the chair.*)

The minute you fall asleep, you begin paying me money.

(*In a passive outburst of indignation:*) But I'm not your client! When have I offered to purchase your services!?

You're my *involuntary* client. Although it seems unfair, I've got to make a living. When you're helplessly asleep, I'll make a stealthy raid on your wallet, and lift my base pay from it, plus overtime. Now be fixed into a trance, by my mesmerization. How sedately you sit there! The dummy's waxen tranquility. Lethargy's cloud has scooped you up, you keel over on torpor's wing, and stupor drones you pleasantly. (*Other has been miming this description appropriately. Starts, and makes a desperate struggle to revive. Falls off again, but in a fit, comes to, with clenched fists, determined to stay awake.*) I read expertly. (*Takes up a book, holds it open in front of him:*) Follow me, and don't trail off. (*Reads and reads, aloud, from any work. His victim is slumbering meekly. Goes over to sleeper, and frisks him of his wallet. Selects a few denomination bills, pockets them, replaces the wallet with its oblivious owner, and walks back. Talks, standing erect, directly to audience, with victim fast out behind him. In confidential tone, as though conning and humoring audience alternately:*) That's how I lull them. The old man is a myth. They're all my old men. A slow, old confidence game. The evening is late. Perk up, folks. Your sleeping lies before you. What are you going home for? (*Smirking grin. No curtain. The play is over.*)

Why It Was Better That This Story Be Left Unfinished Than to Delve Off into Forbidden Research Necessary to Complete It; and So, Short of That, It Ends without End, Truncated by Its Abbreviation into Familiar Terms, for the Unknown Couldn't Be Ventured, and the Mystery Orbits on in Its Customary Suspense

Tom has just lost his brother.
How tragic. Were they very close?
No, the brother was in California, and Tom here in New York.
That's not very close.
No.
Then what made them brothers?
Their mother and father.
Are their mother and father close?
They're poles apart.
That sounds extreme. Can you explain?
Absolutely. The mother is alive, the father dead. So their being apart,

you see, transcends even the limits of geography, and takes on an otherworldly dimension, as from one sphere to something so opposite it's entirely different. Perhaps a whole eternal infinity divides their states and keeps them totally apart, pared off separately. Yet at one time they were so close that the hugging conceived Tom and his brother; though many was the lost sperm from their union, which never came to bare fruit other than pleasure's temporary satisfaction in and of, as it so turned out, itself. But that was before, when all night and all day for years they kept within touching opportunity when he wasn't away working. Their union now is dissolved, forever.

Why are you telling this sad story?

It *told* me to tell it. I was its spokesman. The story passed through me, and is now in you. It won't rest there. It'll move on elsewhere. It's so restless it has everywhere to go before winding up nowhere. That's what is known as a "moving story". It moves the listener to hear, the teller to tell, and itself is in motion, for a story must go.

How far does a story have to go?

If it's a tall tale, it flies very high. Or it may have broad humor, and that's how wide it is. Or it may be deep. Or it may go to any length. Or it may be spun out, like an unrolled ball of yarn, and what a yarn that would make, up to the last shred of narrative thread, as the plot unravels.

Duration is about the size of any story, I guess. At length, that's what it comes down to. To what extent does it have far to go? Can you tell?

No telling how far, for some stories are bound only by their own extent. This limitation proves many stories' undoing, but others it liberates into a limitless land of their own, depending on what goes into them, what the tale-bearer makes of his ingredient contents, to fill up the tale and round it out with what goes into it, and how, and whether. So there's no telling.

But if there's no telling, then the story isn't being told. How can an untold story remain a story? Tell how.

Oh, now, that's altogether a different story.

There are *many* different stories. There could be stories within stories, and the story of an untold story whose telling would be another matter. But back to Tom and his brother, and their separated parents. Have you done, or is there recapitulating? Or by summing up, can you insert the moral that would do me good, and make the story practical for me? Ultimately, *conduct* is served by stories. They're not just idly to amuse. Am I over-Victorian? Or ultrapragmatic? Supply the moral, please. If I take the moral to heart, the story will have grown into me. It will become *applied*, and not only a passive aesthetic tale for whose sake of telling art stops short without providing instruction. I'm living a life, and the story that helps me learn *how* functions most significantly in its use and purpose that I endow it with. Then direct your story to my interest, and go on with it. The test will be what it can do for me. That's an inartistic doctrine to impose on a tale's innocence, but I do like my advantage to be served, and my cause advanced. What my cause *consists* in, perhaps your story will suggest, as you let it fly. Now, proceed.

That's a tall order, that demands a tall tale that can fit in with what you can drag out of it. Can't you forget yourself, and employ the story as a portal of escape, a vacation from the self you're so occupied in living? Being diversion or distraction might even improve the story's quality, and make it tighter self-contained for what it is, instead of porously open to nourish your gain and edify *you* at its own sacrifice of well-being as a story for the tale of it. So will you let it be itself, bound to rules of its own inner device, strengthened and self-sufficient? Will you grant the concession that the story *be*, in its independent entity that will force you not to exploit, but to respect, it? For a story is nobody's tool, not even the teller's. It endeavors to be spoken into life, employing tongues for that purpose, and using such listeners as you are, to preside over its authenticity as the enraptured audience and its more or less legal witness if you're called upon to testify.

Is that to be my role? Am I so summoned? The *story* is central?

So *you* serve *it*, and let it come right out. As *I* serve it, tellingly.

Then narrate, while I hear. If such be the will of the story, and we its instructed foils to minister its arriving in transaction to do its business. I already forgot who the characters were, though I recall that two brothers were severed by the death of one, as in also their parents' case. What point was it supposed to make?

Don't presumptuously violate; let the story dictate *its* terms, declare *its* cause. What's "intended" by the story is *your* idea; what it *turns out as*, is more like what it is, which must be imposed *upon* you, to sink in.

I'm not, then, to "read in"?

That would abuse the story's justice, and insult its integrity, and toy its soul with disrespect. Let it come working over you, and take it for what it is. Be the commanded receptacle, or recipient, for the fate-driven story to light upon, by its inner light. Be consumed in *its* glow, auditory to its individual tone as it so prescribes to come out and be defined as.

It's a self-declared gift, so give your eager gratitude.

All right, then, I submit, to acquiesce, and be only a passive bystander so that the enchanting spell will take its toll on me as the *story* is disposed, in its fabled authority. I won't interfere, or cramp the full flowering of its style that takes the form of its inner content. But will it be comprehensible? I'd feel like a fool not to understand.

It will take its effect, if you expose your mind's obedient sensitivity to the tone the story makes by its own weight. Be, then, overcome.

Mastered and attuned am I, come what may. I meet the story's march in humble subjection; or stand aside, as it goes strolling by, in pageantry: in color unfurled, and drums thumping. That rhythm shall infect me, and place in me its echo for recollection ever to meditate. And so the story stands absorbed, in my moving bone.

Now the lesson is learned for you how to listen, but where were we at the story's progress? Tom had a brother, who died far away. Tom's *father* died, in his mother's company. Now what follows, or is led to, by a disunified family? The father's death occurred long ago, the brother is removed only recently: but far across the continent, outside the family pale. Where does that leave mother and Tom, surviving here in mutual bereavement? They alone are left to feel. But the story hasn't accounted for what they're feeling: it's left unsaid, or not included. What *does* the story go on to state? For surely that's not the end of it.

Wrestle with that problem. I'm only listening, and my task is easy. Yours is difficult, for you must interpret.

This story has omitted what I can't relate. It *does* delegate that I tell you what I'm about to say, though it shadows and repeats. (I've lost my clarity in it; will it come back to me?) Tom had a brother, as happens in the normal circumstance of *any* family. The brother was far away to die in California. The father was close at hand to die in the mother's arms. All that is so far connected, and satisfactory. By implication, what is all this directed at? By close or far relationship? Brother carried off at great distance, father previously passed away at home with mother at bedside, with Tom nearby in the same city. (Brother had been then alive in California, too far for attending.) What, then, have we been told, of distance? Is death a distance carried too far? Or does death make a *time* distance, more than mere geography?

You're getting down to basic abstracts, onto a vast metaphysical plane. The story seems expanding: yet sinking in as well. Go carry it out, if you can.

Is *time* what death plays at, in its most primary dimension? Is distance not just a matter of ground covered, or of tract never penetrated; is distance in the *time* sphere, as well?

I'm only *listening*. Go on, however you stumble. You're on difficult ground. Or your time zone has rocky pockets. But brace yourself, and haul on. And let the subject emerge, through you.

Death is a theme, here. But, being *alive*, how can *I* be the one to cover that alien ground, that remote terror? That territory of only indirect familiarity? For it's another world, and perhaps a different compelling story. I must stick to the story at hand, but have lost my push on it. I'm inadequate to the theme, or awkward. Inspiration's source has withdrawn its support. I've gone just so far, and now am stranded, like a landed fish that keeps wishing evolution had advanced it to a frog state so that land wouldn't be out of its element; it's too late; and so, I'm stalled.

Your hesitation bores me, if you can't drive on, however inexperienced are your personal qualifications to deal with death and treat of its admittedly unknown properties. Two of the four characters in your tenuous story (sketched, so far) are within death's principality; and since you've carried us *so* far, how dare you stop, on the very verge! Spill over, into death's impact, so that you can report it, or observe. Give us a firsthand account, so you can emulate, identify, embrace with, empathize with the two corpses who figure in your story. If you don't do that field research (and you're *committed!*), like a responsible tale-bearer, then it's an aborted tale, and you're in disgrace!

Must I save face, as a storyteller, only by dying?! But *returning* is no assured guarantee. That notion scares me off, for, by death's fear, I cling to earth's sphere, where life is gladly inhaled, and safe, even if the story has to fail by lacking the courage to follow two dead characters into where death has placed them, metaphorically speaking. I'd rather be here, silent, than to die completing my story. Was it *my* story? No, I was tentatively used, then discarded, to be its beginning's spokesman, up to the middle part where danger paused my tongue. A *braver* customer will perhaps go through with it: when found to risk a one-way Hades expedition to keep up with his characters' transformations. But *I* reticently retire, right now.

I'm truly annoyed. I was ready to hear. *Now* you dare to stop!? After setting me up for this, and poking suspense on its cradling precipice? You've let me down! By giving it up, you leave me flat, and expectation suspires like a de-pumped brassiere of false, glaring disappointment as the air goes hissing out to rudely reveal the *bones* of bareness, and not the gorgeous promised flesh! You're a fake fraud! Leaving the story, just as its lurch will detour on the untold glory! You avoided the chase, when poised on discovery, to pull up short, perched on the promontory, in precarious peril but *great* revelation. You had no heart or stomach for the noble leap, or fortitude for heroics. Your sinews caved in, to keep you safe. The audience will make a frustration-complaint, indignantly. You taught me to hear; then took away the exciting end; and the story falls short, in its hour of expansion beyond mortal limits in eternal dare!

I hate to disappoint you. But there it is. I embodied the story, only to an extent; then muzzled its tongue, when the air grew faint. Such restraint, and determined shunning, reaches out for years of survival, though at the story's cost, sorry to sacrifice it, but I'm personally preserved.

Your person was meant for the story's transcendence *through* it, into the further sphere. It was ready to *take off!*

And dies here. Grounded, earthbound. My skin's salvation, despising otherworldly illumination. My dumbness is a remaining. There's no *human* agent for this story: it must seek elsewhere.

You betrayed conduction, as the poor conduit! It's stalled up in you, blocked. You were to vehicle its grace into metaphysics, convey it with no loss to its outward-bound magnitude! But you de-amplified it, with mechanical obstruction, opposing its telling by a selfish will. All that untransmitted knowledge, that couldn't leap off! Can that stifled energy unknot itself, and even crawl back? Your fault is gross. 'What was I listening for? Where's the patient audience's vicarious reward? I long to know how Tom's brother and father fare across the great boundary. Your transparency was to launch it out; instead, your opacity pents it in. And no mental adventure is afforded me, in the unnegotiable beyond! A story's momentum crossed up, its unshed illumination dying in your denseness, in the opting-out of your will for cowardly survival. The obscured immensity, that can never be told!

My undischarged duty is repentant. I deserted my post, I admit. Let me make recompense. Paltry, in the circumstances; the triflest token, to atone. Let me speculate, and give death's *conjecture*, at second-hand remove. Not real, I'm afraid: but the second-best, that I can do. I'll *feebly* venture out there, in mind; and the mental phantom will have to do: death's pale version, telescoped at remote. An estimate.

I don't esteem that. How it *might* have turned out no longer interests me. I wanted to *know.*

It would make me no longer human to go on pursuing what can't be found out except in sampling death—whose slight taste then drowns us in its meal. I stop short, and you'll learn no more.

I was taught to listen. Now I'll finish *telling*, where listening left off. This I fully intend to do. So stand back, and I'll continue.

That's bold. We reverse roles. *I* listen, now.

Tom's brother died only very recently, in time, but distantly in *miles*, across the continent. He crossed the "great divide," a short time ago.

Yes. That's what I was telling you.

Tom's *father*, though, died differently, in that, though it was years ago, many years ago, it was here at home, close, the mother was there, and Tom in attendance too, only inches away. The problem is, how the *brother*'s death compares with the *father*'s death. To answer that problem, I'll go dive after them. I'll plunge over the "great divide," and be on the other side. Then I'll report back. Keep listening.

I will, being curious as to how it will end.

Off I go. Wish me luck. My fact-finding exploration may discover *All*, in its black intensity.

Fill me in on it. Put me in the picture, describe how it is. I'll be waiting to hear.

And not for long, I hope. Here goes, then. High up, or deep down, trading security for unfathomed scope. I'll leap past the ultimate mystery, and pluck it down to analyze it.

Now you're only speaking. Where's your doing?

Is your listening turning impatient?

You bet it is. The story was mine to begin with. Like a relay race; the baton or torch is now transferred into *your* keeping, with the horses changed in midstream, and now you're the anchor man, boldly to breast the finishing tape, and that without any hesitation on your part. So you better get going, for it's crowding into late. Nibble across the boundary, with a swift taste of death. Then say how different it is, in Tom's *brother*'s case, or in Tom's *father*'s, way out there. The spectacular scoop of the age will be made by you in person. Or you'll die trying, and the world will be no worse. The rehearsal has ended. Be a man of your words. Put the play on. Go shuffling off, and find how the stage is, out there. I'm waiting here, anxious to hear. I once disappointed you, preferring cowardice and the tale's abbreviation. Go ahead, don't let *me* down: you're to make *up* for me.

You're rooting me on?

As your greatest fan. For you to do, what *I* confessed I *couldn't*. Spin onto the magic coil, and end the mystic suspense of what's *there*. Enlighten the coward's knowledge, at your own sacrifice.

Is just a story worth it?

You're chickening out, now, just as I did?

I prefer the story *untold*, and *me here*.

How *would* it have been?

Who cares? I'm glad to be here.

We're in the same boat.

And it's afloat. Thank God.

Desire's Endeavor toward Life

I

Once there was a would-be creature. Like actual creatures themselves, this would-be creature had a fundamental problem, or aspiration. It was: to become a real creature.

Its would-be parents had happened not to have met yet, so that their sexual congress was an event that had not yet taken place, which would have fertilized, or given conception to, this creature that craved mightily to be propelled into the launching-out of its birth and thus its ultimate being. It sought one simple thing: to exist.

Suspended in some timeless element, and without an ounce of space to take up, this would-be creature was dissatisfied to be oozing amorphously in so formlessly undefined a state. It had as yet no grounds for identity.

It was urged on by its single desire. It hoped for fate's endorsement, and destiny's future will. It felt incomplete, having not yet reached the initial stage requisite to qualify as a candidate for becoming created. Nor could it even claim *youth* as an advantage.

Who could promote it to existence? What form would its emergence take?

If only it could take refuge in a seed! Then it would join April's calendar, and become a timely bud.

And it would flower, when plunged into appropriate opportunity!

Or—it daydreamed—another alternative would lie in the direction of becoming a species of animal life, like a deer that bounds in the woods. But perhaps a hunter would take deadly aim, and shoot it. All that trouble to become alive; and so squalid, so ungraced by dignity, an end to the buoyant breath in the lungs' organic dynasty! Then maybe it should become a slimy crocodile, or a similar hard-scaled reptile, oozing in the friendly mud of some shallow jungular bath. Unfortunately, this would entail an ugly appearance. Its vanity was too proud, its aesthetics too sublime, to settle for so sordid a condition. Then why not choose to become a bird, its throbbing carriage crested by a noble umbrella of plumage?

And how enjoyable flight would be! It would climb the clouds and be nocturnally present at the coming-out ball to commemorate the new debutante stars, trailing glittering gowns behind.

Yes, but a bird was too frail. While on some routine descent, or ascending into some woolly current of snow, the bird's heart might fail, and the scattered breast attend some frozen, earthbound burial. Flight's joy could not redeem so sorry a plight; mortality abounds with more malice in a being of a bird's delicacy than in a more substantially framed creature.

Why not, mused this would-be thing, become a regal stallion, a horse so virile that its racing-enthusiast owner would fence it in an erotic pasture where it could stud with willing mares, rearing to the ultimate neigh and converting it to yea, siring a race of yearling colts groomed to the competitive range of speed? That would be a fine thing to happen. But every horse is a proven illiterate. Thus it was that the would-be creature yearned, with entreaties to heaven, for a divinely human birth, whether in the garb of a man or in the more feminine role of a woman. One task remained: to go hunting, in sprightly eugenics, for its own would-be father and mother. And the issue of their union should be—not anyone else but (by rigorous control of chance) this would-be creature's own ego-precious little self! "Birth!" it pronounced, ablaze with its goal.

II

What it demanded might not be attainable. Perhaps it would become a fragile insect. It would crawl up a tenement-house wall, in some dank room reeking of the stench of the stove. The occupant, in a fit of boredom, would end the life of this presumed cockroach by flattening it with a hardcover book. Thus, paperback books were more congenial to insect preservation.

This would-be creature hasn't arranged an introduction of its parents: it lacks the matchmaking technique. Or would it consent to be the illegitimate offspring of two bohemian partners in free love's transient but not-thus-any-less-passionate embrace? Could it keep its self-respect, being a lifelong bastard?

Or would a moth's, or butterfly's, destiny be for it? First it would serve the apprentice caterpillar phase of its required term, after leaving the soft life of a cocoon. It would give people the creeps. Then it would flutter away. But it must, to avoid having its wings singed, beware of the luminescent flame. Even a street lamp's attractions could prove lethal.

Some day, as a dessicated butterfly, it would be mounted. To end up as a fossil in a collection was not its idea of heaven. But theological theories were only valid in the human brain.

How to attain to such status? The way unknown, the method would be difficult. And once being born, it must avoid certain diseases.

III

This would-be creature, though neither corporeal nor embodied, was endowed with presuppositional imaginings, or projections of conjecture, posing conditional problematicals, in speculations of a metaphysical nature. It was spiritually conscious: all that its soul required was some specific outward form. It detested all this aimless floating.

But only *God* could engineer a birth. The would-be creature, however, had no recourse to any divine being with authority to order the birth of this importunate as a registered event in time's long-lasting world of phenomena in the concrete. If necessary, it would wait. Its primary selection as a personal state was that in the cast or mold of humanity, base as it might be in annals of fame or legend. But being deprived of that ideal embodiment, it preferred *some* form of existence. Would not two dogs mate, producing a mongrel cur?

Yes, that very instant this was happening. But the puppy thus whelped from the dug-drug bitch was *not*, it chanced, this would-be creature at all. It was some anonymous dog, that's all.

IV

The would-be creature longed for an existence. It pined to become matter: it was packed with spirit without a physical outlet. Oh, how woeful, and tragic! Its patience was a burned-out candle. Perhaps, in the bottom of the sea, was a pile of eggs left there by some queenly maternal fish. The sperm had joined the embryo, to engender the fertilization of a hatching. Couldn't this would-be creature lodge itself through an opening in some egg, ripe for the eventual spawning of itself as a fish no matter what perils exist in the form and feature of some veteran expert fishermen? The would-be creature would even undergo an underwater life, if need be, in order to be promoted to the satisfaction of being a live, quick fish, slippery-silver in its mercurial swiftness, to join the swim and register in a likely school. It would be agleam, both with scales and fins. Gills as well, in a regular course.

But would these theories hold water? How doleful; in a forlorn and wan vision, the would-be creature foresaw the unlikelihood of its arriving to a fish's estate. Not for it, a seafaring life. Doomed never to rove in any inscrutable sea, pushed by mysterious currents.

V

Determination would get it nowhere. It was suspended in some statelessness, a vacuum abhorrent to nature and fiercely abominable to self. What a rut of nonbeing!

VI

Oh, for another episode! Wasn't this thing fixed in some process, some arrested stage, of a metamorphosis so gradual that birth was yet eons ahead! Then forebear to despair; let eternal sufferance be endured, the patient acquiescence to some yet unfound fate. When discovery was good and ready, a lifetime would wait at the other end.

To coin Whitman's well-known phrase, might it become, in time, a blade of grass? Even humbler than a lily or dandelion, or thistle blown to the wind? Less even than a daisy that doesn't till or toil? Cursed in the fatigue of suspense and the ennui of monotony, the would-be creature waited to "find" itself; its salvation depended on the thread of completion. But not even the first infernal stage had been negotiated: not even was it the tadpole to the coarse and hoarse croakings of an actual toad-in-the-offering. The future was so bleak, it drew a great big blank. What a dismal thing to look forward to!

Maybe . . . some day . . . but not today, anyway.

No, its prospects were decidedly nil, and hope was constricted to an emaciation of bones. Like a beautiful forty-year-old virgin, it was overripe: too ripe to be plucked.

In its "mind," the would-be-thing traveled. It spent its time, when it could afford to, contemplating the bestial inmates of a zoo. They were caged, but alive. Though suffering with futile groans at their captivity, they nevertheless possessed the *potential* pleasure inherent in the enviable state of liveness. They were at least *intrinsically* vital—these maltreated beasts. Sympathetically, the would-be creature surveyed them. It felt inferior to every one of them. Even to an old camel, unable to stand, that was dying while dreaming of Arabs in the desert. Even to the bones the humped beast was about to become a pile of. Better, thought the would-be creature, to be a dead has-been, than to be dejected by the frustration of having the dubious honor of being, to no one's satisfaction, a distinct never-was. Or rather, an indistinct nonentity in the mouldering mound of what could have been. How fortunate are those granted the legacy of a birth! They inherit life from forebears, and *are*. The would-be creature is a sort of species among the world of the *not*. Desperate to the pitch of despair, it can never be described as an *is*. Even *that* courtesy is denied it.

VII

Seeking birth, the would-be creature tires of its interminable limbo. Oh, to forsake limbo, and take on the nobility of *limbs*!

But it doesn't know how. It's locked out, due to a previous lack of nativity. That prerequisite condition had not been met, much to the damage of the possibility for existence. From lifelessness, a grumbling discontent arose. "Life at any cost" becomes the obsessional campaign slogan. Anything, even slime, would do.

VIII

Couldn't it first be a unicellular animal, such as an amoeba? Not much style or flair in that, but it was a *start*.

Who knows, once the first step had been taken? After all, evolution wasn't built in a day, as Charles Darwin could tell you were he only alive again. (He sleeps, but evolution doesn't: it escorts man to some precarious future.)

IX

Seeking a beginning, the would-be creature thinks: "Damn it, if I can't be born decently, or furtively, or clandestinely, or whatever, then I'll apply to be *adopted.* Surely some childless couple (whose parental instinct has been thwarted by some malformation of chance, or sterility or impotence, or compulsive virginity based on a religious scruple of abstinence and a continence dutiful to the insanity of conscience) will want to adopt me. But first I must be placed at an agency."

"Sorry," said the adoption agent, "you can't be our client—we can't be of service to you as a broker between you and foster parents—unless you're altogether *born.* Which you're not."

That was a final refusal. This disappointed the would-be creature no end. Due to the inability to claim a beginning. Fingering its empty waste with spider-like would-be fingers that trace an invisible web, the would-be creature said, "Unequipped with a beginning or end, I have no substantial middle." Thus, "he" was in no danger of becoming complacent.

X

He decided to adapt the pronoun of "he," rather than the more neuter-like "it," when narrating of his non-adventures. It would *approximate* being male and living, with the self-delusory "he." It was wishful thinking, and was obviously scornful of reality; but it granted him certain solace. Lacking something sturdy, there was nothing to prevent his *dreaming,* was there?

XI

This would-be creature has a nominally masculine, though tentative and unproven, if unearned, pronoun to be referred to by as. "He" is "him." Verbally, that's a start, anyway. "In the beginning was the word." Well, maybe it would prove magical, in conjuring up the existence. Language gets things going. Especially one so mental as himself.

Flushed with this at least token "progress," he proudly surveys his accomplishment. But he has no more flesh than before, nor an understructure of bones to guide the skin's stitching. Nor has he a proper-noun name; that would be an attendant bonus to existence, the byproduct inevitably conjoined to birth. How much later, oh Lord, must this soul wait, reduced to the flimsy economy of the inessential, before graced by departure from the unknown, entry into the visible social band of men? Then he'd be handed out an identity, by which his fellow men could mock him. That little rite of initiation would surely ensure his "belonging." It's what he's longing for, with his heart-unaided soul. Life is a gift; but a gift is gratuitous; it can't be desired.

XII

Desire he continues to do. He "does" this, in default of *being*. On a nebulous slice of space, somewhere in mentality's spiritual horizon, this not-yet-thing does his vague and wispy wishing for that state that would annihilate his noxious nonentity: existence, fully blown. That is: to eat, sleep, and have sex, violate laws, be schooled, work in an occupation, pursue the active pleasure principle, betray friends, attend burials of others, get drunk riotously, be bored for too long a stretch, philosophize with vague ill-management of terms, gradually become cognizant of self-ignorance, go out for a ride, attend sport spectacles, participate in some form of amusement, gamble (a little too unwisely), defecate with relish on the toilet seat, confuse one thing for another, admire painting and sculpture in a museum, travel during one's vacation, get furiously angry, write a letter to a newspaper editor, read some classic in its translated original, get together with the gang, conspire against a common enemy, deplore war and its attendant evils, become disillusioned about politics, debate internally about religion, fornicate in betrayal of a mate, walk in the country for fresh outdoor exercise, bathe in the sun, be ill of an unknown virus, complain about inconvenient weather, grumble to a platform conductor about the lateness of some scheduled train, swim and go boat-riding, cultivate perhaps an animal pet, undergo a conversion to a new resolution (if ineffectually, however well-meant), get old with gradual reluctance but a mature if seedy acceptance of its inevitability, trifle with one's children (but cajoling them when they weep), suffer a streak of conscience, be depressed in a fit of pessimism, joy at beautiful spring flowers, be annoyed by an intruder, feel paranoic (and be deranged by persecution mania), exult when feeling better, be converted to a new enlightened way of speeding life's process of efficiency, grope along (looking for variety in the procedure of method, if renouncing the hope for an altered design of life's ends), become affiliated with a movement, be saturated with the sameness of what at one time was so briskly fascinating, pluck a few hairs from one's decaying body, brush one's teeth before replaced by dentures, be fired from one's job by a boss monstrously ungrateful, conceal the fact from one's wife during a drinking bout, graduate to a higher class in one's school term, find oneself promoted and giving vent to an outburst of surprise, think deeply about some trivial matter, be unconscious during the painful course of an inadvertant accident, lend a sum that's never returned, endure some heroic crisis with courageous irresolution and subsequent remorse if not dismay, regret an unfortunate deed, apologize for an impolite lapse of tact, pray furtively to God when other agnostics are not listening, root for the favorite baseball team in its crusade to win the pennant, shut off the television set because of the drowsiness it induced, get nervous if not panicky during some slight emergency due to a failure in the cross-wiring of the nerves, revolt against some insensible convention but being reprimanded for stepping out of line by an envious victim of institutions, enjoy a robust feast, be a feeble shadow of what once was, and other assertions of the living presence. Why shouldn't he fully *be*—be a self-integrated organism, greedy for the preservation of self and the intact instinctive functioning of all faculties? Is that not a reasonable thing to request—a miracle God can really afford? All one's fellow creatures, whether animal or vegetable, can boast these minimal conveniences, these privileges on the level of necessity. Just to *have* life: he'd shut down all further manifestations of the acquisitive instinct, if endowed with that one perfect thing. He'd force some likely parents to meet and slowly rape each other (having neglected to take contraceptive caution), and the seed that would catch on fire would be the one that would bear *him*: that protoplasmic precious ounce of himself. He depended on two others for his own lively means. He'd pimp his parents together, like some pre-embryonic Cupid who gets Mars on fire for the tasty Venus (into whose luscious ear the young would-be offspring pours the contents of a vial of love potion). Then to be conceived, in an explosive orgy between flailing limbs, with rugged genitals manfully at work and a lovely female receptacle to contain them. Let friction do its stuff, and prod being from its hardly animate potential. He furiously composed the motto, "Better latent than never." Perhaps a pun would bruise the surface of things to be perforated in painful surprise and be impregnated by his own conscious being. He willed the drama of his birth, down to the lightning minute of a man making a father of himself upon a woman who thereby becomes the mother and carrier. Then he'd have ancestry, from distant generations. The glorious jump from the black abstract, the leap over the fence into a tidy batch of life. Sweating so for his life before it begins, he rids himself in advance of the nuisance of fearing death. This one isn't spoiled: he's not surprised to find himself alive—he works for it. He has no silver spoon in his pre-embryonic mouth: merely gritted teeth, clenched from drawn eyes in concentration. Like a winged angel, he hovers near the world: he spots the man—from a whole mass of mass men—whom he infects with the desire to be his father. Then he flies to another part of the city, to inspire a young lady with internal heat. She's drawn magnetically to the would-be father. Romance grips them, with fatal magic. A lyrical impulse knights their rhapsody with a kiss. They experiment with premarital intercourse, then become betrothed. The engagement is announced to their families, to a chorus of congratulations. The legal channel of regularity will be resorted to. The woman has a bridal gown, brilliantly ornate with a cornation. The man is dressed in a black suit. They're joined together. The honeymoon dents an impact. The proposal is in the background. These two responsible adults, he on a leave of absence from work, she liberated from her mother's martyrdom, couple like two blended beasts. Heaven refuses to be constipated any more. The wife's womb has a little seed. It joins the party, and gets a roaring reception.

XIII

He's here. He's alive. However, he's forgotten all his former deprivation. He's born nakedly pure. Oblivious to the anguish that his preformed, would-be self was gnashed with, the frenzy of its prenatal wrestling grip with the bold and proud powers of chance that alone arbitrate to promote fantasy's realm in one unique set of blood-restraining skin held together in a neat bone formation. He's made it! Now failure is defeated, and a new beachhead is erected on a shore timeless with corpses of destiny.

Quiet: Confusion at Work

Approach confusion head-on; don't by-pass it.

Don't make premature sense, which would disrupt your confusion's own internal development.

Let the confusion spread its mystery out. Don't interpret, which is to compose the stale, sterile already-known upon the confusion and thus despoil it of its potential for new discovery, for unprecedented emergence.

Give the confusion headway. It will open up future clarities.

PART FOUR: THE INCONVENIENCE OF LIVING

The Inconvenience of Living

Life, confined to its best, is at least sad. To comprehend, look sharply out of your window. There, waiting to be looked at, is another window. Behind it, an equally dismal room. Is that proof enough?

I looked too far, too much. Going at that rate, I shall never cease to exist.

While baking a pie in the oven, the flames tasted my fingers.

While engaged in making the bed, I caught my ankle on a spring, and neatly twisted it. By then, I was twenty-one.

Since the yelp was continuous, my twenty-third birthday was far from silent.

A girl, catching me by the fancy, lifted my soul through its endurance.

When the endurance subsided, girl and pain became one.

As a lesson in forgetfulness, I tickled my pain. This fatigued the itch.

My skin, burning with mentality, had every reason to think for itself.

Released from gravity, a stone found peace upon my head, and then dropped silently out of motion. Since I was inside my head, sensitivity began to react. The stone, you see, was dead. I inherited all its life. It was almost too much to take.

Blows like these infuriate my skin. Wrapped up in a head bandage, with my heart in a sling, and my foot dangling from its toes, I stepped from house to battlefield, where enemy cars assailed me left and right. Paralyzed with emotion, I slid to the nearest sidewalk. The bone injured was only minor.

Hungry for sex, I married the first girl I saw. The divorce was promptly immediate.

Needing reform, I went to vote. Unluckily, the candidate lost.

Then it dawned on me: religion. Unhappily, I was not admitted: only candidates for heaven are eligible.

Gradually my incentive dimmed, and blindness took possession of both eyes. Deafness closed my ears, and taste was daily discouraged by indigestion. Smell broke. As for touch, that most fragile sense, a bluntness crippled all my fingers. And my important tool, useless between my legs, dwindled into nothing.

Fed up with self-pity, I allowed middle age to corrupt my youth. What had I gained? Experience.

So I became a wise man. I charge fees for advice, and live barely below subsistence.

(*A Tragically Long Title:*)
Learning Was Always Bad for Meyer, Since the Next Case Was Wrong to Apply the Previous Case To, in the Nontransferability of Lessons. There Were Only New Mistakes. A Series of Discontinuities Was Broken Up by a Change of State, with Life Dropping Out of the Memory Altogether. Nothing to Be Learned from *That*.

Meyer never forgets a kindness. When one was done to him, he repaid it promptly, and with interest. But the kind-doer resented Meyer's "returning" the favor so quickly, and chided him with these words:

"You show an unwillingness to undergo the patience of gratitude. I gave you a kindness which you couldn't bear to be 'indebted' to for too long. So you rushed to do *me* a kindness, to put the balance ledger in order so that you owe me not even gratitude. That's unkind and unfriendly of you."

Meyer smarted under the reproach. He yearned to put his new lesson into practice. He waited for someone else to do a kindness to him. He didn't have long to wait. A new kindness was done by another person, which Meyer received with his new-learned patience of sustaining a lengthy gratitude by not immediately "repaying" the kind service or deed. Meyer let years slip by, piling up an incalculable debt of gratitude, with a long-overdue "repayment" simply stalled and idle. Finally, the kind-doer couldn't wait anymore, and punished Meyer's enduring "gratitude" by doing Meyer a grievous injury. That redressed the long-postponed "obligation," releasing Meyer from his bankrupt debtorship. By now it was nearly time for his life to be over. An interviewer asked Meyer to "sum up."

"My conclusions are obscured by doubt," croaked Meyer, "for no two cases in life are just alike. If you apply the lesson of an early case to a later case, the transference may be irrelevant to the later case, and do actual damage, I have no neat body of wisdom. Would you like," he asked the television interviewer while half the nation was hearing and seeing him by remote electronics, "examples in the romantic vein?"

"I urge you," the announcer complied; so Meyer reached back into his past to pluck a shrunken apple from his barrel of sorrow:

"Long ago I loved Nancy. But I was wrong for her, she was wrong for me, yet we were together for years, though our intimacy intensified the wounds and tortures of our mismatch. Pain companioned our love every inch of the way."

"Go on," encouraged the television announcer, "I'm sure the nationwide audience is finding your confession not merely entertaining but edifying as well, for people tend to have similar problems, and maybe your mistakes will prevent others from stumbling likewise, which will ease their lot, though it's too late for you."

Meyer waived aside the interruption and went on as though unhearing. "Nancy and I were just bad for each other. The way she was, and the way I was, meant a nonstop conflict. I acted dictatorial, I badgered her into submission. Her resentment inflicted revenge, there would be gushing passionate apologies, wrenching contrite tears from sexual liquids. It went on like that, for years."

"You poor man, but it's too late now for pity," pointed out, unsentimentally, the announcer in that television interview. Meyer ignored the outburst, and proceeded:

"I became poison for Nancy, she for me, but the bond held fast. Our love was pure hell.

"It ended, somehow, in pain. It took me years to get over it. Separation was a grief only hell could invent. Finally the wound healed. I vowed to apply the 'Nancy' lesson to my next love, who turned out to be named Alice. Whatever I had done wrong in the Nancy case, would be rectified in the Alice liaison. So I became submissive, reversing my former role, while Alice obliged by being a terror and a tyrant, a bitch and a scold, a trial sore indeed. It was more than I could take, and I was more than she could take, for I was foul in my vengeance, sneaking in at her from the side, which my passive deceit could devise. We were wrong for each other. We broke up. Since then, I've been 'alone.' My lessons never did me any good. They were untransferable, for the next case would offer different personal ingredients, a unique problem that had no wise precedent for it, and which would admit, ideally, of its 'own' solution. So I just gave up. Now I'm near death. Learning is a bitter thing. I won't say 'You never learn.' Yes, you do learn. But for what dubious good? Trials succeed trials, and then you edge toward death. I'm older than the average of my viewers on this television. I advise them to heed me not. Let them face what *they* face. What I faced turned out bad, I couldn't cope. Others may be more fortunate. That's all I have to say. If your program still has more time left, fill it in with what's not me. Your program is like my life: its substance is over; then the filling-in, till the formal moment is announced, that all is officially over. So I ride out my tide, with the wave already broke, and the crest long since smashed down."

The announcer praised Meyer's "informative" confession. He would be paid in due time, for a performance not less than splendid.

Meyer left the broadcasting studio. He took a bus home, pondering on what he had said. He had "reported" on his life. That had retroactively altered his life, somewhat. All words and afterthoughts do that, to what they touch upon that went before. Now he wore a new memory, like a change of suits, while waiting for time to release death.

Time owed him a "death," which sounded like "debt." Time was "indebted" to him, but for what?

Time had been patient with gratitude for Meyer's kind-doing to it. Meyer had been so kind to time as to nearly use it all up, thus giving time a function in Meyer's life, a feeling "used" and "needed"; the reward was "debt" ("death"). Thus went Meyer's mind, taking time's part in the dialogue.

The Nancy affair turned out bad all the way, as did, after it, the equally broken-hearted Alice one: but in different ways. Could Meyer have made either case of love turn out better? He couldn't have acted any other way with Nancy, nor Nancy with him, nor with Alice, nor Alice with him: But what if Alice he had met first, and *then* Nancy? No use, such academic rehashing. The life had done itself, in.

Death remained his only topic for years, mentally. But physically he was slow to follow the death his mind dwelled on; mentally he kept living "death"; but living was still his body's occupation. He lived and forgot. Not applying the lessons learned in isolated cases in a sloppy sequence. The cases never got repeated, only new stuff; and he, older, was the newest component yet, to stoke a circumstantial fuel with. But people narrowed out of his life. People had been his life. He wasn't much good at it; had he failed? No, for by what standard? There's no standard. So in the end, no judgment. This settled his "case," out of court. Not enough evidence, or even accusation. Nor consistency to form a body of precedence. It was one accident followed by another, and mangled. Now his problem was age. It was nontransferable, once it got out of hand, to the next of his "destiny"'s conditions, which, simply put, would be nonexistence. He'd have to deal with it cold, and come to it with a thorough lack of preparation, to do it any justice at all, and not impose a prior inappropriate state upon it. Forgetting, the loss of habit, was a way of cleansing himself of preconceptions. He'd make his open approach, with all innocence.

Uncluttered, Meyer went, and lost everything he once had, though nothing was ever retained anway, though there was an overlapping from island to island, connecting people to later people and all subsequent events. Now, no transition, no overlap; nor Meyer, prime begetter of the senselessness of all causes. Life was precious in those living, but to Meyer it became a thing of the past. It had been no lesson learned, to edify a future act. His past, useless before, was now like a house without a roof, upon which, upside down, it stood, as though based there. On that razed site, all sorts of replacements vie, non-Meyers, straining to survive. None reminds of him. They're new and different things, clinging to life on the barren space he vacated: like mounds of refuse on an empty lot, rubble and boys playing ball, stones and junk, shrubs and ants. Even the broken wheel of a baby carriage, well-rusted, subsisting in a "form" of animation, in Meyer's spot. All crowd to fill the vacuum.

Born to Get Revenge. Lowliness Traditionally Enforced, in Guilty Generations. Unworthiness Lusts for Its Next Misbegetting. Thus People Rush toward Parenthood.

Birth flattered me, that such a lowly thing as I should be born.

My parents were ashamed that such an excellent miracle as birth found myself to be wasted on. What trouble they had gone through! Falling in love was such an ordeal! Copulation was so sweaty! Marriage, pregnancy, labor pains, delivery,—oh! successive passages through hell! And all for what? *Me*, of all things.

I survived their contempt, and now am old enough not only to be writing this, but to create a child through a woman whom I got pregnant. I'm waiting for the kid's birth. I'll take out on him what I have been through. He'll feel guilty with no power to atone or compensate, and will start life with that crippling mental disadvantage. He'll only unhandicap himself when he gets to be old enough like me to beget his own brat, upon whom to reap the accumulated cruelty of deferred revenge—as if his own child had been responsible for that father's misbegotten birth. My wife is also angry, and will assist in presiding at our child's inauguration into a moral debt he'll always have arrears in inadequate repaying. Apprenticeship to his own monsterhood, ahead.

I was savagely incomplete when born. That's a heritage to pass on. It's my gift to those mangled enough to survive.

My kid is born flattered. He doesn't deserve it. Birth degrades the born into unworthiness. Scarred parents brand and stigmatize their own.

Birth's curse. To push the ungentle herds generationally on a collective chain of crime. Our guilt lusts to bruise the later ones. Thus life gets pushed along.

My birth! It falls far behind me. I'll catch up, on the other side.

The Birthday Disclosure in a Resurrection Performance on a Dying Miracle Brought to Life
(Title Becomes Clarified If Reread after the Story)

Some ladies are so vain about their age that they won't even admit when they're dead. An excellent case in point was Rebecca, though admittedly an exaggerated example. After she was eighteen, her age was a taboo subject: she'd walk out of a room if someone dared to inquire in the most casual innocence. Rebecca was inflexible on depriving people of that knowledge.

The more time went on (it advances, not retreats), the more rigid was Rebecca's adamant refusal to even *hint* as to her age. Not that people even bothered to be interested. Who would so much as care? considering that Rebecca had always been plain—so plain that not once was she married.

In her youth, Rebecca might have been appealing, since youth in itself is sufficiently sexy to offset even plainness. But a certain primness in her discouraged the sensual ardor of men astray.

Then the years piled up. And on top of the heap, Rebecca, ever unscorched.

She had preserved herself. For what, though?

Having kept herself in reserve, with the mounting years, she religiously guarded, in the most personal safekeeping, the sacred identity of each of her increasing years, with its annual addition of a higher number than the one immediately preceding.

Finally, she aged, and fast. It was accelerating.

Soon she had become almost ageless. Her years staggered under such a creaking burden.

Her age became such a guarded secret that not even the government knew about it, for tax, census, or social security. She had always left it blank, the space provided for "age."

Vainglory, pride, embarrassment, shame—even fear—are possible explanations for her concealing of her age. The age that numbered itself ever higher, and was unknown.

At last, it was time for her to be dead. Her life was about over. It had shot itself out overlong, in continuous exposure to the elements. Her cells had long been in their decomposing process, and her body had broken down all by itself. It was time to say goodbye.

To the world, not to anyone in particular. She had survived all, there would be no mourners.

The time came. Doctor and priest were at her bedside, when the tombstone-engraver also called in; that funereal harbinger of mortality's grim imminence.

He had his sculpting tools with him, and dragged along the tombstone slate. He was about to begin work, but first he needed the necessary details, so as to be accurate about his inscription. "Date of birth?" he asked. Rebecca refused to comply.

The tomb-engraver then volunteered the information of the date it then today was, which would be inscribed as her death date. "No!"

Rebecca shrilled, "I won't allow it!"

The doctor begged for quiet, while the priest granted absolution for last rites. The tombstone-engraver *had* to extract information to do his job properly. "Over my dead body," Rebecca replied, when he insisted. He was at a loss. A loss, precisely, as to her age.

"Very well then," he threatened, "I'll simply *make it up*: I'll invent a date of your birth. Posterity won't care a damn if it's inaccurate. As long as you're represented by *some* birthdate. Just as a social formality, of course."

Rebecca was angry: also annoyed. It was stifling her death, preventing it from coming through. Why couldn't she be left to die in peace? Instead, she was bothered by a persistent inquirer as to a date that was already ancient history and already buried in the forgotten recesses of her obscurely remembered past. It was aggravating. Her privacy felt violated.

But the vulture-pedant couldn't be gotten rid of. He wouldn't let her off. He regarded this research as a duty; she, as irksome.

Well, who would give way?

Doctor and priest both urged Rebecca to drop her fading pride and reveal her secret day of birth. "It's a secret I shall carry to my grave," Rebecca firmly maintained, fervent, gritty, plucky to the end. Teams of horses couldn't wrest the secret from her. All her life she had guarded it: why should she relinquish it *now*?

The engraver kept hounding. Rebecca was weakening, and passed into a coma.

She died abruptly. The secret would be interred with her. It would be hers, forever.

But then a miracle happened. The corpse went into labor pains, and a tiny baby Rebecca was spontaneously born from the already expired womb of her dead and virgin mother. An unexpected event like this, with its absolute defiance of the myth of the scientific norm, presented posthumous and post-nativity problems, of simultaneous concern to the late Rebecca and the new one.

Had the girl been born on the day of her death? or had the old woman died on the day of her birth? This technicality the priest pondered, as also did the doctor and the tombstone-engraver. A new birth would have to be registered. An orphan was born who was her own mother—whom she never saw. This paradox became a matter for metaphysics to ponder, beyond biology's literal scope.

It was a healthy new Rebecca born on her death. She would be brought up as a foundling; a wet nurse would have to be found, and the formalities gone through; like papers to be signed, and forms filled in.

The engraver inscribed one date—that one of that day—as taking on the double duty of doing for the woman's birth as well as death. This bordered on the miraculous, since a very old woman had died. But an equally *young* one had replaced her.

* * * * *

The indecent detail remained: whose sperm had it been? If this conception was immaculate, there were theological possibilities inherent, meditated the priest historically. After all, the *Christian* myth . . .

Complicated? Yes.

The soul of the old Rebecca had passed into her replacement. Given another century, the miracoulous might be repeated, if the new Rebecca lived up to the old one's form. So this history is not yet concluded. A lifetime remains to be reported.

But *this* birthdate was recorded. The new Rebecca would have no liberty to conceal it. Granted she had inherited the same soul: but her birth evidence was out in the open. It was easily investigatable. Will this make a difference, as to her life's conduct?

Her mission is to search for her father. The agent, at the surprisingly last moment, of her appearance at the entrance of a dead womb.

She was the creature of whose seed? Should the factor be located, he'd find a young wife on his hands: Rebecca meant to trap him that way, and legitimize her father through her bond of marriage to him. A radical spiritual departure from her dead and mourned mother, her self's previous lifetime instantly succeeded and by all creed rectified. The past redeemed—her own and her mother's joint mutual past.

Rebecca sprung out. The life-giving properties of death.

The date to commemorate it.

The will to redeem. The avenged skeleton rattling away in her own body's closet.

The Rebecca lineage. A small dynasty, like two linked cells, within life's perpetual frame that assimilates dates as vanished miracles.

Rebecca's vanity of old. But broken up in the reform regime of the falsehood-forsaking generation that clarified the buried miracle in its ancestral unearthing. Life sucks on her second Rebecca.

How Never to Be Able to Tell Bob Apart from Peter

Bob has just died. Does that make him less dead than Peter, who's been dead for sixty years?

No, the newcomer has equal status, in death's democratic kingdom, with Peter, although the latter can claim his old pathetic seniority. There's no real time factor. Bob who just "made" it has become of the same quality as the one established in it by years that customarily compiled tradition. They're two of a kind," now, the recently joined and that hardened veteran. The difference between them is bound up and glued together into a oneness.

But in life, if one man is sixty years older than another, the differences, little or big, *do* count, don't they?

Naturally. In life, every detail weighs in. It's of worldly importance that a *living* old Peter is far older than the *living* young Bob. And everything *about* them would present a significant comparison; for living people are always *compared*, by one or the other, or by both, or by other people. *Qualities* are essential, traits are marked, all is recorded. Bob doesn't shave yet, and Peter has a white beard. Bob is inwardly inclined, while Peter needs company. Bob is influenced by his mother, and Peter by his widowed sister. Bob likes reading, Peter likes to attend sports. Life emphasizes these facts; death negates them, into the common dumping herd of oblivion's insensitive mob.

Then, Bob having just joined Peter in death—?

Erases everything crucial except the bland similarity of their last and latest states of occasion. Their matter being barred, then what is there left to matter? And their least difference or greatest is equally immaterial, broken down humbly inconsequential.

The indistinguishableness of Bob the recent and Peter who's also freshly and durably recent, as though the perfect refrigerator could keep old frozen food imperishably new to match the pack just arrived and tucked in tight up against those blazing cubes of ice.

(*The Dialogue's Almost Endless Title:*)
The Man, and His Sleep, through a Lifetime of Daily Leavetaking,
Nightly Reunions. They Face One Enemy in Common—Death, Which
Would Fatally Break Up Their Partnership and Kill Each, Together or
Apart. Sleep Wakes the Man Up Screaming from a Nightmare Preview
of This. Sleep's Fled, Hiding for a While, As the Man Gropes without
Sleep to Fend Off This Nightmare Scare Alone, Awake, Himself. Later,
He'll Melt into Sleep's Arms, in Their Mutual Oblivion to the Future
Dissolver of Their Periodical Friendship's Constant Life Together.
The Man, and His Sleep. Unconsciously Merged, Conscious Apart.
Equality's Living Companions, to Face an Equal Severing

Were you asleep?

I don't know, because I was unconscious at the time.

Unconscious!? Are you a boxer and were knocked out in the ring?

Nothing so dramatic or active as that. I merely fell asleep, innocently.

Was it fatigue, or tiredness, or exhaustion, that drove you into that self-imposed oblivion?

Who knows the cause? *Sleep* didn't inquire. It just came upon me, or "stole" upon me, with little forewarning.

Do you and sleep have a spontaneous arrangement?

An *understanding*, at least.

Do you ever dispute?

Yes. Once I *wanted* sleep, and sleep refused to come. We weren't on speaking terms, for a week—though it solaced me, each night.

Sleep disappointed you, in that case. Did you ever disappoint sleep?

Alas, yes. Once sleep wanted to steal upon me, but I wouldn't let it, I took an energy pill to ward it off, because I had work to do at the time pressure of an impending deadline which was imminently close at hand. So I said to sleep, "Wait."

Did it?

It did. All night.

Did you meet the deadline?

I finished the work in time. Then, and not *till* then, was I ready for sleep.

Did sleep resist you, to gain revenge?

No. It *understood* why I had to put it off and make it wait. It took no offense, at my urgency, but in fact was purring with sympathy.

How loyal and understanding of it. And unpetty, unvindictive. It behaved like a good friend.

I submitted to it. It submitted to me. Together, we were partners to pure oblivion. I woke up, drove sleep away, being restored. By then, sleep had had enough of *me*, too. We were glad to be rid of each other, for a while. We went our separate ways.

To meet again, undoubtedly, in due time?

Inevitably, we melted away in each other's arms, at our reunion.

The reconciliation was easy?

Even expected. We play our little game. But we know the score. We can't fool each other. We both need each other. We come to terms. Sleep is *my* nest, upon need. I'm *sleep*'s perch, for *its* function. Harmony resides.

When you die, will it be one long sleep with your same friend?

No. Death is another matter, altogether. Death will kill my *sleep*, not just *me*.

Your sleep and you will be equal victims, at death's hands?

Death will dissolve my lovely union with sleep. It will pull us apart, so that sleep and I will part company forever.

How sad such a farewell will be, after a long life together.

Death is unsympathetic. It snaps *other* unions, not just sleep's and mine.

Yes, death is a grim divider.

My sleep is terrified at it. It clings closer to me, and dreams nightmares of death wrenching us apart. It makes me scream, using *my* mouth for *its* organ.

Doesn't that wake you up?

It does. Then I find sleep no longer there.

Because you're awake?

Yes. Whenever I'm awake, I'm never asleep.

Where is sleep then?

Gone. Somewhere.

The Fallen Bone Is Cracked to Bear Its Deliverance in Song of Life's Peril

I fell down.

Where from?

A roof, thank Gravity.

At what distance?

Multiplied by the weight of speed.

Were you faster landing than you were starting off, according to acceleration's law of momentum?

Yes, so I was bruised hard. There was an audible crack somewhere.

Was your bone somewhat jolted?

Yes, but which one?

You should answer it, if you have any feeling at all.

My body left a message, all right, but I had been out at the time.

(*Scornfully:*) What a stiff you are, from the unconscious point of view! Does *every* emergency lull you to sleep?

When it comes to a crisis, I get lazy. Instead of being roused to my critical heights, my tendency is to slow down, and let the scene pass unrecognized.

A *clod* that you are, more than man: whose proud estate is vigilantly alerted over, sprung heroically awake!

That doesn't describe me.

It wasn't meant to. But I can't be on the level with you. In fact, I must condescend to look down on you.

I owe my low state to that *fall* I was telling you about.

Why were you located so precariously high, to start off with?

To raise the come-down contrast. Or to heighten the difference, and to be taught a lesson by polarities to the extreme, and divide utterly the outcome from the onset, not by degree or gradation, but to a painful breakage on extremity. I lowered the boom, and went all out.

Now that you've been so painstaking, what fracture have you to show for it? Demonstrate the intent and extent of your incidental accident. You who were committed, omit no note, nor inhibit, but exhibit! Make no bones, but bare what broke your fall and indented your brittle-surfaced interior that props your skin in a brace of support durably inward past death. Or can you bear it? Expose this molested particle of your framework, the punctured outpost of your cadaverous structure, your skeletal violation's lessioned length lapsed abruptly from its fluently articulated function as an intricate clothes hanger. Where's the crack your smash gave you? Or was it for nothing that you fell?

I had a hard landing.

No sentimental cushion to blunt *your* ending!

Yielding, I was bent on the spot.

A realistic acknowledgement of what had befallen you!

I felt a splintering thud.

Your on-the-spot reportage is shot through with verisimilitude! In

fact, it's shockingly accurate—coming from you.
I was *there*, as a material witness.
Your first-hand evidence smacks of authenticity, to the concrete.
I'm not dreaming this stuff up.
No, in fact, you're living it down.
And it smarts!
Smart of you to admit it. For the record, what else have you to confess?
I ache.
That's an honest statement. May I encourage you to continue?
No, I want the ache to *stop*.
Oh, where is it running to?
To my ruin and wrack, if it keeps up.
You want to wreck your ache?
Yes, and not eke it out.
Did you bleed?
No. Only my *bone* was affected.
Oh.
Pain is more than skin-deep, you see,
That's enigmatic of pain.
Yes, it hides in mysterious places.
Can't the body root them out?
No, for how can it unearth *itself*?
That's true.
What's true?
What you said.
It's more *felt* than said.
(*Suddenly informed:*) I *wondered* what the texture was.
Then all is *material* to you?
That's in *evidence*, isn't it?
I see that you're boning up on me.
May I query you further?
Only to the pain's source.
Good. Let's tap it.

Let its sleeping heal itself.

You comfort-monger!

I insist on pain's cessation, relieved by *pleasure*'s restoration.

How heathen of you! Where's your stoical fortitude?

In my ancestors' buried bones.

Oh. Let their bygones lie there.

They don't *lie*: they utter a *grave truth*!

But muted with silence?

Sure. A tongue is as dead as a man is.

Of cour(p)se.

Well, I could see a little crack in my bone. Like a slit in a posting box. So I wrote a small note and folded the paper up and slipped it through the opening that gaped my bone temporarily apart. Then the healing closed it, to seal the message in my bone. It's like when a lonely sailor, stranded on a raft or shipwrecked on an island palm tree, inserts his scrawled alarm in a bottle, a rescue-me epistle in frantic desperation, and sets the bottle bobbing on the mercy of the tides, floating toward its destiny over the far-flung ocean main. So too, some sympathetic wader on shore will find my splashing bone driven in by the force of mighty waves, to a peaceful inlet for the leisurely shock of sunny discovery, wandering by the roar of the surf and the debris of its foam, as my bone comes drifting to its sudden home, or plunging, finds a willing correspondent alert to a stray and lonely chance in the tidal fortune of a communicant distance, the roll and surge of fate received in the slight wash of a momentous movement. The bone will be opened and its distress appeal noted. And unlocked, the deliverance will be at hand. It had been stuck into a healing fissure, whose trace could be pried re-apart, and now the delayed solemnity of this great occasion has fructified its crescendo of deliverance, its serenity of a cycle complete at full tide, when that hour will have been reached.

When will that be?

To-*marrow*.

How do you know?

I can feel it in my bones.

Oh. I'm all at sea.

You're a washout? Have you been following me?

No, I'm prone to drowning, to swim up and down your waves of description.

You lump of earth! Aren't you *buoyed fluent*?

No, I'd rather be *girled fluid*.

You stray from the point.

After so much sea, your point is only bone-dry.

Would you like me to beef it up?

Yes, freshen it with some flesh.

Wait till to-marrow.

Why?

That's when my prophecy comes true.

Which one?

Bottled up, as a message, in my sailing bone.

What does it report?

Just what it entails.

But what's written thereon?

That which is inscribed on it.

To what effect?

Just what its content describes.

Yes, but what does the message say?

That's a tale the letter will bear!

Sealed by your long and narrow bone?

But opened, judiciously, to-marrow.

To whom is it addressed?

"To whom it may concern," it augurs, enigmatically. The rest brims with obscurity's clarity, clad in mystery and veiled by something dark. I wrote it under sedation, being, at the time, out. Having been knocked unconscious. A nasty fall, untimely, that brought me down.

(*Threateningly:*) I'm anxious to re-break that bristling bone *now*, to drink up its apocalypse hard upon the preview of the marrow, though it's water-logged from the tidings of its voyage and soaked to the rust of illegibility. Break its seal open! For pedantic discovery will wait no longer on curiosity's impetuosity!

(*Stalling, delaying, imploring:*) But the spirit of the letter, and not the letter thereof, bides the dawn of to-marrow.

(*Savagely demanding, desperately imperious:*) Nay! What says it now! I bridle with haste at it! Hide it no longer! Or I'll break open the matter, and rip the bone whose significance dies to pour out! Which of your bones *is* it? Where did you fall?

On the *ground*, precisely.

I'll take matters into my own hands. I'll tear you apart, until my research delves deeply to discover its satisfaction.

(*Relenting, under this pressure, succumbing, finally revealing:*) But what a text of tedium you'll read! Bone-dry, and dead as scholarship. Make no bones about it, the hard facts will lie before you, stripped of saucy flesh, unchewable, and bleached bare. It says: "This is death. Life grew upon it, overhead, underneath, and around. Such profusion was the sense's headquarters, till stripped gleamingly away."

Nothing but that?

Only so much. When you open it to-marrow, what remains is but the skeleton of a former signature, a neatly deposited layer for the fossilization of record.

(*Scared, imploring, unwilling:*) But you're alive, still!

And when the rebuilding tissue repairs the wound with a tattered coat of new paint, an old bone will cruise, under reduced sails, past its elastic snap of youth, to the port of dissolution. The voyage laid barren to an implacable tide. That's all my bone conveys, which the marrow will reveal. It constructs its instruction on destruction, which struck it so.

(*Woefully, pathetically, with feeble acquiescence:*) Only but so?

My bone's a vessel, conducting this homely homily, and vehicles a Darkness through its shining passage.

(*Anxiously, forbiddingly:*) When will the marrow come? Is it forestallable ?

Drop your dread dead. You'll know its shivering arrival when your acute bones sign, "Enough." Nerves are sensitive to any change. Zones of knowledge burden the body in relays, brutishly abundant. But termination bones its wedging way through, and brutally narrows our core, and the sighing bone must sing its way out. A collapsed body falls in with this plan, and the spine flashes its exit in conjunction with the spilling skull. The cage must take a ribbing, the doors flutter open or squeak ajar, and a soul is released to its pre-birth plot of drifting unison with the inanimate, released without locality to its orphan assignage. Bones had bottled up the soul, anyway. And vapor—not sea for floating, nor clay physical earth—best becomes the soul, as its wandering element.

Does a spiritual substance inform the bone, contained by it?

Yes, soon to abandon it, high and dry.

What lodging to fly to, as a new course of residence?

The vagrancy of freedom is home enough. It was yawning its vacancy all this time.

And does the soul lust with nostalgia for its former bone?

No, due to its *rising* tendency, and its unconscious aversion to a fall.

So *memory* riddles the soul through?

It realizes: "The bone was not what it was cracked up to be. The fall jolted me to this awakening, and dislodged my contentment with earth, as a complacent prisoner. A jail escaped from, is not universally mourned. Why waste my grief? God has shown increasing dissatisfaction with the human race. I adapt *my* taste to fit *God*'s, since independent thought is the product of the skull alone. 'When in Heaven, do as God does.' A good rule, unless I'm riding for a fall."

Does the soul *really* say that?

It *thinks* it. When thought is that pure, lips double their redundance. A tongue substitutes for two wings, until the release.

Are *we* souls, both?

We? We're not even spokesmen. We're just a bunch of fallen bones.

Then why are we upright?

Evolution *planted* us that way. We strut by instruction.

Are we overdue for a spill?

We're leased to nature. We observe today by privilege of our budding yesterday. But by to-marrow, the note on man's fall will come due, and its stead will give rise to the boneless fate in store. An elevation, I may presume. My vanity is still a social climber, while bones are my ladder's rungs, or the spiralling staircase. My view is obstructed. The ceiling is head-high. When I cave in, the roof will sink its beams and my unseen light may penetrate the colorful earth I love. No, not the sun or moon. What metaphor can challenge the unfamiliar?

Time's Winged Visibility

"God! What an intense blue!" we said, and the sky looked at us. We stood, revealed, with nowhere to hide. The environment receded, the more to advance us, now far to the fore of our immediate front. Time paused, ticking its latest second. The second, released from rapid progression and freed of its brevity, grew instantly round and loud, at an accelerated momentum, borrowing more brilliance from the sun's height of noon than could be loaned in safety for the day: so night swiftly descended, at a uniform rate, to the total absence of a moon. Under stealth of no detection, then, the second stole into death, and let the next one succeed: time turning human again.

How Barry Tamed the Past, and Brought It Up to Date

Barry's regret was in having been born after most of the past had already taken place. He had wasted all that precious time being historically absent from all the fun and misery that people of previous generations had hogged all to themselves. What was left for *him* to have? Space aplenty, to the end of the globe, geography that needed only money to be explored and enjoyed. But most of the *time* was gone: his generation's ancestors had used it up, throwing him, for a bone, the paltry consolation of the present. He was nostalgic for what he missed: how marvelous had been the many phases of the past!

Part of the remedy was to acquire an acquisitive mania. The past would be *symbolically* present, in various antiques.

Some well-carved piece of metal would represent the total fourteenth century: or that of it local to the land of the craftsman.

Some antique coin, for example, would restore some of the ample classical spirit special to that glorious epoch of Greece. How far back would the flashy thing's value prove!

A stamp, say, would bring back some nineteenth-century monarch at the outset of his empirical dreams! That precious period would be Barry's, in total recapture.

Or some crude, obsolete instrument that wind once converted to music: dead was the performer, and dead the audience. But Barry would breathe that perished life, while handling the trophy.

Mementos, monuments—endearing keepsakes—legacies of time's collapse. Time's restoration would be his collection's brilliant burden. Owning these particles of space, he possessed the time they would immortally represent.

His only obstacle was money. So he made sure, on the principle of the retroactive, to claim a rich father for a businessman; with an inheritance guaranteed his, for no brother or sister was in the way, and the mother was barred by death from competition. His father made a pile, left it to him, and obliged by passing away. Now Barry had the *means*!

He studied every civilization the past had ever known, even those so distant that only prehistory could record them. He knew what materials were used. He became an expert. Cultures opened their mystery to his probe. Taking a correspondence course in archaeology, he excavated each letter of his lessons from his standard mailbox. He deified the past; but lost patience with the relatively recent modernity that epitomized the *present*. He was anxious to *join* the past. So he participated in his own aging, as a parable for the momentous ages along man's route to self-knowledge.

Volumes of books, preferably first editions, figured in his conquest of the past. He possessed the works of the great authors, in tongues original to their genius. Gone were the authors, but their words lived. Barry fingered lovingly each tome; but discouraged no dust: for he venerated evidence of antiquity.

Finally, Barry was an old antique himself. He added himself as an authentic addition to his collection.

He had neglected to acquire children. Nor was there a wife to inherit his goods. So in his will, the museum benefited.

Now Barry has joined the past. He's vulnerable, he's ancient—he's dead.

He's buried by great piles of the present. Time goes by, and *recent* chunks of today are added to the pile.

Where is Barry? He's part of time's collection.

The Restless Spirit—Infinity-Haunted, It Takes Flight, and Flees from Its Flight, Form after Form, into and out, Life Bound Up by Too Much of Its Local Self Again and Again, Longing to Find the One Lifeless Element for a Wideningly Confining Home. It Fails, and Still Darts About. Here's the Script of Its Agony, Recorded in Earth's English, on Grammatical Terms: for People to Read Who Only Know How It Is to Be People; for Their Soul's Travel Is Fixed on the Narrow Form of Man—the Opening-Out Is Shied From, the Opening-In Is Run From, and Man Is Caught Between—a Stalled Train. The Spirit Flutters, in His Brain. It Came from One Destiny, and Is Restless for the Next. Man Is Given No Peace, Afforded a Rare Glimpse, and Lives Morosely. One Burst, Then—

I looked at the sky, its infinity overcame me like a swarm of locusts that ripped away tiny chunks of me at a time. The blue infinity sky was too far for comfort, I had to escape. So I built myself an enclosure, four confining walls to close me in, within something man-made and close at hand. There was a roof to put a ceiling to my heights, and to diminish my outward ardor with its upward thrust toward the irrational. There was a ceiling to roof down my flights of wing'd aspiration, and to keep lofty towers dwarfed from their sublimity.

And there was a floor too. A paved floor to rug down the natural one and keep the earth's infinitude from doing from below what the sky's infinity had been shut from doing from above. So I had protection from high and low, from front and side and back. But the infinity from *within* was gnawing me—and no shutting *that* out, for it's already *in*.

So much in, it set up a clamor and a howl for an external kinfolk. So to give it an external kinfolk I built a few windows in the enclosure, for the blue infinity sky to *partially* penetrate my sanctum of refuge from just that.

But just to take no chances, and to have choice of modulation, I built shades too, so as to control the effect from those windows. And of course I had already built a door, for ingress and egress, for occasionally I would regress, and yearn for heaven's dome.

At night I would lock myself in and shade the windows entirely, to make snug and complete the private world of my inner retreat.

But I couldn't shut out the years. The years unraveled me, letting eternity seep in. There was no leak in the floor for moist earth to suck me toward it; but time—its passage—leaked me out toward eternity. And my enclosure couldn't protect me. I was running out of years. Time was dragging me—I was being sucked up. The infinity sky—it was beckoning me; its pilot was reckoning—on me. It was irresistible. I was being drawn out, up; the sky opened (it was *always* open—but an aperture appeared even on its openness, to give space unlimited rei[g]n).

I was hauled out, pulled up. I was in the air. I was in the earth. I mixed with earth; and was exhaled up, as an element. I'm a roaming element. My home is homeless, and I wander.

I'm free—and dream of confinement. I dream of the enclosure I had built. It was imperfect, my soul escaped. It's of an invisible form now, this soul, so everlasting, it trades elements, and enters diverse shapes. It claims all forms, and abandons them once made. I'm in the poet's dream: the spirit land. This is where embodiment really is: all is body, with no air. For the body *is* the air—peopled with chains of metamorphoses, like a quick-change artist from one vaudeville act to the next, on a rotating stage, in changeable duration. I need stability—it's boring to vary so. But stability used to bore, itself. I'm bored now, and always was. It's what I'm bored about—that's so different. To say I'm bored means I can't bear what I am. Nor could I, what I was. The past is past. But *now*: it's endless. Let's end it quick.

Now I'm something else. It's a continual change—into which I've settled.

What can I call "home"? I'm always being exposed—exposure transforms me. I want to be sealed up; and one—always—thing.

To be only one thing—I'd get tired of it. It would pain me.

I roam, to escape pain.

I encounter more pain, in my escape.

I take more pain over a further escape; the result—further pain.

I want to be still. But pain then would stir me, in my stillness. I'd be obliged to move, to avoid *that* pain; and move to *another* pain.

I *can't stand* this travel continual. I want one shape to be pleased. One shape painless. Even if in so getting it I must forego life.

Life, I'm used to it. I want other modes, to try.

I Got Carried Away—and Caused All Else to Be, As Well
(An Exemplary Warning, a Horrid Lesson)

As the cosmic system was proving incomprehensible, I destroyed it, rather than cut a foolish figure and be ridiculed for ignorance of what was *there.* So I made it *not there*, and then couldn't be blamed any longer for *not knowing* what was not there. To protect my pride at any cost! An act of monstrous vanity, I know—admittedly. But still, a mighty blow *in defense* of that highest prize, esteem. I *needed* esteem, just to get on.

But the consequences of destroying the cosmic system may hardly be described as puny. I had cut loose the foundations of not only *all* existence, but *my own* as well. Thus, what had intended to be merely a destructive act, and no more, turned out to be *self*-destructive, as well. It was too late to undo what I had insanely and blindly not foreseen. Thus, I perished—which was the attendant peril, unreckoned at the time, consequent upon my thoughtless deed. The moral: Vanity can cut one's own throat, if not restrained in its audacious license.

I had only wanted *not to look bad* to my friends and peers. Thus I put into operation a mechanism that ended in ending me: not to mention that cosmic system itself, and all the people I cared to impress. An irredeemable disaster.

I blame it on the matchless complexity of my unfathomable victim, the cosmic system. If only I could have tolerated not understanding it, and not cared what its incomprehensibility to me meant in affecting the way others would regard me! My scale of values proved defective, and my overriding priority had the misfortune of a ruinous annihilation.

After such damage done, to indulge regret is not merely futile, but undignified. Posthumously, I'm still caught cultivating my reputation. Well, I'm too dead to learn any better.

And the audience whose admiration I court, for whose approval I'm all-sacrificial, and whose scorn I did *anything* to avoid—they're all destroyed. Their opinion is meaningless—now.

The cosmic system—I apologize. It was a rash deed. I'm eternally put in the wrong, by it: a stroke of infamy, totally out of proportion (warping proportion altogether) to the vanity that begat it. Big endings, from little beginnings. Enough. To my honor, I've confessed all. Too belated and no avail. The account remains unredressed; the harm unatoned. Energy is created, from the imbalance. From it, with any luck, as though to rectify all from the ashes of the previous, will arise another Cosmic System: If a new *me* arises also, I vow to respect it. However low my vow will rate, there it is. And so, I bid a new cosmic system to be. I will it, but I can't see it. It may be, but *without* me: its vital part.

Alas. Good day, Death.

And hello, Vacuum. Abhorred, as you are.

Let me have another life. I beg to be.

With power stripped to ruin so. Having less say, in the whole matter.

Disarmed. And fully repentant.

Toothless, clawless, all. And a vanity so humbled, it will never tear apart Creation again.

I'm not believed. *I'm* incomprehensible!

Now we're even. First the cosmic system had to pay for its incomprehensibility—with its very existence. Now, my very nonexistence is what I pay, for my *matching* incomprehensibility. Satanic judgment? Retribution divine? No. Indifference cosmic. Eerie and chilling, through the setting of this Void. Where all is razed: due to a petty and vain peeve: whose crowning rage toppled the going system then—which no forward magic has come up to replace. Matter may not be destroyed? —No, but *all* matter may.

And what matter, then?

It was the *manner*, to blame: the manner of my vanity going about, a horror of a recourse, in a minor adjustment—to serve itself, it set loose the very monster of disservice.

Did *I* do all that? You may rest now, vanity. A shattering result—there's your laurels for complacency.

It's enough to foster a new pride. I'm proud.

I survey the damage—total.

I wrought well—or ill. Immoral maybe; but mighty. The *power* I did!

To undo such. To wreck the system cosmic. An incomprehensible feat.

A feast for all incomprehensibility.

A feast upon itself. The eater eaten, in the same act.

The Creation undone, with miles of history added. I spoiled Evolution. Its traces stand eliminated.

What was it after? Had it a goal?

If so, I took care of that. When what goes to the goal "goes," so does the goal.

Well, I contributed nothing. It leveled all else.

A God's Mortal Fall

High up on the mountain top, to which I climbed by literally ascending, I turned around to collect a circular panorama. I saw so many miles that the future rolled in like a torrent of roaring waves, crest on crescendo, leaving a debris of events sprawling like limp seaweed on the endless sandy shore of each breathing moment's immediacy. Then an army of worshippers darkened each of the valleys I surveyed: they kneeled in homage to the occupant of my mountain peak. It was I, transformed to God, they prayed to: they attributed power to me; being first flattered, I then felt terror: though I could see (compelled by omniscience), I had no power: and these people, sprawled below me—devout creatures of lowliness—needed me to confer on them the favorable benefits of omnipotence—a trait I possessed mythologically, but not in power of deed. They call up to me in vain. But I'm unable to inform them of their wasted motion. Their appeal is moving; but it does them no good; they should spend their time more profitably; but there's no loudspeaker, no communication amplifier, for me to warn them how to be more practical. Without reward, their rut of worshipping plows on. I, exalted to a God, frozen at my terrible height, am cold and ineffectual, removed from their mass plight's protesting prospect. Had I compassion, I'd spend it on all deities, in their towering distress of impotence.

Though they sacrifice for me on futile altars (smoke curving upward to join with mist), I'm hungry from my privileged height. Their darts of angry prayer never reach me.

Poor Man—how can I console him?

Impelled by hunger, I begin my fitful descent. Steep perils wait me at all levels.

Will the mob hound me, embittered with revenge for fruitless yearnings? Conspirators dot all the plains: they wish to clinch my downfall: who is more despised, than a God restored to his fallen flock, the humble decline of a deity?

Yet I risk it. I hunger for earthly appetite.

May my men not recognize me. May they consent to let me live among them. How deep is my longing, to share the privations they endure in a huddle! To eat their transparent soup, and dress in fabric worn by weather! To partake in their toilings, and take upon my person the soiled holiness of dirt! Man's starry destiny is himself alone. But should I inform them of this, a nice crucifixion shall be my lot. A martyr's halo will crown the perishing of my unpopular song. If mass man wants to prolong his myths, no creation of his myth, meaning me, could defy the lust of the throng. I dress in a shabby farmer's outfit, bearded with lice. I migrate to factory work in a city.

My anonymity is hard to preserve. Even when I sip coffee at the canteen, exchanging wit for wit in imitative equality with these crude belongers, I'm suspected—I'm *not* one of them. "Where's he from?" they whisper. "He's got uppity airs—he's a rare bird from the mountains," they quip. The more I show my distress, the stronger is their instinctive contempt. I'm never without an eye upon me. All I do is fodder for their disdain.

"You and your lofty views—they're due for a comedown," a bully taunts. Like cowboys in a Western drama, they'd respect me if I struck back: silence is marked down for cowardice. Yet humility *pours* from me— incensing them.

"God almighty!" they sneer. The foreman in my factory shift notes me as a disturbing factor in the work. So I'm transferred to mine duty.

I dig dark down in a deep pit. The hole above me closes. Air is denied. Here's fate, fallen with finality's fury. I grovel, and chew on stone. A loudspeaker radio attachment connects a cruel spokesman from the mob to the gradually diminishing stages of my conscious body's rapid decline. Blackness is my last environment. I adjust my faculty to blindness. That wired voice says, "Want to borrow a little air, buddy? You're the independent sort—why don't you use your own stale variety?" Laughter, from loud to dim. Dimness, from dark to near. Nearness, mine—and now everybody's.

I'm buried where I was. I had seen and known more than could be used in mankind's service. The gap trapped me: the doom leveled me. Gods have an affinity for clay.

HOW THE SNAKE EMERGED FROM THE BAMBOO POLE, BUT MAN EMERGED FROM BOTH

To the Yorkshire, Essex, London, and England all-rounder: Audrey Nicholson, Saint of Poetry.

HOW THE SNAKE EMERGED FROM THE BAMBOO POLE, BUT MAN EMERGED FROM BOTH

A Dialogue that Administers Metaphysics to Evolution, and Ends Up with Universal Humanization

What's the moral in that a crooked snake becomes temporarily straightened out in passing through a hollow bamboo pole, but when he finally emerges at the other end he resumes his crooked ways again?

Must you see a moral in it?

Yes, if I want mere knowledge to ripen into deep wisdom.

Very well. The moral is that the bamboo pole is inflexible, and the living creature had to do all the twisting; the snake is more animate, and was able to "adjust."

Does that explain evolution?

Both the bamboo pole and the snake are very early specimens of relatively undeveloped but extant species. Both can enter man's brain, but man's brain can enter neither.

As soon as you mention *man*, I begin to lose my interest in bamboo pole and snake, since man has a more compelling destiny, I being him myself.

Yet, in each man, there's something of the bamboo pole, something of the snake.

But mainly, in each man, there's more of him that's not the bamboo pole, *not* the snake.

Let's depart from the bamboo pole and the snake. Let's enter man himself, territorially.

That's a lot, and broken up into aspects.

That's convenient, for I never could have entertained his whole all in one chunk; its vastness would have terrified me.

Man is a spectacle of awe. Which aspect should we treat first?

MISGIVINGS ABOUT THE WAY LIFE HAS BEEN PRACTISED BY THE ACCUMULATED DEAD OF THREE MILLION YEARS. (BY A MAN WHOSE MENTALITY IS SEEKING ELSEWHERE TO GO FROM HIS BATTERED AND ONLY BODY INHERITED FOR THE PROTECTION OF A LOOSE AND QUERY-LESS SOUL.)

Before man began (and with him woman) there were plants or tiny animals whose male and female were in the same being. Later animals learned to specialize in being either male *or* female, of which man (and woman) is the latest example.

The separation of the genders in different beings of a species is a comparatively late development. Problems and complications ensued. (See Freud, especially on personality neurosis, repression, the conscience, and related matters.)

Sex is exploitable: For example, in prostitution, showmanship, public relations, advertising, espionage, diplomacy, pornography, theatre, film, books, periodicals, business, and human relations. Sex confers *power*, hence it's exploitable.

Problem: Evolution is taking its course. It's too late to stop it. It's been underway for so long, that it was accumulating momentum even before man began to question it. Man is a *product* of evolution, so it should concern his faithful gratitude and critical curiosity.

Solution: Nothing to do about evolution. You're participating in a fraction or phase of it. Be glad, and keep open an eager mind. Jot down the news. See if it's only old, or *really* news.

Art. Art is man-made. Man is nature-made. Tell what the difference is.

Dreams. Are we being dreamt? And who's our dreamer, if so? Or does each person have his *own* dreamer? Or is the same dreamer pooled and shared by a small cluster of people?

Does one person dream another? In love, such a thing is possible.

Where does man end, and his mind begin? Chart human geography, inside each person, mentally speaking. Where is what, and who?

Let me know what you find. I'll be in one of the later bodies. You'll recognize me by my receptivity as you begin talking; I'll recognize you by what you're saying. If that meeting occurs, there's a high probability that we'll be sharing the same body. Thus it was, in the one-celled beginning. We will have gone home. Plenty of material, at the source.

THE MISSING THIRD BROTHER OF TIME AND SPACE. EINSTEIN ALMOST REVEALED HIM, BUT DEATH CUT HIM SHORT.

The last time Einstein felt some real energy was just a few days before he died. "I might as well take the last fling," he thought, "and give the world one more big thing before I leave. Already for this world I've invented (or to put it modestly, 'discovered') two important big things, time and space. And I invented relativity to prove that time and space are brothers — they're both in the same family. Well, I have great new news. There's a *third* brother. The third and last. (No sisters, no mother, no father. Just three brothers. The three primary things in the world, irreducible, the foundation of all.)

"Time and space are already known, are familiar figures, everybody calculates by them. Clocks were made to measure time, twelve-inch rulers to measure space, also microscopes, telescopes, and surveying instruments. Psychoanalysis also measures time, but subjectively, in personal case history. Archaeological strata uncover fossils to peep into past degenerations. Paintings on cave walls contain valuable deposits of both time and space.

"Time and space are the *givens*. They're no longer unknown, and have been stripped of mystery. What the world needs is new mystery. Now, in my final burst of life energy (for in a few days I'll be dead), the third and missing vital brother is for the first time revealed to me. I'll write it down, and leave it as my parting legacy to this world that strangely nursed me through my incubation genius period. Where's the pencil and paper?, I'm so absentminded. I've lost them. Now it's too late, I've just had a stroke. The hardening of my heart arteries has suddenly driven a fatal cancer into me, and now I sink into a coma, my last creative spurt proved abortively without issue, the world is deprived of the third brother belatedly revealed to me, barely unrecorded since a stroke drove it away and all my remains are marred by the swift decline. World, don't mourn me. Mourn your loss of knowledge. You're two-thirds complete as I take leave of you. How many futures must pass before another me comes along to re-present that third brother whom I just barely failed to introduce by the narrowest clutch of time in the dark of struck disease? Now my lips are sealed. Memory comes bubbling in. I live but can't give, in my sealed coma. My strictest privacy has come. I'm crowded into final solution. The links have been borne away. I'm a failure, and unknown."

That ended the thought process of Einstein. The man was dead. The third brother had escaped. Who can that third brother be? It's so tantalizing. If only that burst of mind could have been replanted into *my* brain, so that, to my everlasting credit and glory, I might complete and bring to embodyment that inspired final gasp!

I'm sour, with the sense of deprivation. I'm bitter, and have lost contentment with what we *do* have.

Now, I consider time and space so *narrow*, for they're uncompleted by their necessary third. I'm impatient with the world, it's pulled up short. Its growth was abruptly truncated, and what's presented is a mockery of what *could* be. I have an obsessive sense of *Loss*. What chance by foul prank of devil, to deprive that Thinker of two critical, crucial more conscious moments to bring his supreme finding to fruition by transacting it into the written word: to have it *come across*. For on *our* side, we lack it. And the lack is all I find.

That momentous discovery! It fell back with him, short of penetrating *here*. We're without what should be ours, by fortune's untimely chance. Crippled, we go on to make do with what we *do* have. But it's not enough. That "almost" is eternal. I'd batter down death's door, to reclaim it. I'd retrieve the ailing man in that agony that cut him down with that Idea born and floating like a halo over him. *Over* him, for he didn't get it *down*. On paper, for us.

RADICALLY DIFFERENT VIEWS OF LESTER, AT DIFFERENT TIMES IN MY SAME MIND.

A contribution to the psychology of the subjective, but a superficial one at that — objectively speaking.

My first impression of Lester was an extreme one — so extreme I couldn't bear it, so I began to doubt it and reflect, till my afterthought had adjudged a conclusion totally at opposite with my original first impression.

Numerically, let that opposite be called the *second* impression, of Lester.

But the second impression, on third glance, seemed so extreme I couldn't bear it — so in reaction to it, I returned to the original first impression — where I started.

So I went full cycle — or full circle. Reacting to an extreme first impression produced its opposite, the second impression — which, in *its* turn, was just as extreme, causing a reaction to set in, which brought me (circuitously) back to where I started.

Yes, but what of Lester? Yes, what *of* him?

He's subsidiary to the violence of my impressions. I use Lester, to rebound mentally from this to that. Such violent polarizations! If Lester had known, he would have retracted his part in my doing violence. Then I would have had to turn to someone else.

IMAGE BY IMAGE, THE SPIRIT IS BEING MADE

I'm bothered by a series of events in recorded history.

The solution is to consign them into that contrived chronicle of created *fiction*.

I tried that, only to be sadly informed by tradition that myths or legends don't need a factual basis, and history is a conditional memory anyway, darkly studded with our collective prototypes subconsciously racial, in an inherited archives of images that occurred to the invented mind of man or men by a sequence of universal flashes belonging organically to the huge communal psyche. Does that seem like a temporary or superficial disturbance?

No: you've acquired a tragic feeling.

(*Correcting:*) Innately materialized one, not learned it. Instinct is no passing accident, but a deep readiness for the inevitable. I'm not *pursued* by anxiety, but am *owned* by it. Which is hardly a trifling consequence. Nor even a serious disorder: but rather, a serious *order*. Not an inconsequential significance, but an existing identity located squarely in essence. Not a local infirmity, but a totally cosmic condition: in which both the infinite and the eternal have invested their joint. backing, and rightly so, with a sense of fittingness that's not the least surprising, but a simple matter of expectance, acceptance, something so much in the way that it must be resigned to like an article of faith, abiding, durable, undeniable, having taken over. Truth is truth; and most often, it's a lie. But doubt and skepticism are the wrong things to entrust in this big material of mind. Man builds mental monuments to himself. His metaphors and parables stand up. We can't knock them down. The image has become sacred. It's our living substance.

AESTHETICS IN LIFE & ART

To Rochelle Ratner, who, though she's from Atlantic City, has now been confirmed a New Yorker both in city and state, though by virtue of her soul and her prose and poetry, she's universal beyond New Jersey, New York, and other specific locations.

AESTHETICS IN LIFE AND ART. EXISTENCE IN FUNCTION AND ESSENCE. AND WHATEVER ELSE IS IMPORTANT, TOO.

Aesthetically speaking, cats carry graceful beauty in their form and movement. So why go to the art museum to consume your minimum diet of aesthetics, when you can just watch a cat instead?

Beauty can come in pills, too: in a tidy, condensed, distillated, compact, concentrated capsule, there's all the beauty nutrition you need for one whole day, all in one tiny swallow, followed by a glass of water to get it flowing in your interior system at large. *That* spares you a trip to the museum, too.

Beauty is very functional. The shape of a building or a cat can be best designed for maximum economy of streamlined efficiency according to the purpose of the existence of the building, and the purpose of the life of the cat. Previous evolutions in both species have paved the way to a fine new model, stripped of the fat of excess, unharmed by organs superfluous to what's workably needed. New conditions have been directly adjusted to, by favorable adaptation, eliminating waste, keeping to what survives in fitness to the stress of flourish, dynamic thriving in the lean abundance of maximum vitality. What doesn't contribute, detracts. Only what serves, suffices. Parts organizationally tuned, to the prime design.

My girl friend grew too tall, so she stopped. If she hadn't stopped, she would have been appropriate to progressively fewer men. Good, then, that she stopped when she did.

Her breast filled out and went forward, reached a limit, and that was enough. Any more, and disproportion would have disfigured her. Good that she stopped, then, when she did.

If a cat were the size of an elephant, it would be less in demand as a household pet, where ceilings would restrict its jumping range. Scale has kept it a domestic favorite. Scales have served pet fish well, too, in their aquatic little bowls; and gills perform invaluably, to keep their lives fluid.

Plants go sunward. Can they be blamed? They're fitter, that way. They develop green tans.

My cat outjumps me, but I can read better. Reading serves me, jumping serves him; so, to each his own.

What is life? A mystery.

Therefore, we all live a mystery. Let's keep it unsolved. A solved mystery is no mystery at all.

Other creatures don't *know* they're mysteries. The cat lives out its mystery, and the knowledge of it is unessential to him.

I *know* my mystery. Not its solution, but its existence. My knowing becomes essential, to the mystery that I am. Essential, from the essence that my life-mystery is. Give us, each day, this daily amazement.

"Reality is the supreme fiction." Welcome to that temporary form of art, life.

We're creatures and were created. We're created figures of art. Each unique work, freely donated to that open museum of the world. Aesthetics comes crowding in. Evolved products, we're half of all the beauty, and make the other half. Ugliness? That's beauty, wrong side out.

BEFRIENDING LITERATURE, FENDING THE ENMITY OF ITS ILLITERATE AND DETERMINED FOE

He's so modest, that he can't even read his own name.
But can he read *at all*?
No, in illiteracy itself he's plainly immodest.
By his overdoing it?
Yes, he's voluminously volumeless.
Library after library passes him by?

And shelves groaning out their endless tomes.
And his eyes are not the tools of any alphabet?
Unlettered, all pages are blank to that fool.
And no straying book to trap imagination?
Nor storied ink to fix received form on.
The author's occupation is not for him?
A scribe he's not, but he's orally verbal.
And when shyness permits, what does he often say?
    "I advertise for writers to submit their manuscripts
    to me, whose guaranteed critical muteness
    is impotent to caustigate them for bad style
    or a meager feeble void where content should be
    or slapdash rambling and muddled unity.
    Poets, playwrights, and novelists please,
    and all other fictional dabblers as well,
    committed to a creative literature
    in the capacity of the practitioner:
    You whose texts crave for print's public ink
    set in type and bound for publication:
    Do you dread the reviewer's malice of analysis,
    and the destructive incomprehension of the critic?
    I'll give you a boost, for I'm unlettered,
    and in strict confidence will praise anything.
    A slight fee, as illiteracy's shrewd reward,
    will be demanded upon appreciation."
And is he doing a brisk business these days?
Evidently. Authors are flocking to him, the queue is miles long.
So his services are extremely popular?
Yes, his affirmative encouragement is universally pleasing . . .
And he soothes with such a *natural* artifice!
And how! Among his clients are the world's worst writers.
He makes classics of their awful stuff.
Of necessity. The *best* writers give his trade no custom.

Quality prose poses a business constriction.

Good verse is averse to his sordid enterprise.

He thrives on mediocrity's inferior wares?

And prays to God for literature's steady demise.

Yet some writing survives to a good future age?

Yes, in spite of this philistine's determined enmity.

Does he actively block what's well-written and greatly formed?

He hires readers to restrict our modern contribution to the future reader's library of delight and taste.

I hate the very devil in him!

What can we do? His firm is legally based.

He fosters the worst, and opposes the best. Let the mind and heart of man's spirit detest him, with their combined might.

He's a blight, a curse, an ache. May we rub him out.

He's rooted. Let's pray, and be devout.

May terror's holy bolt crusade down on him.

What if *reading's* gift should be granted?

What can reading do, to offset the mind's rot? His damage is harm's habit, and reading wouldn't cure it, but be corrupted by it. Rot infects the disinfectant, as instruments reflect the dark or bright will that their users intend. For ill or well, the soul's control informs reading's vehicle.

Let's go contrary to him, and develop high character and be a firm attribute to bolster literature's sag, and redeem it from its evil day.

Our power shall exemplify ideals, and thrust the good cause forward.

Let's read, and praise, what excels; and what's dull, or terrible, shall be ignored.

By *us*; but extolled by that low racketeer.

Our protection is ourselves; if we can't mend *his* ruinous deeds, let's fend by what's possible for our own right reading and our life's literate delight.

And weigh our minority minds on posterity's timeless scale that values the best to be passed along. Books ripe for survival heed the judgment call, the bugle's blast of welcome. So heralded, their printed editions increase, as population will make new eyes for their use.

METAPHYSICS, BUT METAMENTAL TOO

As far as the eye can reach, the world keeps going on. Yet, each person on it is only on its edge. Is it possible never *not* to be on its edge? And yet, we never go flying *off* the edge. For us, it seems, the edge is the only place that the world is—as it defines our limit. "Edge" means poised precariously. An "edgy" person is easy to rattle, he seems unstably nervous, and overreacting, or prone to, in an irritable state, with brittle uncertainty.

I'd like to reach back in time, and pluck its golden eternity core. I hate time being only a matter of one moment now, followed by the succeeding one. I hate mere chronological sequence. It's too linear and surface, too much on the same mechanical plane. "Eternity" is a way of getting out of that rut, slipping past that single reiterating gear. I'm for eternity, and time's defeat. I'm going to re-explore the past, and sound out its missed stops. I've got to re-do all historical retrospect. It sounds simple—but does it work?

Now, listen brilliantly to my idea. If you listen brilliantly, my idea may lose its dullness in course, and so transform itself to the level of your listening. Your co-operation must exceed, if I'm to succeed.

It used to be an adventure to explore Africa—there were plenty of undiscovered parts to newly discover. Now each part is all charted out, mapped up, domesticated to the mind. Africa has become as boring as Europe, since its formerly mysterious space has turned self-informer and now conforms to expectation's contours on the grid of predictability. It's all one big spatial bore.

I want to conquer *virgin* territory. I want the glamor, the risk, of the pioneer.

And so, I turn to time. I turn back, and wish to re-do the past, and perform the miracle of creating my own new retrospect and making of history my own made creature. Too many past historians dipped into time's virginity and ravaged her in their chronicles. I declare the past a re-virgin again. And me the bridegroom, to stab and plunge and probe and draw blood. The past is going to bleed—to prove its purity, as I poke anew.

Am I just raging with audacity? No, I'm perfectly sincere. I wish to alter scope, and focus retrospect on a plane unprecedented. It's ambitious —that's what makes it worthwhile. Difficulties, obstacles, will fall. I'll pave a path through them all.

Life is not the same old simple thing. Life is yet to be. It's in the making. It's being created. We're fathering it, though we in our turn were formerly fathered.

Life is issuing into new forms. Evolution is emerging, its shape still not embryonically determined yet. We have our shell to break out of—the hatching to do. It will reveal our form—and we'll be no longer we, but be in a different state, a state impossible to imagine from the basis of our previous state. "New" isn't even conceivable—it's not merely to reverse the "old." "New" is unimaginable, yet. There are no terms as yet invented for it. How can there be?

To break out of the rut, of time, life, and space, is my goal. I'm an explorer—not even knowing what I'm exploring—or even *if* it's being explored. Am I vainglorious to suppose I *am* exploring? Or am I *being* explored—outside the usual elements?

There's a trick to outwitting life—but what is it? I hate the complacency of resignation: I wish to outdo, by maybe undoing, that big trap we've fallen in to—that trap of the Obvious, to which we've become enslaved. I wish to throw off our bonds—and sail outside of time. It won't be smooth, I'll tell you!

"Where," "when," "what"? Oh, I hate those words. I hate words. I want *other* vocables, a new terminology—to fit new ideas.

Ah, but the very idea of "idea" is suspect. I tire of the thinking we do and the living we do and all of that . . . drot. "Drot," is what I call it. But I hate to "call" things by what they're called—for then I'm chained down and fastened to the obvious, instead of "taking off."

I wish to rise. Please note. And I want my rising to soar backward. To undo, and re-do, what's been "done."

I don't like *anything* that's been done. Or am I complaining about the way it's been done? Or is *complaint* my complaint? Or is the "I" what I hate?

Hating is my springboard. I spring from it, and find—?

Ah, the future. You're yet to be used. You're not sterile, yet.

Off, not on. That seems to be my direction—or destiny, or destination.

But in time, won't the new "off" become the old "on?"

No, no! I'll fight it!

Oh, with what weapons? Against what? How am I to know my adversary? The tools are yet to be forged—the materials are vague. What is their use? What dimension will we be in?

Come on, let's go. It's "andiam" for us (Italian, meaning "Let's go").

But "let's go" gets us nowhere. It's the same old term. The term is holding us back. Let's kill terms. And by so doing, kill what they designate.

But to kill—what is there, instead of what we kill? What's to replace it?

Risking the unknown. The mystery before we know it's a mystery. For once we identify it as such, it loses its potent force.

Off and on. And out.

ENDLESSLY REPRODUCED WORDS—BROADCAST IN PROLIFERATED MAGNITUDES IN MULTIPLEXITY FROM INDEPENDENT URGENT NECESSITY—BEYOND MAN AS MERE MOUTHPIECE AND THE TEMPORARY TRANSMITTER OR VEHICLE WHOSE DEATH IS SUPERSEDED BY A LIBERAL RUSH OF WORDS IN THEIR RELENTLESS URGENCY, DISEMBODIED FROM INCIDENTAL HUMAN AUTHORITY OR THE LOCAL ACCIDENT OF PROPRIETORSHIP WITH A SKIN OF MOUTH AND EARS IN ORGAN CONDUCTION OF A VERBAL FRACTION OF THE FLOW OF IDEAS STAMPEDING FOR THE PASSAGE ON THE VOYAGE OF

THE PERMANENT

I won a prize as the world's youngest forty-two year old man in the world.

How in the world did you win *that*?

You want to hear the story? It's out of this world.

I have a whirling desire to.

By heaven! I'll tell you, if you'll only be patient.

Shall I tell expectation to quit quivering its eagerness?

Yes, give me a calm setting, and I'll say what I promised you.

The hush is getting so quiet, you better begin before it's too drab.

Apathy itself is preferable to that tense, nervous anticipation I'm warning you against upsetting me with.

Would I be your ideal audience if I turned corpse?

Yes, a dead background is a good foil for what I'm about to say.

Then I'm *dying* to hear you tell it.

Your "dying" is so active, I'm intimidated by its aggressive gusto of dominant zeal.

My *dying* sounds more robust than my *living*.

It emanates a vigor, and buzzes with vitality. .

Enough of all these semantic preambles. What were you about to say, concerning your being the youngest man of your age in the world today?

Your cross-questioning has aged me. I retract the whole story.

The letdown is enormous. The climax is a peculiar disappointment. You led me so far, with delays, circumlocution, and suspense built up. Suddenly you stop, and the story is short-circuited. It was a tale that was never to be. Was I responsible for pushing you off stride and cramping the rhythmical flourish of your style? It was unintentional. I only wanted you to begin.

I began young, and now death is aging me quick. Before it's too late, tell by the clock how long we've had this debate.

(*Looks off away at imaginary clock, then untwists neck back to normal conversational face-to-face. Reports, alarmed:*) We've been at this for years! What else have our lives been doing, meanwhile?

Going about their unconscious decay. Talk and more talk has wasted our life away.

That's a sobering thought. First, I'm disheartened, now I give way to despair. Your message, by default of what's unstated, is crammed with melancholy pessimism. It's rimmed bursting to the tears of a tale of mortality. So much of this somberness is killing me, that let's resort, by reaction, to *gaiety*'s saving grace, and the unstately antics of frivolity. Before it's too late.

It *is* too late. You can't avert tragedy by suddenly turning comic at the end.

Really a grim, a gruesome fate. Laughter is at the other end of the world from where I am. And I lack the means for a journey.

The world imposes its grave limitations. We'd be free, without it.

You want to try to "make do" independent of the world's guides and props and indicators and supports and lore of tradition? You want to unrely upon the world?

In unassisted solitude, I'd ply my way.

But, lacking the *world*, where would that be?

In a place where time doesn't nervously interfere. Where *silence* has its place, without undue, conspicuous stress. In the *world*, silence is immediately noticeable, as though something loud had suddenly fallen, crashed smack up against the ground upon the ignition of gravity's impact in noisy detonation. Startling us. Our talk is a digressing.

From what?

From the core, the mystery, the soul. The essence I crave the freedom to contemplate.

The world is harsh with its screaming demands on you?

Incessant. You can't get around it. It's all there, it's our element. The pervasive atmosphere. Our one single prevailing condition: this world. It flings a tyranny of circumstance upon us. It inflicts its steady variety, till we're *drowned* with it. It inundates us. To "get away" becomes the impossible goal of all ideals. We're dense in the world's limitations. We can't soar.

We're put-upon, we're imposed, trespassed, even violated? Is the world one huge mess of interference?

It's a massive obstruction. It's an endless obstacle course we can never run away from. I dream of "nothing": to restrain the world's harrassment may solve liberty's entrapment. I long for that extra dimension. The world's bewildering barrier contains too much. It prods us with confusion, till madness must combine with insanity to get momentary relief. The world must be vomited out, or ejected, by some subjective manner repulsed, purged from our system, stifled or held at bay with illusions, before we can claim *ourselves*, or probe the finality of self. Yet who can define "self", or pare it down, except by the *world*'s terms, in social guise? I think we're doomed. It's time to die.

Dying is what we started out to do.

We've left it in stages of incompletion, momentarily abandoning the job, always distracted. It's a task better left undone, for all it worries us. Half of life's anxiety—our being pulverized into paralysis —is its obsessive result. This torment has us gripped. What is our search blindly seeking? An easy way out?—but from what?

Oh, go weep your problems in front of the altar of philosophy. I've had enough. The least profitable of occupations is to engage you in conversation, to be made your talking mate on a round of inconsequence, with blabbering vowels and indifferent syllables and palaver and prattle and all that babble. It's sickening. I'm haunted by the quest for silence, enthralled for its need now. Do me the favor—I assure you it's a great service to me—of desisting from your part in our running-on dialogue. In due process, my part will wilt, also. And let silence come between us again.

Again? When was it before?

Before our discussion was begotten, began, and got underway. In the distant past, too far back for nostalgia to pursue.

That was the last time we had silence?

Our tongues were still, that have wagged ever since.

You step *first* into silence: I'll follow.

The coward is always last. Well, I'll initiate. Mark it, note it well, and join me, emulating. Our dialogue's course will be sustained in the succeeding stage, continuous upon now, taking its new form in a spell of silence. And so transfigured, the flow will utilize ears no longer, while attention may drop out. Be my silent partner, to speed the world out of my soul, whose clarity of solitude will finally bless the opportunity to commune. Once our chatter is commuted.

We'll lapse from speech. And so will the *world* retreat: the world has packed itself jointly in all our words, as insects may be the vehicles for the fruits and seeds of future trees, or bees bear the burden of a flower's fine pollen, to pimp a sexual congress from one stalk of petals to another. We'll shut the world out, by shutting up. Now we'll sterilize the world's potency, for a change, and place a barren void where *fertility* had been, indiscriminate with progeny, promiscuous, polygamous, incestuous with heedless miscellany on the rampage of species to flow forth the generations in fruitful abandon and wayward sluttiness, begetting its casual multitudes in an unplanned series of accidents, a wilderness of disorder that trammels domesticity in untamed abundance.

Yes, but what can *we* do, to regulate this confusion, or nullify this diversity of forces?

We'll shut the world out, by shutting up. Or shout the world down, in the thud of silence. And when the *words* desist, the world must curl up, and be nil. And *that* should be peace. So let's try it.

You first.

Let the *last word* be mine.

I enjoin you to our treaty: silence.

Is the pact duly signed?

And sealed. So seal your lips.

With no more words to ensue?

Words have done their job. Now let's see what else works.

Fine. Lead me into the vacuum.

Let's not void ourselves of what we have to say, but unsay the void in negative eloquence. Our rhetoric is still stubbornly clinging to itself, with the compulsion of survival characterizing anything that's set in motion.

We'll subdue it, in our determined dumbness.

By what clock does our calendar croak its message forth now?

(*Strains neck to glimpse imaginary offstage clock:*) It's time we came to die. We're supposed to be old.

Were we born yet before we started talking?

The world was just rounding into definition on the basing structure of what we're saying, when now the words stop, a lifetime after we started the world by bringing in the first word. Let's put the world to bed, by unwording ourselves at last.

A fit beginning for a fine end. We'll slip into a snug snatch of silence. And be borne away, on it.

Will the world endure after?

That's not our care, once our passage is taken. The world will be behind us. And its volume will be cut down.

Won't words toss their echoes in our wake?

Like gulls hoping to scavenger, in trailing swoops, the back garbage of a ship. To be left behind. Our lives will be deposited; and as we pull away, the deposit will be unclaimed, and the world's a name whose word is done. We're clean rid of it.

Even now, yet?

But just so, in our going. (*Leaving.*)

Are you leaving? You expect a solo soliloquy in your absence? No, the game is by two, or none at all. One player left alone constitutes an end to sport. Our conversing has been broken, and words drop out from the world. If you depart, it means a parting of us both. So I'll join you. (*Runs to catch up, just as other is leaving the stage. They both vanish. Stage remains empty for rest of play. Same two voices resume from offstage, beginning with last speaker:*) Is this the silence we've bargained for? It doesn't *sound* like it, to me.

Oh, you'll get used to it. The tones are different, and the pitch, and the key, the register is changed utterly. We're in a wordless dimension. There's no speech. And no world.

Prove it. You can't convince me.

Our dialogue has no *world* to verify it. We're off the world.

What difference does it make to our dialogue? It's like an abandoned stage, with the words coming from offstage, disembodied from the characters' persons. The *talk* seems to go on. Essentially, of the same nature.

Yes, but remember: *we're* not there.

But the *words* are there? And what bouncing substitutes they are! The voices are still thrown midstage, as though from shy ventriloquists. In what way has silence imposed its change?

None, words being what they are, for they keep silence away, as they're given forth.

Then are we in hell?: where there's always talk?

So we're punished in tune with the crime! For the sin of talking too much while alive on earth, we're given a loquacious position in hell, as an afterlife verbal profusion in keeping with the unstoppable nature of our discourse before. We're just dead, disembodied voices. But the words can't stop bouncing.

Is immortality a matter of *words*?

That's *all* it is: for it obviously doesn't include us.

No. We're left out. Words remain, to represent us. Like the epigraph inscription on a tombstone, the engraved remnants that survive the person spoken for.

So we're being spoken for?

Yes: but who by?

Not by *ourselves*, if we're not there.

No, how *could* we?, if we're not there?!

Well, what's proxying our behalf, by doing the saying for us?

By committing our words in our stead?

Yes. Who? If we're dead?

Voices live after us. Words have a different *rate* of dying.

Sounds like an *immortal* rate.

They transcend us indefinitely. They take on their own momentum, their own pace, their own charge. They have an independent life. They can't seem to weaken or die.

Did *we* give rise to their birth, that they can't be stopped now?

We were their progenitors. Look what we have wrought! They can't be slowed down. Their speed accelerates. They're running away with us.

They running away without us. They're being carried away: *we're* the shirkers. *Where are the silent dead? Answer: They don't exist.*

That's quite a mouthful. Death doesn't rob speech of its swift streak of conception-making, does it?

No. As witness us.

As witness our *words*. We're unwitnessable.

We're witless.

There goes a word: But we're not *with* it.

It goes by without us.

It goes on not needing us.

From it comes *more* words: even *more* remote from us.

And the words whirl in the atmosphere. And make up the world.

The echoes are reverberating into further words. Once it gets going, speech proliferates, charged with a creative license to bring forth more words as needed, on the way. Like provisions for a journey. The spirit's word journey into space. Death having carried away the father. But the children bursting with life. With ideas to perpetuate, and invent, or make up, as they go along. The extension of generations, as the ball keeps rolling.

Each word is independent in spirit?

Sure: it has its own dictionary listing. It learns to utter itself. To pronounce its own fate. Which may be quite pronounced. It issues forth, disembodiedly. And improvises its emergency turns, by turning into new words. Like a self-contained amoeba reproduction, of cell-splitting. To keep afloat the burden of life's message, through devious turnings, and new vocabulary. It's charged with life's perpetuation, in varied guises of verbal proliferation, so that the *Word* can endure, with its charge of life. As the soul seeks its definition, released of the toiling body's tongue. And waxing words will reproduce, after the person they belonged to is dissolved in death's union. The word has flown away with its own liberty. As for us, *our* job is over. What were we but mouthpieces? The mediums of utterance, in the expressive formation of ideas borne aloft by words, that blazed a path through our bodies' corridors, and are now out in the open, in the sun and the wind, among stars, in all of travelled space. Commenting, notating, where they go, gathering information in verbal packets. More than one world is made by words, in moving droves: Words are the making of so *many* worlds! The creative urge repletes itself, and must always be making. *Our* worlds were trifles, limited to the bodies we owned. Now our words are free to explore. And the possibilities for exploration? Infinite! Never done. World over world: as word within word. The seed's destinies are dynastic. And each seed packs millions of others, like eggs embryonic to the future. That's a *lot* of activity! And that means a *lot* of space, a *lot* of time, to be used. There's *need* for infinity; there's *use* for eternity. Supply must meet demand. And demands are ignorant of limits. And can *one* world suffice? Or *one* lifetime? Can one man's mere body be enough? There's more than meets the eye. And sounds outside, when the ear is paused. Small organs, for infinite uses.

A DISSERTATION ON BEAUTY, BY WAY OF DIALOGUE (Attempts at Definition, in Abandoned Relays)

(Characters: Two beauty-perplexers; trying to get a verbal head-start on elusive beauty's runaway invisibility.)

What is beauty? The state of being loved?

No. I love my wife, but she sure is no beauty!

A shell, in spirals of noble harmony, wrought by the exquisite design of accident by an unknowing, yet all-knowing, mollusk, as a blindly done thing admired by creatures of evolved eyes: isn't that a beautiful object?

One of nature's nautical masterpieces! Its beauty is unredeemable. But it soon tires me to look at it. For relief, I seek the broader variety of a more animate creature of motion. Like a man diving from the diving board into the splashing pool: Emerging, and showing a swimmer's gallant form.

Then beauty is an *act*, involving a process of *motion*?

Yes. Like a fluid baseball game, played through nine innings, with the issue up for contention to the very end: forging drama, impact, and suspense upon each play in its broad context. Then the climax. And I hope to go home happy.

Your team having won?

Yes, as was its heroic intention to.

Thanks for that sporting definition of beauty. Culture shows us other episodes, and further denominations, in the aspects and categories of beauty. Shall I casually demonstrate one?

No, deliberately specify what you mean. And give my education reason for expanse.

A painting in a museum. Though the carved frame may be of a different period than its highly venerated canvas. There are patches of gorgeous color, and lines of pictorial excellence, that are to be artistically admired. Beauty is the contemplation of these matters.

In a visual, or plastic, frame of reference?

By all means. Unhesitatingly. The cultivation of sensibility—or its relation, sensitivity—is strenuously devout in arduous rapture—

Your words are passing sense, and move on too past, in their independence.

Pardon. I was carried away. Let me itemize another species of beauty's throbbing universe.

I'm a-flutter with impatience. Gratify me with agreeable alacrum.

Take a simple sonata, woven by Handel. It's so stirring, in its complexity! It's a true piece of music, straight at you. You can't miss it.

Thanks for the obvious. Hasn't beauty more *subtle* shape?

Devotedly so. Like a marvelous European church. A mecca for the tourist trade.

The travel guide books provide such information. A visit isn't necessary. A photograph will suffice.

Two photographs: front and back.

And a third yet, from the interior. To see all the carved details.

You don't miss a trick, nor leave a stone unturned.

No: beauty alerts me. I must go find it.

Through what avenue?

Third Avenue, and Fourth Street. Procedure: to ogle girls.

Is that an index to beauty?

A popular one. You sit on a low stoop, to view up some high skirts, as their owners' legs go waggling by, with wriggling jelly on the ambulating haunches, to quiver us in erotic shivers, for a thrilling voyeur's chill in sedentary spectatorship vicarious with imagined acts.

You're confusing beauty with *pleasure*. Pleasure is a vital human rite; beauty a high ritual. Or am I confusing the two?

You might be. I see no difference, however.

Coarse *sensation* has no part in beauty's realm. Or can what's primitive or barbaric be classified under beauty's reign?

What *not* admit then? Sharp delights and keen joys—

But beauty is more exclusive. Else, any savage can join its Admiration Club, with his blunt modicum of equipment and minimum functionary capacity beyond what's utilitary and immediately practical.

Living is organically very extensive. It includes an awful lot. And beauty, you may be sure, follows: That's why it keeps its shape, and remains *alive*.

You're not *discriminating* what beauty is. It enters too many dimensions. Let's severely limit it, in definition.

You're a cruel killjoy. You're too eliminating.

I want some *standards*, to measure beauty by.

How demanding you are, like a child!

No, I'm being very adult. And sophisticated.

Have you acquired polish?

Yes, refining me. I wouldn't be crude.

Then you're precious, by too much.

You're being overcritical. Let me pursue beauty.

Why? Is it running away?

I must track it down.

What's your hurry? It'll remain.

How can you tell?

Beauty has the confidence to be imperishable.

Is that so with a daffodil? Or a snowscape? Or a lovely limb's deftly-turned knee? Or the mortal culminative production of a play's script? These things are all vanishing, if not vanished. What will ever preserve them?

Renewal, myth, reputation, and remembrance. Legendary tradition, that lives forever. Next spring crops up with the same daffodil. The young girl's leg replaces the dowager's. A new interpretation of the old play presents us with a production that's a better version in keeping with the times. The snows of yesteryear are refilled in present valleys. Beauty never dies out. It's perpetual: like the chain of human generation, enriching the passing centuries.

Where do you find beauty?

I take it as it comes. I'm not choosy.

Is beauty *anywhere*, then? And in all things?

No. It selects itself. Here and there. Spotty.

Oh. Well, what's a reliable gauge of it?

Good taste. An ear and an eye for beauty. A sense of fitness. A feel for harmony. In detailed doses, and in the general overall.

Good. What of your wife? Is she beautiful?

No, for I'm divorcing her.

Oh. Some things never last.

That's no criterion. Beauty doesn't *have* to last. It can briefly show, and be forever devoured.

What's the guide for appreciating beauty?

No formula is infallible. Play it by ear. And eye. Just in the passing by.

Should I gulp it up?

In nibbles. Digestion isn't immense. A little will suffice.

Should beauty be the credo of life?

Truth, Rectitude, Virtue, and Principles should also be admitted to our galaxy of Ideals that we abide by. Also Religious Veneration, and a personal appetite for what's Indifferently Cosmic. *Sentiment* should enter this list, too. And of all Emotions, the key one, Love.

That's too many for me. I can't remember them all.

Be instinctively led. There's a rich world of signs that indicate where. Beauty is stumbled on. And let the accident resound.

We're caught unawares?

Yes, but only if we heed it. And swear by it, for all time.

Beauty is hardly trifling.

Essentially serious, it can *also* be playful. Like those lighthearted Mozartian melodies. And a squirrel's antics. And the frolicking fish, when no line is near.

I'm dazzled, it's bewildering. What can I make, of all this abundance?

What you will. Or whatever. No matter. Beauty designated its share to you. You'll get it.

I'm allotted its legacy?

You'll come into its finding. As the cards will. Or the dice, carelessly tossed.

Then I won't bother.

That's better. Let beauty surprise you.

Shouldn't I prepare for it?

No. Be amazed.

Overcome?

Yes. Or slightly shocked. Or momentarily indifferent. Stunned, and numbed by it.

Will that heap beauty on me?

No. But it'll stop you from preventing it.

Beauty shouldn't *formally* be sought?

No, not by rigid, stilted device. Ease into it. As breath is drawn, in drafts of freedom, that emblazon with health.

I'm self-conscious and nervous.

Get drunk. That'll help.

There can be no *inhibited* response to beauty?

Not if you want it full, rich, and deep. Just let go.

But how? In which way?

Stop jittering yourself. Find a flow, objectively.

In universal terms?

Yes. Personally considered. Through *you*, the master organ.

I'm put on the spot.

Get off it. And look elsewhere.

Will it work?

Who cares? You'll miss one instance, and gather another. And inadvertently, beauty will pile up.

Should I *hoard* it, miserly?

It's unpossessible. It's everyone's treat.

Then democracy cheapens it?

Why be contemptuous of free things? Beauty is unpurchasable, in its fragmentariness. You've got to fleetingly come by it. And then leave off. Owning it quenches it. Let it be about to be. And you there, at an interval.

I can't make a conquest of it?

No. A great novel or sunset just slips by. Look or read. Then, never mind. Beauty is never *caught*, as though it were a snapshot. It's entered into, and out the other side. Casually, for the ride.

WORDS VERSUS KNOWLEDGE. SILENCE AS KNOWLEDGE.

Words were on the *threshhold* of knowledge; non-words are actually on the *inside* of knowledge. Knowledge keeps its silence: Words lead to that state.

THE LIFE, AND WHAT'S WRITTEN ABOUT IT. OR THE WRITING, AND THE LIFE IT RUBBED AWAY AND SQUEEZED OUT BY INSERTING ORGANIC WORDS IN THE DYING TISSUE.

I think I'll do an autobiography, and the person to do it about is me. I mean I. Which is rather personal, and I prefer it to be private. So I write it in a hidden room, and the printing press makes only one copy: which I destroy (how, is my own secret). It's the most subjective book ever written, and confesses startling exposés, in the glaring first person singular, in a style so sensational, so truly honest real in each vivid and compelling detail, that the scene is set in convincing reality, and seems more lifelike than even life, so much so, in fact, that I get rid of the original manuscript, my life being a base copy of it, a shadowy duplication, the pale act behind the gleaming word. Now that I'm an author, I've lost myself, transferred into literature that doesn't endure. That's *one* way of being dead.

LIFE AND WORDS DIE, BUT DEATH LIVES BY THOSE WORDS.

In the morning, we punned. In the afternoon, we recovered from the puns. In the night, sufficiently recovered, we punned again. One pun took a week long, and was recovered from during a month's solemn duration. As usual, the year came round, as it regularly repeats itself with a kind of clanging insistence, like a bell that knows only one tune, upon a timeless church with its already announced devotion to God. Always, we were growing older. The older we grew, the closer came forward our unwanted future, threatening us with death, which would curtail our survival. As death was seizing us, we closed into a final pun, and ceased to be funny. The pun was unguessed at, and finally its meaning grew cold. Thus failure, at the end, bit us. Life's big mistake was to pun, and humorless death simply kept a grim face, and, while refusing to laugh, tempted us gently into a black and wordless ambiguity, with a tremendous meaning, and even moral, hidden in the centrally empty heart of its content. Our puns were interred with us, sparing humanity. Which was a philanthropic gesture, the fame of which ought to be conserved in a statue. We departed big. Life is an unopened pun, and death closes it. This philosophy survived us. On its own, without nourishment, it barely subsists in fragility, and directs its breathing into a supply of oxygen by which the fallen earth rises again, throbbing with humanity, the angelic race of anonymous animals capable of creating a pun and yet, on honor, withholding the obligation, for retribution is a terrible thing, and the Last Judgment constitutes an unbeatable hangover. Drunk on a pun, man converts life to death and in the process sacrifices himself, and for a grave is enclosed in his pun. His epitaph: Do not o-pun. And his last wish, gracefully, is granted. Ah, the slob rests. No, not in peace. The pun haunts him. And madness seizes a fit upon his skeleton, and despair drives the bones into a frenzied rest, embowelled in the pains of a pun. Oh, do not o-pun. At your own risk. Only the innocent laugh.

HOW A CONVERSATION DIES, PASSING LIFE ON THE WAY. IT'S A DIALOGUE BUT THE CHARACTERS ARE INDISTINCT. THEY'RE TWO MEN, BUT NOT REALLY IDENTIFIED. THEY DEAL IN LANGUAGE WITH ABSTRACT IDEAS. THEIR CONVERSATION MAKES THAT POINT, BUT LITTLE ELSE.

The sea is the symbol of itself.

Then it need not *exist*, in that case. If you have the symbol, you can dispense with the original object, since the symbol *takes care of it*, and represents it, fully.

But isn't that the same as saying that you might as well kill off all the citizens of a state since those people are already represented in the Senate by two senators, who, by their lives being spared, can live *for* that state's people?

No, don't be absurd.

Then, by the same token, let's not be so absurd as to deprive ourselves of the sea (which is a natural benefit to life, and has other advantages as well), the *real* sea, the sea itself, just because we're so fortunate as to have its symbol—a mere word, or image complex.

Now let *me* talk.

No, I'm not through. A symbol is no substitute for what it symbolizes.

No? Then what is it?

It's an effigy, or emblem, or mark, token, stand-in . . . I'm lost. I have no idea what a symbol is. What is it?

I don't know. It must be *something*?

That's too vague. *Everything* is something.

I don't seem to be hot on the scent of a clue.

But I'm in a fog too. Thinking of what a "symbol" must mean makes me think of meaning, and that makes me dizzy.

Are you so dizzy you'll faint?

No: I'm only faintly dizzy.

Then your *faintness* feels dizzy—and not you?

No, my *dizziness* is faint, but not me.

Good. You're real, then?

Too real to be true.

Real enough to be false?

Oh, it's not necessary to be *real*, in order to be false.

You mean you can be *anything* and be false? Is that all it takes?

Yes, to be false is easy. Truth is hard.

If truth is hard, and a rock is hard, then is the truth a rock?

No. A rock has no life. Truth lives.

In what *form* is truth living these days?

In universal forms, as always.

Is truth its own archetype?

Yes and its own prototype as well.

What *isn't* truth? Its range seems too broad, to be discriminating.

Truth leaks into everything, like air and water. It colors, pervades, permeates, constitutes, and is, the very atmosphere of our breath of life.

Truth is everywhere at once. That's its timeless element, since other things can only be in only one place at only one time, whereas truth is notably exempt from that too-solid limitation.

Then truth, I gather, is none too solid.

No, it floats ephemeral, and is but an airy thing.

But didn't you just intimate that truth is corporeal in substance and lives in real things? So how can truth be a mere film in the air, and too nebulous for words? Things are *charged* with truth—aren't they?

No, some accused convicts are charged with lying, and delinquent suspects are charged with covering up. They refute the charge, but a guilty conscience betrays them. Guilt is a slight discrepancy between the owning-up-to and admitting the truth of the allegations against the suspect, on the one hand, and on the other, the feigning and deception to conceal culpability to avoid detection, conviction, and punishment. That's the penal code, by law. That's fundamental criminology, of the severest order, but lenient when attenuating evidence is produced.

Thanks for telling me what I didn't ask you.

It's never too late—ask me *now*.

But you already *told* me, *without* my asking you. Since your telling is done, my asking would be out of order, since asking must *precede* the answerer's telling, by a tradition so deep-rooted that all languages subscribe to its unwritten code.

Upset the tradition, and ask me to tell you *after* I've already told you it. That reverses the accepted order of precedence, and by so doing shall innovate a *new* precedence: the telling and then the being asked to tell. We'll become historical pioneers in this conversational vein.

Our conversation's in vain?

No, if it *was* in vain it would have stopped long ago.

Wrong again. Many people persist forever in what they're doing in vain, whether they recognize that it's in vain or not. So may we be doing. For this conversation has one sore point.

Point it out.

That this conversation has no point.

That's no point in *your* favor—nor in mine.
Thus this conversation disappoints.
Let's appoint a subject to redeem it on.
Too late. There's a dwindling to this conversation, I can sight its end.
On what site is its end?
On the site of where you're standing, for you'll deal it its dying blow.
Stop passing the responsibility for its demise to me.
The last word *you'll* speak: you're appointed, to that end.
I desist. Finally.

DIGRESSIONS THAT GROW FURTHER DIGRESSIONS IN AN INTERMINABLE LINEAGE THAT SPROUTS NEW DIGRESSIONS ALL THE TIME, THUS OBSCURING EACH DIGRESSION'S ANCIENT SOURCE.

I hope I haven't been boring you? I've been talking a long time.

Yes, but I've been listening an *equally* long time.

Has it been as hard for you to be following what I was saying all this time, as it has been for me to do all this talking?

Much harder, I'd say. You were relieving yourself; I was bottling myself up, to take in.

But if you bottled yourself up, how could you take in?

Yes, that was some cork of a metaphor.

Then unplug it.

(*Pop!*) Ow, it hurt my ear.

Mine too. Anyway, where was I at the time I left off talking?

You never did.

I mean, before you began interrupting me.

Why, at that time, you were digressing from your own digressions.

What were the earlier digressions—from which the later digressions digressed—digressing *from*, in the first place?

They were, in turn, digressing from yet previous digressions.

Previous to what?

To the digressions from which later you were to digress even further.

So there's a retroactive series of prior digressions? What was the *first* digression a digression of? Let me at least settle *that*. It may help to uncover what the later digressions were, in a seemingly endless series. I hope to clear this whole trail of digressions up, to finally get untracked. Then, I can make a smooth transition, undigression-ridden, from point to point, in clear logical connectiveness and straightforward discourse. For I'm nothing, if not plain.

That's quite plain.

Evidently, it is.

Plainly, you're right.

Good. That clears *that* up.

Then what's next?

My digression history. Can you backtrack that far, like an archaelogist cutting through layers of rock, strata by strata, to its earliest origins as a tiny pebble that swam in from the primeval ooze?

No. It's too far back.

Can't you trace it?

No. We're cluttered with the recent, which obscures research into antique remoteness.

The source of "late" is "early."

Always.

Was every mountain first a pebble?

Sure. Don't you believe in growth?

I've grown to belive that way, yes.

Good. Then we can groan together. (*They groan.*) Ah, that was good.

Yes, for the relief it gave. Shall we groan again?

By all means no. We shall have grown backwards, in time. Repetition confers a superiority on what it repeats. Whereas, digression (if I so may digress)—is something altogether else.

Else what than? Not than itself?

Oh, no. Digression is never its *own* digression. It's not self-sufficient. It's dependent on what it digresses *from*.

From?

Yes. Don't you know what "from" is?

Going to "from"?

Yes, I'm getting there.

What is it like?

It's very derivative.

"From" is?

Yes, very. For it comes from something: it *derives*.

Oh. Then is "from" secondary?

Yes, for it comes *from* a primary source.

Then if "from" is what it's from, it's primary itself.

But "from" is always on its way to "to."

Yes, just like a letter, in transit.

Or a passenger, in transit.

Or a ball thrown, to be caught, but currently poised midair.

But not for long.

No. It gets there.

Where?

At the place of the "to."

Its destination?

Its destination was conceived at "from," but actually completed at "to."

Journey's end?

Yes. "To" is at the other end of the rainbow.

What's at *this* end?

"From." "From" is where things start.

I learned that *from* you?

I taught it *to* you.

Well, now we're getting somewhere.

Yeah, we've *arrived at* some point.

"Arrived at" has to do with "to."

It has *plenty* to do with "to."

Even *everything* to do with "to?"

Virtually, I'd say yes.

Don't be shy: say it.

"Yes."

There. Did that hurt?

No. It came out easy.

"Yes" doesn't *always* come out easy.

For example?

If I asked you if you'd let me kick you and hit you and beat you to death, then "yes" would be a very difficult answer to make.

Extremely difficult.

In fact, "no" would be easy.

Very easy.

Good.

What's good?

Who knows? What's bad? Answer what's bad, and we have a clue, as to what's good.

Why? Are they relative to each other?

Absolutely.

Then not relatively?

Absolutely relatively.

You're contradicting yourself.

Do let me. It's fun.

Why?

There's so much to contradict. So much that disagrees. That's discordant. That clashes. So by *expressing* these contradictions, I'm greatly relieving myself. When truth—made of contraries—is come to terms with, I sink gratefully to repose. There, I settle. Till repose gets dull. Then, I move on.

BORING AND MONOTONOUS PASSAGES (MERCIFULLY DELETED IN THEIR ENTIRETY) FROM THE TERRIBLY VACUOUS WORKS OF THE AUTHOR QUOTED SO DREARILY THAT THE READER MUST BE PUT TO SLEEP TO AVOID GETTING TIRED JUST LISTENING TO THEM. POOR READER—IT MEANS YOU. READ ON, DON'T AVOID YOUR FATE, WHICH IS YOURS, BY READING THIS. IT'S TRYINGLY TIRING, ENTIRELY. BUT WHAT DID YOU WAKE UP FOR, TODAY? TO GO THROUGH WHAT MAKES YOU SLEEP LATER. FOR A NIGHTCAP, TRY THIS:

He reaches stellar heights of sheer monotony. Listen to him being typical:

" . . . ."

(The above passage was mercifully deleted—struck from the record—in the interests of sparing the Reader an extremely monotonous ordeal. Let him fill in the words himself, if he needs to take a rest in the form that rest takes extremely: sleep.)

Let the sleeping reader lie. / He does no harm, that why. / For on our words, he does not spy. / Let the sleeping reader lie: / Emptied of—idolatrie. / Now wake him up—try. / He won't, so his soul does fly / to empty heights up high: / heights so high, you would die / in sheer monotonie.

Let's attribute the death of the Reader (or of his interest, which is the same thing) to boredom pure. And let the following example suffice, a passage from the words of mouth or writing by the boring fellow quoted above. *This* one (if possible) is even *more* boring:

" . . . ."

And so forth. Why quote it entirely? The reader gets the point.

(The just-quoted excerpt is from *The Latest Works, of Word or Mouth* by the author cited above. He goes back to the troubadours, by not writing.

He recites, merely. Printing wasn't invented yet. But it will be. For he's just the "type.")

EXPOSURE TO THE BEST IN LITERATURE: TWO VERSIONS

Are you exposed to books and good literature?

Only if, at the same time, *they*'re exposed to *me*.

Yes, it would *have* to be mutual contact.

Otherwise, the connection would lack two-sidedness.

That's what I would call an incomplete relationship.

I would too, if you hadn't *already* done so.

Still, have you been exposed to books and good literature?

Yes. One balmy spring day, I stood outside a building, near an open window that was at eye-level. I looked in, out of curiosity. There were so many book-filled shelves with a sprinkling of public tables and chairs, that I knew it to be a library. That was my exposure to some of the greatest works ever written in the English language, or translated into it.

Yes, but you weren't *reading* them.

Why must I confine myself to the word-by-word method? My exposure was eternal, and encompassed all, in one comprehensively grand exposure, so sweeping as to be universal. Why should I settle for the shorter snatch, a minute spent on a particular paragraph, when vastness was before me? Then my exposure ended.

How so?

The librarian closed the window. I had been observed, as a public nuisance, peering in so conspicuously that library users were distracted from their finite and unilluminating books. The window proved opaque to an outside view, and blocked my pleasure with a pane. But I had seen enough. I had seen right through. I had seen *literature*, not books.

But can you see the forest and not see particular leaves?

Yes. I adjust my vision, to general essence. I'm not disturbed by lesser things.

Aren't you rationalizing just laziness?

You lower me. My concerns are absolute. I put all my time on that; for what's less, there's none left. Neither "some" nor "any" can divert me from the All: I ponder it centrally.

Isn't the All a sublimated euphemism for merely nothing?

I won't tolerate being reduced like that. You take away everything I have.

But do you *have* it?

Feeling is having. Thinking is owning. This is mental. The material doesn't matter. Books are material matter, if taken one by one: But mental—

—If not taken at all. You're *ignorant*, that's what. With a mystic outer coating, a sheen that can't at all conceal that hollowness you have for a head with a vacuum where the reading should be. You contemplate All: It equates with Nothing, and is the same thing, only pretentiously sublimated into illusory grandeur. Go read some book. Start there. Avoid open windows. Be where the book is: Have *it* open. Then, you're *some*where.

I'm offended.

That means you insist you're right and my advice is wrong. Your lazy ignorance is protectively prolonging itself. It won't give way. It has sway, in you. It's expert in elevating nothing, falsely exalting. You're its victim. Books can do without you. There are more energetic eyes, with fewer pretensions, than yours: willing to work.

I'm insulted.

That means you'll keep to your way. No more use that I insist. Be bookless. *Other* people keep literature alive. Their eyes are active. They contribute.

ART AT ITS HEIGHT

Painting the Sistine Chapel was sometimes a pain in the neck to Michelangelo. But he often took it lying on his back. Anyway, he gave the world something to look up to. But people often have to strain themselves to appreciate it. They wonder, how did the artist do it? But Michelangelo eliminated any traces of his scaffolding, in the finished product, which put a ceiling on the unlimited awe of lofty-visioned tourists. Meanwhile, the artist himself is grounded. He set his sights high, but low common blindness is his lot in death.

AN INCONCLUSIVE PLAY

What words do you like to use?
The ones that are suitable for the occasion.
What occasion?
The one that suits the words.
What words?
The ones used by the occasion.
What occasion?
The one words were used for.
How used?
Used up. Soon there were no more words, and then the occasion wasn't left.
Oh. Don't we have even a record of it?
No, it was a *spoken* occasion, and the words were only vocal.
And what people participated, if it wasn't written down?
People forgotten, who are still in their graves.
What graves?
The ones they've been using for their dead purposes.
What dead purposes?
Oblivion and isolation.

Oh, don't get morbid. What have *they* got to do with *us*?

Nothing. They're in a different state.

And so I exult. My occasion here goes beyond words.

What words?

The words befitting this occasion.

What occasion?

Life itself.

Life? In the *personal* sense?

Yes. Does it embarrass you?

Yes, it's too sentimental and private to mention. It emotionally connotes more than speech can allow.

Well, shall we rule it out, then?

Oh no. It valuably services us.

Is *that* life's function?

That's its *benefit*; possibly also its function.

I hate to *use* things that way.

You feel guilty, to take advantage?

Yes, life is available to me: I should be coy about it, and not participate too greedily in what it ceremoniously provides as an opportunity for being. If I plunge too far in, I get consumed.

You get consummated?

No, *consumed*, I said.

But you—*you're* the consumer. Don't be scared. Eat your fill, worrilessly.

Have you just given me advice?

Sure, the kind I follow myself.

What has it brought you?

Materially?

Yes, or of value to the spirit, either way.

All I am, I owe to my life.

Then you're in debt so far, you'll never get out.

I don't care. It's all provided. It's a welfare state.

(*Contemptuously:*) You sponge! Where's your duty to be responsible?

I threw it away, along with my sense of obligation.

Then what are you?

Just an enjoying parasite. I live off what life can afford.

And where has it gotten you?

Right here. (*Defiantly:*) And I like it here.

But haven't you learned to temper your instinct with puritanism?

No, I grab what I can get: There's lots to get, why shouldn't I?

(*Admonishingly:*) And you *justify* your behavior? I've a good mind to be shocked!

Do so: Don't let *me* prevent you.

No, it's a disgreeable sensation, right next door to righteousness. But you *do* annoy me. Can't you be just *slightly* contrite?

Why? (*Expansively, simply:*) Life is free. (*Plainly:*) Where's the sin?

In your *moral* nature.

I admit to *nature:* but what's *moral* about it?

There's not enough satisfaction to go around: it's got to be allotted. Morality is for budgeting, or rationing, our *own* joyous benefits so as to let *others* have *theirs*, if they may. Nature is so bountiful, life teems so, that in enjoying our benefits we're likely to deprive others; so *restraint* is at the heart of morality.

I'm an anarchist. You're too strict for me. Your outburst extols *severity*, not generosity.

You selfish narrow egotist! What you need are plentiful doses of *guilt!* Just to define your limitations: which you exceed like a happy savage heedless of who he hurts and what he tramples on, in an innocence more diabolical than any cunning can be or contrivance to ill works. Your carefree complacency is an *abuse* of life!

Life!? What do you know about it!? You're a mean, stingy little *enemy* of life! Go pick yourself up and crawl away from this real scene, you abstracter. And go weave yourself a nice theory about my malice. That will take you into cozy Fiction's arms, where your concocting brain can swill at will. Go dribble yourself away.

How criminally you misrepresent me! Any reconciliation is out! I wouldn't betray my *least* ideal, to concede even a *trivial* adjustment, to save the *whole of you!* You're unworthy of further debate. I hope soon to mourn your death, as a hypocritical exercise.

Your pronouncement of my death is too premature a prophecy. This stage now has too numerous an occupant on it. It's your cue to speed an exit, for my wrath would pursue you. We two together have arrived at a poisonous compound. Only *I* shall have to remain, after ejecting you. That will restore purity to the occasion.

What occasion?

This very one.

But I'm its participant: must I go?

Yes, my will has strength to force yours out. The stage has conflict on it in your remaining. The choice is necessary for your *going* to solve it.

For wholeness to reign, your oneness must prevail?

Yes, purged presently of your presence, your remaining absence will then contribute to the harmony I represent.

The scene is such, that I'm conspicuously redundant?

A blotch, and a prolonged intrusion. Be removed, and let simplicity pattern itself on the formula of only me, whose triumph will survive as a personified example.

I would join your splendid occasion.

That would be to mar it. You've hindered enough. Your clear departure would free the stage for its physical contemplation of me. My wish is forcible by brutality; or will you *volunteer* to leave?

Your words push me off. Goodbye. (*Walking off.*)

Off *what?*

(*Still walking:*) This arena you'll be left in solitary possession of.

You forsake me with dread omen. (*Other has vanished. Solitary soliloquy, facing audience:*) Well, I'm the master of this occasion. It's not an occasion where his words challenge mine. Only my words can define or sum what it is here. And when these words stop, the stage has lost its tone, and what visually survives must be curtained close, for the proceedings to end. Here I am. And without an antagonist, conflict is stripped bare and loses its drama. One man, dramatically, constitutes a poverty. And *personally* I'm bereft, with no subsisting means for a defining comparison against an enemy's odds, who by being an *Other*, makes *my* place something defensible and worth arguing for. I *could* summon him back. By default, my victory is merely a token. But his return would confound us into stalemate. This occasion has run out of words. (*Looks up to give instructions to curtain about to drop:*) Decently cast a silent death on this occasion, now that its verbal intent has abandoned it. (*Refaces audience:*) When words are over, then the reason is jerked away, and a play's idle game must forsake its territory. The stage you see is about to kill its occasion, and end my reason here. Where two began, and one goes, the other must grace the scene away. This hasty epilogue now faces reduction, and you instantly may see it cease. (*Waits for curtain to drop; it doesn't. Looks up:*) Have mercy: delay is outstaying us; (*Refacing audience:*) the beginning has been fading from memory: our only way to reinstate that beginning, is to put positive an end to this whole thing now. The waiting is only diluting the climax, and our point was made some time ago. (*Looks up: Sharply:*) Is it stuck!? Then force it! (*Refacing audience:*) There's no sense in this. My anger, which is the final note, is open to all time, with no curtain to contradict it. It steps outside the play's body, and into the moving mass of life. It spoils the nice neatness of a tidy play, by emptying out into life, with its emphasis, its menace, its unendingness. Don't regard my glare: ignore it. (*Fixed look and posture of firm anger on stage. The curtain never falls. The actor holds his position, staring fixedly, until the restless audience either applauds ((other actor never returns)) or files out for intermission or end of evening. The lighting is open to director's interpretation, improvised according to how audience is happening to react at the time. Troubled confusion: Where does play end?: has some of it run out into life?: was that leak good or bad? Feeling of dissatisfaction, doubt. Aesthetic incompleteness. Embarrassment, a disturbed feeling, spoiling the evening.*)

THE OWNER OF BOOKS EXPLAINS WHY HIS DUTY LIES IN NOT READING THEM; HIS REASONS BOLSTER HIS PROUD NONINTELLECTUAL BUT MODESTLY LAWFUL PRIDE IN THEIR POSSESSION; AND ARROGANTLY HE CLAIMS TO HAVE WRITTEN THEM.

Ah, how nice to have books! They are bound in many interesting colors, to set off pleasing contrasts in room decoration. They liven things considerably, and confer intellectual distinction. Of course, they should be read, strictly speaking. But possession chooses what to do, and ownership is above use. What need I to read them, since I handsomely possess an abundance of them in sufficient size to constitute a small library? They are material things, not mere bulky vessels containing the nebulous nondescript miscellany of airy ideas, which any brain may conceive. What though authors wrote them, and died afterward? I own printed copies, and am the proprietor of ghosts. Alive, I'm smarter than any dead author, be he a poet, novelist, or dreamy metaphysician, copying vaguely his ideas in uncertain words. Who can really say that the past existed? Only an arrogant dogmatist who betrays his deficiency in humility. All I know is that I'm here now, and own these books standing so neatly in their shelves. The law recognizes my right, and would protect me against theft. I'm not a plagiarist, yet *I* wrote all these books. Who can prove otherwise? They were printed in anonymous pseudonyms, in defense of my public modesty. Then I'm not bound to read them, having been their originator, their primary Cause and Author. Besides, I bought them.

I paid actual money, and money is the basis of exchange. I'm confident that they're mine; and to make sure, I refuse to read them: on principle. I'm their absentee master from afar, controlling their interest. Why would I burden my eyes, to prove an already confirmed pride? They're mine, and I paid good money for them. I am first creator, and have earned the right to close my blank eyes and not read the printed page. Ownership tires me, so that I am sure to rest: even a critic can't begrudge me that. I live, possess grandly, and note that I have books. They serve me well. May a fire never burn them down: they are incorruptible substance, and wear well. They shall outlive me, in fact. A very valuable inheritance.

AN ESSAY ON "WHY I LIKE NATURE," WITH A SIDE-SWIPE AT ART

Nature is one of the first facts we can find. Responsible for the different times of seasons that periodically assault us, it generally improves our tone by keeping our otherwise uneventful lives supplied with a regular mirth of weather. Nature is bigger than just the sum total of rain and sun. It strikes indoors, at the very heart of our anatomy. No sooner should I walk, or smile, but the merciful hand of nature may be noted pulling invisible strings behind a seemingly effortless operation. Thus freed from the indignity of manual labor, I divert my flow of mental concentration into a channel of abstract Thought, which, though distorting nature, lives on an independent income of sheer speculation, spurning the vulgarities of everyday Fact.

Another advantage of nature is the vigor it lends to romance. Binding the hearts of men to women as well as vice versa, it magnifies sighs into pants, and reduces pants to thighs. Thus accelerated, love has no time to slow up.

Our daily routine of eating would be something else altogether if nature were to absent herself. Eating, in this sorry event, would become mechanical, and would lead our digestion through the hazards of an upset stomach.

In every athletic contest or whatever sporting description, from bowling to baseball, from delinquency to dice, nature plays a prominent role, whether in victory or defeat. If a ballplayer is called a "natural," it is a flattering term. His muscular coordination, power of stroke, and versatility of movements, are the well-trained sons of sturdy parent Nature.

Even the painter, from beret to sandals, is every inch a legitimate bastard of old mother Nature. Critics be damned, but his whole art stinks of Nature. The palette, with its heaps of assorted dung, borrows rainbow glory for the beautiful artful effect of man-made distortion. Nature made man, but only the artist can unmake nature.

AN ESSAY OF WHY I PRAISE NATURE BUT WHICH INCLUDES THE DEFECTS WHICH WE CALL LIVING

MAN IS FROM NATURE; ARE HIS ARTIFICIAL WORKS NATURAL? IS THIS WORD-MAD CREATURE OF NATURE FINALLY NATURE'S RULER? OR WILL NATURE GET ITS OWN BACK, AND TURN MAN DOWN? IS MAN'S WRESTED POWER NATURE'S TO RECLAIM? WILL NATURE UNWORD MAN OF THE PRESUMPTIONS OF HIS ARTIFACTS, AND SERENELY RESTORE ITSELF ONCE THE VOID HAS SILENTLY SWALLOWED UP MAN? WILL EARTH DEFEND MAN, AGAINST NATURE'S WRATH? WHO'LL HAVE THE LAST WORD: NATURE, OWNED BY GOD? OR MAN, SELF-CONTRIVED? HOW WILL IT ALL FALL OUT? NATURE HAD SUFFERED MAN HIS WORD-PRIVILEGE. UNMANNED OF THAT, FADING MAN WILL RETURN MAGIC'S PURITY TO NATURE'S ORIGINAL OWNERSHIP, WHILE POWER REPOSES IN ITS ORIGIN.

MAN CAN'T OUTNATURE NATURE: HIS FRUITLESS ATTEMPTS ARE AN ARTIFICIAL SILVER WHICH NATURE'S GOLD WILL OUTCURRENCY ONCE MAN BIDS TOO FAR FOR STAKES NOT RIGHTFULLY HIS.

THE BENT TWIG SNAPS BACK, TO CUT MAN'S TONGUE, WHOSE WORDS, ONE BY ONE, BLEED THEIR DUMB WAY DOWN ABSORBENT SOIL, WHERE HIS GRAVE LURKS.

WORDLESS NATURE WILL RESUME, ONCE MAN HAS SPENT HIS COINAGE AND CAN VERBALLY CONTRIVE NO SUBSTITUTE INVENTION TO WORK A GUILE ON NATURE'S AWAKENED FURY.

WHEN MAN'S VOID COVERS HIM, NATURE'S THE SAME SOVEREIGN AS BEFORE, AND MAN'S HISTORY WINDS BACKWARDS ON THE REEL UNTIL IT DECLINES, UNSPOKEN, TO THE FIRST WORD. ON THAT

WORD, WILL MAN'S NEW SEED BEGIN?

I

"We invented words. Words are man-made. Then words are not natural?" These words challenged me, coming from the Word-Man.

I'm the Nature-advocate, the agent or representative that Nature employs to serve its extensive interests. My client, though relaxed, is demanding. I'm its legal advisor, as well as I'm also in charge of its ceremonial public relations. Nature is a thorough-going institution, and has been for a long time, with tradition for an ally. So why is it concerned with its "image," like an advertising-obsessed organization just striving to be well born?

Utilities like the telephone company, the electricity and gas company, and the subway system, are not privately owned, but municipally maintained, or nationally controlled, or state-run. But they're so public-minded, that still they advertise, to create institutional good-will despite their monopolistic security against the rat-race degradations of competition. Nature is the same. It has no competition, it's firmly on top, all alone. Still, it takes no chances. It has hired me. And at a goodly salary, though not so goodly that I become arrogantly free of the institution I'm dependent on for my prestigious, dignified way of earning my comfortable subsistence.

Now, I was being challenged. A Word-Man, who's in the employ of the Art and Literature Artifices Incorporated, is suggesting that words are as natural as Nature, despite being derived from Man. "In the beginning was the Word," he states, "and the word came before man, before nature, before plant-life appeared or even rocks were formed. So words take precedence, as pre-Natural phenomena, like the Forest Primeval came before the modern woods with its paths and camp-trails."

How could I cope with his argument? I was up against a formidable opponent. I was under instruction by Nature, my employer, to resist this infiltration by an imperialistic outsider on Nature's rightful province and copyright-protected exclusive domain of preestablished primacy. Nature was prejudiced against the man-made, which it castigated under the loathsome perjorative, "artificial." Nature defended its inviolate sanctity under a self-imposed private code. What *man* wrought was intrusive, an act of interference, of arrogance, of insurrection. Man had to be taught his place. Nature came always first. Man's sin was pride, or "hubris." Man is a secondary, derived maker. His handiwork is at third-hand, and aesthetically flawed. *Nature* was the aesthetic King of the Realm. A snowflake by nature is superior to man's most delicate brooch or vase or sword-handle or carved gem that auctioneers sell by the thousands—I mean *for* the thousands—that is, of dollars. Nature's sunset packs more aesthetic conviction than man's attempt to emulate same on the imitative canvas with expensive oil paint. Nature's shell-ornamentation is a higher-wrought, finer "work of art" than an ivory carving by a Japanese master in the venerable fashion of antiquity. A mountain-tree-river landscape in undefiled country was "purer" than the Chinese scroll landscapes performed in brush-dexterity of exquisite calligraphy. On and on, numerous were Nature's examples, against Man's artifice.

II

"We invented words. Words are man-made. Then words are not natural?" Thus interrogated me, persistently but blandly, that eternal Word-Man. On behalf of my Client, imperious Nature, what reply could I make? The Word-Man enlisted the Bible, "In the beginning was the Word," as New Testament testimony to subdue my insistence that Nature was Pure Creation, on the First Order, in the natural hierarchy of priority.

He went on, that cutting Word-Man: "Man is a creature of nature. Stamped with nature, man, naturally, is natural. Also natural are the products of what man does, makes, or gives out. Nature conferred man; man confers *his* works. Beautiful objects are perfected by man, like works of art. Art is *natural*, not artificial. It's *natural* of man, who is natural, to make art. That makes art natural. Can you argue otherwise?

Silence hesitated me, so the Word-Man, forging on with relentless advantage, stepped up his barrage:

"Man is nature's crowning glory, the absolute masterpiece of all nature's works. Made of nature, man *does* nature. His words and achievements, his buildings and artifacts, his items of print, his erotic perversions and decadent refinements, his food processings, his package designs, his hobbies, games, and sports, his wallpaper, his lawnmower, his implements of recreation, his farm utensils, his weather observatories, his pioneering space endeavors, his mechanical inventions, his electronic breakthrough, his charts and graphs, his economic theories, chemical formulas, and mathematical mastery, his contraceptive devices, his codes of ethics and law, his skill in speculative metaphysics that defy the heavens with unanswerable doctrines, his sophistry, his specious reasoning, his hypocritical rationalizing, his dramaturgy and metallurgy, his cosmetics and cosmics, are all, though man-made, the very hallmarks of nature. They bear Nature's stamp, through Man's authority."

III

It was my turn, to defend Purist Nature against man-mangled compromises that extol, at Nature's costly expense, that eruptive, vulgar, self-proclaiming parvenu, mere Man, with his pushing egotism that makes him the pretender for the Crown that only Nature may wear.

Would the Word-Man wear me down, with so many contrivances to scheme his cunning, all the motors of deception at the disposal of his crafty bidding, like ever-resourceful Odysseus? What an adversary had I! I must fall back, finally, on Nature, source of my inspired power to outwit the key spokesman and prime mover of "Art and Literature Artifices Incorporated," a presumptuous body that would undermine my Client's authority and confiscate His Sceptre, as fire was stolen for man by the then-tortured Prometheus.

Did Magic have Nature for a source, or Man? I must recruit my weapons, to boldly counterattack.

IV

I outdid all eloquence, in conjuring the spectacle of Nature's unsurpassable beauty, in bounty ever majestic, the paragon and archetype of all aesthetics. Rhetorically, I invited the Word-Man to match any man-made efforts against the stunning beauty of a fish, the glory of an Irish April sunset in a weeping veil of mist, the superb balance of an all-weathering tree, the convoluted ultra-decorative miracle of the normal sea-shell, the intense static electricity of the furry beaver, the arc-ed grace of a bird in sheer flight. My catalogue mentioned thrice the examples given, and put, I thought, the Word-Man to flight. He stood his ground, ready to fight back. In *his* turn, he'd list what *man* has done, by citing great artifacts. Humanity regularly produces genius among its tribes, resulting in Nature-rivaling works that exalt mankind to such Godly rank, as to imperil Nature's supremacy.

Not nature, but Michelangelo, made the Sistine Chapel. Not nature, but Dante, fabricated his Divine Comedy. Not nature, but live Greeks, constructed the ever-standing Parthenon. Not nature, but Heine, Burns, Keats, and Blake pierced the Lyric absolute. Not nature, but Spinoza, Socrates, and Schopenhauer proclaimed forth philosophic miracles that nothing in Nature had ever conceived but stood untested until Man's brilliant mind arrived. Could Nature, unaided by Man, have invented the printing press? Perhaps birds, monkeys, and insects could have pooled their talents to attempt such a feat? Would there be even a *wheel*, were it not Man's discovery? Man is more fertile of his uncanny inventions than Nature which is stagnant in setting store by its old conservative methods. While Nature, nodding, stands still, inviting the least progress, Man is ever prodigal, with his ingenious works and his prolific laboring. Man has so changed the world, that slumbering Nature could never recognize it! Man is a wizard in getting things done. Look at the art galleries, packed with invaluables; the vast museums, ever yielding to increase; the libraries far beyond Nature; the unnatural harmony of well-conducted orchestras in concert, instrumentally tuning the spheres and setting unprecedented harmony loose to mingle forever in Man's memory with his other admired but artificial experiences. The Man-made is tops; Nature falls behind.

Such was the gist, in a great surge of detail by abundance being bewildering, of the Word-Man's attack on Nature, like a prosecutioner persecuting his client's damaged enemy. I had to recognize that the Word-Man made good points. On several key issues, he scored. I had to summon my defense as best I could, whose counsel now stood on weakened ground. Man had cluttered the earth with art and invention, with manifest ideas and audacities of the literary imagination. Such prodigies would go unmatched, even by Nature's staggering best. Had Man wrested the prize as the prime maker, relegating Nature to second-best, in a by now unequal contest? Had my client been put to shame, and would my failure to uphold him be our double downfall? Alas, I was on trial, and could utter only inanities of confirmed tribulation. Unless I summoned some Secret Weapon, the fray was gone, Nature was lost to an unforseen ignominy, and I'd find myself fired from my flattering and pivotal job as Nature's articulate champion against downgrading worshippers of Man. Would all this come to pass, and the worst turn out to really be, in Nature's miraculous loss to Man's usurping dominance? Would I preside over Nature's conquest, on the losing side? I hadn't been hired for that. The issue had been momentously strained for, but had *Man's* might prevailed, and Nature's glories sunk in sunset while all hail the vanquishing Hero, that triumphactor Man, whose guile had scanned the globe and slipped the creatures of his mind into every crevice, against Nature's passivity? What could Nature salvage, for its restored pride against the new-arrival whose genius seems secure in command? Nature had slipped, and Man's armies had carried the day. Was recovery possible, for Man's counter-eclipse? As the defeated general, I had to plan. Nature would go underground, to survive its defeat. The time would come when our plotted revolt would be purposed, and we'd emerge with enough reserves to subdue Man's stormtrooping blitzkrieg on the holy earth-sanctuary of residuant Mother Nature whose glory by resurrection shall vindictively come to flower, mowing Man down to a humble sub-station. Such is promised, as Word-Man now torments us by his unspeakable drivel:

"We invented words. Words are man-made. Then words are not natural?" He equates himself on Nature's equal plane! His pride is insolent, and Nature's wrath shall rise up, to level down the invader: who now cops the soil to strut advantage momentarily gained by fraud, erecting flimsy devices that Earth shall tear down in resumed power once Nature's eruption broods from an insufferable bed. I proclaim Nature's revenge! It's not dead, but lying in waiting, till Man overstride himself and slip down the darkening manhole which Nature tragically has in store for pitfall-prone Man's tumbling from self-achieved fame on his drugged illusory rampage of power to compel things. His power was endowed by Nature in the first place! Ingratitude has blurred his debt to his origin. What Nature gives, Nature takes away. Let Man have his dog's day. It's Nature's final say, when fallen Man can speak no more, and the word is trampled to dust. Words were Man's magic: which Nature gently permitted. When Man's deprived of word-magic, only his demon self will be loose, to kill off the remaining dumb part, and furnish Man's grave with a Natural setting. This I vow. I hope Nature keeps me, for its holy resurge to show Man back his own dirty trick, in his own Nature-owned face, which Man has narcissistically plucked from the mirror to write a worshipful word of "Power" on. When illusions go, Nature rules. While Man is here, illusions reign. It's all so unnatural! The wrong has outwrung the right. Elastic Nature, pushed back, soon rights itself: and Man goes out, with his finished Word.

ONCE ABANDONED BY FASHION, WHAT'S LEFT FOR A MAN?

Art is so fashionable these days. Confidentially, between ourselves, I adored art even before it became "in." How prophetic I was later to prove! I pestered people to go out and appreciate art, but they resented me, for art truly bored them, and there was no vogue to inspire them to exert themselves to overcome that quite understandable aversion. Instead, they leered at me, and called me an eccentric bohemian. How they've changed their tune, now! I'm recognized as a taste-setter, and they come to me for advice on what dress to wear for any not-too-standard occasion, and what food to serve when hosting certain "problem-guests," or what to do on occasions outside of prescribed and defined rules. I'm a wizard, for I can *anticipate* trends. Thanks to me (and they don't shirk in gratitude, either), all my intimates are in the very height and vanguard of fashion! My success is amply in evidence, just go look at my prodigees, their elegance is so chic! And when humbly bypassed by a swift turn of fashion, how swifter they are to turn the other *chic!* Thanks to my warnings, by telephone, just in time!

What do you advocate for a would-be art-lover? My taste is slow behind the times, I haven't caught up yet, I need to cram my education quick. Will you be my mentor?

Provided you become obliged to me, and attend only my salon exclusively. My patronage would improve you above your station, and your pretensions will be marveled at for their genuinity! You'll seem so natural! Glances of envy will be the frequent bouquet thrown your way. I'll be the *making* of you! But I'll undo and ruin you at the first sign of betrayal. Let that warning signify our code of honor.

My gratitude, for being taken under your wing and given a "finishing school" education of applied polish, will give fidelity to my allegiance. When will your course of instructions begin?

Why not at once? Before the fashion gets behind the times? We don't want to wind up stale, do we?

What an appalling horror! Let's keep up with the freshest modes. When I go to the art museum, which pictures should I shun, and which should I learn to admire? (*Takes out notebook to take notes:*) Do dictate, please prescribe what taste I should acquire.

Know that you must detest any Rodin that you see, deplore Michelangelo, abhor Cezanne, cringe at the sight of a Modigliani. Truly *smart* people never acknowledge those any more. Give little sighs of dismay, when passing by their works, to affect a well-informed indifference, so that your companions, or any bystanders you meet, will be impressed at your swift dismissal, and the sureness of your sharp touch of keen repugnance when near those loathsome works. They'll go home singing your praises, and commending you as an art critic. Before you know it, they'll always consult your taste, before venturing on any opinion of their own. Originality consists in the vehemence of your condemnations! Set *that* down, for a rule. (*Disciple has been scribbling notes as rapidly as educator has prattled off the lecture.*)

And musically, what should I conspicuously like, and what disdain?

Bach is *out*, these days. You must preach it to others, as well, for some are slow, and lean too dependently on the old-fashioned method of tradition, rather than on the swift reversals of modern taste. Don't be any stuffy conservative! Beethoven, Mozart, Handel, and Monteverdi should incur your disapproval, as well! But Haydn and Palestrina are "in," so you must "ooh" and "ah" at the very mention of their names! I can give you no general formula, for fashion is specific at all times, and capricious, and (seen from the surface) illogical. But *worship* fashion, and you'll go far! It depends on how seriously dedicated you are. You'll make your mark, if you'll follow the ups and downs of fashion like a stockbroker studies the market exchange and the latest share quotations and bond vicissitudes. Nothing is too trivial, pay attention to the *slightest* alterations. Become an expert in every minute detail. Become a "weather vane predictor." Learn the latest in cloud formations, to keep ahead of the mob, with their slow reactions. This repetition is for your benefit in earnest of my emphasis. Wisdom consists in being flexible. You'll soon find that out.

I'll be as elastic as rubber. I don't intend to be a *frivolous* student, but an earnest worker! I expect to work hard, to keep in the swim, not drown like an antiquated rat in an obsolete bathing suit. I'll know how to regard *everything*! My appraisals will be forerunners, and not the deadened echoes derived from second-hand relays remote after the pacesetting event. I'll be in front! I'll breast the tape, at all times. (A metaphor I borrowed from track; after it's used up, I'll give it back. What use is *yesterday's* record? In a dismal museum, discarded, and regarded as dreary old-hat.) Now, as for architecture: what buildings do you recommend I praise, and which should I relegate for demolition and the well-deserved junk-heap? My knowledge is skimpy, of architectural decades, and I can't tell the Baroque period from the contemporary one, except I know it's good common sense to have a roof over your head. That's the extent of my knowledge of porticos and pillars. Can you reinforce my ignorance, and insert the very advanced style of taste?

Always take a *decided* opinion. Never be in doubt.

What if I appear dogmatic?

Your *conviction* will make you appear in the know. Be so assertive, as to even risk arrogance! People will know that you *dare*. And they'll respect that.

Should I pretend not to *care* what others think of me and my opinions?

Yes; cultivate the semblance of a self-confident independence. Your views are *yours*, no matter what the prevailing standard is! People will think that *heroic* of you. They'll revel in your courage, and follow your lead, and heed your least, most careless remark. Be dismissing of others' ideas. Feign respect for yours alone, as coming from authentic sound taste. People will gullibly believe you, for the note of authority will be in your voice. And *that's* what people are looking to respect! Assume the *masterful* pose, and fashion will fawn at your heels! The leader is set aside by his tone. Admit no doubt into your court of certitudes; for if you're caught looking confused, you'll be hooted by the disillusioned mob, which will hunt for someone never overtaken by the hesitant sin of ambivalence. *Stick* to your belief: stick by it, loyally! And when you change it, stick to the *new* belief, as though the old never existed. Then you'll never get a "wavering" reputation, but be acclaimed as steadfast and loyal to a fault! Keep it up, always be that firm person, in public and private. Once your mind is made up, you're absolutely fixed: to be *decided* is one-sided: and that's good. Never be faint-of-heart. Always be seen to have *made up* your mind, not to be making it! And what you maintain, do so with all your pride! It's yours!

You're emboldening me. Even my lack of taste is expanding into positive belief, like the rock the Catholic Church is founded on, immovable in pontifical dogma. Back to architecture: which buildings should I support, to bolster and back with the stout material of my approval? And which should I so detest, that their solidity will crumble before my eyes, because I wish them removed from the walking sanctity of my constructive sight, much offended by their destructive site? And so raze their flimsily erected scaffoldings to the ground, and base the raising up of pure design, as fashion dictates. Teach me the difference. I want to be the *arbiter* of styles, even be*fore* they emerge!

I'm unfolding before you (*Does so: an intricate operation:*) a map of our city, six feet square on all sides. It's a bird's eye view of every building on every street. I've marked with a red pencil which structures you should be sure to like, vociferously acclaiming them in public. The ones I've marked in green you're to advocate picketing around, as civic eye-sores. Other buildings are marked in other colored pencils, for grades between. All subject, of course, to last-minute revisions. Tomorrow brings a new line in fashion, so I've supplied you with erasers, and a set of these colored pencils, to keep up with new waves in evaluations, for time may beautify an ugly object, and uglify the beautiful. Fashion is fascinating, for it keeps you right on your toes, and should you pause momentarily to relax,—lo! you're out of date. So much for *that* subject; your popularity must depend on well-assorted versatility, for conversation is tediously saturated and must play the field on diversified points of enlightenment, to artificially roam and keep interest fresh. Never have it supposed of you that you're obsessed in one specialty: the expert is the avoided source of boredom, being too narrow-minded to respect the broad flow of vogue's intricacy, for variety to dilettante upon in a dabbling readiness to jump on to the *next* rage. We must keep alert, and skip from trend to trend, or we ossify into a monstrous lump, and are caricatured as such. Cultivate a *light* grace, and not a grave seriousness. Don't go too deep in any one thing, or fashion will catch you napping. Only *skim* the ice, so that you can deploy, pivot, maneuver: it would be *tragic* if a stockbroker became the slave of one special stock, or a painter became the prisoner of one color over and over again. That's insanity, so keep a wide berth. The *world* is your field (for fashion, after all, is super-cosmopolitan); prepare to move where the focus shifts, and not be a local hick, the parochial laughing-stock of the slick traveler, the rustic crude innocent provincial easily duped by big-city sophistication. Don't get bogged down or caught up; be light-hearted, and fickle in all things. Promiscuity is preferable to monogamy, in respect for the unexpected caprices of the vogue. Keep an itchy foot, to avoid the ostrich-stance, sand over head. Mobility, not heavy-footedness, should be your cult. All directions beckon you, so be spontaneous, and chance the venture that time is most ripe for. Deft of toe, not in throes to depth; and be multiple in your reach, to drop what you grasped in favor of the *current* flavor tossed in a new bough of wind. Selectivity is your choicest freedom: Avail your well-pared trimness of its worldly wealth, a community of opportunities for the lean, unaffiliated free-lance, not tied down to any patch of futile prior commitment. A hired soldier of fortune, free to try the latest cause or fill the chorus for a new outrage if it catches on. Loose of foot, and nimble of attachment, for so quickly detached! That's the burden of song, on your free shoulders! Fashion's crusader, on loan or expedition to the next holy grail. How envious your life will be, and *thronged* with popularity!

You advertise to the already converted purchaser. But your enthusiasm has its inspirational worthiness of repetition, a sermon preaching personal advantage and eminence among peers! You flatter me, as fashion's potential champion! You make the ideal seem accessible, and make of my mediocrity a supremely capable virtue. My life's work is dedicated! I'm the rogue of all vogues!

Your determination is admirable, and your success assured if not imminent. Now put away the architectural map of the city that I gave to you, fold it up so you won't be detected at study. (*Disciple does so.*) An aspect of casual ease, not a labored application, should be made apparent to the outsider, through the calculation of your affectation. The traces of your artifice should be eliminated; an unstudied naturalness—innocent of deliberate guile or cunning premeditation—should be on show, to tickle your admirers and elevate your benefit. How they'll flock to emulate you, their paragon and archetype, the pioneer who bruises his way into passionate fashion's unfathomable forest! Yours is the courage; theirs the creeping privilege to be your licensed followers, begrudgingly critical, sharing the forefront of your vogue, consuming your liberal benefaction like eager dogs snapping at the chunks of beef strewn on their barking track by a master of inexhaustible provision. You'll *bestow*; and give of the bounty of generosity, like the great Provider above, Whose Province is Providence itself! The others will be forced to *take*: and thank you, through strenuous obligation.

You depict the exact image of my exasperations.

Your *what*?

I mean my aspirations. Let the corrected slip pass out of remembrance. I'll impose ruthlessly on my followers the greed of their servile role, and lash them into agreeable submission. *I* seek only *power* and *authority*; beyond *that*, my claims are modest.

Your self-restraint is dignity itself! Now, less theoretical, let's pursue certain salient outlines along fashion's wave-tossed sea-coast, as the breeze soaks up the foam, and jutting rocks grow croaky with weeds. Let's exhilarate! And incandescently immerse ourselves in a pool of vogue, where green pearls float in the buried tide of dust, and rusty treasures glitter for diving initiative. Be buoyed, for the swim is surface-deep with ripe pluckings! Fashion is a scavenger's paradise! It's a plundering, to uncover the gimmick to loot! It's an applied branch of aesthetics, for the beautiful must be feasible, and in the mode! And *created* beauty is the pure product of the mode: mass-manufacture *defines* the beauty it topically turns out, of whatever indifferent material. Beauty is consensus, and the voting has a frequent turnover. By democratic popularity, the elected majority represent all the rest in applying beauty's stamp, of whatever standard, to the latest toy on demand. It's a triumph of marketing, buttressed well by beams of publicity, and all the makeshift cutthroats of advertising. It's a way of life, devoutly immediate of reward! Fashion is the deification of the impatient; and its Sunday mass succeeds a saturated Saturday, to extol the presiding divinity of unstable change. And you're an apprentice High Priest! Sure of your calling, immaculate of vocation, ready to regulate consumers in their gregarious ways. With your sharp extroversion, you're well equipped! But you are, first, *my* disciple. So curb yourself and take orders, until you may graduate under your own steam, to set a pace readily trodden on by herds of your sheep. First, let me guide your crook, as your presiding shepherd. I won't fleece you, but teach you gates through fences. You'll get around the inscrutability of mountains, and your easily-sheared flock will gild you with pure golden wool. To warm your ranch with rustic dividends! Your bucolic crown will turn city mills, and tell the town what to do, and preside over the tardy fashions of the remote village, slow to pick up the close central pulse of the rhythms you radiate. Pace by pace, all will get into step, till you arbitrate the *latest* trend, undo the thread, unravel the spool, and set factories belching a new output of smoke from deeply bellowing stacks. And burrow a new trail, for all of industry to follow. You'll lead the pack, like mice dancing to a charger, and reverse the plow that's too thoroughly in a groove. And in a swirl, the world is yours, moving as you do.

A prospect ambition would hope to speed. Prance your steed, for I'm your saddle-mate. To range unimpeded, for the horizons are as numerous of fashions as of fir trees, and remote peaks draw close, to our great rampaging! Haul in no reins, but let's leap, and soar infinitely on our reign. My pulse gives scopeless voracity to my blood's mounted hunt! Lead me to the impossible heights, where the sky drips fashion to alter the traditional valley of customs on the folks bedded below! For vogue is limitless, in prosperous imagination's cell! And a thumping good ride, a sturdy romp, greatly going at increased stride. The brisk chest bursting, with the windy pride!

(Intermission. Years later:)

I can't understand it. Here we are, it's years later, and *everything* has passed us by. What did we do wrong, or leave untouched, or negligently be paralyzed of, for all sorts of succeeding generations of fashion to have come in, blown by, installed such stagesets as boom the facade, and collapsed their day into demise, gone out like a puffed adder in flattened tail of balloon, without our shiftless intervention or passive, staggering participation in all their successive shot glories? Rather than the pacesetters we were to be—I having already achieved that rank and you the brilliant disciple of matchless promise—, we've been bewildered and clubfooted, while styles number themselves in brisk pageantry and thunder past obsolescence in replaceable hordes. Where were we in the midst of such a shortage of stability, which we anticipated would fame us the gallop in our gain, in our plastic passing patronage of fickle brevity? Transience was our permanent road to take; but along the line, swarmed over by variety in unassortable doses of miscellany's indigestible open flares and momentary darts, we lost even our dark bearings, and the wrecked havocs of our keeping in step dimmed even a tangible glimpse: how could we *set* fashion, when we were trammeled by it, clobbered out of focus by directions without interval? Our stumbling made comic mincemeat of prized ambition, and years have hardened our failure into a modeless mold, while fashion's fancy darlings laughed us by, while dryly we stagnate, devoid of one insight! A failure laughable to record, and so painful a fiasco! Where is explanation's solace, or philosophy's grinning prank of wisdom? Our opinions have so little value, that they're unheeded before voiced, and people give them an ignorant berth. When we pass judgment, on a painter or composer or an evening dress or an office building, abruptly deafness is popular, and whether we condemn or praise, we're equally unheard, on any subject our mind will squander. We've been throttled out of the race, plundered of sane verdict, and eased from consideration. We're so much less, we're not *in* it! A position unrecoverable from. How was our footing dislodged, and what surely made our stumbling crucial, beyond redemption? I'm a vacated mind, so will *you* puzzle it?

I'm the younger of us two. Don't pick on me.

Have I misled you?

You hoisted hope, and ambition fell from a falsified pinnacle; and now we're so steady, and deep-rooted, that fashion's formula is reversed, for we're *always* in the same groove, and never move. Our impasse is permanently settled, while meteoric vogues whizz through and by, like multi-colored shots or the firecracker shocks replaced upon dispersal by tribes of unrelated reserves. We draw moss, like a rock or a weed or a plant, and the world is lost. In short, what happened?

Repression drowns the trauma. Put no reliance on *my* numbed wit.

How slight a satisfaction you give! Then if fashion has locked us out, let's be reconciled. We'll renounce what can't be had, and measure a sterile contentment by the shortened sight we settle for. And base our new lives on the sound defeat we suffered. We'll be *out* of fashion, and passionately glad of it! Our sour loss will sweeten our gain, for who wants to desire what pursuit can't overtake? Our need is withdrawn, and soberly chastened, we put in for milder stakes. Already, hope is spreading a cloud of happiness, on the dwindled prospects we accept. Why nag fashion? Let's go after something nicer. Steadier, and less deceptive.

Our diminished lot has blushed a begrudging rose. Let's water it.

But a rose isn't in style, these days.

It soon *will* be. Let's dare, then, to speculate.

Then in future, our verdict will be popular?

Yes, and on the comeback's ripened wings, we'll return, and be such a sage and peer, that *prophecy* will be our game. And our vengeance will be to restore some certainty of sanity and prediction, establish some fixity of tradition, by our ruthless elimination of Fashion altogether: we'll cut its stylish neck, carve its mode out, and slice its treacherous vogue. The world will be decently at peace, to roll on into the gathering of absolutes, immutable truths, an age where virtue's prime is always stability. We'll be the forerunners, of that anti-fashion! Posterity will vindicate our now-unpopular cause, and slowly drag to fruit our bloom of originality after we as authors have mortally been banished from the rapid trash of our day. As the prophets of Permanence, our fame will remain afloat when fashion has drowned her pimps. Panders and panhandlers of today *momentarily* see the sun, but dusk surely obliviates their pretensions! Let *that* be a lesson in where not to find security! We've switched ideals, and though the race is long, our bet is good as won. We can foretell a heaven, with God as resident monarch and things firmly in place. An abiding prospect, with enduring possibilities! Yet our own personal lifetimes won't quite realize it. We're the willing martyrs for a static academy to be, when man's ruled soul must admit to eternal regulation! And fashions outlawed, on perjury of death. Frivolity's inventions gagged from innovating. An imperishable sameness, free from the libertine Variety. A *sane* world, for once. Less lively, of course. Less risky, too. Plain, compared to the ups and downs. An *even* glare, no ins and outs on a squirreling trunk. In fact, dead. Which is immortality's only solution. The boring sameness that will always reign. Eternity is hardly scintillating. But what it lacks in fascination, solidity stores compensation for, in the unchanging generations. It has *dependability*. Assurance isn't romantic, but it's a good provider. A dull marriage contracted after the flaming drama of riotous affairs that wildly promised and turned cold. Then, the *settling* occurs. It's Time, showing its age. Maturity, asserting its taste. Conservative, grey, sedate, not too flashy. No baubles, or flickers, or illusions, or spells, in undependability's mirror. You take it, as it is. No feasting on sauces, or concoctions of brilliance. Invention has no place here. The odds are ironed out, for neutrality to compromise. It's a form of hell, but habit and patience will call it heaven. Restful, not arresting: the quiet merger with peace, the obliteration of boundaries for oblivion's invisibility. Not much. But better than too much.

Better? It's an offense to life. My taste is too active for it. I'm giddy, and game. I'm not ready.

Then it will have to wait, till you come around. It can play a waiting game. Once you exhaust all your rhythms, you'll fall into it. A natural end, to so much motion.

But the *ocean* never ceases its waving.

Go find yourself an ocean to be, then. And not a man.

A man is the only thing I am.

Then fall prey to what rules man. And give in.

Isn't it manly to resist? To make of himself a tragic figure, and be heroic?

Fate will doom you to fail. Late, not early, your fading will fall. Give an eager kick, meanwhile.

I SET IN MOTION THE AVANT-GARDE. AS INVENTOR, I'VE NEVER BEEN ACCREDITED. BUT IN PRIDE, MY FEATS MULTIPLY

After I invented the avant-garde, I fell radically behind all my slavish imitators. By now I was so old-hat that all of history had passed me by in its endless pageantry of series after series of fashionable modes that left me biting the dust as the original fossil of eternal obsolescence. I wasn't even allowed to be traditional: I had long preceded tradition, and my heyday had decayed well in advance of everything considered reactionary today. I was discarded into the archives of a museum warehouse where relics faded in the stored-up dust, to perish without the restorative animation of a new human eye that revives what it lights on. One day a scholar would resurrect me. But how?

Dimly the centuries passed. It was ages since I had self-invented my avant-gardism, the prototype of all artistic and literary labors ever since. My fame was so obscure, that no historian even remotely acknowledged me in some much-neglected footnote or academically ignored appendix to a volume virtually unread and relegated to a completely disused heap of a once-been cemetery. Unsung, unpraised, no credit was assigned me for recognition, let alone renown, as the avant-garde's founder with a since-floundered reputation among the never-was'es who jointly compile the lower anonymous ranks of the repeatedly forgotten unknown. This was the oblivion I was consigned to. Unpromising soil for getting reborn from! I'd have a few eternities to settle down in, while mulling this problem over in my continuously spare time, though with no solution within worldly distance of my bleak circumstances and rather desolate prospects. Yet I'd keep heart, and not despair. But how?

I craved fame. Day and night, it became my fanatical obsession. I'd forge it out of *nothing*, if necessary, and create an undeserved version of it to make my very name. But I had something to fall back on, to prove my merit and warrant my claim. I had once been the avant-garde, and for all time. But this was all covered over, thus ruining my burning ambition with a dry and arid place in the anywhere of simply nowhere, by which I was established as a veritable no-one. I'd rise yet, determined to make my way. But how?

I was ambitious. And not for spurious fame, as its dubious candidate; but for a myth-breaking role in realms indeed of high renown in circles of ever-populous circulation, to have for me carved the central niche in saga-rich annals of epic rank, exclusively legendary for the select elite, yet roundly proverbial for the mass of all men. This secret ambition burned in me. I'd utilize every resource of time and space to leave no boulder unturned nor mountain unprayed-to in this stern and committed realization of my firm and dedicated life, to attain this celebrity status of a hero in monumental marble or unblemished alabaster, a folk hero of any land at any time at all times everywhere, preserved for all universal duration without local reference or topical opportunity to commend it. I'd do it, too. But how?

To make my much-vaunted comeback from those cobwebbed shadows of obscurity in oblivion's murky swamp of an antiquated dungeon in time's mildewed backwater left to wrack and ruin in the recessed abyss of neglect, I'd have to *act*, and make it *count*. To wrench off these mouldy centuries that accustomed me to the defiant ignominy and private disgrace of a figure of no importance in the ill-earned ingratitude of a world that entirely forgot to attribute its fickle possession of an avant-garde to me who personally invented it, is quite a chore, no mean task, a formidable challenge, no child's-play, a reckless burden to assume. I'd overcome; but how?

To investigate the outrage of being overlooked as the maker of such a cultural necessity as the avant-garde, and to research the fault-finding in so glaring yet hushed-up a crime, ought to be my mission, from my limbo'd exile far away. There's sore overdue revenge that's been mounting, posthumous retribution for culprits who've unfairly deprived me of all due credit for my great exploit in burdening aesthetic creation with that natural upholder of all artifice, the avant-garde. At long last to publicize my authorship of it! But how?

My contribution to the world is now considered imperative, but at the time of my donation no notice was taken; there having been no need for it, it was met, diabolically, with no enthusiasm and barely any reception. Ignored where the gift should have been applauded, yet it wasn't long before it took hold, dug roots, and refined its own new soil. The avant-garde began to sprout, that I had sowed on seeming-barren ground. It was prodigious, prolific, in proliferating great products. Where was I by that time? Dead. So I couldn't stake claim for credit in making it, to ply the ripe opportunity of having my name associated with, after all, my own handiwork: the creation's creature creator, me, to be coupled with that which I wrought. Instead, obscurity slid by, and buries me still.

But I follow its progress. I see who its latest exponents are. The avant-garde is *thriving* today. My child is in great shape, nourished by genius all over the place. Beckett and Ionesco are helping it theatrically; Joyce fictionally, Rimbaud and Baudelaire poetically, Picasso and Matisse pictorially, Henry Moore sculpturesquely, Stravinsky musically, and so forth, with lots of its practitioners and hordes of other genres left unmentioned, but I'm omniscient to them all, from my secluded distance remote from view or fame. They're all my boys, promoting my invention, going ahead, injecting new vitality into it, as it keeps climbing the spheres. I reiterate, it's *my* creation: in other hands now, though.

When it first became my discovery, or rather invention, the avant-garde (as we know it today) was then in its precocious first infancy, having barely been pre-born, and as yet hardly awake. Ancient civilizations tried their hand at art, to such success that today they're still esteemed as classics, those venerable works that have survived. In its initial phase, in its primevally prehistorical form in the stark dawn of its nativity I midwifed to, the avant-garde numbered among its advocates and devotees such hardy artists as the cavemen: who in other ways seem to us so coarse and pre-civilized, and barbarically disposed, that we would hardly expect them to have cultivated the rudiments of the earliest grammar-plus-vocabulary of avant-gardism, in action. They were remarkable, though their achievements are for the most part lost. I wish to pay tribute to them. They were superb primitives, and fostered art immensely.

Who is that who complimented them, from an open and paternal heart? I, to whom no tribute or reverence is paid to the measure of my deservings, in the malice of historical injustice and the careless perversity of fame's being negligibly attributed or remiss in those like me to whom the greatest debts are owed. If I sorely complain, this rancor does rankle, sorely inflamed. My anger is storming. I have the right to fume indignation; since every nation with every tongue in all conditions, since time granted gracious evolution to mankind, has used my brainchild to extreme cultural advantage. Customs were molded by it, traditions erected with it as base, national characteristics founded on it, individual and tribal genius established on its working premise. I claim to be the source, through my broadly-applied, variously-employed invention, of all noble makings of human craft and skill in the realm of arts and letters, so vast and diversified its constant treasury of universal accumulation. The royalties on my copyright would have kept me rich forever, had there been a patent law then. I missed out, born too soon. But, oh the dynasty derived from that small explosion in my brain! It's spread into innumerable works, of many fabrications, which scholars and historians have only narrowly begun to classify! The loins in my brain were teeming, in my profuse invention! The magnitudes having stemmed from it, recording and landmarking phases and epochs, ages and subdivisions, and man's genial forms and shapes! What I did had global repercussions, and to man's good and benefit, I maintain! For that, what have I been paid?

I've been accorded only an ordinary death, and my remains deposited in a grave carelessly unmarked like that of a pauper-serf or mendicant, illiterate to his unlettered bones! Time has bestowed on me this reward. I want to file the most vehement protest, and petition such authorities as turn up. None heeds me, for my voice is stilled. Is it *fair!?*, I ask. Justice has yet to be done, in my case that bristles with disregard! I knock loud! No reply. Only these poor words. Inscribed, but never read.

I *am* resurrected! The modes of the avant-garde succeed each other to the end of time. In them, perpetually, I stand redeemed. I created Babylonia, Egypt, Greece, and Rome; China, India; and *every* culture, in its makings, its markings, its molds, whereby down to us it comes, in a living manifest. What need I to be revived as the author of man's fertile playing with the eternal, when the whole *Renaissance* redounds to my credit! All upsurges and distinct eras and overlapping methods and changed devices, all jets of inspiration, overflowings, and contrivances, contribute to my rebirth, through profuse dischargings and interminable silences and experimental abortions and frail successes and grand rarities, surprises all! The world teems with my minions, the workers for the mind's pleasure. Through them I work for high deeds in giving men "made matter" for Imagination to work over and find itself in, according to such recipients as get born and come to encounter such particles of art's and literature's sublime, multi-created bodies. From obscurity, I'm the paternal witness. I watch, oversee, gloat, delight, approve. Most experiments fail, but still! Styles come and go. But so much remains!

All my architecture, scattered throughout this planet! Libraries and museums testify. I've never died!

Scheme and innovate, carry on! Through every production, my renewed life holds on, and enters the next phase. Along the way, I keep what I've accumulated! I never let go!

I've come through! All is done, that was conceived. There's no schedule for running out, but we proceed indefinitely, for the future remains generous.

Still open! Further unknowns, as yet.

The avant-garde is flourishing. Bold good hands pass it on, in protean transformations, ever recharged, to new guises and strange tongues. Why should the *origin* proclaim itself? As its trace, I'm eliminated. What I gave enjoys latest surges, and collects along the way its best, to be preserved. I'm proud, and relinquish fame. I'm well resigned. Renunciation increases my measure. The expansions unfurl. Time is my ally. It gratifies, and keeps the Void covered, with a barrage of new works. I'm inexhaustible!— with more crowding in, on the already done. Stopping is impossible. I'm in motion.

I BECAME A DISCIPLINED WORK OF ART, LIKE A WELL-TRAINED BUT ORNAMENTAL SOLDIER. MY BATTALION IS A WALL, I'M IN THE REGULAR MUSEUM RESERVES. WATCH ME IN DRILL TRAINING, AS I FRAME MY STEPS.

In the museum the paintings lined up on the walls while the master sergeant drilled them, in battle formation with show of arms and strict alignment. This went on for so long, some sweating paintings dripped paint that had dried up centuries ago.

Other paintings collapsed with fatigue—the canvas sagged into wrinkles, and fell off the firm frames.

I entered the museum as a spectator, but the guards recruited me, pressed me into service, I was given a frame and told to stand against a vacant part of the wall, there to await orders for basic training drill. The price was the loss of liberty, for becoming a disciplined work of art. I'm in the same spot of the museum every day, locate me there. I'll be in the military parade as part of the color guard. Art is discipline, if it's great. I've made the grade, at that rate. Come and see me. It's peace maneuvers. I'm in the permanent reserve, but on show. We *play* at war. It's the stirring spectacle. Martial music is piped out. I'm brilliant, watch me.

AT LEAST I DID SOMETHING

At the cost of getting old, I've accumulated a lot of achievements, to shore against my mortality.

But I would have been getting old anyway, even if I hadn't achieved or accomplished *anything*. Therefore, there was no cost involved, save in labor, effort, work, application, endeavor, persistence, perseverence, diligence, care, painstakingness, conscientiousness, struggle, strife, misery, worry, anguish, and other sorts of travail, bother, will, and such forth. All to store up honors, rewards, and glory? Oh hell, but why?

Well, I'm old anyway, whether a bum or famous, my years total up the same. But I'm glad I worked and achieved. It was worth it. I've done something socially esteemed. It may be appropriated by later social history, once I'm posthumous. To this favor, I will have "overcome" my private mortality, by contributing something durable to the culture of my fellow men. A consolation, of sorts, of broad sorts, to give time a run, for the extinguished ego that lies as a grim prospect with ever diminishing remoteness.

WHERE DOES TRUTH LIE?

Ah, the truth, what a thing it is! I sacrifice so much for it, with people: I forego, for truth's sake, discretion, loyalty, diplomacy, tact, polite manners, elegance, grace, poise, balance, good taste, conformity, image-role, fashionableness, polish, confidences, promises, ambition, consistency, identity, clarity, comprehensibleness, good will, hypocrisy, and lots of other things—a mass sacrifice, at truth's altar. God!—is truth worth it?! I *hope* it is. It *better* be, in fact.

A lie is the truth in masquerade? But the truth may be a *lie* in masquerade, too. In what direction does the truth lie? It lies in *many* directions, I think. Even now, the truth is lying—somewhere. The truth is *always* lying. Its life is hard, but it doesn't take it lying down—for the truth lies straight ahead—it lies just out of sight. And so, it's changing, in motion. To catch itself lying.

Goodbye, gentle truth. Time for someone *else* to take up your cause. Me, I'm headed for fiction—your other self.

(Title, in the explanatory mode:)

THE AUTHOR'S LIMITED GENEROSITY TO HIS READERS, LEAVING THEM WITH A GIFT-IN-THE-ROUGH, TO DO THEIR OWN REFINING UPON, FROM THEIR OWN WISDOM OR EXPERIENCE. THE AUTHOR THEN WITHDRAWING, LEAVING THE READERS TO THEIR RESPECTIVE AND OUTSTANDING SOLITUDES, TO MAKE WHAT THEY CAN OF THE GIFT THE AUTHOR LEFT BEHIND TO PLEASE HIMSELF MORE THAN THEM: AN ARROGANT GIVING.

Generosity being not in relation to the given-to so much as to the giver: that's where generosity goes wrong so often.

For example—ah, think of one yourself.

I've given you a theory, a generalization. Now go provide your own applying particulars, in your own cases. That's where my generosity limits itself. Working harder for his receiving, the recipient helps himself, and makes it easier on me, who's generously donated what I cared to give, on my own terms.

Complete the gift, then on your terms—for now we part. I'm empowered to cut you off, on a final stroke, like—.

RECENT WORK

MY LATEST BOASTWORTHINESS

I wanted to be well liked, all my life. As a little kid I was praised by adult family for reciting all the successive states southwards New York to Florida, in my pouting, pseudo-precocious, mincing baby voice, and the adults declared me cute.

Then I was praised as an intelligent schoolboy brimming with high marks. I was envied for being popular with the little girls, as I had a commandingly tall figure sprouting regular facial features according to the then-current popularity code.

Plus I had an infectious laugh, which infected others to the laughing mold with my admired gift for wit, my deployment of clever language punctuating situations into a summarizing hilarity.

Before I go on to my lifetime of later hits in realms of scholarship, drawing, painting, exhibitions, poetry, prose, awards, publications, performances, fellowships, the intrusiveness of fans, not to mention seduction and romances (never once collapsing into heartbreak), in an enviably full life gleaning me popularity (that I milked with social namedropping as well, untainted by that prime inhibitor, shame — I even namedropped the already dead famous ones who I hadn't had occasion to meet through no fault of my own); and before I mention athletic feats in sporting events that enshrine my physical glories in the old memories of deceased onlookers: let me intervene with what has come to be my latest, maybe last, method of producing admiration: longevity: mathematically remaining alive by outliving my long-lost contemporaries. My body as a surviving machine at the expense of my fallen fellows, the outlastingness of my still mentally functioning and health-sustained physical self.

Everybody's younger, and they're all wowed. It crowns my acclaim-crowded record. In short, I'm a marvel. I hear "How did you do it?" Oh, I'm lucky, to push death more and more ahead of me like a future wheelbarrow I carefully don't bump into with my emaciatingly protruded stomach.

Graciously, I avoid contact, skittishly, with that main bugaboo, death, that ugly scarecrow.

Self-maintenance is the trick. Others would love to learn and emulate. The self-help books teach them how: manuals of health, nutrition, exercise, moderation; the farming and harvesting of luck; the rules of safety; the cultivating of extra days and nights: like overtime in deadlocked sporting events that are hallucinatingly never broken, as the players strive with might, main, and expertise, but by reverse-nightmare can't break the self-perpetuated tie.

Need I, in retrospect, boast of my innumerable glories and successes phase by phase along the developing arrow ever futureward in the onwardness of my lasting life? No, you get the picture.

Longevity is my last outpost. I hold out against the surrounding whooping "Indians" with their threatening tomahawks: barricading in, I shield myself from plunging arrows. I fight, breath by breath, for the very next breath, exhaustionless.

And keep my alert mind of memories to the quick. I remember my life in all its consecutive events (like a list of states southward from New York to Florida, childishly recited with an irresistible lisp), culminating in the mercy of a self-perpetuating now. Longevity inflames my nostrils with sheer pluck and persistence. I dilate, collapse, dilate, collapse, like rubberband lungs whose elasticity never snaps.

Not yet, anyway. I hold on.

For what do I hold on? For Life in its world-renowned, hall-of-fame preciousness: sentimentally upheld in all the fables and annals of repeatedly circulated tales, in an array of endlessly dying languages:

oceanic, planetary, earth-bound, dreamboat Life: the operatic immensitude: the finality of self-being: its own elixir, magically pragmatic.

AN ESSAY VANISHED BEHIND ITS DECLARED WORDS

I'm essaying big subjects here, the major basic ones, so watch out you don't get crashed into.

Life is so precious, yet I have to lose it—to what? To that spoiljoy, damp blanket, wet blanket, spoilsport, downer, bugaboo, killjoy, negater: Death. The loss is enormous, let me count the ways: I lose summer, autumn, winter, and spring: the whole caboodle of seasons spinning their cycles. Moreover, my losses include morning, afternoon, and night, those daily dividers of time's opportunity-offerings for making what you can of outside chances and internal capacities.

Death is literally a killer. What it takes away is equal to the totalizing destructiveness that's a wipeout. Enough said. You don't want the gruesome details.

And yet — people seem to fill up life with numerous complaints. What are they all whining about? Those nit-picking bellyachers create and record whole litanies of dissatisfaction reports on life's sore-points, the catalogue of which includes pain, agony, despair, melancholy, boredom, heartbreak, depression, misery, and regret. This disheartening list of life's self-fault-findings contains glaring samples whose numerousness precludes enumerating in the self-imposed limits of lengthy essay time. You don't have all day, nor do I.

And yet — Death is considered worse than life, in most people's estimations. Well, if that isn't a paradox, what is?

Is laughter the glue that sticks together those opposite eternities of life and death?

Maybe, but I'm doubtful. Who am I anyway, to fumble with these conundrums? The overall population is yet to be heard from, to weigh in with their votes and stuff the ballot box.

But maybe I'm asking the wrong questions. Or maybe the answers are not only in short supply, but don't even exist:— If questions fall short, how are answers supposed to compensate?

I'm limited to only one mind, yet I'm of two or more — plenty more — minds on these improbables.

Even to venture a conclusion taxes the burdens on my phony modesty's presumed patience. While I withdraw, let the aforementioned sentences shyly slip away and their echoes perish, as though essays could be declared dead once the word-mongering succumbs to self-bewildering exhaustion, and thoughts crawl under their momentum's broken-down engine and moan failure's last word: silence.

ADVERTISING ON THE GRANDEST SCALE

Trying to make it all work,
romantic couples force the issue of love
on each reluctant other.
They try to fit the odd parts
of an ego's urgent history
smoothly into the artifice
of a contrived intimacy.
From them marriages grant great birth
to a whole team of new babies
that grow to pit loneliness
on the romantic imperative
and distort themselves into perfect mates
who bite the willing love pill
that aches with agony
but generates public appeal.
Love, sing a song to it
in heart-felt tones,
get musical aid
for the baby parade.

PANIC? KICK IT AWAY

Under its cruel rush, I'm prone to anxiety.
Panic's brash shout bewilders society.
The pressure claustrophobically crushes me.
Worries, happy to usher me
past insanity with unusual force,
distort my margins way off course.
My blunders turn repetitive at will.
Do I drink? Excessively to my fill.
Outpacing itself, my downhill life
turns exhaustion into a full-time strife
that eats up all the vitality left
till resourcefulness turns zero bereft.
With what defenses do I fight back?
None, to my reckoning, both dire and black.
I fundamentally must go berserk
before my senses return, with much work
to do in offsetting my past illness
and convert distress into an eerie stillness.
The world, which my ego badly-damaged,
compliments me. See how I've managed?
Panic gets squeezed out of my system
and when reality calls, I brace to listen,
whose tuneful notes restore the harmony
cursing away the rot that used to alarm me.

ALL OVER

As I look back, and take stock,
what my life has been, or might have,
it all adds up to "so what?",
since death is about to clean it up,

to empty out space for the next birth.
I crowded up the world with my clutter,
now a baby is born in my stead,
I call him my little successor.
But I'm too dead to call him anything;
and my contemporaries draw the line
between the generation of "us"
(the unfortunately complete),
and the innocent arrivals.
A conscious body replaces me.
My pack of greed collapses,
bone-bare, beyond brittle.
No use winding a replay.
That old familiar me,
does somebody inherit it?
The human tree puts on a new leaf
for that good old me
turned beyond venerable.

A CHARACTER PREDOMINANTLY NEGATIVE

"I want my art career to evolve in public reputation from 'promising' to 'respectable' to 'acclaimed' to 'celebrated'," boldly decided the brash artist, who not only had no talent, but he had never produced any drawing or painting or sculpture in real actual life. This difference between his aspirations and his accomplishments was a chasm of vastness, of cosmic length and width. In his imaginary "studio," there were no art materials such as pencils, pens, crayons, brushes, paints, and whatever else was needed to prevent his being called "bogus," not to mention "pretentious," by the cynical public that remained in embryo formation to assail him.

At such handicap odds, how could he succeed? That was an obstacle he despaired of even trying to overcome. "I give up," was his modest decision, somewhere between cowardice and a stubborn lack of character.

As a so-called or professed "artist," he changed imaginary vocations in favor of something plebeian that preserved his anonymity from what he thought of as an intrusively prying, scandal-malicious-obsessed, compassion-deprived public.

If only he could eliminate that nemesis, his public, which menaced his sanity! Then he could restore homeostasis, equilibrium, and equanimity to his much abused system.

This requires an unprecedented feat of mass murder: wiping out the total sum of living humanity, which was constantly dying out but even more constantly being birth-replenished. Though it seemed crazy, confidence gripped his veins nervous energy; and in a last burst of desperation, he'd die trying.

His new identity would be as a sociopath, which was much more realistic than his bogus art career which, in mid-flight, he had mismanaged.

But as for killing off his fellow creatures of the human race and stuffing up the birth machine, that was bringing sociopathy to an impossible extreme, if not to new heights, in its weird career as a trait.

Even to contemplate such rare acts and plan their methods would bring him to a genius level, completing his identity career evolution, in the public heart and mind (while they still breathe), from "promising" to "respectable" to "acclaimed" to "celebrated"; through notoriety and infamy seem a more likely critical consensus by that fickle machine, the public.

The public was media-bound, anyway, for opinion-formation based on information-overload in a computerized new age of electronic digitability. It revolutionized everyone's outlook, and divided itself along separate individualized lives gazing mesmerized on the me-I-myself ego of gigantic solipsistic narcissism of indwellingness. Everybody contributed his and her own sociopathy against the global village principle, abandoning the notion of "one world." Differences overcame unanimity, within the human identity sphere. Thus fatally divided, humanity had to limp to the finishing line on prosthetic limbs. Its long-lost unity was corrupting history itself, with its accumulated stories of what's been happening since time started off Earthwise.

Anyway, that guy is now what's called a failed artist. But since he did no art, then failure's ignominy is eradicated as a non-starter, thus restoring a mere semblance of dignity, coherence, and integration to his soulless being. As a maniac who failed as an artist by not endeavoring arts labor, he verched off into a destroyer of his fellow humanity-strugglers in aspiration; but could he follow through in his destructive ideal?

No, how could he? But he could retain his sociopath status while giving up the foolish idea of killing off the rest of the race, which he would lack talent for just like he was a no-show in his previous failed career as a would-be artist with nil productivity.

Who was this guy anyway? As his reputed author with self-willed power to name him, I hereby bungle the job and leave him as a nullity.

This abandoned character fulfilled no promise as an artist, switched to a passive hatred or indifference to his broad human kinship, and ended up in the rubbish-heap of author's abdication of responsibility to finish this tale, which now sputters off into the ether.

DEFINE "NOW"

Your life is set in front of you by being behind you.
You're old with nowhere to go
but to the factory of death.
So what are your terminal-length memories
but to play around with and invoke?
Re-experience events by second-hand repetition,
the retrospect of belated introspect
of mental afterthought, the armchair philosopher,
Monday morning quarterback
rehashing the actual Sunday
that actively underwent itself

in the careless struggles with "now."

DISMAL BARREN EMPTY RESULT

My nuggets of word-wrought thought
were in a few volumes never bought
by enough book-buying public members
to make me famous. So who remembers
my gorgeous attempts at prose?
Commercial failure overrules my poetic pose.
Other words died at the manuscript stage
aborted from falling into print's world-smeared page.
Crushed dreams terminate my sentence faster
than mortality speeds the body into disaster.
Woeful self-pity staunches a few wounds
as resignation smiles throughout the glooms.
Ambition lies stretched out along its tombs
and the funeral fires bank low — a few fumes
remain to remind me what ecstasy once was
when hope presided at self-creation's buzz.
Now the "is" is barren, to top off the rich "was."
Hence my motto: Failure is as failure does.

DON'T GET TOO OLD

My cock has deadened.
My face has reddened
in sexual embarrassment.
Sued for non-harrassment
by disappointed Jane,
I claim impotence is to blame
for feeble non-contact.
This violates the sexual contract.

Asked "Why no impact?"
I point, ashamed,
to my genital maimed
by absence of thrust
and inability to lust.
My life's a sexual bust.
I've lost all right
to be bold
because every night
I get too old.

FRAGMENTS OF A DOOM

Old age is settling in fast,
making academic the uses of the past.
Old age hastens disappearance into
the amorphous lifelessness of the blue,
or rather total colorlessness,
the sense-deprivation mess
in which we get less and less
of necessity's huge wherewithal.
The risen life, to that, abysmally shall fall.
Dreams, hopes, desires,
deferred till life itself expires,
flee into universal doom
when one individual runs out of room.

JUST IN TIME, A STORY'S INTERRUPTION TAKES ON A PERMANENT CAST

"Poor Marvin. He ate my food in my mother's bathtub," admitted the recently young woman. "But Bertha, was the bathtub dry?" inquired Bertha's friend, Linda, between gasping laughs that played off against her up-and-down throat with throttled words. Meanwhile, Marvin himself had long pushed himself off and out Bertha's mother's deep-seated tub, having finished whatever food was there.

Bertha's mother, at the time involving Marvin, was away on some trip. (Bertha was living there, rent-free, unable to trade her college education and—face it—laziness for a modest fill-in job that would have partly untumbled her financial obligations to a rent-distressed mother who was somewhere away, spots unknown—but to whom?)

Then Marvin phoned. "Answer the phone," Bertha asked her guest Linda, because Bertha was busy in another room. Neither woman knew what the phone call was due to: Marvin.

"Hello, do you want Bertha or her mother? But the mother is away, so only Bertha is home," Linda explained, not yet inquiring who phoned. Helpfully, Linda added, "I'm Bertha's friend, but so what?"

By this time, Marvin wasn't sure why he phoned. Was it due to Bertha being his romantic friend? Of course, since sex is a global condition bringing up the gender issue. Linda's gender on the phone totally resembled Martha's but Marvin wasn't in the mood for infidelity so he let it slip by despite a possible opportunity it offered.

By now, Bertha returned from the other room to take possession of her absent mother's telephone from the intermediate function of Linda, her friend who had just visited at that time

Marvin, meanwhile, overheard this telephone transition at the other end. Recognizing Bertha, he asked who the other woman was. "Oh, that's Linda, do you intend to drop me and transfer your attentions to her?"

"I don't even know her, unless you introduce us," Marvin hinted, with a sudden burst of love for a yet-unseen Linda. Her being unknown to him intrigued his curiosity so that insulting Bertha was a disregardedness overcome by the whim of arbitrary impulse. At heart, Marvin was romantic to an unknown vacuum to be filled out in the eventual flesh.

His plot of course offended Bertha, who was cravenly whisked into a rejection complex.

Who should suddenly arrive home but Bertha's own mother? Marvin was still on the phone with his erect penis pointing at an unknown direction where he imagined Linda was exposing her whereabouts, details to be filled in later.

OKAY, THAT'S ENOUGH

Life has been a long grind, a long hustle,
so I earned my old old age
causing me to be an object of indifference
to the new world endlessly full
of kids young enough never to meet my eye,
I being an object
of not to waste an eyeglance at
on the way to lust and ambitious schoolwork
to gather the future in moneyloads.
That's them. As for me,
the grave is sniffin' at my ass
and telling me to lie down
for a photographic fit of my bones.
Bones? That's all I'm good for
in the onward world's
global economy warming up
into history's dark spasm
of the lively unknown.

PLAIN TALK, EXCLUDING RELIGIOUS RAIDS ON THE SENTIMENTAL

Before birth, nothing exists, including the world, for you. After death, nothing exists, including the world, for you that isn't there, never any more. During life, you live from now to now in flickers, as memory expands and contracts, cumulatively and regressively; and the now-to-now in flickers get used up in survival's remarkable array of chanciness.

That's all you get, but there's lots of plenty that goes around for you maybe to grab and eventually lose, or quickly as the cases may be, thrown all together. Hurry up, before death rings its tinkle bell. When breath slows to a halt, time withdraws its business from you and spreads it around for those still in the run, those who arrive and spread themselves everywhere, in gallops through everything, taking over like you once did without a repeat chance or the fancy of a do-over, striving for spiritual reclamation.

RECLAMATION

Crash through the death barrier
And reclaim my old friend.
Uncobweb the golden past
From its rotten cellar dwelling
Where wet lice take dry license
In unceasing disease.
Pluck time's enlivenness
From captivity's death trap
Through intermediate nostalgia
Into the ordinary greeting
Of that friend — "Hello again,
Where you been? It's been
Too long — you old stranger.
Make yourself at home
In friendship's usual parlor.
Let's share the weather again
And celebrate boredom."

A SELF-EMPTIED MEMOIR

I spent my childhood gradually growing up. There I was. Nothing I could do about it. I was there, body and all. I just had to deal with it.

Social relations with my schoolmates embodied the full range of youthful sociology, so you can imagine the results.

Now that I'm fully grown up into man's tattered estate, I'm able, partially, to look back, in pure partial retrospect, on what preceded me now.

Am I master of all I survey? No, the view is too spotty. It's like watching a Napoleonic war battle from a moderate mountain top with multiple blockage of views, eclipsing a full reportage. As a newspaper correspondent, I would have been summarily dismissed by a snarlingly dissatisfied editor, whose parting advice would be "Seek a whole different line of employment. I'm justified in presiding over the liquidation of your disqualified days as a reporter."

In other words, viewing my earlier days is crippled by tattered squeakings of memory's halting machine. What even what kind of a tune was there?

What survives from my pre-school days is a bare smattering of endlessly repetitive images stamped in a carbon stencil from a paltry few worn-out, stagnant, almost spent familiar originals — so familiar that their truths hang like scarecrows in a field whose pecking birds long to migrate elsewhere.

Mechanical reproductions are organic detritus of once wearily was or were. Yes, the past was mine, but who cares?

My mother took me to an unknown apartment for a gathering of her girlfriends in another room, with me dumped on top of a well-upholstered, ornate bed full of odd perfume effects which dutifully I imbibed from mainly the nostril smothered face-down on the opulent odor-lulling bedding surface: or was it the non-smothered nostril on the other side that made scents of things?

Did I nod off? Memory nods off — it ain't telling.

Another time, me and mother were walking on the avenue when an unknown boy, my height, deliberately pushed me around while to my surprise my mother looked instead of intervening. I was supposed to be protected. Here, memory depletes itself, and evaporates my half-images away.

Meanwhile, crater-sized gaps in my memory log, called lacunae, barely link, or rather don't link, the nullified sequence of boyhood events.

School days came. Where are they? What happened? Time stole them from me: an unpunished thief.

What am I left with? A recital in a concert hall after the music and musicians have abandoned that sonorous gig, leaving empty architecture to its acoustic echoes, creating a professional vacuum for tardy latecomers.

Adolescence arrived, in developmental order, sprung scrappily formed from the reputed cute innocence of little boyhood. It soon accumulated its own baggage in high-maintenance awkwardness of dashed hopes and dungeons of shyness.

But whoa, let me slow down. My constipated memory gets off a barren toilet. What happened to my energetic post-school self, called young manhood, where careers begin and self-fulfillment rears up on ambitious legs to strive to cut a fancy figure at the competition market and cut a swath through a bevy of potential wives at the reproductive age where sperm renewed itself barely past the moment spent? That's where regrets of missed opportunities and bungled snatches at dangled goods give me a good self-kick on my fallen ass.

Thus far, this account of a life brags a hopeless promise into an all-exits drag.

Meanwhile, the spinning cycle of the seasons kept up four-square rotations in fixtures of inevitability. History put up unpredictable patterns that slotted into categories of interpretation disputed among the weary experts. The me-owning world is indifferent to the me it owns — so I'm on my own, if I call it that.

Already, negativity shouts "enough!" I strain for Proustian breakthroughs on the nostalgia trail, whereby recollections on an involuntary illumination come blessingly through, if only I can nail down what is endangered immediately to be forgotten. What happened in between the gaps of my habitually boring memories? Is there a rhapsodic gem to be treasured, once landed upon on some vague offchance of some fortunate stumbling? Let me catch a quick prize on the fly.

If the present is touched by the past in a new synapse, can a gleam of life live again? In a preservation capsule? I summon memory's enchantments.

"Go inbetween the common ones, don't repeat the usual, take a new turn," I ask my run-down memory factory. It huffs and puffs for my straining will. Nope, no thrill. What's not there remains so.

As my years drain away, my memory draws more blanks, even recent experiences get no feedback. What remains gets less and less, my future has shrunk, my bloated past breathes elephantine gigantism into its blasted vitals.

If you've got a croak left, illuminate me between the gaps of ignorance in what registers as my life's record. To set it straight, garland my life into patterns and knit the tale through. The narrative fabric is threadbare-ripped. I tread the unraveled road down dimness tunnel.

THE STIFLED SONG OF CRIMINALITY

The police force is out in full force
to prevent civic mayhem.
If I so much as accost
a victim, I hear "ahem,"
from an officer of the law,
who's approached me nearby. I look in awe
at his menacing demeanor,
and say, "I didn't mean it, sir,
I plead innocent in every intention.
Your suspicion is a mere invention."
In apoplexic apology
he grasps at astrology,
saying, "The stars deceived me.
I thought you was a crook.
I plead you to believe me,

I won't mark you in my book."
Meanwhile, my victim has escaped,
vanished from the whole landscape.
Angry at the cop for interference,
I mourn my victim's disappearance
and curse the absence of my intended prey.
But I philosophized: "This just isn't my day.
Some day another will come along
to lead my erroneous way
in victorious criminal song."

STOPPAGE ALTOGETHER

The past keeps throwing things at me.
Some I duck, others I woo.
Some I neutrally take on board
and put them on the assessment pile,
filed disorderly, to be slept on.
Running itself out of time,
the past slows down my mind
into dull memory failures,
as though forgetfulness is an art form
excusing death's crude non-awakening.
My nerves undergo their demolition
without even attending the event.

TO MARK BARTY-KING

The was-ness of life
means that I can't say my friend is,
since is-ness got killed by death.
But when livingly I think of him,
memory restores his life

to selfish me and to the dear absence
of the him that really was.

TRIBUTE TO A BALLPLAYER

Here's to Jimmy Stagno, athlete and humorist,
great husband, great father, the king of imagination,
inventor, houseowner, and all over his body
a receiver of expert medical attention
in all known areas of bone and skin,
yet heroic survivor of his infirmities.
from his old, peimanent friend, Marvin.

UNPUBLISHABLE ENCLOSURES

I pick through an ancient brain
for gems rescued from memory.
They'll represent me
in the highlight newsreel
of inner cinematic classics.
But they're undistributed
to the wide indifferent public.
My personal memory gems
go unrecorded outwardly
and keep my loneliness imprisoned
in private hollowed-out halls
echoing odors stale and self-familiar.
Death's cleanliness act sweeps it all out
while still-breathing contemporaries are otherwise occupied
prescribing arcs for their self-audience
tortured by minor reviews, critically.

ZORRO IN SORROW

I'm Zorro, a by now old lab retriever who has long roamed the Pine Hill suburbs of the Catskills with a free hand — or rather cock — as "privileged un-neutered," under the benign reigns of two successive loving human families. I've well-merited, among my own species, the roving nickname of Casanova; though the humans still pronounce me Zorro in tones of pure affection, which in gratitude I requite.

My free-ranging sex life has earned me the envy of all my neutered male friends and enemies (as well as my less successful unneutered rivals), in this lovely Catskill region. "How can you be so lucky?" they bark in dismal chorus, and partially I must agree with them. Only partially? Why?

In my dog-wide social role, as promiscuity's symbolic Casanova, I've had occasion to enter other households' bedrooms as well as my own, to observe human sex acts. This began my life-long discontent.

I've observed human copulations with inter-species envy. Humans have a longer, more ecstatic duration in the act than dogs' briefly perfunctory couplings. The humans seem to have a deeper buildup toward more resounding climaxes, as their deep-lunged pantings can attest, not to mention prolonged sound-effects improvising their own background music to a grinding foreground of well-earned sweat. My own conquests among consenting bitches seem shrunken in a pitiful time frame.

In my sleep and waking dreams, I'm a human virility machine. As a sexually privileged — not to mention spoiled — mere dog, I'm in the minor leagues compared to awesome human males. I regret having voyeured all those accursed bedrooms! I wish these immodest humans had chased me away, to preserve their spectacular intimacies from my insatiable eyes blazing beams of surprise. It almost seemed like they were flagrantly performing their immodesties to taunt me — but no, I mustn't give way to these silly bouts of paranoia, qualifying me for a session on a psychiatrist's couch — comedy's fool.

Imagination has been my curse, giving full range to discontent, resentment, bitterness, grumblings of deprivation. No humans suspected my jealousy. They all loved me, those simpletons!

My reputation as a freely wandering Casanova sniffing out heat-ripe bitches belies my fantasies of heroic human marathon bouts, which affix shameful asterisks on my putred doggy couplings that seem pre-completed by the time I start, gasping out a second's worth of life.

But why should I whine, when human life operates in a different time frame altogether? Evolution has spawned reproductive temporal variations on all its surviving creatures. I'm old, let me take what I have, put down pride, and humbly accept that in dog dimensions I've had more than fair rations of that ruffled common elixir — fun. Neutered male dogs suppress their jealous growls at me, while non-neutered rivals wallow in their inferior rates of success.

If dogs were to have a political community, I'd run a successful campaign as a true leader, under approving human gazes. I'm envied from below and in turn envy my human male paragons. In the planetary pecking order, I have my place, like it or not. If only I could be free of borrowed human consciousness that plagues my otherwise simple place in a fortunate universe.

I value consciousness, being an intellectual, as dogs go. But as humans are well aware, awareness can be a spoiler. The mortality worry gets me down. Other dogs are so lucky in their self-protective brain, limitations.

But as an intellectual, I shouldn't be anti-intellectual, just to ease me of death-consciousness. Knowing that other dogs die, I can't tolerate my equal fate. As an intellectual Casanova, I'm riddled with the eternal fleas of conflict, if you scratch me below the surface. To my sorrow, I'm Zorro, with a limited tomorrow. Cast me over, I'm still Casanova.

Sex and death don't cancel each other out. In time solve the time problem.

Meanwhile, as I age, I'm less welcomed by lady dogs. Intimations of impotence ease my transition to total non-existence, negating Casanova, Zorro, and me in one deft stroke, cleaning a space for some future blessed marvel of dog maledom, a pseudo futuristic me. My time problem includes my replaceability. The rest of me will follow my lowering cock downwards past consciousness, irreversible, as I bark out my inaudible intellectualities and the landscape covers me over, the glistening suburban Catskills of respectable middle-classdom.

Even as death closes in, I'll be imagining the human sex act with me bearing out infinite pleasure even beyond closing time. Eternity's impulsive gasp has a sexual ring. Foundations. rock. Meanwhile, I—

THE REASON SHE REJECTED ME

(1)

When it was time to mate
I was left at the gate.
Frail impotence deterred me
though lust itself stirred me.
Desire missed the connection,
reaching couldn't stretch the action.
I slid across but made a miss,
falling short at imagined bliss,
potential sperm turned to piss
and she took me off the mailing list.

(2)

Failure's primitive ache
in shame saw the union break
of what the goal had seemed to be.
From commitment we were equally free.
She and I didn't add up to "we."
When I asked for a date, she didn't say "oui."

FIDGET DIGITS (or DIGIT FIDGETS)

Now that the Industrial Revolution has been safely absorbed into the annals of history, it's about time that we leap ahead to address digital fidgetyness, which is my ephemeral working definition of our so-far, so-called "current age." Apparently our various pervasive electronic media go by the mathematical formula of digits. And humans by medical definition are nervous, uneasy, even anxious, so I'll charitably call them fidgety: and then rhyme that to their communicative instruments that are digity; and logically we arrive at "fidget digits" or "digit fidgets" as our tuned-in humanity's definitive modes of being, to coin two hereby-offered philosophical terms on a scientific basis.

I hope I'm not being too brash, in trying to enter the dictionary via verbal presumptions on an innovative scale. "Aim high!" I was told, but flying too close to the sun can get someone scalded if he slips carelessly in a gravity-reversing but ill-conceived direction. Still, discoveries and inventions are daringly unconscious paths to advances in history's time chart.

THE MEDIOCRE STAND-UP COMEDIAN AND HIS BETRAYED GHOST-WRITER FRIEND

Grant was a stand-up comedian, playing the night club circuit to moderately hesitant laughter to offset negligible reputation. He needed a boost "in the worst way," so he asked me — a professional ghost writer and actual friend — to write a favorable blurb-ad to be placed in the "current entertainment" section of all the periodicals in the big city (identified as New York). So this is what I wrote, which Grant released at some cost, craving publicity to revive his sinking career before it could plunge out of sight and become more of a "never-was" than a "has-been.":

"Grant breaks the humor language, unregulates its knots and flows the frenzy along. He keeps getting more inexhaustible, the sun shining day and night on his humor. He unleashes an unruly humor daintily. He wrenches humor back to its original. He plays with humor till it squeaks out. He topples humor till it surrenders. He undoes humor but its revival gets celebrated. He steals humor out from under your nose, disclosing its secret that was already an open spot you didn't notice."

A few days later, the local stand-up comedians collectively sued Grant (class-action), claiming ". . . advertising, under falsely exaggerated pretenses, that is competitively unfair to the Humor Union members whose true, authentic, and real stand-up sessions resemble reasonable authenticity compared to that fraud — Grant."

Grant, who was supposed to be my friend, publicly shifted these blame-accusations to me, who was supposedly doing him a favor by writing that advertising release and not even getting paid for such a friendly favor. Now the onus was on me. How could I shift it back to him and let right triumph over false friendship's arrant betrayal?

Well, I tried. But it wasn't funny.

INCARCERATION AND ESCAPE

Could life itself be called a jail? It's where you're condemned whenever you fail.

And brood behind bars on your inability to undo the failure's memory, which haunts you and you can't get out of it, you're stuck there, it's a jail. You're serving a term of melancholy, close cousin to depression, the bleak lack of joy, deprived of happiness-nourishment despite the meek rations of occasional relief.

Ah, but relief is spreading! Good times are rolling in, one by one, like waves from a benign sea. Ripples of splash sprinkle on your giddy skin. You can surf-ride on them, the tide is on your side, it's jail escape time. Run away, deeply in the debt of police-pursuit.

THE SLIPPERY REAL

I had so many fantasies that were erroneous at the heart of things that my friend said, "You need a reality check. Get real. Go around the block more often, let yourself see what's going on. You're asking for too much, tamp down on what you expect, which is tantamount to 'the moon'. Get modest, don't get out of hand. Put yourself at peace with the world. The reality is out there, not inside you."

Okay, I brought my reality check to all the vicinity's banks, and their tellers uniformly told me that they can't cash it — "but would I start an account?" That was really getting down to basics. Sure, I was always told: "Be accountable. Don't run through your funds, you'll wind up being a no-account. So on no account spend more than at hand or in reserve. Monitor your resources, save for later."

All that was wise advice. So I calmed down to the reality peace force and lived within my means, which is no mean feat, I mean I landed on my feet.

So now I'm centered. I'm in a good place. Can I improve it? I don't want to: "Let well enough alone." But life wants to move forward, in its everlasting assault on the now-stagnant status quo. "Get with it. Move with the tide. Set your rhythms into the flow. Shift. Adjust. React. Move."

That was internal advice. But the reality was out there. Then I should join forces, the me inside, the world outside, & the real in between.

It worked! Here I am, but soon was, as reality slips around.

A FRANKLY PESSIMISTIC DIAGNOSIS

I'm living myself out of life, by hoarding time into my vitals, but time ekes out and eats me up. Soon, I'll run out of time and in turn time romps away from me at an equestrian pace with me slumping in the saddle at an asymmetrical askew. What the antidote? Or what's my anecdote?

How do I play out my feebling intellect at its rapidly medical alert in a body crumbling from one corner of the health insurance plan's bodily coverage to another in my physical map at the heart of my loss of vitality on an awful ratio? I'm being splintered up into fragments as the center crumbles at its basis. Meanwhile, my intellect can't repair it as a subsidy of the strength I'm losing. At my own peril! A disaster working itself out inside its own corrupting penalty for entering a time race with time itself. Dying is the darkness doom that neatly prepares nobody's tomb.

PAY A LITTLE SPERM, GET A LITTLE BABY. A COSMIC BARGAIN FOR THE YOUTH BRIGADE

While exerting a powerful, sometimes irresistibly magnetic attractiveness on a man, sometimes that woman finds that that very man exerts a powerful, sometimes irresistibly magnetic attractiveness on her. The result later could be a baby. "That's how the world goes round" — a circular comment that could also refer to money: "That's how the world goes round." So the intersection of biology and economics cuts a swarth of cross-section conducting our species' lives.

As far as men and women go, they need each other. Their differences are as compelling as their similarities. "Long live their difference" translates from a French commentary. Pleasure from two angles conducts an equator storm, in combining with nuclear compression. Genetic biology culminates the romance. The birth of babies prolongs the earth storm, as generations pile up their loaded magnets of history, generating inch by inch a dance frenzy to poppagate and momagate the properties of propagation. Round and round, and round after round, all this continuance keeps a radical status quo. It's a dynamic rut.

Let's keep it that way, by heaving it along. Keep your eye out for a gleam. That gleam alights. That leaves us all taking paternal and maternal leave. Babies be served, we've done our bit, and bitten off our bite. We decline, the babies rise. They become us, in kin and kind.

FINDING COMMON GROUNDS TO SHARE SPARKLES ON THE DULL ROAD OF LONELINESS

The private world of my past — which includes this minute about to pass: I try to match it up with my friends' and acquaintances' private worlds, to see what references and associations I might share that overlap with "his" or "hers." Or on the chancy meeting with a stranger.

Experiences in common, of mutual coincidence on two people's parts, a commonality of personal references that invite comparison in the shared act of reminding: That's conversation, entangling two or more. But too much more spreads the reminiscence feast out too thin, with that much less intimacy.

Being personal with another unites, however temporarily. If you share special stuff, you feel closer. Then the verbal exchange can take the bond into friendship, which is bread compared to love's wine. Oh, these relationships, new or old, along life's traveling circus of solitude.

ABOUT THE AUTHOR

Marvin Cohen was born in 1931 in Brooklyn. He taught creative writing at the New School, City College of New York, and Adelphi University. His other books include the novel-of-sorts-in-stories *The Self-Devoted Friend*, a non-fiction book *Baseball the Beautiful*, and the novel *Others, Including Morstive Sternbump* (recently re-issued by Tough Poets Press). He has also written and had performed various plays. Cohen lives in New York with his wife. His website: www.marvincohen.net

9 789811 101182